PENELOPE'S ZOO

PENELOPE'S ZOO

By Robert Leigh James

DODD, MEAD & COMPANY
New York

ISBN 0-396-06332-2
Library of Congress Catalog Card Number: 78-147133
Printed in the United States of America
by Vail-Ballou Press, Inc., Binghamton, N. Y.

This book is dedicated to my daughter,

ALEXANDRA

who delights in being a Washington girl

❧ 1 ❧

THE empty store front near the Mayflower Hotel on Connecticut Avenue was emblazoned with signs in red, white, and blue, *Charles Frome for President; Frome Headquarters; Frome's First.* A tall, thin, sandy haired man peered owlishly out into the street from its single glass door. Inside the cooled building, shaded by an ancient survivor of the great trees that once arched over the avenue, it was pleasant enough, but outside the air was humid and heavy with the sultry oppressiveness of Washington in mid June.

The man watched the flow of tourists in their brightly colored cotton shorts and skirts, already stained and limp from the sweating bodies they covered. *Homo Americanus* he thought sourly. My God! We'll never make it. The high school kids were something else. He watched them stream out of a line of buses and pour into a cafeteria across the street, prattling happily, determined to see everything in their allotted forty-eight hours. He realized with regret that he had never shared that school age excitement at seeing the Capital for the first time, realizing with awe that the scenes in the dog-eared history and civics books could come to life. He had been born in Washington, the son of a veteran bureaucrat with an astringent view of politics and politicians. The city had never been glamorous and exciting for him as it was for the kids piling out of the buses. Maybe he had been

1

cheated. It helped to start with a few illusions.

He lit a cigarette and, holding it between nicotine stained fingers, continued to gaze out on the street. An impatient glance at his wristwatch told him that it was ten past nine. Damn Barney Harcourt! He had promised to deliver the desks and filing cabinets at eight-thirty. He had to be back on the Hill for Frome's press conference at ten. The telephones weren't even in yet. The signs were up outside and on the window and there was nothing inside. It was bad timing; it made things look totally disorganized. God damn it! He had wanted everything ready inside, furniture, telephones, and staff ready to go before the signs went up. It was working out just the opposite, par for the course. He wondered why he didn't have an ulcer. But then it would come. He'd only been working on it thirty-four years.

Frowning into the distance he gradually became aware of a girl of college age looking at him speculatively through the window. His eyes met hers. She did not look away but continued to look at him solemnly. Then her thin, freckled face was transformed by a sudden smile that creased into little lines at the eyes and lifted the rather thin lips into a beguiling expression of artless happiness. He smiled back. He even felt like laughing.

The girl made an almost clown like gesture toward the signs and then, looking beyond him into the empty store front, raised her shoulders to suggest mock deprecation. When she returned the guileless gaze of her wide set blue eyes, he laughed out loud. He stepped over to the door and opened it, still grinning.

"You have any suggestions?"

She walked inside. "You need fewer signs and more people."

"That's just what I think."

The earnest eyes sought his. "I was going to apply for a job. Is it too early?"

He glanced at his wrist. "No. You're hired."

2

She laughed, suggesting embarrassed disbelief. "You're kidding!"

He fished in a coat pocket and extracted a red, white, and blue Frome for President badge. He solemnly pinned it on her blue blouse. "You are now inducted. Your first job is to take my place at this window and look for the van of Harcourt Furniture Rentals. A lying bastard with red hair will be sitting beside the driver on the front seat. He will deliver six desks and ten metal file cabinets and will tell you that he was held up on Rhode Island Avenue in the morning traffic. He'll give you an invoice to sign. If the count is right and the merchandise sufficiently beaten up to be appropriate for a Candidate of the People, sign it and keep one copy." He tossed her a key and started for the door.

"Hey! Are you leaving me alone?"

"Why not? I've got more important things to do on the Hill."

"But you don't know me."

"Right. Neither does Barney, but you're at the right address. He's a trusting soul."

"But who are you?" She called frantically as he opened the door.

From outside in the street he pointed up at the Frome for President signs and turned and ran to hail a passing taxicab.

Fifteen minutes later a green van with Harcourt Furniture Rentals in gold letters drew up and double parked. A short, bandy-legged man with red hair swung down from the cab and walked across to the store front.

"We got your delivery, Miss," he said gruffly as she opened the door.

"O.K. It's about time. We thought you'd got lost."

"No. Nothin' like that. I know this town like a book. It was the traffic. We really got hung up out on Rhode Island."

"You don't say?" She grinned.

He grinned back. "Well, what the hell? So we got a late start. Me and all of the boys will vote for Frome. O.K.?"

3

"O.K.," she said extending her hand. "It's a deal."

When the furniture had been unloaded she signed the invoice and carefully put the blue copy in her purse. Barney sat on one of the desks chewing gum. "This Frome guy, pretty hot stuff, huh?"

"We think so."

"Think he can handle it?"

"Sure. Why do you think I'm here?"

The gum was chewed slowly, speculatively. "It must be interesting, being on the inside."

"Inside?"

"Of politics."

"Oh. Well, yes. It is."

"I know how it is at the local level. You know, you give a little, you get a little. You know how it is."

"That's the way it goes."

"Exactly. That's what I say." He scratched one ear. "I suppose when it's a President it's different."

"Some different."

"Like what?"

"Like you say."

"Yeah." He scratched his ear again. "Well, good to know you." He hesitated. "What I mean to say is, if you need some help, remember me."

She cupped her chin in both hands and smiled at him. "I'll remember, Barney. And don't forget our deal."

"Our deal?"

"The votes. Three votes. We need all we can get."

"Oh, yeah. It's a promise."

"And we shook on it."

"We did at that," he laughed delightedly. "I can see you're already in business."

"Yes, sir. All the way."

The sandy haired man returned at five-fifteen. The six desks had been arranged and the filing cabinets were in an orderly row along one wall. The girl was sitting at a desk ear-

4

nestly talking with three middle aged businessmen. "Frome is a fresh new voice, a man who is both an inspirer and a problem solver."

"But is he a leader?" one of the men asked.

"That's my definition of a leader." She glanced over the shoulders of the men around the desk and grinned impishly at her newest visitor. "Yes, sir?"

"I just dropped by," he said dryly. "Is Mr. Frome in?"

"No, but please come over and meet three voters for Frome. Mr. Henbury, Mr. Wentworth, and Mr. Blount."

"Winslow, Davis Winslow," he said, extending his hand. "And your name, Miss?"

"Penelope Benton."

"It's a pleasure."

"For me, too, Mr. Winslow. I always like to put a name to a face." She turned to the visitors. "We'll have literature and pins tomorrow, gentlemen. Meanwhile, you don't mind if I count you as sure votes for my first day?"

There was a rumble of assent as she walked them to the door. Locking it she turned to him with a grin. "Well, boss man?"

He pushed a freckled hand through his thinning hair and nodded his head.

"Great. You seem to have landed running. I'm sorry to have left you alone all day. I expected to find the keys inside the letter drop with a note telling me to go to hell. On second thought, maybe I didn't deserve the note."

She shook her head slowly causing the fine brown hair which fell to shoulder length from a side part to swing back and forth.

"No strain. I enjoyed it."

"What did you do for lunch?"

"The telephones were hooked up about one. I looked up a sandwich shop in the yellow pages and had a sandwich and coffee sent in. There's a john in the rear, so I made out swell."

"You must have wondered if I'd return at all."

"I have been too busy to wonder. I've had a stream of drop-ins, but if I had, I would have guessed you'd be back as soon as you could make it. You have that little conscientious furrow between the eyes."

"I'll buy you a drink and stand you to dinner. O.K.?"

"Scrumptious!" She grinned at him, her blue eyes meeting his, the tip of her tongue unconsciously running along her upper lip. "I'd like that."

"Where are you staying?"

"At the Statler."

"Seven?"

"Seven." She handed him the key he had given her that morning.

They sat in rattan chairs before a low, plastic topped cocktail table in the Sky Lounge of the Washington Hotel. Beyond the green tree encircled ellipse the shaft of the Washington Monument rose majestically from its sloping hill. The fifty American flags that flew from high staffs around its base made a bright circle of rippling color beyond which, across the tidal basin, the perfect white symmetry of the Jefferson Memorial appeared to float on the edge of the mirror-like water. To their right, surrounded by century old trees, the White House seemed only a large, comfortable suburban home from which a few window framed lights glowed in the summer twilight.

Penelope took a deep breath and looked at Dave Winslow. "I can see why you chose this place."

He smiled and sipped his scotch and soda. "Every new Washingtonian should have this bit of stardust thrown in their eyes." He watched her for a moment as she sat eagerly absorbed in the view. "Does everyone call you Penelope?"

"They usually call me Penny."

"Then I'll call you Penelope."

"You like to be exclusive?"

"That depends upon the person."

6

"Now you're giving me a line." She looked at him out of the corner of her eyes.

"God forbid."

"You sure never got through school being called Davis?"

"Dave."

"That's better."

"Where have you come from, Penelope?"

"Indiana University. I got an A.B. in education four days ago."

"Why Washington?"

"It's an election year. I thought it would be exciting."

"Do you need a job, or are you one of these gals who work for kicks?"

"I need a job."

"The one you've taken doesn't pay much."

"How much?"

"Four hundred and fifty a month. You could do a lot better elsewhere."

"I can live on that. Don't forget I'm a lean, hungry college kid."

"You can't stay at the Statler on that."

"I'm only at a hotel until I find something else. I'm in what they call a mother-in-law room. The only difference between it and a broom closet is that it has running water. But it's the minimum rate."

"Are you interested in politics?"

"I think it's fun. At least it was on campus."

He made a sour face.

"You don't agree?"

"Politics are necessary. I never thought of them as fun." She sipped her drink.

"I suppose you have just finished four years as a popular co-ed and you think that is politics."

"No. Not really."

"Come on, 'fess up."

"I was president of my sorority."

7

"And?"

"Head cheerleader."

"And?"

"Associate editor of the student newspaper."

"Bully for you."

She looked at him. "What about you, Dave?"

"I was a pretty decent newspaperman until I hired out to Frome."

"Why did you hire out?"

"He's going to be the next President of the United States."

She gave an ecstatic little shiver and ducked her head over her drink. "You see? People never said things like that in Bloomington."

He laughed. "If you're interested in pompous statements, this is the mother lode."

"Why is he going to be the next President?"

"One: he is good looking in a craggy sort of way. He'll look great on Mount Rushmore. Two: he is a veteran of the House of Representatives—eight terms—yet he is only in his early forties. Three: he is the best orator this country has produced since William Jennings Bryan, and Bryan didn't have television. Four: he is a genius at spotting the gut issues in any campaign. Five: he has the money and the judgment to hire the best talent whether it is idea men, speech writers, public relations men, or administrators."

"Including you." She said it sincerely.

His ironic glance slid away from her. "I'll do."

They ordered another drink.

"The regular crew arrives tomorrow, Penelope," he said quietly. "It won't be like today."

"I noticed there were six desks."

"They all have know-how. They know Frome. They've been around."

Her eyes widened guilelessly and sought his. "I'd like to be a part of it. Can't I be your girl Friday? I'll answer the telephone, I'll stuff envelopes, and I'm good at re-writing."

8

"How about typing?"

"Sixty words a minute, less time for erasures. I can't spell worth a damn."

He nodded slowly. "O.K. We'll try it on those terms. Can you get along with women?"

She looked at him in surprise. "I get along with everybody."

❧ 2 ❧

PENELOPE peered from the window of the taxicab at the narrow yellow facade of the frame wooden house on Thirty-fifth Street. "Is this it?"

"It's the number you gave me, lady."

"I didn't think it would look this nice."

The taxi driver cocked his head, "It's O.K. Kind of old fashioned. I like the new suburbs. They're more with it."

"Georgetown is supposed to be old fashioned."

"Like I say. It's O.K."

"How much?"

"One-twenty."

She paid him the exact amount. He pushed open his door with a grunt and walked around to the rear of the taxi. The rusty hinges of the trunk lid creaked as he opened it and swung two bags onto the sidewalk. The trunk lid slammed shut with a soft crunch.

Penelope smiled at him. "Be a pal. You take one and I'll take the other."

The taxi driver blew out his cheeks. "I'll take 'em both," he said in a tone of resignation. "It don't look right, a lady doin' it." He carried the bags up the five steps of a narrow brick staircase and put them down on a stoop.

She looked at him uncertainly. "Should I tip you, do you suppose, or would you rather I didn't?"

The taxi driver stared at her, then mumbled, "It's a pleasure." At the side of his taxi he turned around and called as his face broke into a broad grin. "I'll make it up on the tourists, little lady."

Penelope smiled brilliantly and with a horizontal movement of the palm of her hand acknowledged his implied accolade as she turned and rang the doorbell.

A colored cleaning woman answered the door.

"I'm Miss Benton. I'm moving in today."

"Yes'm. I been told about you. You leave your things right here in the hall. I'll show you the room Miss Wilson said was yours." She turned and preceded Penelope up a narrow flight of stairs which rose beside the hallway leading to the rear of the house.

The room was small, but filled with the morning sunlight that filtered through translucent white curtains caught in a tuck on either side of the narrow window overlooking the street. The single bed was covered by a simple white coverlet. A bureau, a table with a lamp, and a small slip covered slipper chair completed the room's furnishings.

"I'm so glad it's wallpapered and in yellow," Penelope said, turning about in the center of the room with her hands clasped together, "It's my favorite color."

"It's got a nice closet over there," the cleaning woman gestured.

"And I am so glad you are here, too," Penelope smiled at her. "That's why everything looks so fresh, I'm sure."

"I tries," the woman said simply.

"What is your name?"

"Lillian."

"How nice. I like the name Lillian."

"It's a family name."

"When will the others be home?"

"They gets here about five. I leave at four-thirty."

"Then I think I'll go downtown to my job. Did Miss Wilson leave me a key?"

11

"She left an envelope on the table in the hall downstairs."
The envelope contained a door key and a short note.
"Welcome. I'll see you about six and will tell you what all
this costs. Jean."

Jean Wilson sat on a slightly worn sofa in the narrow livingroom off the downstairs hall. She was a tall girl with short
bobbed black hair and a brisk impersonal manner. "I'm really
relieved, Penny. I really am. It takes four to keep the cost of
this place where it belongs and when we're missing a gal it
costs that much more for the rest of us. On the other hand,
we all have to be compatible. All we need is one bitch and it
would be sheer hell. Absolute, sheer hell." She emphasized
each of the last three words and reached for a cigarette. "So,
when Dave mentioned you, I held my breath. After all, I
thought, what does a one time loser like Dave know about
women?"

"A one time loser?"

"He's divorced. Didn't you know?"

"No. I didn't."

"Last year. I didn't know her. Maybe she was a creep; anyway, I did hold my breath until we all had lunch together
yesterday and, when I met you and learned that you were a
Kappa, I knew it was going to work out."

"I'm glad."

"Sue and Mary didn't hesitate a minute either."

"I like them too."

"Well, let me fill you in. I work for Senator Clinton up at
the Old Senate Office Building. Sue Gort is a secretary for
one of the assistant secretaries of defense and Mary Totten is
over at the State Department in one of those frightful air
conditioned catacombs, the office of AID to something or
other. So we all keep office hours five days a week. That
solves a lot of our problems. Evenings and weekends, we go
by the numbers." She opened a black leather notebook.
"There are four bedrooms in this house and one john, in a

12

converted storeroom at that. This house pre-dates inside johns. Then there is what the real estate boys call a powder room off the downstairs hall. This means," she consulted the notebook, "that while you can bathe any night of the week, you can only do a major overhaul, hair wash, nails, leg shaving, on Tuesday and Saturday nights. No bathings on week day mornings. We all have to pile out of here by eight A.M. Well, I won't go on. It's depressingly regimented, really. I'll give you a list. All other uses of the facilities are by arrangement. We all cooperate, even swap nights if we want to, but it's all agreed to in advance."

She pushed out her cigarette in an ash tray. "Now, let's see. No meals served here other than a get-your-own breakfast. Of course, if you want to cook a meal, that's up to you. Just sing out which night you want and bring in your own groceries. We take turns each week buying the breakfast things. Lillian. Do we still have Lillian? Yes. Lillian comes in five days a week and does cleaning and our laundry. No cooking. All clear so far?"

Penelope nodded, a serious, intent look on her face which made her features seem thinner and emphasized the tightness of the fair skin over her cheekbones and thin nose.

"Now, costs. Rent for this place furnished is $400 a month. Lillian gets $200 a month and utilities are another fifty dollars. That's $650 split four ways or $162.50 a month. Georgetown elegance at bargain prices. O.K.?"

Penelope nodded. "O.K."

"You can give me a check for seventy-five dollars for the rest of June and the full monthly amount the first of every month."

Penelope opened her purse and extracted a folded checkbook. "Is an out of town bank all right?"

"Sure. Make it out to me. I'm house mother, it seems."

Penelope carefully filled in the check stub and then wrote out the check. She waved it back and forth until it was dry and handed it to Jean.

13

"Many thanks."

Penelope put the checkbook back into her purse and closed the purse with a snap. She smiled happily and slowly shook her head. "I'm in Washington with a job, part of a Georgetown house, and four new friends, all in two days. I can't believe it."

Jean lit another cigarette and looked at her with friendly amusement. "Pray no one drops out. Costs go up like sixty."

Penelope stretched, pushing her hands out before her. "Don't you find it just thrilling?"

"Washington?"

Penelope nodded.

"I suppose so, when I can get off the treadmill long enough to look around. Most of the time I feel like Eliza crossing the ice except that I leap from filing cabinet to filing cabinet in a blizzard of carbon paper."

The door to the street opened and, in a flurry of conversation, Sue Gort and Mary Totten entered. "He didn't!"

"Yes, he did."

"I don't believe it. I simply don't. He never could stand her before."

"Well, he's changed. Whenever he sees her now, he snorts and paws at the ground." Both girls broke into hilarious giggles as they entered the room.

"Well, hi, Penny. Moved in?" Sue asked.

Penelope nodded as Jean said, "I've got her money."

"You're moved in," Sue agreed.

The two girls threw themselves into chairs and regarded Penelope in a friendly, interested way. "Your hair is nearly a chestnut color," Mary announced. "In that dark little hole where we had lunch I thought you were a brunette."

"Sorry," Penelope said pleasantly.

"It's very pretty," Mary murmured politely.

"What do you mean, 'dark little hole'?" Sue bristled. "I picked that restaurant. I had my first date with George there."

14

"I know, dear," Mary said sweetly.

"George and I go there all the time. We like it."

"For dinner, yes. At lunch it appeals to businessmen having noontime assignations on the cheap."

Jean laughed. "What an imagination! Who would want an assignation over egg foo yung at high noon?"

"Highly sexed vegetarians?" Penelope said tentatively.

The girls burst into laughter. "How do you like Frome?" Mary asked in the silence that followed.

"I don't know," Penelope said. "I've never met him."

"Well, I didn't think you had, dear. What I meant was, do you agree with him?"

"I don't know what you mean."

"He's been engulfing the country with television appearances, radio speeches and magazine articles on foreign affairs, civil rights, race relations, crime, transportation, economics. You must have heard or read some of it."

"I have been pretty busy with final exams and graduation."

"Well why are you working at his headquarters, for God's sake?"

"I'll let you know before the summer is out," Penelope said evenly, "if you can wait that long."

Mary looked discomfitted. "O.K., touché," she said. "It's none of my business anyway. Nothing personal."

"Of course not," Penelope smiled. "We haven't known each other long enough to get personal."

Jean was grinning at Mary. "Live and learn I always say. Live and learn. You gals dating tonight?" They both nodded. Jean glanced at Penelope. "I'm going over to a little place near the Georgetown University campus for a sandwich. Want to come along?"

"Sure."

They sat in a booth under a ceiling with a gridiron of heavy oak beams and ate a huge hamburger from a paper plate with beer served from a can into a paper cup.

"College life," Jean said. "Though I never went to college, I love it. And the food is cheap."

"Yes," Penelope said.

"I suppose you're kind of fed up with it."

"Not really. I'm just ready for something else."

"Marriage? Kids?"

"Someday. Not yet. I just want to meet grown up people off campus—to be a part of things."

"You think you'll like your job?"

"I know I will," Penelope spoke with enthusiasm. "It's exciting, so alive."

"Politics." Jean said the word with a flat, downward inflection.

"You don't like politics?"

Jean lowered her voice. "I see too much of it in the Senator's office. Ugh."

Penny looked troubled. "Don't you like Senator Clinton?"

Jean laughed. "I like him as well as I'd like any pompous old goat with a phony laugh and a leering eye for any woman under fifty."

"If that's the way you feel, I'd quit."

"Why should I quit? The pay is good and the hours aren't bad."

"I'd want to feel a part of his career."

"His career is over," Jean said flatly. "He'll find that out at the next election." She glanced at Penny. "It's different when your boss is a young politician on the make."

"I guess so."

Jean lit a cigarette. "So, you like politics?" The tone of voice was unconsciously patronizing.

"I like people. I like to work with groups. I like to win."

Jean studied her. "You pick the winners?"

Penelope shook her head slowly. "No. I avoid the losers."

"It's the same thing."

"No. It isn't. It isn't the same thing at all."

16

❧ 3 ❧

DAVE WINSLOW walked into the Connecticut Avenue headquarters from the heat of the street and stopped at the desk immediately in front of the door. "How's it going, Penelope?" he said over the clatter of typewriters and the intermittent pealing of telephones.

"Swell. I'm having a ball."

"I'm glad we made you our receptionist. I hear glowing reports about the way you handle people."

"I'm happy." She looked up at him with a coquettish look. "I haven't seen much of you, though. Do you have the busies?"

He sat down on the edge of her desk. "You said it. The Congressman is really pouring it on. There are only three weeks until the convention in Chicago and the delegates committed to the other candidates are beginning to become unstuck. That irresistible ground swell of public opinion Frome's been talking about is actually beginning to move."

"You sound surprised."

"The expression 'public opinion' always puts me off. I'm going to be as surprised as hell if it turns out there really is such a thing."

"You're not as cynical as you pretend to be. You know voters are out there somewhere beyond the District of Columbia line."

"So they tell me. Something is stirring out there on quiet summer nights I'll admit. Maybe they're beating skins stretched across the ends of hollow logs."

"I was wondering," she said directly, "when you were going to take me to dinner again."

He looked vulnerable. "You really want to repeat that?"

"I do."

"Well," he glanced at his wristwatch. "It's possible tonight. All I can do is feed you and run, I'm afraid. I've got to finish a speech draft tonight whether I get to bed or not."

"Tonight it is."

He studied his watch as if it were an appointment schedule. "Let's see, it's two-thirty. I have to be up on the Hill with the Congressman. God knows when he'll be free. I tell you what you do. Come on up to the Rayburn House Office Building at six o'clock. You may have to wait awhile. We'll grab a bite to eat up on the Hill, O.K.?"

"Oh, I'd love that. I haven't been up on the Hill yet." She used the expression self-consciously and gave a little bubbly laugh of anticipation.

His glance up from his watch was almost shy. "Well, O.K. Six it is. The suite number is 2106. The guard at the door will tell you how to find your way about in the labyrinthine depths." He moved on into the clatter of the headquarters, greeting the young men and women at the desks until he disappeared behind a six foot high frosted glass partition in the rear.

Penelope sat in the dull black leather chair in the small anteroom of Congressman Frome's office. A seemingly endless parade of people had walked by her since six o'clock to enter the Congressman's office. They had ignored her, but then they had usually ignored the receptionist at the desk too as they had pushed through the half opened door to Frome's office to join the rumble of voices, the clinking of glasses, and the occasional bursts of laughter that came from inside. At

18

seven-thirty the receptionist, a pretty, slight Negro girl of about twenty firmly cleared her desk and got to her feet. "I'm not doing any good here," she announced, "and tomorrow is another day. I'm going home."

"Is it always like this?"

"Since he started moving up in the polls. Each point he makes on the polls, the more visitors we get. We've got a national constituency now and this office was too small even to handle the visitors from the first Maryland Congressional District." She looked at herself briefly in a compact and reached for her purse. "Will you be O.K.? Your date is in there somewhere, but I can't promise you when he will be out."

"I don't mind waiting. It's fascinating."

"You're a jewel. Well, goodnight, then."

Penelope sat alone in the anteroom, gazing at a relief map of Frome's congressional district, the autographed pictures of the famous and near famous of his party, apparently all convulsed with laughter at the moment the shutter snapped, and a number of conventional souveniers of patriotism: a model of a new jet fighter, a silver replica of the American flag planted on the moon, and a picture in color of Frome on the bridge of an aircraft carrier.

She arose from her chair to look more closely at the colored picture and decided that Frome was very handsome. The parka hood of the navy blue jacket he was wearing was thrown back and his hair was tossed by the sea breeze. He had a distinct air of command. She gave a light sigh of excitement and happiness and, opening a door across the reception room from Frome's office, peered into the room of the staff. It was filled with desks, typewriters, and filing cabinets and gave an impression of crowded, disorganized clutter. She made a face and quickly retreated from this vision of the prosaic.

She sat down again. She preferred to listen to the murmur of voices in Frome's office and imagine what the voices were saying. She told herself that they were at work making a

19

presidential candidate beyond that paneled mahogany door. She could feel the tension in the air. It permeated the office suite and affected her as well. To think that she was sitting just outside the Washington office of a presidential candidate and a month ago she was still in Bloomington. Maybe Dave would introduce her to Frome. She sat back in her chair, her heart pounding. What would she say? What would she do? Did you shake hands?

Gradually the inner office emptied as more people emerged than entered. About eight-thirty a comparative hush settled over the inner office and at eight-forty-five Dave Winslow emerged at the side of the familiar smiling figure Penny had never met. "My God, Penelope!" Dave said stricken, "I forgot completely. Have you been waiting all this time?"

Charles Frome smiled at her as she arose. "Have I done this? Then I am sorry." He took both of her hands in his and held them for a moment in a firm, warm clasp. "I am Chuck Frome."

Penelope felt her face flush and she smiled up into the handsome face with the square jaw and the short cropped jet black hair. "It's nothing, Mr. President. I was glad to wait."

Frome threw back his head and laughed. "You have me nominated and elected already? You better just call me Congressman for a while, yet, sweetheart. We aren't counting our chickens yet."

"This is Penelope Benton, Mr. Congressman," Dave Winslow interjected. "She works for you at the Connecticut Avenue headquarters."

"Well, do you now? In that case, young lady, you weren't anticipating. I'm as good as elected."

Penelope kept looking directly into his eyes, smiling, but she could think of nothing to say. Frome took her by the arm. "You waited all this time? What a shame and what a waste. You could have been in with us. We could have used a pretty face among all of that political granite, hey, Dave?" He led her into the hallway followed by Dave Winslow and moved toward a private elevator leading to the garage under the building. "I'll drop you two off wherever you're going. It's the least I can do."

Dave sat across the table from her at the Rotunda restaurant on Capitol Hill. He looked weary as he sipped the martini before him.

"Why don't you unbutton your shirt collar?" Penelope suggested. "You can't relax as long as that shirt and tie has a stranglehold around your throat."

Dave unbuttoned the shirt and gave his tie a sidewise jerk. "Thanks. That does help. I could feel my pulse beating in my neck."

They drank their drinks in silence.

"Shall we order?" He asked.

"Let's have one more drink. I think you need to relax before eating."

When the drinks came he smiled across at her.

"I'm damn sorry about keeping you waiting. Nearly three hours. My God, you should have walked out."

"I enjoyed waiting. I've never been so close to a presidential candidate before."

"He's quite a guy. A slave driver, but quite a guy. He smells political blood and we're really driving now."

"I think he is wonderful."

"You think he'll get the women's vote?"

"Every last one."

They ordered steaks and a salad. Over the coffee he sighed and rubbed his eyes. "Now, damn it, I have to get to work. I'll take you home."

Penelope looked disappointed. "I feel like Cinderella after the ball, Dave. It's been such a wonderful evening."

"Most of it you spent waiting for me in Frome's reception room."

"I loved every minute of it. I never dreamed that I'd get to watch presidential politics close up."

21

He grinned at her, warmed and amused by her enthusiasm. "I'll try to keep our other evenings at the same high level."

"I'd love other evenings, Dave. I really would . . . unless I'm a bore."

"A distraction, maybe. Never a bore."

She held his eyes as she laughed and placed a hand over his on the table. "You aren't *all* politics, are you?"

"No, ma'am. I keep a little back for other diversions."

She gave his hand a squeeze and then reached for her purse. "Good. Then maybe I won't lose you entirely to Mr. Frome."

"Not a chance."

Penelope stood on the corner of Wisconsin Avenue and "N" Street, her hand protectively held by Dave Winslow. Around them swirled the shambling variegated crowd of the young and the pseudo young that in recent years had made Georgetown's sidewalks their own. Dave sniffed the air and glanced disgustedly at a barefoot foursome dressed to simulate both independence and poverty which had just passed them by. "You can get high on pot just by sniffing the night air in Georgetown these days."

Penelope shrugged. "They're the losers doing their thing. Let them lose. It reduces the competition."

"I wish to God they would do their thing in a part of town as unattractive as they are. Why ruin Georgetown?"

"Potheads are quaint," Penelope shrugged. "Georgetown is quaint. Naturally, they got together."

"Georgetown was having a rebirth of its eighteenth century soul in a completely natural and unselfconscious way until Kennedy stood on the stoop of his "N" Street house and announced his cabinet appointments. Then the newsmedia 'discovered' Georgetown. It became the 'in' place to live and, as real estate values rose, it was already on its way back to the twentieth century slum from which it emerged. Another dream smothered when too many people embraced it."

22

"It's not that bad, yet, Dave. Georgetown has more beautiful eighteenth century homes than any other place in the United States."

"Yes. You can step from your eighteenth century living-room onto your eighteenth century front steps and get a late twentieth century crack on the head. It takes a lot of imagination to overlook things like that. Fewer and fewer people have it."

Penelope laughed. "You're jealous because you live across Rock Creek Park from Georgetown. You can get a late twentieth century crack on the head in front of your late twentieth century apartment house. Also, I don't think you liked your dinner."

"I don't like hamburger flambé, no matter what they call it. Besides, I've got to give birth to another damn speech for Frome and I've run dry. I've ground out six in the last three weeks."

"What is the subject?"

"The importance of young people. He's addressing a safe college crowd out in the corn belt. We've cased it for student activists."

"You mean he's going to talk to college kids about the importance of being young people?"

He was raising a match to light his cigarette. He hesitated, glancing at her over the flame, then he lit the cigarette and slowly waved out the match. "When you say it like that it sounds fatuous, doesn't it?"

She nodded. "I've been listening to Mr. Frome on television. He has to be careful about that. For example, one of the girls at the house says he sounds like his speeches were carved on stone tablets."

"Thanks," Dave said dryly.

"She was referring to his delivery."

Dave pushed a hand through his hair and stared at the smoke rising from the end of the cigarette. "You're right. Penelope. I know that you're right; I've felt we were going stale

23

on Frome's speeches, but I don't know what in hell to do about it. I'm tired and I'm always working against a deadline. Under the circumstances, all that comes out of this turgid brain is banalities."

"A speaker has to be careful about what he says to college kids. In the middle of a serious passage they can begin to laugh if they think it is phony. Then the speaker's had it."

Dave shuddered. "Laughter would suggest that Frome, the youthful Congressman, couldn't communicate with young people. It would be fatal to the image we're trying to project."

"Most kids want to be involved. How about, 'Your Role in a Frome Administration?' Then he could take the offensive, challenge them to come out of their ivory tower and become problem solvers."

Dave puffed on his cigarette. "It's an angle." He glanced up at her with a crooked grin, the cigarette dangling from his lips. "You just talked yourself out of a night's sleep, Penelope, baby. You're going to help me write this speech for the college crowd so that I don't put a foot wrong. We're going to make Frome sound like a real collegian."

Penelope's eyes sparkled. "Can I help, Dave? That's really great! You see? This is what I love about Washington!"

They worked together on the speech until five-thirty A.M. behind the partition of frosted glass at the Connecticut Avenue headquarters. In the grey light of dawn, the speech finished, they looked out of the store front window into deserted Connecticut Avenue, its empty pavement suddenly revealed in the absence of traffic as patched and lumpy where sewage, telephone, and electric line workers had torn it up at intervals.

"City streets look shabby at this hour," Penelope said.

Dave yawned. "You aren't supposed to see them at dawn or early on Sunday mornings. Their glamor depends upon the movement of crowds, and on expectations. No one expects anything at dawn and the crowds are in bed." He

24

glanced at his watch. "At eight-thirty we should be back here. No point in going to bed. My apartment is four blocks from here. Can I offer you breakfast?"

"Sure. Don't tell me you cook?"

"Scrambled eggs. I offer them at all hours to my friends —plain for breakfast, with mushrooms for lunch or dinner, and with anchovies in the late hours when the impulse for seduction courses strong."

She laughed and looked at him out of the corner of her eyes as they stepped outside into the cool morning air. "I'll have mine plain."

Dave Winslow grinned at Penelope across a cup of coffee in the coffee deck of the Mayflower Hotel. "The college speech we hammered out together last week was a great success. Several college newspapers have printed it in full. The University of Chicago Daily Maroon gave us a new slogan in its editorial, 'Frome speaks the language of youth'. We taped the speech, though it wasn't on television live. Now that it's a success, we're going to run it in prime time. The boss gave me kudos for a fresh approach and I gave you full credit as my college age consultant."

Penelope smiled. "I'm glad it clicked. I was afraid we might have overdone it."

"Not at all. It hit just the right note—the young Congressman and presidential candidate who has not forgotten the idealism of his college years." He finished his coffee. "Incidentally, you've lost your job at the Connecticut Avenue headquarters. We've replaced you with a dumb blonde. You're going to work with me up on the Hill, giving the youth slant to our speeches and publicity handouts. As Frome's Administrative Assistant I now have a spacious working area nearly eight by five feet right off the Congressman's office. You will have the sole use of a small table in the corner. From this cramped and ill-lighted space I expect you to have inspiring and ennobling thoughts twenty hours a day.

The remaining four hours are yours for personal hygiene, recreation and sleep."

"Maybe I ought to go back to Bloomington."

"And vegetate? I'm offering you all I possess, you ingrate, migraine headaches, acid stomach, and nervous tension, and you hesitate!"

"How can I refuse? You put it so touchingly."

He held the door open for her into the hotel lobby. "Incidentally, and it is incidental, you'll get another hundred bucks a month."

"I guess crime pays."

"Whoever said it didn't?"

They spent little time in the office on Capitol Hill. Dave Winslow worked frenetically from slips of paper stuffed in the pockets of his wrinkled summer weight suit and Penelope quickly learned to keep skeletonized records in a thin folio of red vinyl with "Courtesy of Your Coca-Cola Bottler" stamped on it in gold. Dave had thrown it at her on arrival at the office. "When it overflows, throw some stuff away," he said airily. "That will hold all of the problems we can cope with at one time." They spent most of the days that followed flying in either commercial or chartered airplanes, touching down at airports in key states for conferences in nearby motels, or dashing by taxi to vital meetings of principal supporters in city centers. They saw little of Frome. He was crisscrossing the country with a small entourage of aides, speaking on carefully chosen occasions, calmly developing his claim to the presidency in a deliberate, contrasting counterpoint to the frantic, hectic campaigning of the other candidates. Dave spoke to him several times a day by telephone and, as the dates for the nationally televised speeches approached, they met to go over the script and arrangements in meticulous detail.

Ten days before the convention for the first time, Frome

topped fifty percent in the public opinion polls as the prospective nominee of his party. He had a ten percentage point lead over his nearest rival within the party and ran four percentage points ahead of the prospective nominee of the other party for the presidency itself. Dave Winslow grinned across the cramped little office on Capitol Hill at Penelope. "This poll enables us to call on the convention to nominate 'the People's Choice.' In the hard sell for delegates behind the scenes it enables us to use the best old tried and true gambit in politics. 'Back the winner when he needs you or miss your chance at the pork barrel.' We are already referring to our supporters as 'Frome *before* Chicago' men. Everyone in politics knows what that means if we win the election."

"What does it mean?" Penelope asked.

"It means that if your name on our list is followed by 'Frome before Chicago' or 'F.B.C.' you will be mothered and embraced in the warm, protective arms of patronage. If those magic words or initials don't follow your name, the next four, even eight years are going to be very difficult, disappointingly difficult. As a party man, you'll get your chunk of beef, but it will be 'choice' not 'prime.' The dams in your district won't be as wide and high. The highways will be one lane narrower and some miles shorter. The judgeships will be less impressive; the ambassadorships in the southern hemisphere rather than the northern. Get the idea?"

"Yes," Penelope said thoughtfully. "It's a rough game isn't it?"

"Anything that's for real is rough and politics is for real."

Penelope hugged herself with her arms and smiled at him. "Men have to be rough. That's why they're men."

"And women?"

Penelope laughed. "I'm hardly the one to tell you all about women!"

Dave arose and gave her a hug. "You're my girl Friday. That's good enough for me."

27

She leaned against him for a moment and then drew away. "Now you're letting your sentiment overcome your judgment."

He looked at her seriously. "You recognize it as sentiment, Penelope?"

"Yes," she nodded. "I recognize sentiment." She moved away toward her small desk.

"Do you mind?" He said to her back.

"No, I don't mind, but we have a job to do."

He lit a cigarette and did not answer. She sat down at her desk and began to work over a series of typewritten questions and answers.

"Penelope?"

"Yes."

"Would you like to go to a party?"

"A party?"

"A very exciting party with people who are bigger than life?"

"I'd love it."

"I'm not really bestowing the invitation on you. The boss thought you ought to come. He appreciates your ideas and you gave him a big charge that first day he met you, calling him 'Mr. President' so matter of factly."

"Really?"

"It's a little party of about fifty that Mrs. Rumbaugh, one of the Congressman's principal financial supporters and fund raisers is giving at the Chevy Chase Club. She calls it a Poll Party to celebrate the boss's showing in the polls. Actually, it's a chance for the inner circle to get together and relax before Chicago."

"The inner circle? Really? And Mr. Frome wants me to come?"

"Yes."

"Oh, Dave!" She rose from her chair and kissed him on the cheek.

28

Dave Winslow swung his dusty green Volkswagen off Connecticut Avenue, through the gate of the Chevy Chase Club, and into a parking space near the soaring white pillared porte-co-chère that framed the entrance to the field stone club house. The Negro houseman in his beige linen jacket just inside the door quickly recognized them as nonmembers and murmured politely, "May I be of help?"

"Mrs. Rumbaugh's party," Dave answered.

"Down the hallway to the left and up the staircase on the right, sir. It is the room at the top of the stairs."

They walked through the quiet luxury of a recreated eighteenth century colonial interior and up the deeply carpeted staircase. A burst of laughter drifted out from the large, high ceilinged room at the head of the stairs. A tall, florid woman with iron grey hair in a short bob, wearing a knee length summer cocktail dress in a vivid floral pattern of reds, blues, and yellows, greeted them at the door. "Welcome, Davy," she said in a hearty voice. Her shrewd, brown eyes turned to Penelope. "Is this the new girl friend?"

"Penelope is working on the campaign, April, and doing a great job."

April Rumbaugh threw back her head in a hearty laugh. "I knew that, honey," she said to Penny. "But he hasn't answered my question, has he? I'm so glad you came, dear. We need a few school girl complexions in this crowd." She took Penelope by the arm and led her into the room. "I'll introduce you to the first group, Penny, then it's up to you. Are you shy or gregarious? You haven't said a word yet and I can't tell."

"I like people. With some I feel gregarious and others make me feel shy."

April Rumbaugh pulled her head back in a mock grimace. "Don't tell me you feel shy with me!"

"A little."

"Oh, for heavens sake! I've overdone it again. One drink

29

and my personality goes up to mach two. Do you know what mach two means?"

"Not exactly."

"Neither do I, but it sounds frightfully modern and 'in', doesn't it? I wear myself out trying to be 'in.' Sometimes, late at night, I kick off my shoes and say, 'to hell with it.' I suppose that's when I'm smart." She grinned at Penelope. A broad smile stole across Penelope's face. "My God, you're beautiful when you smile, Penny. The little waif look when you're serious is appealing, but that smile, it bowls one over. No wonder Dave is hooked." Her eyes moved across the room where Dave Winslow had joined a group by the window.

"He isn't hooked," Penelope protested.

"Don't tell Aunt April. I may get my romance on the late show these days, but I still recognize the male in love when I see it."

Penelope felt color rushing into her cheeks. She found April Rumbaugh both fascinating and rather disconcerting. She made her feel slightly off balance, almost dizzy. The room, with its scenic wallpaper depicting an idyllic early view of Washington's Potomac waterfront, its great chandelier, and its beautifully proportioned period furniture, projected an atmosphere of calm, of continuity, to which her hostess's frenetic personality was at a strange counterpoint. Penelope wondered if she were as open as she seemed and concluded that she was not. She was playing a part. The guests were the audience and Penelope the ingenue, standing slightly downstage, providing the occasion for the delivery of the lines.

She quickly decided that it was important for April Rumbaugh to like her and if she were cast as the ingenue to the female lead, she had better play the part and well. There were worse roles and she was realistic enough to realize that she was not yet fitted for any other. Female leading roles in Washington, as elsewhere, took time to develop. Penelope's smile returned as she met April Rumbaugh's eyes. She was prepared to spend the evening being an observant understudy.

April Rumbaugh put her arm around her. "Come on, honey, let me introduce you while you still have that pretty blush. No one has had the grace to do that in Washington politics since Dolly Madison and I suspect she faked it."

They moved toward two men in their late fifties and a tall, leathery looking woman in her thirties standing near a window overlooking the deep green of the golf course. "Penny, this is Patty Winston. She looks like a horsewoman from the Plains, but she really rides the Congress. You've read her column, 'What's Up?'"

"Yes," Penelope lied. "Hello Miss Winston."

"Mrs. Winston, Penny," the voice was dry and flat. "Three times over. Dick Winston is the latest."

"You notice she said, 'the latest' not 'the last,'" April Rumbaugh said in a good natured bantering tone. "I'll have to warn Dick. Where is he, by the way?"

"He's home drinking."

"Home? Isn't my liquor good enough for him?"

"No. Not any more."

"Well," April Rumbaugh said after a momentary hesitation, "I can't help that. Dick knows where I stand. Penny, this distinguished looking man, politely listening to this hen talk while I keep him waiting to be introduced, is George Williams, former national chairman of the party and Charles Frome's new campaign manager. What did it, George? The polls, or the way the money is beginning to flow in?"

George Williams, balding and blandly imperturbable in a carefully tailored navy blue linen suit, smiled faintly. "Both helped, April dear. I only manage winners. Winners are all that count in politics. But don't accuse me of being a Johnny-come-lately. Charlie Frome didn't want a formal campaign or a manager until last week."

"And this is Senator Baur, Penny," April said, turning

31

from Williams. "He is the leader of the Senate establishment. Southern Indiana's gift to the nation. He declared for Frome at four o'clock this afternoon. If I had any doubt that Frome would be nominated, it disappeared when Herman Baur said those fateful words at a press conference in the Senate caucus room."

Senator Baur, heavy set and rumpled with unruly grey hair in which a suggestion of the original brown remained spoke with an Ohio River valley twang, a linguistic survival from a century and a half earlier when the Ohio flowed through "the West" and the "frontier." "Charlie's always been my boy. I was ready to speak out whenever he gave the word."

His pale blue eyes behind horn rimmed glasses caught Penlope's stare of frank interest and he winked at her broadly.

"I'm from Southern Indiana, too, Senator."

"I thought so. I thought so. We have the prettiest girls, you know. I haven't lost my eye for that." Penelope caught herself blushing again. "Where are you from, dear?"

"Bloomington."

"Go to the university there?"

"Yes. I just graduated."

He sized her up, smiling. "And now you're in politics."

"Oh, no. I just help out."

"Sure you do. And don't minimize it. No candidate could ever win without folks 'helping out.' That's a good Hoosier term, Penny, and you're a good looking Hoosier girl." He gave her cheek a gentle pat.

There was a chorus of voices at the door to the room and April Rumbaugh turned away to greet her newly arriving guests.

"What plains state do you come from, Mrs. Winston?" Penelope asked politely, turning to Patty Winston as Baur and Williams moved slightly aside for a chat.

"Plains state? I live in Virginia."

"Oh, I thought Mrs. Rumbaugh said you were from the plains."

Patty Winston threw back her head and laughed. "The Plains is a small village in the Virginia hunt country, honey. I've never been west of Cleveland."

"Oh. I'm so stupid."

"Not at all," George Williams said kindly, returning to hear the end of their conversation. "The Plains is only famous for saddle sores on prominent behinds."

"People or behinds, George?" Patty Winston asked.

"Often both."

Penelope looked up into George Williams twinkling eyes. "I like what you said about winners being all that count. I believe that."

"In politics, Penny. I suppose we must tolerate a few losers elsewhere."

"I suppose so, but losers are depressing."

Patty Winston looked at her with interest. "Are you a winner, dear?"

Penelope looked at her solemnly. "Yes."

"Good girl," Senator Baur said jovially. "All we want around here are winners."

There was a stir at the door and a scattering of applause that swiftly rose to a collective shout of greeting and hand clapping punctuated by a single rebel yell as Charles Frome entered. He kissed April Rumbaugh on the cheek and turned to the group with a grin, holding up both arms extended for silence.

"Fellows and gals, thank you. Let's keep our cool and not disgrace sister April by getting thrown out of this august club. We are here not to listen to the candidate talk. I'll only inflict that on you in prime time from here on in, but to hoist a few together to celebrate our winning the election in the public opinion polls." He quieted a shout of excitement with a gesture. "That's great. We had to do it, but it is only fun and games. Now we have to get the votes where they count, on the floor of the convention in Chicago and at the polls next November. So drink up. Have a good time on April's chit and then let's go out and continue to work like hell." He waved with both hands above the crowd and began to move among them. In a few minutes he reached the group including Penelope. "George, Senator, Patty," he looked at Penelope, smiling, "And this is the youngest soldier, I take it?"

"Yes, Mr. President," Penelope's voice was faintly impish.

"Of course, Dave Winslow's girl. He tells me you have been a great help. Fresh ideas. That sort of thing."

"It's been fun."

Frome grinned boyishly, "Hasn't it though?" He turned to Senator Baur before moving off. "Thank you, Herm, for that statement this afternoon."

"My pleasure, Charlie. It got good coverage thanks to George and Patty, here."

"It topped a day of good news from every quarter. Very good news."

"I didn't hear your last name, Penny," Patty Winston said as Williams and Baur drifted away with Frome.

"I don't think Mrs. Rumbaugh knew what it was. It's Benton."

"Benton? Isn't that a New England name?"

"It could be. I'm from Indiana."

"I see." Patty Winston looked at her brightly. "Did you go to school in the East?"

"No."

"But you went to school?"

"Yes."

"Where?"

"Indiana University."

"That's a state university, isn't it?"

"Yes."

"What does your father do, dear?"

"He's dead."

"And your mother?"

"She's a mother."

"Don't you want to talk about your family?"

"No."

"Most people do."

"I think it is a very uninteresting subject."

"Weren't they all winners?"

"No. They weren't all winners. What about your family, three names back?"

Patty Winston lit a cigarette and removed a flake of tobacco from her tongue. Then she smiled, throwing her tanned, muscular face into ridges. "Your looks are deceptive, dear. You can't be pushed around, can you?"

"No."

"Forget the prying questions. It's my news hen instinct. How long have you been in Washington?"

"Seven weeks."

Patty blew out her cheeks. "And you made this little inner-sanctum get together in seven weeks?"

"Well, I'm here." Penelope looked around with interest. "This seems to be a well-heeled white group. I didn't think politics could be that exclusive any more."

"Negroes are important in politics in season. Negro politicians deliver a segregated, bloc, black vote. Frome is bidding for that. He'll pay a fair price, but votes are a perishable commodity, not power. Real power must be there all of the time. Real power is money, influence, connections. It's built up over generations. In this room is the core of that kind of power. That's why I called it the inner-sanctum. These are the donators of big money, the political pros. No Negro is in this league, yet. There's no way to desegregate raw power. You either have it or you don't and this room is full of raw power held tenaciously. It's carefully doled out to a political candidate, usually to obtain more power. The Negroes haven't any power to give and no one is going to give them any. That's why they are not here. It isn't discrimination, it's cold reality. If you ever see a Negro in a group like this, then you'll know that 'Black Power' is more than a slogan."

Penelope shivered. "I can feel the power. It's thrilling.

35

Some day, I'd like to be a part of it."

Patty looked at her speculatively. "You've made a good start, baby, if you know where you're going."

Penelope smiled. "What about you, three names back?"

"Three names back I was Patricia Phelps of Harrisburg, Pa."

"Connections? Power?"

"None. Just a lot of brass and an eye for the winners," her eyes twinkled. "I'm here because I have a rich mother-in-law and can raise hell in my column."

"I like you, Patty. You're genuine."

"Heaven forbid." She reached out and squeezed Penelope's forearm. "I see Dave Winslow coming this way. Good luck. Don't press too hard. You'll make it."

❧ 4 ❧

THE days of the convention in Chicago were long, hot and frenetic. Penelope spent most of her time in a small suite of mezzanine rooms converted into an office at the Conrad Hilton, seeing Dave only briefly each morning before he drove out to the great convention auditorium set amid the blowing papers and broken glass of the city's west side slums.

She was only dimly aware of the fight for delegate votes in the crowded hotel rooms and corridors of Chicago and on the convention floor. Her days were a blur of activity, directed by Dave, usually over the telephone; the typing of memorandums of conversations, checking lists of names, or relaying cryptic telephone messages.

Charles Frome sat in his suite at the Palmer House calmly waiting for the balloting, receiving the leaders of the party and introducing them to his gracious, smiling wife and two teen-aged sons who had avoided the nominating campaign but now suggested by their manner and appearance that they would help win the election and ultimately grace the White House.

He received the nomination on the second ballot and appeared with his family and that of the Vice Presidential nominee, Governor Perry of Texas, on the convention dias to accept the nomination with an eloquent, graceful speech. Balloons and confetti drifted down from the ceiling, illuminated by the probing shafts of light from the spot lights as the auditorium organ thundered out the strains of his campaign song. At last the hot, disheveled, excited crowd dispersed. The lights in the auditorium went out and the election campaign began with Charles Frome taking a midnight plane to Iowa City. He had pledged no rest, no relaxation until he was elected in November.

Penelope stood at the window of her room at the Conrad Hilton as a cool breeze off Lake Michigan billowed out the curtains around her. The lake was a pool of inky blackness broken only by the red and white flashes of offshore bouys, and the lights from a distant water pumping station offshore. Though it was past midnight, the endless flow of automobiles on the outer drive continued, the red tail lights and white headlights creating twin ribbons of flowing motion. She had watched the acceptance speech on the television set in her room and now she felt very alone and a little sad. There had been such excitement and now it was so quiet.

There was a tap on the door. She opened it and Dave Winslow walked in.

"No lights? No air conditioning? Don't tell me that you are going native?"

She smiled. She was glad to see him. "I was enjoying the view. It's the first time I've looked at it since we arrived." She turned back to the window.

He moved to stand beside her. "It's been pretty hectic," he said after a moment. "I hope you enjoyed it."

"It's been thrilling."

He put his arm around her shoulder and she turned, kissing him lightly on the lips, but when he tried to embrace her and prolong the kiss, she broke away.

"No fire?" He said huskily.

"I take a long time for these things, Dave. The kiss was a friendly gesture, that's all."

"It's nice to have a friend."

She switched on a table light.

"I didn't really come up here to seduce you," he said with forced lightness, putting a cigarette between his lips. "I wondered if on the night of victory you'd like to exchange a few hours sleep for a late supper and some dancing?"

"I'd love it. I don't feel like sleep."

"I know a little place on Rush Street where they never heard of politics."

"Give me ten minutes."

"I'm going to give you all of the time you need."

She laughed and touched his lips with her forefinger. "It's a deal."

Charles Frome's campaign for the presidency subtly suggested the inevitability of his election. He gave the impression that he was not campaigning, but moving about the country consulting with the people, learning to know them better so that he could perform the great works for them that their needs and aspirations had shown him were necessary. The newspapermen said that he travelled about the country with the air of a president-elect but the people did not find this presumptuous. He won in a landslide, 430 electoral votes to 105 and a popular plurality of 12,000,000 votes.

Dave Winslow sidled between the desks and tables that filled the suite in the Rayburn House Office Building of the president-elect of the United States until he reached his own desk jammed in one corner and almost hidden under a mound of papers. He grinned at Penelope, who looked up from her adjoining table, and mouthed the words "good morning" over the clatter of the typewriters and the ringing of telephones that blended with a score of speaking voices to inundate the suite in noise. He glanced at several telegrams and telephone messages on the memo sheets with "urgent" printed in red block letters across the top and then stepped over to Penelope, putting his lips close to her ear. "Let's get the hell out of here."

They stepped out into the snow falling gently on Independence Avenue. "Where are we going?" she asked as he hailed a taxi cab which almost drowned them in slush as it skidded to a halt.

"I'm going to buy you a cup of coffee far enough away from the bedlam of the birth pangs of the Frome Administration so that I can talk to you."

She smiled at him as she got into the taxi. "It's about time."

They sat in a semi-circular booth upholstered in red leather in a hotel coffee shop. He sipped his coffee and glanced about the nearly empty room with its decor of stylized circus animals. "This is more like it. I feel like a fugitive who has found sanctuary."

"I know you have been terribly busy."

"Every person close to Frome is on the hunted list these days. Appointments, favors, 'background briefing.' God, I'm bone tired. Frome has holed up over at the Eastern Shore estate of April Rumbaugh. We poor bastards on the firing line, filtering the messages and callers to him, are the ones to be pitied. For news media purposes his headquarters is a small brick eighteenth century courthouse in his home county. He looks great on T.V., casually pulling a piece of paper out of one pocket and making a political announcement from the courthouse steps as if it just occurred to him. The public doesn't realize twenty people agonized over that announcement for two weeks and spent five hundred dollars on telephone calls clearing it with all interested parties."

"You don't want them to realize it, do you?"

"I'm out on my ear if they do. I'm the keeper of the image, you know. But sometimes I wish it weren't so easy. I'd feel better if the public were smarter."

"You're just tired. It isn't just an image. President Frome is real. He'll be a great President."

Dave lit a cigarette. "I've been too close to it. The metamorphosis from Congressman to President seems phony when you're too close to the man. Yet, I know it's occurring."

40

"Your image building helped, but the man was there. He's the man that got elected and he's the man who will be President."

Dave regarded her, a little smile playing about his lips, without speaking. Then he said, "I didn't really bring you across town in a snowstorm to talk shop. It's four days to Christmas and I hear you're going home."

"Yes. For a week."

"First time since you came to Washington, isn't it?"

"Yes."

"You'll feel like the walls are closing in on you in Bloomington."

"Potomac fever?"

"We all get it." He reached into his pocket and with a touch of shyness put a small package before her. "That's for Christmas and because you are you."

She touched the package with her fingertips and looked into his eyes earnestly. "How sweet, Dave. How very sweet. May I open it now? Or must I wait?"

"Open it now."

She undid the wrapping and removed the lid. A small pin of tiny rubies set in gold in the shape of the Capitol sparkled from a pad of white satin. "Oh, Dave! How wonderful!" She leaned toward him and kissed him. "Thank you, so much, darling."

"I'll pin it on," he said gruffly. "I hope it will remind you of a wonderful six months."

"It will. And of you."

"I hoped that too."

A waitress in a brown and white uniform with a yellow ribbon in her henna'd hair, came over and filled their coffee cups. "Isn't that pretty!" She said leaning over Penelope. "Is it real?"

"Yes. It's real," Dave said shortly.

"I never seen one like it."

"It was custom made."

"Real nice, doll. I love it." She moved away to a nearby booth.

Dave grimaced after the waitress. "I have some news, too, Penelope."

"Good news?"

"I think so. The President-elect has asked me to become a White House Assistant."

"Dave, that's grand! Simply grand! But I'm not surprised. He couldn't get along without you."

"I'll sort of be an assistant without portfolio. Still the keeper of the image. The builder of the legend."

"That's very important. He has to get re-elected."

He looked at her wryly. "My God, but you're practical! I doubt if even Frome is thinking about re-election yet."

"I'll bet he is."

"I'll tell you what he *is* thinking about."

"What?"

"He wants you on the White House staff."

"You're kidding!"

"No. He wants to use the 'Before Chicago Team,' as he calls it, to fill all positions physically near him. Where he can be frequently seen and overheard, he wants loyal people he can depend on."

"But what can I do in the White House? I'd be scared stiff."

"You do just what you do now."

"Help you?"

"Sure. Keep me in touch with the younger generation."

She relaxed and smiled. "Well, why didn't you say so, Dave, darling. That's all right then. You frightened me with that 'White House staff' stuff. It sounded so official."

"We'll get you double your salary."

"Double? I'm not worth it."

"I say you are. Anyway, this is politics. We won, Penelope. It's the winning that determines the pay. If Frome had

42

lost we'd be out on the street. It's double or nothing in politics."

"You have convinced me. I'll take it."

"Would your mother like to come to the inauguration?"

"My mother?"

"Yes."

"No. She doesn't travel much. But thank you."

"Any other family members?"

"My mother is all of my family."

"Home town friends?"

"They all voted against Frome."

"That's that then. More coffee?"

"No. I'm jittery already."

"Then I guess we'd better get back."

"Dave?"

"Yes."

"We're having a little pre-Christmas party at the house tonight since all four of us are leaving Washington for Christmas. Would you like to come?"

"Would the other girls mind?"

"No. They're impressed by you—a man so close to the President."

"I'll have to wear my suit with the broad shoulders and the statesman lapels."

"It's for dinner at seven." She put a cool hand over his. "I do appreciate the gift and the wonderful news about my job. I'll have a little gift for you tonight."

He looked very pleased. "I'll be prompt, ready, and willing. Will there be mistletoe?"

"I'll go out and buy some, now that a man is coming."

Penelope awakened in the low ceilinged room at the back of the house and for a moment did not know where she was. Then she recognized the wallpaper with the yellow buttercups. She was at home in Bloomington. It was early, barely light. She turned to the small leather framed travel alarm she

43

had placed beside her on a night table. It was seven o'clock. She stretched in bed and listened. There were no sounds. The students upstairs were at home on Christmas vacation and her mother wasn't up yet. She got up and walked down the hallway to the floor's single bathroom. She was back in her room dressing when her mother appeared.

"You're an earlybird, Penelope." Mrs. Benton had a blue flannel robe over her nightgown and her close cropped iron grey hair was awry from sleeping.

"Yes. I've gotten in the habit of getting up early in Washington."

Mrs. Benton yawned. "I rather expected to sleep late. This is as much vacation as I ever get, with the students gone and all."

"I know, Mom."

"Eight bedrooms is a lot to straighten up every day and there's no help to hire, at least at a price I can afford."

"What about Hetty?"

"She quit last month; said it was rheumatism. I think it was because she finally found out she could get a government check."

"I'll get breakfast. You needn't bother."

"No. You're home for a rest. I'll get it."

"Coffee and toast is all I want."

"No eggs?"

"No thank you."

"I've got eggs."

"No thank you."

"You on a diet?"

"No."

"I'd think not. You look trim enough."

Penelope did her mouth. "You're pretty," Mrs. Benton said. "You'll be getting married next."

"No. I want to stay single for a time."

"That's right. Waiting don't hurt. Marry the right man, not someone like your father."

"Dad was all right."

"Sure he was all right. There wasn't anything bad about him, but look how he left me."

"He didn't know he would die of a heart attack."

"He didn't plan anything. That's what was wrong. He left no pension, no insurance—nothing."

"And no debts. Allow him that, anyway."

"No one would give him credit the last few years. That's why he had no debts." Mrs. Benton leaned against the doorjamb into the bedroom. "He threw over his job on the railroad when he was thirty-five. That would have given him a pension, but, no, he was too good for the railroad. He was going to make it on his own. And the insurance. He used to have $5,000 in insurance. How was I to know he had stopped paying the premiums and let it lapse? It was all I could do to give him a proper burial. I increased the mortgage on this house to do it. I never told you that, did I?"

"No. I never knew that."

"Well, it's time you knew."

"Dad was a good man. Everyone liked him."

Mrs. Benton's expression softened. "Yes, he was a good man, a loving man." Her voice trembled. "I miss him."

Penelope started to push by her mother. "I'll get breakfast."

"No, really, dear. You are the visitor."

"You're not dressed. I am. It will be ready when you come down."

Mrs. Benton watched her walk down the hallway to the head of the stairs. "It don't seem right."

Penelope had an egg after all. She fried an egg and two strips of bacon for each of them. She had the breakfast laid out on the large square table in the window that overlooked a narrow kitchen garden extending to a ragged privet hedge running along the cinder alley that bisected the block. She had covered the table with a red checked tablecloth and had placed a small table lamp on one corner to fight the gloom of

45

the gray winter's morning.

Mrs. Benton appeared, looking neat and competent in one of the pale green dresses piped in white she wore while working in the house. "Why that looks real nice, Penny. You're a regular little homemaker."

"Thank you," Penelope said quietly.

She eyed her mother over their second cup of coffee. "I wish you wouldn't wear those dresses, Mother. They look like a uniform. Someone would think you were a servant."

"They wouldn't be far off," Mrs. Benton smiled wryly. "But they are practical. They wear well and launder easily. I like them."

"I think you glory in it."

"In what?"

"In your difficulties."

Mrs. Benton pursed her lips. "It's like old times. I wondered just when you were going to start."

"Start what?"

"Start picking on me. I've never suited you. You've always acted a little ashamed of me."

"That's not true."

"Yes, it is. I scraped and saved to get you through the university. I even let you join that fancy sorority. All it did for you was to give you outsized ideas—make you harder to please."

"Remember, I worked too. I never lived on campus. I was always a 'townie.' I had to fight for all I got. We did it together."

Mrs. Benton sniffed. "That's all I ask. Remember we did it together. I only want credit where credit's due."

"I'll remember. I'm getting a raise next month. Maybe I can send you something."

Mrs. Benton's eyes filled with tears and her lips trembled. "You don't have to do that. I don't want to be a burden."

Penelope got up from her chair and came over and kissed her on the cheek. "Mother, I want to."

Mrs. Benton began to cry and held Penelope to her. "I'm so proud of you, baby. I really am. A college graduate and now down in Washington and knowing our new President and all. It seems like a dream. It really does. Your dad would be so proud if he were alive."

Penelope uttered a deprecating little laugh and gave her mother a hug. "I'm only a secretary, but guess where I'm going to work, Mom?"

"Where?"

"The White House!"

Mrs. Benton gave a little scream. "The White House? Right in the White House? Are you going to be the President's private secretary?"

"Oh, no, Mother. It's a big place. I'll continue to work for Dave Winslow, but I'll be on the White House staff."

Mrs. Benton beamed at her. "Oh, I'm so proud! My stars! I really am." She sighed. "It shows what an education will do for you. My! My! Well, I never guessed. I just never did."

She sat a moment, sipping her coffee, then she glanced at Penelope shyly. "Do you suppose I could visit you in Washington some day, Penny, and you show me all of these wonderful things? I'd just die if I could shake the President's hand."

"Of course, Mom. I don't know when, but when I have a place of my own we'll try to do it. I share with three other girls now."

Mrs. Benton was starry-eyed. "Just think. Going to Washington to visit my daughter who works in the White House! It's just a dream. That's all it is. It's just a dream." She looked at Penelope fondly. "I'm so proud of my little girl I could just bust! I really could!"

❧ 5 ❧

PATTY WINSTON sat back in her chair in the West Executive Wing of the White House with a sigh, regarded the disorganized pile of papers on her desk with a bored expression on her face, and lit a cigarette. Penelope entered and laid a publicity layout on a comparatively empty corner. "How's the Press Secretary?"

"Slowly choking to death on administrative details. If I'd known I was expected to be an administrator, I never would have taken the job."

"You couldn't resist the honor of being the first woman Presidential Press Secretary."

"Maybe not," Patty said morosely, "But I'd rather hand it out in my column than take it here in the White House."

"The press corps is treating you very politely, it seems to me."

"Oh, I'll get some special consideration on the sex angle for a while. It's not that the bastards feel chivalrous. It's just that they know the public expects it of them. As usual, they're the victims of their own clichés." She drew on her cigarette. "How are you making it, Penny?"

"All right, I guess. It isn't as exciting as the campaign."

"Winslow's kind of a droop. Isn't he?"

"Dave? Why no!" Penelope protested. Then her eyes met the shrewd eyes of the older woman and she giggled. "Well,

I guess he is, a little."

"What kind of men do you really like?"

"No special kind. Older men, I guess, who have accomplished something."

"Why?"

"They're more interesting. They know more than I do."

"And they don't make passes?"

"Well, I'm not speaking from experience. On campus, the only older men were professors. That isn't what I mean."

Patty yawned. "I forget how young you are. So indecently, boringly young." She coughed. "At least you have the grace to be selfish and self-centered. Most of you young are so banal these days—hung up on this social conscience thing. Maybe we're going to create a whole generation that doesn't know how to have a good time—like the Victorians. The only difference is the Victorians suffered in bone stays and stiff collars and our new young go in for long dirty hair and muumuus."

Penelope grinned. "You sound like your column."

"Do I, dear? Thank God. I was afraid the juices were drying up." Patty pushed out her cigarette in an ash tray with a prodding finger. "The President said something nice about you the other day."

"The President? I thought he had forgotten I was around. He smiles at me in the corridors, but it's the same smile he gives the tourists; you know, the shining teeth from the tanned figure surrounded by Secret Service men."

"Don't be irreverent. That's my department. Yours, if I'm not mistaken, is sweet, feminine guilelessness."

"What did he *say?*"

"We were discussing an idea of yours and he said, 'why that's as bright as Penny!' "

"Did he really?"

"So help me God. Do you think I'd make up a corny play on words like that? You only think like that after fifteen years in politics."

"Gosh. That was awful nice, wasn't it?"

"I thought so. That's why I passed it on."

Penelope stood a moment, smiling into space, then she turned to Patty. "Thank you for telling me. Remembering that will always make me happy."

Patty waved a hand and reached for a file of papers. "Glad to oblige. Why keep one of Frome's few spontaneous remarks to myself?"

The next day Penelope invited Patty to lunch at Sans Souci. They sat at a table for two on the little balcony overlooking the main dining room with the heavily framed reproductions of the French impressionists on its brocaded walls. Patty sipped her martini. "I shouldn't have had this second one. Dick is the lush of the family and I'm having a press handout this afternoon."

"Anything exciting?" Penelope asked idly stirring a scotch and soda with a plastic cylinder protruding out of the glass.

"The boss is going to Japan."

"Oh." Penelope looked around the small room. "I notice the Postmaster General, the Secretary of Commerce and two Senators down there," she said with shining eyes.

"If they could only see you in Bloomington, huh?"

"It's still exciting to me to see famous people I read about in the newspapers and magazines, yes."

"You haven't mentioned the important people in the room," Patty said.

"I haven't? Who are they?"

"I won't point them out. It would be too obvious, but if you watched the crowd down in the pit for a few minutes you could guess yourself. They sit still. The others come to them. There's a newspaper publisher from New York, the mayor of Chicago, and a nationally syndicated political newspaper columnist known for his sudden shark-like forays. There also is a famous television personality, best known for the way her derrière moves when she closes a car door on a T.V. commercial."

"Yes, I recognize her," Penelope giggled.

"One of the nation's richest men follows her advice in making political contributions, believe it or not."

"Is she that smart?"

Patty studied the menu. "Hell no. He must figure because she's good in bed, she understands politics."

Penelope laughed.

"That's not as far out as it sounds," Patty grinned. "But I may be complimenting her at that."

They ordered. Penelope toyed with her food. "Patty," she said into a prolonged silence.

"Still here, baby. Spill it. I know you have something on your mind."

"Patty, I thought what the President said was awfully sweet."

"What he said?"

"About something being as bright as Penny."

"Oh, yes. Trite, but sweet."

"I know I seem terribly small town when I say this, but I'd like the folks back in Bloomington to know he said it."

"Swell, write them about it. Quote me."

"It would sound like boasting and they wouldn't believe me."

Patty cut into her minute steak, saying nothing.

"What I mean is," Penelope said intensely, leaning forward, "Couldn't you give the story to one of the newspapers? If they printed it everyone back home would believe it."

"Plant it, you mean?"

"Whatever you call it."

"I didn't realize you cared so much about what the folks back home in Bloomington thought," Patty said drily.

"It could be a human relations angle," Penelope suggested hopefully.

"It's not original enough or, present company excepted, important enough."

"Please, Patty."

51

"No," Patty said definitely. "I can't play that game with the President of the United States."

Penelope's mouth drew into a thin, stubborn line. "You sound awfully damned pompous all of a sudden."

"Pompous or not, there it is. Your investment in my lunch was wasted, unless it enables you to improve your technique next time."

"I didn't ask you to lunch for that," Penelope said sullenly. "You can say the most wounding things."

"I know," Patty said wearily. "This restaurant is always packed with people who just love each other's company."

Dave Winslow looked in on Penelope late that afternoon. "Do we still have a date tonight?"

"Yes."

"I'll be by about seven-thirty, God and the President willing."

"Dave, it's such a wet, stormy night. Come by at seven for dinner and we'll stay in."

"Dinner? Well, O.K. Sure. Didn't you want to see the movie?"

"Later. Not tonight."

"Don't go to any trouble."

"No. I'll stop by Cannon's for fish. Otherwise, it will be frozen side dishes."

"Great. Will the resident Witches of Endor be there?"

"No. They'll all be out tonight."

"Great. You've made me a happy man, Penny."

She smiled. "Don't let affairs of state interfere."

"I'll be there even if the hot line is ringing."

The fire in the small Victorian grate burned low. Dave sat slumped down on the sofa unconsciously turning a brandy snifter in his hands. Penelope sat on a hassock nearer to the fireplace, holding her hands toward the heat. "It's cold tonight," she said.

52

"Yes."

"February is always the coldest month. It is back home, too."

"Penelope, I suppose I'm taking advantage of the evening alone with you, but do you ever think of me seriously?"

Her eyes turned to him. "Yes, I do, but I'm not ready for that."

"My divorce becomes final in March."

"I remember your telling me."

"Well?"

"Let's talk about it in March."

He leaned forward toward her profile outlined in the firelight. "I am in love with you, Penelope."

"I know," she said softly. "Thank you, Dave, dearest."

He sat back against the sofa. He lit a cigarette and after the match had flared in the semi-darkness and had been extinguished he said with forced lightness, "Well, I never claimed to be a great lover."

She reached over and squeezed his hand. "I'm not indifferent, really I'm not. Things take time. I like what I am doing. I'm not ready for a change."

"I understand."

"Dave," she said after a moment.

"Yes."

"Did you hear what the President said about me the other day?"

"No."

"He was pleased with an idea of mine and he said, 'why, that's as bright as Penny!' "

"I'm not surprised. Among the younger gals you are his favorite."

"I was thinking, Dave, looking at the importance of emphasizing his human side, if we shouldn't try to play this up as a human interest anecdote about the President? Of course, I know it involves me, but we could color me any color you want for effect. I don't care."

"Human interest?"

"A busy, burdened man who still maintains a warm relationship with his staff and is amused by their humor and personalities. It's sort of the youth bit again. In other words, he relates to the younger generation who work for him. He remembers their names, digs their talk—I just happen to be an example."

"Yes," Dave said slowly. "We might be able to do something with it. I like human interest stories to counteract the natural tendency for him to disappear in the clouds around Olympus. You wouldn't mind the publicity?"

"No. Actually, to be frank, it would please my mother."

"O.K. I'll look into it tomorrow."

"How will you handle it?"

"Oh, I don't know. Maybe a no attribution, background bit for the columnists. We're about due for one of those."

"Can I help work on it?"

"Sure. It's your idea and you're part of the color."

She hugged her knees. "I just love working with you, Dave. It's such fun."

"You don't find me maudlin when I get sentimental?"

She kissed him softly on the lips and moved over to the sofa.

Jean Wilson squealed at the small breakfast table in the little house on Thirty-fifth Street. "Penny! You're in Sy Corman's column!"

Penelope looked up brightly from her coffee. "Really? What does it say?"

"Well," Jean said excitedly, her eyes racing down the news column, "It's about President Frome and his schedule around the White House, there's a lot of stuff about his family, his days, his health exercises in the gym and in the swimming pool and then it goes on about his morning office routine. Now get this," her eyes raised to Penelope's over the top of

54

❧ 6 ❧

THE telephone in the downstairs hall of the house on Thirty-fifth Street rang about nine-thirty the next Sunday night. Jean Wilson, her hair in curlers, got up from a chair in the livingroom with a sigh and walked to the telephone table, the index finger of her right hand marking her place in the book she had been reading.

"Yes?"

"May I speak with Penelope Benton, please?"

"Who shall I say is calling?" Jean asked in her best secretarial manner.

"Duane Miller."

Jean shrugged her shoulders and rocked her head as she silently mouthed the name. It meant nothing to her. "I'll call her. Just a minute. 'Penny!' " she shouted up the stairs, "Telephone."

"Coming," Penelope's voice came faintly from her bedroom.

"Who is it?" She asked Jean from the livingroom doorway as she tied a red dressing gown around her.

Jean looked up again from the book she had resumed reading. "Some fellow by the name of Duane Miller."

"Don't know him."

"Neither do I, but he's hanging on the other end of that line. You made the papers. You can expect crank calls. Either take it or hang up, Penny. I'm expecting a call from home

the paper and she giggled, "President Frome is the third youngest President in history, after Kennedy, who was six months younger on inauguration, and he is fighting hard to postpone the loss of youth to middle age. He has surrounded himself with a youthful staff and is amused and stimulated by their enthusiasm. One of his favorites is twenty-one year old Penny Benton, a sprite, ingenious Hoosier gal, fresh from the Indiana University campus who has become a symbol of the sparkle President Frome wants about him. If a thing seems particularly apt to him, 'it is as bright as Penny,' otherwise, it's dismissed 'as dull as lead.' These days to be 'in' at the White House, you have to be contemporary and if you don't know what contemporary means, just ask Penny Benton. The President of the United States does." Jean put down the paper. "How *about* that! I didn't know you were that close to the President, Penny."

"I'm not, really," Penelope replied. "You know how columnists exaggerate. Sy Corman is really a sports columnist anyway substituting as a political columnist until the *Tribune* can find Patty Winston's replacement."

"But, sweetie, there must be something to it."

"Well, he does use the expression about me."

Jean picked up the paper and re-read it. "Gosh, wait until Sue and Mary come down. Will their eyes pop out!"

Penelope finished her coffee. "Mary will discount it. She always does where I'm concerned." She rose to go.

"Well, I think it's great, Penny. Simply great. At last I've read something in Sy Corman's column I can believe. I'm on the inside, roommate with a celebrity!"

Penelope giggled. "Don't ask for an invitation to the White House or you'll find out how unimportant I really am."

Jean smiled at her. "All I know is what I read in the newspapers."

Mary entered the kitchen a few minutes after Penelope had

left it. Jean smiled at her and handed her the newspaper. "Look at Sy Corman's column."

Mary read it through and then laid the newspaper down to pour her coffee. "How did our Penny work that?" she asked acidly.

Jean frowned. "What do you mean, 'work?'"

"Well, things like that just don't happen."

"It's a quote from President Frome, Mary. Are you suggesting that Penny put words into his mouth?"

"Presidents get misquoted or quoted out of context. All I'm saying is that Penny's an operator. If you can't see that, you're pretty thick."

"You certainly got out of the wrong side of the bed this morning. I think it's great. You're just jealous of Penny."

Mary sipped her coffee. "If Penny wants to promote herself, more power to her. I just insist on recognizing it for what it is. I'm not going to fall for that 'my gosh, how sweet everyone is to me' routine."

"You don't like Penny much, Mary, and it's beginning to show. Remember, we do have to get along in this house. Roomates don't grow on trees these days, so be careful."

Mary vigorously buttered some toast. "We'll get along. I just don't think she's Shirley Temple. She's on the make."

"On the make? For what, for God's sake? Maybe for Winslow but what's wrong with that?"

"Not for Winslow. I don't know what she's on the make for, but for whatever it is, she's at it full time."

"I don't see why you say these things. She's always nice to you."

Mary made a little grimace. "She's always nice to everybody in the same superficial way that doesn't cost her anything. She knows that she's an ambitious nobody that can't afford to offend anyone. Wait until she's a somebody. Then you'll see her claws."

"Have you noticed yours lately, dear?"

56

Mary lit a cigarette. "Oh, go to hell. She's taken I'm wasting my breath."

Jean flushed. "Yes, you are. I don't buy it."

Mary gave an elaborate shrug with her shoulde the room.

57

on the Sunday night reduced rates."

"Hello," Penelope said tentatively into the receiver.

"Hello, Miss Benton," a masculine voice spoke easily and unhurriedly. "I am Duane Miller. I am one of the contributing editors of the *Georgian*. You've heard of our magazine, I hope?"

"Yes. I've read it."

"Bully for you! Then you know we are a slick paper magazine with a Georgetown slant that covers the scene in Washington. That's scene in the old sense without the capital letter."

"Yes."

"I was intrigued by the little paragraph about you in Sy Corman's column this last week."

"Oh, that!" Penelope's voice was deprecating.

"I'd like to build a feature for the magazine around the idea. Would you mind?"

"Well, I don't know."

"Can you have lunch with me tomorrow? I'll explain my idea in detail."

"I only have an hour."

"That's enough."

"All right, I'll listen, Mr. Miller."

The laugh over the wire was warm. "Duane, please. When you see me you'll see how ridiculous it is to call me, 'Mr. Miller.'"

"I'll meet you at the gate on East Executive Avenue at 12:15."

"It's a date, Miss Benton. I won't waste your time."

Duane Miller was waiting for her on the sidewalk when she emerged from the White House East Gate, holding an umbrella above his head against the light, cold rain which was falling. His freckled face broke into a grin. "Hi. Miss Benton?"

"Yes. You are Mr. Miller?"

59

"All five feet four of me, honey chile. My mama raised me to be a jockey, but I get sick way up there on top of horses." He hailed a passing taxicab. "I'll take you to the Press Club family room. No innuendo intended. It's close and the food isn't good enough to distract you from what I am going to say."

When they were seated, Duane Miller leaned across the table. "Drink?"

"No. I'll just have a hamburger and coffee."

"That's great! I've only got about ten bucks for expenses on this story from my parsimonious editor. I love gals who like the simple life. It's all I can afford."

"I could get by with a hot dog," Penelope smiled.

Duane Miller held up a restraining hand. "Please! There are standards to be maintained, mademoiselle. We will compromise no further." He ordered and turned to her. "Here's the idea, Miss Penelope, ma'am. I want to do a two page spread on the young, unofficial members of the Frome Administration. You know, running the country is only fun when you're underpaid, overworked, and have no responsibility for the decisions. I figure it's a natural to build this idea around you, the President's favorite girl Friday. I was waiting on that curbside in the rain, waiting for a homely bag to appear and blow the whole idea, but just my luck, out walks a dream, fresh, engaging, beautiful smile, the all American girl and we're on like gang busters!"

"Are you proposing, Mr. Miller?"

"With more stature and more dough, the answer would be yes. I'd throw you across my saddle horn and we'd ride hard to reach the castle by the wood before darkness fell. Lacking both, I can only spread my calloused ink stained hands and say, 'no, my lady.'" He bit into his hamburger. "What do you say?"

"To what?"

"The idea, the pictorial spread."

"Will it be friendly? Or poking fun?"

"Friendly? I throw myself at your feet and you ask? Of course it will be friendly."

"Who will be in it, besides me?"

"Guys and gals under thirty. You can help me pick them out."

Penelope sipped her coffee. "What's your circulation?"

"Circulation?"

"Yes. If we go to this trouble, how many people are going to read it?"

"We print about twenty-five thousand copies. The readership is about three times that. We hope."

"Not much, is it?"

"No, but we are widely read in Washington."

"In the Congress?"

"We give every member of Congress a free subscription."

"That doesn't mean that they read it. If it's free they probably don't."

Duane Miller's face clouded. "O.K., so we're small time. But we try harder."

"If you have this idea, why wouldn't *Look* or *Life* have the same idea?"

"I don't know. Have they called you? Do they buy you hamburgers with pickles and onions, yet?"

"No. But they might."

"I tell you what I'll do, I'll throw in a free subscription. For life or for as long as you can stand it."

"I'll tell you what *I'll* do, Mr. Miller. Think big. Get *Life* or *Look* interested and I'll cooperate. Forget the *Georgian*. Go free lance. Hit the big time."

Duane Miller looked at her solemnly. "Maybe you're right," he said after a moment.

"Of course I'm right! You have an original idea. You've got a White House contact who will cooperate. Why waste it on a neighborhood magazine with a circulation of twenty-five thousand when it will sell as easily to a magazine with a circulation of seven or eight million? They can afford to pay you what it's worth."

Duane Miller's fingers drummed nervously on the table top, then his face broke into a grin. "You're right, doll. Absolutely right! How can I thank you?"

Penelope reached over and squeezed his hand. "You can keep me front and center in any story you sell."

"That's all?"

"That will be enough."

"Are you giving me an exclusive?"

"If you deliver."

Duane Miller glanced at his wristwatch. "I'll start right now."

"Lovely. Call me at home when you know something."

"To think you did all of this for me on a hamburger. Think what would happen if I bought you a steak?"

Penelope leaned her chin on both hands and smiled deeply into his eyes. "Frightening, isn't it?"

Three days later Penelope answered the telephone at home. "Miss Penelope, baby? This is Duane. I've done it, by God. We're doing the spread for *Life!*"

"Duane! That's wonderful! But when?"

"For the Easter issue. How about that?"

"Come over and tell me about it."

"Right now?"

"Sure, right now."

"I'm on my way."

Duane Miller leaned back in the big chair and beat his hands on the chair arms as he grinned at the ceiling. "Christ! What a day, Penny. What a day! I had a hell of a time getting inside, see? Then they liked the idea. Then they liked the layouts of other stuff I've done, they liked the photographic techniques I've used."

"Are you a photographer?"

"Penelope, baby, I'm a one man army, limited only by union rules. Anyway, everything goes along swell and then they call New York. Can you believe it? New York doesn't like the idea! So we all fly up to New York on the shuttle and after we all get smashed on cocktails, they agree to do it. We sign something in an alcoholic stupor and I fly home and call you."

"Do you have control over the format?"

"Absolutely. They keep editorial control, but I produce the raw material."

Penelope hugged her knees as she sat on the hassock and looked at him. "I've been thinking. My birthday is the first week in March. Let's make it my birthday party and I invite all of these people in. Then you take pictures of us having fun and you can identify us and editorialize if you wish in the captions and leader paragraphs."

"Say! That's great. We need some occasion to hang it on."

"Hang it on my birthday. I'm supposed to be front and center anyway. Remember?"

"Will do."

"I intend to work very closely with you on this, Duane. It indirectly concerns the White House and I want to know just what is happening."

"I can understand that."

Penelope sat toward the rear of the first tier box and listened to the tumultuous music rising from the stage at the end of the ornate, gilt encrusted ballroom of the Mayflower Hotel. She smiled wanly at Duane Miller. "I have a hell of a headache."

"Yeah, it's pretty wild, isn't it?" He peered down onto the crowded dance floor."

"Uh huh."

"Don't you dig this, Penelope, baby? Remember it's all for you. That's supposed to be your gang down there."

"Most of them I've never even seen before."

"Well, sure. If we'd only invited your friends we wouldn't need the Mayflower ballroom. We could have had it in a

Mac Donald's drive-in or a phone booth, maybe."

"Oh, shut up, Duane."

"I'm sorry this is not your style. We had to create a party that would sell magazines in Peoria. In Peoria they believe this is the typical Washington get-together of the golden youth. That's what we created."

"I'm not complaining. I just want to know when I can go home."

"Anytime. We've got all of the pictures we need of you having a good time."

"Then I'm going."

"I'll take you home."

"No, I'll take a cab. You're itching to get back on that dance floor."

"To be honest, I figured a little action down there would be one of my fringe benefits."

Penelope looked down at the gyrating crowd. "Nobody down there matters. They all look rather underdone, mentally moist, and a little mushy."

"You'd better keep that opinion a deep, dark secret, sweetie. You're supposed to be the spirit of the young in Washington."

Penelope reached for her handbag. "Don't worry. I always remember to smile when I see the little birdie."

Dave Winslow nervously puffed on a cigarette as he gazed out of the window. He did not see the first green signs of spring or the swelling buds of the tulip magnolia. His expression was closed and he looked inward.

"Did you leave word for me, Dave?" Penelope said from his office door.

He swung around in his chair from the window and faced her across the desk. His hand fell on an open magazine. "This is quite a spread about you in *Life*."

"Yes. I'm simply thrilled."

64

He cleared his throat. "I didn't even know it was your birthday, March sixth."

"Well, Dave, darling. I have to have a birthday sometime. That was it."

He picked up the magazine. "Quite a group you had; every photogenic secretary, administrative assistant or minor political appointee in town. I didn't realize you had met so many people in Washington or that you had such an unfailing eye for comers."

"The magazine made up the guest list," Penelope said evenly. "They wanted to make a point. The party was the excuse."

" 'Penelope and the People under Thirty the President Trusts.' That puts the rest of us senior citizens in our place."

"It wasn't meant that way, Dave. You can't blame me if you're over thirty."

"Oh, was it only age that kept me away? I thought I wasn't to know, until too late."

"I don't know what you mean."

"Don't you think this is something I should have cleared before publication? It affects the President."

"*Life* was covering *my* birthday party, Dave. They wouldn't have cleared it with you and you wouldn't have asked. That would have been censorship. Besides, I didn't realize it would have that slant." She stood staring at him, a defiant pout on her face. "Anyway, I think it's great! It's about a nice group of people and it emphasizes again the youth bit for the President."

"It won't do him any good if the public believes he is running the country with junior achievement winners."

"What does the President think?"

Winslow made a sour face. "He likes it. He congratulated me on the idea," he said grudgingly. "I hadn't read it at the time, so I grinned like an idiot and said, 'thank you, Mr. President.' "

"Well, I'll be damned!" Penelope exploded. "You bring me in here on the carpet like a school girl, frighten me half to death in thinking I've made some awful *gaffe* and then it turns out that the only thing bothering you is your injured pride or maybe your jealousy."

"I'm not jealous of you, Penelope. I'm hurt, yes, and I don't think it's pride. I thought we worked together. I thought you confided in me. I thought we were friends, hopefully more than friends. This thing hits me right between the eyes."

She moved across the room and sat on the edge of his desk, placing one hand over his. "Why, Dave? Just because I work with you? What if this had been someone else's birthday party and I was only a guest? It's just a story. It wasn't personal. I didn't even think of it involving the President or you, not really. I suppose I should have mentioned it, but I didn't know how it would turn out. If I have offended you, Dave, I am sorry. You are my dearest friend in Washington, maybe my dearest friend anywhere. I wouldn't hurt you for the world."

He squeezed her hand absently and then smiled. "O.K., Penelope. Forget it. You can't help it if you're good copy. I guess I should be thankful *Life* identified the Administration with you and not with April Rumbaugh. April's been around too long to lend the Frome Administration the freshness it needs. Her money is green, but April isn't and the press was beginning to notice."

"Then I'm forgiven, Dave?"

"Sure."

Penelope got up from the desk, walked to the door and closed it, and returned to the desk. She leaned over to Dave and kissed him firmly and warmly on the lips. "I'm so glad. I hate tension between friends." She did not resist when he pulled her onto his lap and kissed her again. "Do they allow necking in the White House?" she murmured.

"At appropriate moments," he said huskily.

She nibbled his right ear. "Will you take me out to dinner tonight?"

"Sure."

She rumpled his hair and got up. "Silly boy, but I do adore you."

❧ 7 ❧

JEAN WILSON looked up from her breakfast as Sue Gort entered the kitchen of the house on Thirty-fifth Street. "Well, you're up early for a Saturday morning. I work for a slave driver, but I thought you would sleep in."

"I wanted a chance to speak with you, Jean," Sue said, pouring herself a cup of coffee.

"Confessions in hair curlers?"

"You seem to understand Penny better than I do. I want to ask her a favor and I'm wondering how to go about it."

"She doesn't mind being asked favors. I think she enjoys it. Sort of middle western *noblesse oblige*."

"Since that *Life* article, she's sort of become the spokesman for us government girls. You know, T.V. panel shows, radio interviews, fund raising activities. What I mean to say is, she's sort of a celebrity."

"I know what you mean. She agreed to put in a private telephone so the rest of us could still reach the outside world on the old black reliable in the hallway."

"Well, that's why I'm afraid that she wouldn't do it."

"Do what?"

"Act as chairman of our block party to raise money for St. John's."

"Just ask her. If she says no, what have you lost?"

"I hate to get turned down. But Penny would be a natural

for it, she knows everyone in Georgetown."

"So it seems," Jean said drily. "You want me to ask her?"

"Would you?" Sue's plain face brightened. "If she says yes, then I'll give her the details."

"When is it?"

"May first. The police block off the street near St. John's and we have stalls, music, sidewalk cafes. It's really great fun."

Jean glanced at her wristwatch. "O.K. Can I do it tonight? I've got to run."

"Tonight will be fine. Thank you, Jean."

"Glad to." Jean swallowed the rest of her coffee and left with a wave of her hand.

Penelope sat in a red free form plastic chair supported by four thin black iron legs and gazed earnestly at Perry Paulson, a gaunt, saturnine television master of ceremonies who wore his black hair long and affected a drooping moustache. His stock in trade was recruiting cheerful panelists for his show and then cutting them down with a sharp, biting cynicism. He shrewdly cast himself as the villain and wore a black turtleneck sweater under a black suit relieved only by a scarlet pendant suspended around his neck by a red woven nylon cord. His punch line, delivered in a weary, flat voice, was, "You don't really believe that, do you?" Perversely, a large television public had decided that they liked him and his punch line had become a popular cliché around Washington. The cheerful panelists were considered expendables who had their brief time around Paulson's flame before they were sent away again with singed wings.

"Ready, kids?" Paulson asked. "When the lights come on, you'll know we are on camera. Try not to squint or blink. I'll start off with some nauseating remarks about the product of our sponsor and then I'll zero in on you. It's all good clean fun—don't take it personally." He gazed solemnly, in turn, at Penelope, a husky, young, red haired athlete with Olympic ambitions, and a small, dark haired girl who wrote poetry. "Good luck. Happy landings."

Penelope wet her lips and was smiling as the lights flared on. She listened intently as Paulson extolled his sponsor's product and then as he paused to begin his questions of the panel, she spoke. "Perry, I enjoyed the commercial. Why is it you don't seem to believe in anything except the products you plug on the show? Could it be the money?"

Paulson blinked at her in surprise. Then he rallied. "What have I got here? A cuckoo in the nest? *I'm* supposed to ask the questions."

"Well, I didn't come here to squirm for your viewers like a butterfly on one of your pins, and as for the commercial, you don't really believe that, do you?"

A slow grin spread over Paulson's face. "No. We all know that we aren't going to change nature's odds by what we swallow, drink, smoke, or smear on ourselves, but as long as sponsors make that pitch, there are guys like me that will mouth it for them."

"For a price?"

"Sure. I've got mine. What's yours?"

"I believe you're paying us twenty bucks apiece."

"I'm not sure you're worth it."

"Because I don't roll over and play dead?"

"No. Because you're one of these gabby females that won't let me get a word in edgewise."

"It's your show."

"It was. Now I'm not so sure."

"O.K. I'll shut up for awhile."

"Be my guest. Don't forget this is being taped. I can always cut you out."

"This may never get on the air anyway. You admitted that your sponsors might be putting us on."

"Oh, they're tolerant folks, besides I'm tax deductible." He turned to the little poetess to his right. "Well, sweetie, I hear you write blank verse. Does that refer to the meter and

70

rhyme or the content or both?"

The half hour was soon over and Perry walked across the set to Penelope. "Say, you're a pretty fresh kid. Where did you get that approach?"

"Watching you. I just got in my licks first."

"Well, I think it went O.K. I need a foil on this show. If I still have a job after we broadcast it, how would you like to be a regular?"

"At twenty bucks? You must be kidding."

"Fifty."

"No. I don't want to be a regular. I'll get typed as a performer. The White House won't like it. I'll come back once in awhile if you want me, just as a participant."

"O.K. I'll be in touch." Paulson grinned. "I really had a ball. I had something to push against, you know? Usually I get cream puffs."

"I'm no cream puff."

"That I can believe." Paulson put a mint into his mouth. He sucked on it as he eyed Penelope. "I'd say you were a tough little minx under all that charm."

"I'm just as tough as I have to be."

Paulson nodded. "Have you come a long way, kiddo, or do you have a long way to go?"

"I'm going farther than I've come. I don't know how far."

"You play it by ear?"

"Don't we all?"

"I guess so." Paulson stared at her seriously for a moment and then broke into a grin. "Next time, fifty bucks, O.K.?"

"If you want me."

"Sure. I like to live dangerously."

Sue watched Penelope carefully make up her face at her dressing table. "I'm so glad you'll be chairman of the block party, Penny. I know you are terribly busy."

Penelope lightly touched her full eyebrows with eyebrow pencil and glanced at Sue's reflection in the mirror. "I'm pleased to be asked, Sue, but why did you feel you had to put the question through Jean?"

"I thought you were too busy to do it and I have a thing about people turning me down. If I think they might refuse, I feel very shy."

"That's rather silly, isn't it?"

"I know it's silly, but that's the way I am."

Penelope turned around to her. "Don't tell me I put you off? After all, we're sharing the same house."

"No. It's just that you are so busy. I see very little of you. You are always out somewhere."

"I always have time for friends. Tell me, how many people come to this block party?"

"About five hundred."

"From Georgetown?"

"Mostly."

"How do they learn about it?"

"At the church. Then we have posters and tickets in drug stores and book shops."

"Sounds like an old fashioned approach."

"I guess it is."

"Any famous names?"

"A few. Those who live nearby."

"I have made a few contacts in television and among publicity types lately. Maybe we can jazz it up a bit."

"That's why I hoped you'd be chairman, Penny. I knew that you would have ideas."

"I've got to run. We'll talk about it tomorrow."

"I'll take you to brunch at the Georgetown Inn after church."

"Great idea, but we'll make it dutch. Why should you treat me?"

Duane Miller sipped a Bloody Mary and blinked into the sunlight pouring through the glass curtains of the window of the Georgetown Inn diningroom overlooking Wisconsin Avenue. "Where is this gal?"

"She's in church, the one the block party is for. She'll be here soon."

"I thought God was dead."

"Only for newspapermen and related types. You only believe in what you can promote, so promote a church function. You may rediscover religion."

"Why are you interested, Penelope? A church charity is pretty slow stuff."

"Because a friend asked me to help."

"And?"

"You're cynical. That isn't becoming on Sunday."

"Look, sweetie, you and I have been around the floor a couple of times since last winter. I begin to see the pattern. I don't mind selling the product. I'm doing better than ever, but let's don't kid ourselves. You're the product, not St. What's-its-name."

"That's why I wanted to go over it, Duane, before Sue shows up. I think we can make this a real success if we handle it right. It's too soon to interest *Life* again, but how about *Look?*"

"We could try *Playboy* and maybe get you the center spread."

"Look, Duane. Aren't you up to a little success? Do you want to go back to your rut on *The Georgian?*"

"I shouldn't try to be funny on tomato juice, even if it is spiked with vodka. I'm sorry, Penelope, ma'am." His freckled face broke into a grin as he tugged at his forelock.

Penelope grinned back in spite of herself. "Oh, don't be such a fool."

"Seriously, Penny, where are you trying to get? You want to be another Betty Furness, opening and closing ice box doors?"

"I don't know. I'm just going where it leads, but isn't it fun?"

"Except on Sundays with a hangover."

"That's what money does for you if you use it to buy a

73

Saturday night. And speaking of money, please remember *you* are making all of the money. I'm not."

"You're getting the buildup."

"I'm good copy."

"What's the buildup for, Penelope?"

"When I know, I'll tell you." Penelope poured herself a cup of coffee from a pewter pot. "Now, we've only got two weeks. Sell it to *Look* as a local political and social story. Talk up the Georgetown types and the politicians on the Hill. Leave the White House out of it and play me down, a picture casually making the point that I'm chairman will be enough."

"Not front and center this time?"

"Not this time. We don't want to risk overkill. Besides, I'm more interested in broadening my acquaintanceships right now than in more publicity. The publicity is bait to draw the big names to the party."

"You handle that?"

"Yes. All you have to do is get coverage in *Look*. I'll get the big names through the staff people I know and through the church. Sue doesn't know it yet, but she will handle the actual organization of the block party with her church members. The average church deacon is a whiz at that sort of thing. At least they were in Indiana." She looked up, smiled brightly, and waved as Sue Gort appeared at the dining room doorway.

The block party had been in progress for over an hour when at dusk the electric switches were thrown and a myriad of Japanese lanterns winked on in the trees. They bathed the milling crowd below in gentle multi-colors as a low sigh of collective approval went up. Penelope stood to one side at the bottom of a flight of steps leading to a private house, a smile of happiness playing about her mouth, as she listened to the music and the murmur of hundreds of voices, punctuated by laughter. It was a success in every way. She had personally greeted everyone who had filed through the entrance gate at the end of the street, standing diffidently beside Father Martin of St. John's who had introduced her with considerate kindness as "our lovely young chairwoman," until several hundred people had filed past and her mental calculation told her that most of the famous guests were now present.

A tall, slim man in his early forties with an unruly shock of reddish-brown hair flecked with gray above a serious, aquiline face stood near her.

"My congratulations, Miss Chairwoman. You are standing here so modestly, looking out over the biggest block party St. John's has ever had, when you should be taking a few bows."

Penelope turned to him feeling an unaccountable thrill of expectation. She laughed lightly as she met calm, gray eyes. "They wanted to interest the younger crowd this year so they chose a young chairwoman. I'm as surprised as you are at this crowd."

The muscles around the gray eyes tightened into an amused squint. "But I'm not surprised. I know something of the organizing effort that went into this. I have two advantages denied to most."

"I'm afraid I don't recall who you are," Penelope said. "I must have met you at the gate and I'm sorry to be forgetful."

"No, I didn't come through the gate. That's advantage number one. I live in this house." He indicated the Georgian brick mansion on whose steps they were standing. "I just came down the steps behind you. I'm Marc Haywood. I detest street fairs and block parties. Since my house is three doors down from St. John's, I am involved each year whether I like it or not. I was going to follow my usual practice and leave town tonight. Unfortunately, business prevented it."

"I'm sorry if we have inconvenienced you, Mr. Haywood. I suppose we do inconvenience the entire neighborhood."

"No. It's well done. Very well done. I admire a good performance."

"Thank you."

"I see a little sidewalk cafe has sprung up down near that lilac bush. May I buy you a coffee?"

"Yes. I'd like that."

Penelope sipped the hot coffee which burned her fingers through the thin paper cup. "You mentioned a second advantage, Mr. Haywood, what is that?"

"I am the publisher of the *Washington Tribune*."

"I should have known that."

"Why? How many people read the masthead of a newspaper to see who publishes it? I may even be wrong in assuming that you read the *Tribune*."

"Oh, yes. Of course I read it. But then it's the only morning paper in town."

"You don't exactly sound like an enthusiastic reader."

Penelope gave a little laugh.

"Well, we won't pursue that," Haywood made an involuntary sigh. "It confirms in my mind that we need features for young swingers." He extracted an oval cigarette from a gold case, after Penelope shook her head in refusal, and lit it. "How long have you been in Washington, Penelope?"

"Ten months last week."

"Amazing. You seem very widely acquainted, particularly among Junior Washington."

"I've been lucky."

He drew on his cigarette, reflectively watching the smoke rise in the still night. "Do you trust anyone over thirty?"

"Of course. That's a silly theory."

"I am reassured at last. I wonder if you would be willing to come into my home and have dinner with Mrs. Haywood and me?"

Penelope felt the pace of her heartbeat quicken. She was intensely aware of this man's physical presence. She felt vulnerable. "Just like that?" She said, her mouth dry. He was married. She shouldn't let him affect her like this.

"Just like that. We are that happy couple who have no ser-

76

vant problem. Ruth will just set another plate. Ruth is our cook and has fed me carefully since I was a small boy."

"What about Mrs. Haywood?"

"She will be delighted." He sounded as if it didn't matter.

Penelope looked into the grave gray eyes and laughed in a self-conscious way. "Well, sure. If it's like that. I'll take a chance."

They retraced their way through the milling crowd to the steps leading up to the Georgian mansion. The foyer with its marble floor in black and white squares lit by a small brass chandelier seemed cool and quiet after the noise and confusion just outside the thick walnut door. "Claudia," Haywood called.

"In here, dear," a calm voice answered from an adjoining room. Haywood took Penelope by the arm and led her into a paneled library. A patrician looking woman, sitting in a wheelchair, with blonde hair framing a finely featured face looked up from a book with a smile.

"This is Miss Penelope Benton, Claudia. She is the chairwoman of that mob scene going on outside our windows. I've asked her to join us for dinner."

Claudia Haywood extended her hand. "It's so nice to have you, Penelope."

"I hope it isn't an inconvenience, Mrs. Haywood. I'm afraid Mr. Haywood extended the invitation on impulse. I probably shouldn't have accepted."

"Nonsense. Marc often brings people home to dinner this way." She smiled. "They are always very nice, interesting people and I look forward to it."

"Sit down, Penelope," Haywood said, "And I'll alert the kitchen that we are three and see if someone will serve us cocktails. What would you like as a chaser for St. John's coffee?"

"A martini, please."

"Plain or on the rocks?"

"On the rocks."

"Claudia?"

"That will suit me too." She turned to Penelope after her husband had left the room. "Now the first thing you must do, Penelope, is drop that little sympathetic look lurking around your eyes for a youngish woman confined to a wheelchair. A cantankerous mare threw me last October and then fell on me. However, though I proved to be breakable, I also mend and the doctor tells me I'll be riding again in another year. I already can leave this chair, though I'll admit it tires me."

"Oh, I'm so glad, Mrs. Haywood. I was thinking how beautiful you are and what a tragedy that you were crippled."

"There's no tragedy. Only damnable bad luck and temporary inconvenience. Well, now we've got that straight. Tell me, aren't you the girl I saw in *Life?* One of the young swingers on the White House staff? Or have I got it wrong?"

"Right about me. Wrong about swingers. We work too hard at the White House to swing. We may weave or wobble, but we don't swing."

Claudia Haywood laughed a clear, amused laugh. "I can see that I'm going to enjoy you. Marc's taste in people is impeccable."

The dinner was a clear soup and a salmon mousse served with a chilled, dry white wine on a long polished mahogany table under a crystal chandelier that dimly lit the green, gold, and silver of the scenes depicted on the room's heavy, hand blocked wallpaper. They sat at one end of the table, a single candelabra throwing additional light on the thin, translucent china and the damask place mats.

Marc Haywood turned to his wife with a smile, waiting to interrupt until there was a pause in her conversation with Penelope. "We like her, don't we?"

"Penelope? Why of course, she's a dear. Imagine what you saved us from tonight dear," she turned to Penelope. "Marc cracking nuts over sherry and damning the newspaper guild."

78

"I'm going to invite her to join us for the Gold Cup Races at Warrenton next weekend." Haywood announced.

"Do you like horses and cross-country racing, Penelope?" Claudia Haywood asked.

"I like horses. We don't have cross-country racing in Indiana."

"Would you like to come?"

Penelope glanced briefly at Marc Haywood.

"Yes. I would," she said in a low voice.

Claudia Haywood noticed her glance and the high color on her cheeks.

"Good. It's settled then. I'm going out to Hollywood, our country home near Warrenton, on Friday. Part of the race is across our land. You can ride out with Marc on Saturday morning. We will have a few friends for luncheon and then go up on our hill to watch the race."

Haywood smiled at Penelope. "We'll have people in their twenties, too, so you'll have a good time."

"I couldn't have a better time than I have had tonight," Penelope said, "and all the more wonderful because it was unexpected."

"That's the theory of the newspaper business, go out and meet the unexpected. Sometimes it makes for a pleasant evening as well. We both thank you, Penelope, for taking a chance on us. We might become good friends."

She met his eyes directly and frankly. "I hope so," she said.

❧ 8 ❧

PENELOPE looked into Patty Winston's cluttered office. "Do you have a minute for me, Patty?"

The older woman peered through the smoke of the cigarette hanging from one corner of her mouth. "For the symbol of youth in politics, I've got nothing but time. Come on in and sit down, if you can find a place to sit." Patty looked around her. "I used to think that I was well organized, but this job defies organization. If I were a man, I'd say I was flying by the seat of my pants, but in a woman I guess that would be indelicate."

Penelope sat on the forward edge of a leather chair which was otherwise occupied by a stack of file folders. "You worked for the *Tribune* for many years, Patty. What kind of a person is Marc Haywood?"

"You've met him, I take it?"

"I had dinner with him the other night—and his wife."

Patty smiled non-committally at the key board of the typewriter before her. "What was your impression? As a dinner guest?"

"He seemed gentlemanly, almost courtly. Considering that he can't be over forty, he acted pretty dignified, as if he were playing a part."

Patty nodded. "He inherited the newspaper at twenty-four from his father, Black Jack Haywood, as tough an operator as they come. Black Jack became a widower and made his money before he was thirty publishing racing forms, pulp magazines, and cheap book reprints, more than a little on the blue side. He then moved into Washington, bought the old *Potomac Herald and Tribune*, and became respectable, a crusader for civic causes—usually conveniently removed from Washington. He sent his only child, Marcus Danforth Haywood, believe it or not, to St. Pauls and Harvard and married him off to a Virginia blueblood from an impoverished family. Marc had just started at the newspaper when Jack Haywood choked to death wolfing rare roast beef and left his fortune in Marc's hands. Marc fell back on the dignified, blueblood gambit to make up for his age and now he is stuck with it. I think he is a little bored both by his role and by Claudia. She is that wispy, indefinite blonde type that shyly remains barricaded behind a few million dollars and a select group of pallid, undemanding friends."

"You don't like her?"

Patty shrugged. "I'm indifferent. The type isn't very important."

"What about him?"

"In his way, he's as tough as his father. In fifteen years, more or less, he's eliminated all of his competition in the Washington morning newspaper field; he has a network of television stations, a news magazine, and he's just bought a New York publishing house. Black Jack would be proud of him. The Washington Tribune Company is well run and prosperous. Marc has mastered combining the soft sell with ruthless competitive tactics."

"That sounds like an exciting life. Why is he bored?"

"I think he's bored with his pose as a gentleman. I think he would like to mix more with the common folk, get his hands into something real. In business he lives in a world of abstractions, even the *Tribune* is an abstraction."

"Politics?"

"Maybe. But his image for that is all wrong and Claudia

would have a fit."

"I liked them both. They were lovely to me."

Patty lit a cigarette. "So, what's the problem? I sense that this is more than idle curiosity."

"They invited me out to their home in Warrenton for lunch and to watch the Gold Cup Races this coming Saturday."

Patty's eyes met Penelope's. "So?"

"Well, he's awfully attractive."

"You wonder if you should go?"

"Sort of. I really wonder what's on his mind. Do you think he would make a play for me? Is he that sort of man?"

"You kind of hope he would, but it scares you. Is that it?"

Penelope felt the color rise in her cheeks. "Well, he's awfully attractive, Patty. I don't want to be a home wrecker."

"I wouldn't worry about that," Patty said dryly. "How did you meet him?"

"At a little block party we gave for St. John's in Georgetown. He invited me into his house. It was located in the middle of the party area."

"I heard about that party," Patty said. "Claudia was there?"

"Yes. He invited me in to dine with them both. She was sweet."

"Didn't that reassure you? The wife present, acting sweetly?"

"Yes, but the sophisticated type of wife sometimes connives at that sort of thing. She may be tired of sex and he isn't."

"You've been reading too many avante-garde novels, chick. The sex life of this town is at least as dull and unimaginative as its politics."

"But why would he invite me into dinner like that, almost as if they expected me, and then invite me to their country home? It seems like an awful lot, awful fast."

"He's a newspaper publisher and you are an interesting

new Washington phenomenon. He is curious. He wants to put you under his glass. He won't make a play for you. Claudia may bore the hell out of him, but he doesn't realize it. He has made a fetish of living by the conventions. That's a habit difficult to break. He's loyal to Claudia. He may even love her."

"You think it's all right to go, then?"

"Are you curious too?"

"Yes."

"Then I would go. After all, you haven't met the horsey set yet, apart from me, and I am a little synthetic. I learned to ride in Central Park."

"What should I wear?"

"A tweed suit, low heeled shoes. It's one of those occasions where you sort of throw it away. The women you will meet, for example, will have on a worn suit of the very best tweed and tailoring, runover shoes and a priceless strand of pearls."

"I don't own pearls. Priceless or otherwise."

"Finesse it. Don't wear any jewelry at all."

"I don't know much about horses or racing."

"Be a good listener. They'll adore you."

"Well——."

"I wouldn't pass it up, Penny."

"It's just that it's a different group than I am used to, older, richer, with a different set of interests and I'll be alone."

"No Dave Winslow, you mean?"

Penelope nodded.

"I notice you haven't been together much lately."

"No. We've both been so busy."

"Dave Winslow couldn't help you in Warrenton, Penny. If it will make you feel better, Dick and I will be there."

A look of relief flooded across Penelope's face. "Wonderful! Well, why didn't you say so? My gosh!"

"You didn't ask. I thought my presence might even cramp your style as a recent Washington high-flyer."

"Oh, no, Patty. I don't feel that way and I can't help it if I

83

have had publicity lately."

"Since I'm functioning as the house mother this morning, may I give you some advice?"

"Of course."

"A little publicity is helpful. But this town is the most cynical, publicity-wise town on earth. Your appeal is that of the youthful innocent; but innocence doesn't last long in Washington and the town's callous observers are quick to see when it's gone. Then you'll be just another gal on the make with Potomac Fever and the play will get much rougher. Believe me, I know. If I were you, I'd turn away from these publicity gags before the cynics catch on. Preserve that aura of wide-eyed innocence while you can. You'll never get it back, once it's gone."

Penelope bit her lip and looked at her hands in her lap. "You *are* unsettling, Patty," she said in a subdued voice.

"Believe me, I say it because I like you in spite of myself. You do want someone around that understands you, don't you?"

Penelope arose with an embarrassed air. "I'll look forward to seeing you at the Haywoods."

Marc Haywood made casual conversation until the chauffeur driven automobile had crossed the Potomac into Virginia. "I have some work I must do, Penelope," he said, unzipping a narrow leather briefcase and extracting a sheaf of papers. "Please forgive me and enjoy the countryside. It's a beautiful drive, even if it is raining." He read steadily, occasionally making a note on the paper margins with a thin gold pencil, until they turned up a narrow gravel drive between two rows of giant holly trees. He looked up at Penelope with a smile. "Now you know why we call this farm 'Hollywood.' It predates its famous California namesake by a hundred and fifty years. It comes to us from Claudia's side."

"It's beautiful," Penelope said as the car passed a small lake and swung in an arc in the broad circular entrance drive to stop before a long narrow house of yellow brick covered with ivy except where it had been cut away from the white frame windows and the limestone lintel of the doorway. The light rain had increased in intensity and now fell in sheets making puddles in the fine cream colored gravel between the automobile and the house entrance. "One moment, Sir," the chauffeur said and slid out the front door. He re-appeared at Penelope's door and held an umbrella over her until she had walked to the shelter of the doorway. He returned for Marc Haywood and then reached beyond Penelope to open the door.

"Beastly weather," Haywood said as they stepped into a broad entrance hall. "It is going to change the odds on the race."

An elderly Negro woman with a fine, sensitive face, dressed in a grey maid's uniform trimmed in white lace took their raincoats. Haywood smiled at her wordlessly from years of long familiarity and passed his arm through Penny's. "I hear the others in the library. Let me introduce you."

The large library with its high ceiling molded in plaster to give the effect of a shallow ornate dome suspended on the square wooden columns protruding at intervals from dull green panelled walls and bookcases was filled with men and women dressed in tweeds and flannels in muted shades which complemented the worn leather spines of the books on the shelves and the faded oriental rugs scattered over the heavy oak plank floors. Patty Winston was standing near French doors with a formal garden of English boxwood beyond, green and glistening in the spring rain. She was talking to a man of middle height wearing a jacket of gray gun club check closely tailored to his elegant, slight figure. A white linen handkerchief arranged in a fluted pattern protruded from the upper jacket pocket. A single button, under some strain, pulled the jacket in at the waist.

Haywood gently steered Penelope toward them. "Patty, I am sure you know Penelope. Mr. Ambassador, may I present,

85

Miss Penelope Benton. Penelope, the Ambassador of France, Monsieur Piccard.

The Ambassador spun about with alacrity at the first sound of Haywood's voice and bent over Penelope's hand as she extended it. "Enchanté, Mademoiselle." He turned with a smile to Haywood. "Such a lovely girl, and you bring her to me first, Marc. What a thoughtful host on a dark, rainy day."

"And I'm taking her away again, Yves, before you overwhelm her with Gallic charm." He slowly took Penelope around the room, introducing her to groups, until they reached Claudia Haywood, sitting in her wheelchair by a low burning wood fire framed in a mantel of yellowed, veined marble. Haywood leaned over and kissed her on the cheek as she turned from a group to whom she had been talking and extended her hand to Penelope. "Isn't this rain a disappointment, Penelope? They tell me it will stop by this afternoon, but even if it does the field will be sodden. Has Marc introduced you to everyone? Sit down on this sofa beside me and tell me about the Georgetown block party. Was it the success I hear it was?" Haywood smiled and moved away after directing a servant with a tray of drinks to offer them to Penelope. She took a gin and tonic dubiously.

"It is early for a drink, isn't it?" Claudia Haywood said watching her. "Eleven forty-five, not really legal yet for most of us, but we must have lunched by one-thirty since the race starts at two."

"I'll just sip it," Penelope answered.

A fleshy man in his early forties just over six feet stood gazing down upon her. His flushed face was still strikingly handsome, though blue veins were visible around his nose and eyes. "I'm Dick Winston. Marc just whisked you by my group as if he were ashamed of us. Damned outrage." He turned to Claudia. "Isn't she pretty? Dates the rest of us. What's Marc trying to do? Suggest we're no longer 'the young set'?"

"We haven't been, Dick, for some time. Please go talk

86

with Patty. I have a conversation with Penelope to complete."

Dick Winston stood irresolutely for a moment, then smiled. "I'll be back. Better yet, I'll catch you away from our imperious hostess. I want to find out who you are. You must be somebody?"

"I must be," Penelope agreed solemnly. "I am, therefore I exist."

"Ah, ha! A brainy gal! A thinker." His eyes moved around the room until he saw the servant with the tray of drinks. "I'll be back. I'll be back."

Claudia looked after him with an impatient frown. "It's too early for that. Really, Dick can be annoying."

"He drinks too much, doesn't he?" Penelope said.

"Like a fish. His mother has always dominated him and when she wasn't dominating him she smothered him with misplaced kindness and indulgence. I suppose he's just bored. She's left him nothing to do with his life."

"I should think Patty would be good for him."

"Patty? She has her career. The last thing Dick needed was another strong, self-sufficient character in his life."

The French Ambassador dropped down beside Penelope. "Two lovely ladies alone? This must not be. Tell me, Miss Benton, haven't I seen you before? On television, perhaps?"

"Yes. I have been on some television programs recently. I am on the White House staff."

"Of course! You are the young girl who keeps the President youthful!"

Penelope blushed. "Not really. It was just publicity."

"But charming. Rather more French than American, I think. It has made the President more appealing."

Claudia Haywood swung her wheelchair around. "We should go into lunch now. It's an informal buffet. Yves, you take care of Penelope. I'll see to the others."

The buffet was set out on an extended mahogany table in the dining room and on a massive side board against one wall.

A number of small tables had been placed about the room with service and napkins. The Ambassador solicitously helped Penelope to creamed chicken and salad. "Let us sit by the window," he suggested. "There is a lovely view of the azaleas in the flower garden."

"Is Madame Piccard here?" Penelope asked when they were seated.

"Alas, no. Madame Piccard died some years ago."

"I am so sorry. I didn't know."

"Of course not. And it is life, Mademoiselle."

An elderly woman, her plate carried by a young boy came over to them. "I think I'll join you," she announced. Her voice was dry and high pitched.

"Of course," Piccard said, scrambling to his feet. "We are delighted, Mrs. Winston. You know Miss Benton?"

"How are you, my dear?" Mrs. Winston sat down slowly in the offered chair. She leaned forward toward Penelope. "I haven't met you before, have I?"

"No. You haven't."

"I thought not. Where are you from?"

"Indiana."

"Indiana? I don't know anyone from Indiana," she said flatly and took a forkful of salad. She ate it with a rabbit-like movement of her thin lips.

"Are you all right, Mother?" Dick Winston bent over her solicitously.

"Yes, yes, of course. Run along. Eat something and don't drink so much." Dick Winston squeezed the frail shoulders in an affectionate gesture and moved away.

"You're the Ambassador of France, aren't you?" Mrs. Winston turned accusingly to Piccard.

"Madame," he said with a little smile and gesture, "I admit it."

"What do you think you're doing over there?"

"Madame?"

"In France. What do you think you are doing?"

"We exist. We do our best. Nothing more."

"I don't like it."

"I shall remember, Madame."

Patty Winston stopped by Penelope. "Bring your plate, Penny," she said firmly, "There are some people I would like you to meet."

Mrs. Winston looked up annoyed. "Taking her away? I wasn't through talking with her yet."

"You can see her again later," Patty said over her shoulder.

"Thanks, Patty," Penelope whispered as they crossed the room. "I didn't know what to do."

"She'd ruin your lunch, Penny."

"Poor Ambassador Piccard."

"He deserves her. Let's find someone a little younger. You'll think rural Virginia is an old people's home."

"But I enjoy older people. Young people aren't very interesting."

"Everyone at this luncheon is interesting, Penny," Patty said dryly. "And even the young ones aren't all that young. They've lived a little." They joined a group in a nearby sitting room eating from plates in their laps and listening to a George Shearing record.

9

THE telephone was ringing Sunday evening in the hallway of the house on Thirty-fifth Street as Penelope and Jean entered from an afternoon spent walking on the tow path of the Chesapeake and Ohio Canal.

"Penelope?" Marc Haywood's incisive voice asked.

"Yes. This is Penelope speaking."

"I have something to discuss with you. Are you free to have lunch with me tomorrow?"

Penelope hesitated, biting her lower lip, her heart pounding.

"If you are committed for tomorrow we could make it later in the week."

"I could make it tomorrow. I only have an hour for lunch, from one until two."

"Wonderful. I'll send a car for you at one. Tell me which gate, and will you arrange for the car to be passed? It's a dark blue Cadillac limousine with District of Columbia plate TRIB."

"The West Gate will be best. I'll be right outside the executive offices."

"Good. It's a date. We'll lunch at my office and I'll show you something of the newspaper. Would you like that?"

"Very much."

"Until tomorrow, Penelope. Goodnight."

Penelope hung up the telephone.

"Who was that?" Jean asked.

"Marc Haywood. He asked me to lunch tomorrow."

Jean arched her eyebrows. "Three invitations in one week! Isn't he rushing you?"

"I don't know," Penelope said softly. "When I am with him, he doesn't act too interested. Polite, attentive until he can turn me over to someone else, but rather detached otherwise."

"Maybe he's shy."

"He's married, damn it."

"Have you met her?"

"Yes. She's been with us both times."

Jean shrugged. "Where's lunch?"

"At the newspaper offices."

"That sounds matter of fact enough."

"Yes, it does. He is a very matter of fact man." She sighed. "And terribly attractive."

Marc Haywood smiled at Penelope across the small table set in a private dining room that was a smaller replica of the diningroom in his Georgetown house. "Did you enjoy the tour?"

"Very much. I had no idea that putting out a newspaper was so complicated."

"It only seems complicated because you made a fifteen minute first visit. By the way, I called the White House. I can have as much of your time as I wish, so we needn't rush."

"Did you speak to Dave Winslow?"

"As a matter of fact, I spoke with the President. I was calling him on another matter and so I just mentioned it."

"Oh."

"Now, let's see. We have a very straightforward menu, Penelope." Haywood held a pencil over a printed card. "A clear soup or a fruit cup?"

"Clear soup."

He made two checks with the pencil. "Lamb chops or a minute steak?"

"Steak."

"Medium?"

"Medium rare."

"Coffee?"

"Later."

"Well, we have that done." He handed the card to a waitress with a plain Irish face. "I hope you enjoyed yourself at Hollywood last Saturday."

"Very much. It was a whole new world for me."

"I suppose it was. Useless, inconsequential people, for the most part."

"Oh, I didn't mean that!" Penelope protested, confused.

"I know you didn't. That's my opinion, based on a lifetime of close observation. Most of those people are mere witnesses of life, living on money accumulated from ancestors who were doers. Since their heirs really have nothing to do but spend money, they devise a stylized form of life to pass the time. This they call Society."

"You don't like them."

Haywood lifted a spoonful of clear consomme. "Yes, I like them. They are old friends or the parents or children of old friends. I can relax with them, secure in the knowledge that they will observe the social conventions. But they are boring. Even their troubles and tragedies are boring, because they don't really matter. Fortunately, I live in the publishing world five days a week and I find it restful to be bored by congenial friends the other two."

"Patty is a doer."

"Yes, Patty is a doer, but she's married to the most accomplished non-doer in the Commonwealth of Virginia."

"I thought he was sad."

"Dick Winston doesn't matter," Haywood said with a wave of his left hand. "He never did. He never will. I've known him since school days at St. Paul's. Patty is another matter. When she left the *Tribune* to become Presidential Press Secretary she had to end her column. We enjoyed the prestige of a member of our staff becoming the first woman Press Secretary, but we regretted the loss of the column. We also regretted the loss of revenue. We syndicated the column to 87 other newspapers."

"Couldn't someone else do it while she's gone?"

"That never works. We'll have to wait until she returns. Sy Corman tries with a similar column, but, frankly, it's a misfire."

He watched the waitress serve Penelope her steak. "How did you enjoy the race?"

"It was exciting, but I got terribly cold and wet on that hill."

"It was a miserable day."

"I didn't see you."

"No. I had to return to Washington before lunch. I understand Piccard brought you home."

"Yes. He's a dear."

"All Ambassadors are dears. That's their profession." He sipped his coffee. "You are wondering why I invited you here, aren't you?"

"Yes."

"How would you like to write a column for my newspaper?"

"A column?" Penelope looked surprised.

"You wrote one for the *Daily Student* at Indiana University. Very creditable, nice pert style."

"You read the *Daily Student?*"

"When I got this idea, I checked up on you. I had a year's file of the newspaper sent to me, corresponding to your senior year. I also noticed that you were frequently newsworthy. You were very active in school. I wonder when you found the time to study and to graduate."

"The Dean of Women sometimes wondered that too," Penelope giggled.

"I'm not interested in your scholastic standing. I am interested in your one outstanding quality—you seem to get around and people confide in you."

"I like people."

Haywood carefully lit an oval cigarette with his initials on it from a small silver cigarette box after Penelope had refused one. His eyes rested impassively on her face. "I'm not sure that you do, but at best that's a tiresome cliché. You don't have to like people to get to know them or to make them like you. You have to be interested in them. That's what most people crave, Penelope, some assurance that they matter."

Penelope was silent.

"I want you to write a column about the people you know and understand. Junior Washington."

Penelope looked doubtful. "Junior Washington? People like me? But they aren't interesting. They do the menial, routine jobs in Washington."

"You have made them interesting, Penelope. Through you, people have suddenly become aware of this army of young people in Washington. Some genius, and I suspect it was you, suggested that young people in Washington were important because they kept the President young. Now, the idea has caught on and the public wants to know more. Americans have always worshipped youth since Ponce de Leon sought for that elusive fountain. The idea of a source of youth from a glamorous junior bureaucracy fascinates them. And who can tell it better than the young photogenic Miss who started it all?"

Penelope's eyes were shining. "Oh, it's a wonderful idea, Mr. Haywood, I'd love to do it. Do you think I could?"

"Yes, I do. If you will be willing to take close editorial supervision."

"Oh, Mr. Haywood! How wonderful!" Penelope impulsively got up from the table and kissed him on the cheek.

Marc Haywood blushed unexpectedly and patted her

94

hand. "Thank me now. In the end, you may be sorry. I'm an uncompromising perfectionist and a slave driver. Ask Patty Winston."

"I know just what we can call it," Penelope said enthusiastically, sitting down again. 'Pennysworth.' "

A spasm of something close to pain moved behind Marc Haywood's eyes. "I am afraid we have the column's name for you. Penelope's Zoo."

"Zoo? Isn't that a little unkind?"

"Of course. The people reading the column want human interest, that means seeing people like they are. You can't tell it like it is, Penelope, without being a little unkind. But then the people in your Zoo will forgive you. Why? Because you noticed them. You rescued them from their desperate, drab state of anonymity."

"Well," Penelope said doubtfully.

"Think of your friends a moment. What makes them interesting? I'll give you five minutes." He inhaled his cigarette and lifted his eyes to the exquisite little crystal chandelier hanging over the table.

After a few moments with her forehead in an exaggerated pucker, Penelope laughed. "I see what you mean."

"Exactly," Haywood said dryly. "The interesting thing about people is the difference between what they are and what they pretend to be. It is this difference, as they play it out each day, that is the grist for your mill. You must have enough malice in your column to report this difference. If it weren't for avarice, sex, and pomposity and those infrequent glorious moments when idealism or selflessness triumphs over the whole sordid lot, this newspaper would go out of business."

" 'Penelope's Zoo,' " she said slowly.

"Consider it settled," Haywood said firmly.

Penelope gazed across the table at him, a forefinger touching her lips. "What are you going to pay me, Mr. Haywood?"

"Twice what you're making now, plus a percentage of syndicate income."

"No matter what I'm making?"

"I know what you're making."

Penelope tapped her lips with her forefinger. Then she broke into a broad, artless grin. "O.K. It's a deal."

Patty Winston sat with Penelope in the Carlton bar. "I'm not too surprised, Penny," Patty said as she put her dry martini on the rocks down on the small table before them. "It's history repeating itself."

"Repeating?"

"I was a brash young political reporter when Marc Haywood selected me to write a column. It turned out to be good for all of us. *Penelope's Zoo* will be good for you, too."

"Do you think I'm brash?"

"I was describing young Patty Winston, not young Penelope Benton. No, brash is the last thing I'd call you. You are too well—oriented."

"So, you think I should do it?"

"My God, yes. It's a wonderful opportunity. You are a natural for it."

Penelope's eyes sought Patty's earnestly. "Will you help me if I need it, Patty? You have so much experience and you are so level headed about things."

"Sure, baby, but the best advice I'll ever give you, I'm going to give you right now. Dig, dig, dig. Learn all of the facts you can, but don't tell all you know. The Washingtonian that has the reputation of knowing more than he tells is irresistible and people tell him more and more. What you don't tell will be more valuable to you than what you do tell."

"I'll remember, Patty."

"You'll remember all right. We'll have to wait to see if you understand."

Penelope turned a swizzle stick over and over between her

96

fingers. "Patty?"

"Right here."

"It's sort of a personal thing to say, but do you think I could dress more as you do on my income?"

Patty laughed and squeezed Penelope's hand. "That's one of those nice, unconscious compliments that come along once in a blue moon. Thank you, darling." She lit a cigarette and turned, smiling, to appraise Penelope. "I spend more at this point than you could afford, but before I married Dick and had my column I was on a tighter budget. I had a few tricks I can pass on."

"I don't want to overdress, Patty, but I want to get away from that 'money matters' look so many women on a budget have. I hate the feeling that other women can look at me and guess where I bought my clothes and how much I paid for them."

Patty snubbed out her cigarette. "Do you mind wearing hand-me-downs?"

Penelope wrinkled her nose. "I was an only child. I didn't have much, but what I had was new."

"We'll strike that idea off, then. There are a number of good 'nearly new' shops off Connecticut Avenue and in Georgetown where you can pick up a few quality things cheaply, but if you'd feel uncomfortable wearing them, there's no point in it."

"I would."

Patty glanced at her watch. "Do you have a couple of hours now?"

"Sure."

"Let me take you out on the beltway. Radiating off that lethal suburban concrete raceway is the curdled cream of America's culture, a living testimony to the fact that we've flubbed it. Among these commercial and cultural temples, beautifully situated in a sun baked parking lot, is a discount dress store. If you know the ropes you can get some real bargains."

"Do you shop there?"

" 'Shop' is not exactly the word. You'll understand what I mean when you see it. I used to get all of my dresses there. Then I got soft."

"Soft?"

"A customer at a discount dress store has to have a certain aggressive competence. Acquisitive women shoppers can be damn competitive. This place is a sort of a southern extension of Seventh Avenue, so brace yourself. To make it pay off requires mental and physical preparation."

"I feel as if I'm going into a fight."

"You're not far wrong."

As they reached the beltway and Patty accelerated up the access ramp, she glanced briefly at Penelope. "Are you familiar with the better dress makers?"

"Yes, I think so."

"Good. These dresses are all out on racks. Good buys are mixed in with rags. You have to know what you are looking for."

"Won't the salesladies help?"

Patty gave a short laugh. "Salesladies? Wait until you see this place."

They turned from the beltway and took an off ramp into a heavily traveled secondary road. For nearly two miles they drove through a forest of signs advertising gasoline, pizzas, furniture, tires, hardware, garden supplies, and shoddy forms of entertainment. Just before reaching a four way intersection, Patty turned into a huge parking lot. Across a patchwork of yellow parking lines and parked automobiles Penelope could see a rambling one story brick structure that looked like an abandoned warehouse. Her heart sank.

Patty noticed the expression on her face. "It's no boutique, baby. That's why you get a discount."

They entered a huge room lit by parallel strips of florescent lights which cast a shadowless glare on a score of long clothes racks extending from wall to wall and turned human

98

flesh a pale purple. The racks were filled with hundreds of dresses hanging in dispirited multi-color rows. Large square cards held in metal frames divided the dresses on the racks into sizes.

"What is your size, Penny?" Patty asked briskly.

"Nine."

"Nine. Where in hell are the nines?" Patty looked about her, a cigarette hanging from her lips. "Oh, there they are, over to the left."

Patty glanced at Penelope. "Should we start with the basic black?"

"I can't spend over fifty dollars," Penelope said. "That's all I have with me."

"If you're spending more than fifty, darling, you shouldn't come here. For bigger money you can get a carpet on the floor and even a saleslady."

"I'd like to get a beige woolen dress, too. Will they take a check?"

"It's serve yourself, cash and carry, no returns. I'll lend you some money for the second dress. Let's see." Patty lifted a dress or two from the crowded rack before she selected one. "Try this one, Penny. It's forty dollars and has a very good label. I know I've seen it at a shop on Connecticut Avenue for seventy-five."

They walked along the row, past other women pushing the dresses back and forth, looking for something that appealed to them, until they reached the dressing room. Patty turned to Penelope with a little grimace. "This is where you earn your bargain. Ready?"

She pushed open the door onto near bedlam. About forty partially dressed and a few almost nude women milled about in a small, mirror lined room. Two teen-aged girls in black uniforms busily moved about sliding zippers in the back of dresses up and down as women robed and disrobed. A narrow wooden bench ran around the edge of the room on which discarded clothing had been cast. "There's a place,"

99

Patty said, elbowing her way to the side. "You can change here."

Penelope slipped out of her dress and into the black one. A faint dew of perspiration was on her forehead and her hair was already disheveled. "Delightfully tropical, isn't it?"

"Those two bawling brats don't help any," Patty said in an annoyed tone, looking at two, hot, unhappy children in strollers who were sitting, ignored by their mothers, at opposite ends of the room. "I think they are competing with each other. Let me look at you." She turned Penelope around. "Yes, that's very becoming. How do you like it?"

"I like it. Isn't it rather plain?"

"That's the idea. It's adaptable because it is simple. With different accessories you can wear it almost anywhere, cocktail parties, the theatre, even to black tie dinners."

"It seems very nice."

Patty looked at it more closely. "This is a quality dress, Penny. Let me show you why. The snaps are covered; the seams are finished; there is a generous hem; it's lined and faced." She looked inside one of the shoulders. "There's a lingerie strap."

Penelope looked at herself fleetingly in a segment of mirror that was temporarily unobstructed. "It's so hard to tell in here," she complained. "Even if it is a bargain, it's still forty dollars. I want to be sure."

"Of course you do. To use this place you have to know exactly what you want and recognize it when you see it. That's not easy in a mob of gals like this."

"I'll take this one."

"O.K. How about the beige? Do you feel up to looking for it to-day?"

Penelope's face was flushed. "I might as well."

"Is this for the office and maybe going on later?"

"Yes."

"How about a shirtwaist type?"

"I think so."

"O.K." Patty said, "stay here and I'll hit those racks again." She pushed forward, past two heavily tanned, over-weight women whose corpulent bodies were clothed only in scant, bikini-like rayon panties. "Pardon me, ladies," she said briskly.

"That's a nice dress," one of the women said hungrily, eyeing Patty. "What rack was that on?"

Patty looked at her sardonically through the smoke of her cigarette. "I got it some distance from here, dear."

"Where? How far?"

"You wouldn't know the place. It's about ten years away." Patty pushed the door of the dressing room open and re-entered the huge display room, her eyes darting alertly over the racks. "Beige nine," she muttered, "now where in the hell were those nines?"

Marc Haywood read the double spaced manuscript pages, his eyebrows drawn down in a characteristic frown of concentration. Penelope watched him intently, unconsciously running her tongue along her upper lip, and met his eyes anxiously when he looked up with a smile.

"I like it. It swings along and has the jaunty air I was hoping for."

"I'm so relieved," Penelope said, her face lighting up. "I really slaved over that. I know that the first column is so important."

"They are all important. Sit in this chair beside me. I'm going to use the editor's prerogative and cut and transpose a bit."

She sat down beside him, feeling a moment's giddiness at being so close to him, and then forced herself to concentrate on what he was saying as the thin gold pencil flew over her manuscript, making proof-reader's symbols.

"You don't always have to agree," he said after a time. "Defend your stuff. I could be wrong."

"I can't imagine it," Penelope said softly.

101

Marc Haywood turned and looked at her sardonically. "I appreciate your vote of confidence, but we are never going to develop a good column if you engage in that sort of thing."

"I'm sorry. You just affect me that way."

"I've noticed. And I've noticed how attractive you are, but that isn't the point, is it?"

Penelope flushed with pleasure at his compliment. "No, it isn't," she said in a low voice.

"Then be a good girl and stick to business."

When they had finished he leaned back in his leather swivel chair and lit a cigarette. "How do you like your office?"

"Great, I've never had an office of my own before."

"It's a hole in the wall, but I wanted you on this floor under my thumb. It was all that's available."

"I like it. It's cozy. Besides, some people tell me that I don't rate an office at all."

"Oh, they do, do they? So you've already experienced the staff stiletto?"

"Sure. I'm used to cattiness. It doesn't bother me. After all, the column isn't about the also-rans on your newspaper's staff. It's about young Washington on the go."

"You don't like 'also-rans,' do you?"

"No. They depress me. They're frustrated. They think small."

"Someone has to do the plodding work."

"I know. And I intend to leave them to it."

Haywood initialed her column. "Take this along. They'll run it tomorrow. Someday you won't need my initials on the manuscript, but, for the moment, I intend to edit it closely to see that it has the flavor I want."

"I don't mind."

"In time, you will. Now run along to your cubby hole and let yourself be seized by inspiration. This is a daily column, remember. I want six like this every week."

Penelope arose. "This is fun, not work. I'm going to knock myself out over this column."

"Don't overdo. All I require is a sixteen hour day."

Claudia Haywood looked up from the copy of the *Tribune* she was reading in the livingroom of the Georgetown house. "Really, Marc, this child gets better and better. I think you have something."

Marc Haywood grinned. "She has a way with words, hasn't she?"

"Not just words. She seems to see people from a surprising angle. It's a little disconcerting. I'm not sure I'll be comfortable around her in the future."

"This column is about Junior Washington. We're safe."

"Well, I don't feel *that* senior."

"This column is for those under thirty."

"Touché, darling."

"We are going to undertake syndication next week, based on the column's first six months and a reader's reaction survey."

"How nice for you, and for Penelope."

"I'm going to take her down to a small editor's meeting at Williamsburg this weekend and introduce her around. It will help promote the column."

Claudia Haywood looked pensive. "I thought you were coming with me to the Bryants this weekend?"

"Business comes first. Bill Bryant will understand that even if Ruth doesn't."

"I'll explain that carefully, though they may not believe it."

Marc Haywood looked at her calmly. "What do you mean by that remark?"

"Nothing at all, but you do seem very pre-occupied with Penelope. I'm afraid that you are overwhelming the girl."

"I'm pre-occupied with *Penelope's Zoo*. It's going to be a leader for our syndicated items. I intend to make a lot of money with it. My interest in Penelope certainly isn't personal."

"Of course not, dear. But what about Penelope?"

"What about her?"

"She's mad about you. People notice."

"Oh, for God's sake, Claudia."

"It's true."

"It's a school girl crush. After all, there's the generation gap."

"Not quite a generation."

"I'm not going to discuss it and I don't give a damn what people say."

"I do."

"Well, you shouldn't. I'm merely building up a property for the newspaper."

"I know that, dear. I don't mind what you are doing. I do mind what people say you are doing."

"Then take it up with them, not me." His eyes dropped back to the business papers he had been reading.

They flew down to Williamsburg in the helicopter the *Tribune* used for the traffic reports of its radio station and landed on the sweeping lawns at the rear of the Inn. Their arrival caused a mild flurry of excitement until the other guests realized that an important political personage had not arrived. Marc Haywood took a suite and Penelope was given a pleasant room on another floor overlooking the golf course. They attended the editor's conclave sessions and its social events together and on the second night Haywood had a cocktail party for the thirty editors and their wives to whom he hoped to sell *Penelope's Zoo*. After an hour and one-half of chatter and hearty fellowship they were left alone in the smokey clutter of the suite.

"How did it go?" Penelope asked.

"They liked you and a surprising number had heard of your column. So far, so good."

Penelope dropped down upon a sofa. "I'm glad. This was the soft sell?"

"You could call it that."

"Who handles the hard sell?"

"Professional salesmen." He ran a hand through his hair and rubbed his eyes. "How about dinner?"

"Dinner can wait. Can't we stay here for a few minutes and catch our breath? It's been quite a whirl."

He sat down beside her on the sofa. She moved slightly and settled into the crook of his arm with a little sigh.

"We shouldn't do this," he said after a moment.

"Don't be silly." She leaned up and kissed him on the cheek. His lips sought hers. The kiss was long and ardent. He gently disengaged himself and got up. He walked over to the fireplace mantel and picking up a paper packet of matches, lit a cigarette.

"This isn't what I want for you," he said huskily.

Penelope sat silently, watching him.

"You're making a success as a columnist. You have a wonderful future. We'll spoil it all if we have an affair."

"Why?"

"I'll lose my objectivity about you. I'll be emotionally involved."

"I am emotionally involved. I can't help it, Marc."

"No. You must sort your emotions out. You're impressed with me as your editor. You may be grateful that I gave you your chance. You may respect my judgment. You may be excited by all the new things that are happening to you. But you don't love me."

"I'm afraid that I do," she said quietly.

"No," he was positive. "We won't have that."

"Your kiss wasn't platonic. We made waves."

"That's why I'm not going to repeat it."

"Chicken."

"You've heard of wiser and cooler heads? That's me."

"I'll remember that kiss. It won't go away."

"So will I, but we are going to keep our emotions out of this. That's an order."

"All right."

"Save it for the right boy."

"Compared with you, there isn't one."

"You'll discover when the stardust is out of your eyes that I'm a slightly shopworn piece of merchandise."

"How can you say that!" Her protest was half angry. "You're wonderful, simply wonderful!"

He gave a deprecating little laugh and patted her cheek. "We're both wonderful. Let's leave it at that and go have some dinner."

"Alone?"

"Alone."

"I'll buy that."

❧ 10 ❧

P ENELOPE looked up from her desk in the small office at the *Tribune* at the figure lounging in the doorway.

"Where did you come from?"

Dick Winston smiled down at her. "I called on ol' Marc and thought I'd drop by, Mis' Cinderella."

"You've been drinking."

"Why, sure. What else is new?"

"Run along. I have copy for my column to do."

"How about lunch? I do eat lunch, you know. No matter what Patty says."

"Have lunch with Patty."

"She's stood me up. The President's decided to get gabby with the press again."

"Does Patty know you're asking me to lunch?"

"Don't b'lieve she does."

"Patty's my friend."

"I know. I know. I know. You're true blue. If it will make you feel better, I'll confess it all to Patty, including the number of calories."

Penelope laughed and laid down her pencil. "All right, Dick. I'd rather see you eat than drink. Let's go."

Penelope stood at the tall windows of Patty Winston's office in the White House and idly watched the traffic move by on Pennsylvania Avenue, visible at some distance through the trees on the north lawn.

"I'll be with you in a moment, Penny. I have one more thing to polish off." She turned to the secretary sitting beside her desk with a pencil poised over a dictation pad."

"No hurry," Penelope murmured almost absently. "I can wait."

Patty finished her dictation and spun around in her chair with a grin as her secretary left the room. "Now, I am all yours, chick, unless that buzzer from the oval office sounds."

Penelope dropped into a chair and slowly took off her gloves. "Any personal angles for me today?"

"The White House dog, Burton, choked on a bone this morning. Mary Fenton got bit on her index finger extracting it. She can't type for a week and the President has promised her the pick of the litter of Burton's next family as a reward. I understand Burton was very apologetic and follows Mary around, looking even more hangdog than usual."

Penelope smiled. "I can use that. Burton's pretty prolific, isn't he?"

"There's a great demand for his progeny among the politically faithful. The President may start a new breed single-handed with Burton."

"Where did Burton come from?"

"Someone dropped him in the letter slot of Mr. Frome's home when he was a Congressman with an uncomplimentary note. Burton was only a few days old. They fed him from President Frome's very own silver baby bottle until he could be weaned."

"That's a wonderful story. Why hasn't it been told before?"

"I don't know. Maybe because it's so natural it sounds contrived."

"May I use it?"

"Why not? Better check it with Dave first."

"Will do."

"*Penelope's Zoo* is about to have its second birthday. Con-

108

gratulations. It's been a real success."

"It's pretty trivial, don't you think?"

"It's original and popular. That's what counts," Patty said earnestly. "It has a little bite between the lines. You're developing a style, whether you realize it or not. You have a subtle way of suggesting to the average reader that he is being shrewd and perceptive in understanding your stuff. In other words, that you are writing on two levels and he is smart enough to understand the second one."

"Thanks, Patty. But don't analyze me. I'll get self-conscious and lose whatever touch I have." She was silent for a moment. "I'm seeing quite a bit of Dick these days."

Patty lit a cigarette. "He's taken quite a shine to you. Does it worry you?"

"Only that you're my best friend and he's married to you."

"I appreciate that, baby, but don't worry. Dick is harmless. Believe me, I know. If he bores you or gets in the way, that's different, I'll tell him to cut it out."

"Oh, no, he doesn't bore me. He's really wonderful company in an off beat way and, unlike most men, he gives you his undivided attention—one can't help but appreciate that."

Patty smiled with a touch of tenderness. "He *is* sweet, isn't he? Vague, alcoholic, indefinite, but sweet."

"He's really useful to me when he gets to prattling about social life in Washington, Maryland, and Virginia. It's killing."

"Dick was born to be socially conscious. I'm sure he enjoys a new audience."

"You don't mind that we lunch together once a week? It seems to have become a ritual lately."

"No, Penny. Not at all. I think of you as a friend, too."

"Well," Penelope said with a little sigh of relief. "I'm glad that's settled. I enjoy Dick and I wouldn't hurt his feelings for the world, but I don't want to risk our friendship either, Patty."

Patty smiled at her. "It's no triangle. Agreed all around?"

"Agreed."

"Then let's go to lunch before the ship of state starts shipping water."

Duane Miller sat with Penelope on a red leather settee at the Jockey Club and looked about the walnut paneled restaurant with its heavy low ceiling beams from which subdued lighting bathed the well dressed luncheon crowd. "I like this place. It may be high noon outside, but it always gives me the impression that we are having a clandestine midnight rendezvous, secure in the knowledge that your jealous husband is attending an iron monger's convention in Pittsburgh."

"I'm meeting Dick Winston here at two o'clock."

"In that case you can pay the bill."

"I intend to."

"Then I'll order something expensive, like broiled picked brains."

"You don't like giving me information?"

"It's a living. Two years ago when we gave you the big build-up with *Life* and *Look* I thought I was on my way as a free lance something or other, maybe a journalist—maybe a publicist. I wasn't sure which. Now everyone says, 'What have you done lately?' It doesn't take me long to answer that. Giving you Duane's Dirt helps pay the bills, but it's dirty money, if you don't mind the play on words."

"Don't go ethical on me—you'll ruin lunch. I hate ham acting."

"At least you never use the stuff. No one gets hurt. What am I? A charity case? Or don't you believe me?"

"I don't write that kind of a column. I write of the happy doings of Washington's under thirty group. You know, 'Ann Wilscam returned from Congressman Black's *Aircade for Votes* foray into the southwest just in time to make all three of the costume charity balls given last night to raise money for Children's Hospital. It's not surprising that she came dressed as an airline stewardess—Japanese yet. Sayonara."

"I'm familiar with the style. How about an answer to my question?"

Penelope studied the menu. "I'll let you in on a little secret. I'm bored with writing spritely columns about Junior Washington. I'm ready to write a column about Senior Washington. I'm accumulating your dirt for the column I'm not going to write."

"I don't get it."

"You know the old joke about the one legged hotel guest dropping one shoe on the floor and the guest in the room below going crazy waiting for the other shoe to drop?"

"I've heard all of the old jokes and I've been trying for years to forget that one."

"I've been here just long enough to learn that everything that happens in Washington is motivated, usually by the desire for sex, money, or power. Your dirt confirms this. The unqualified appointee turns out to be the son of an old mistress of a famous man who may or may not be the father. A senator's persistent partiality to a business buccaneer is the result of a substantial unsecured loan twenty years ago. The reason a much heralded investigation never began is a sexual triangle with the husband and wife setting up the innocent bachelor. A famous Congressman lets his career be jeopardized by his administrative assistant because he is in love with him. I'm not going to write about these motivations. I'm simply going to write about the two dimensional image these people project, the image of ideals, beliefs, minor prejudices, endearing human traits, and ambition masquerading as the urge for public service. However, once in awhile I'll drop a subtle hint that I know the image has a third dimension."

"You call this dropping the single shoe?"

"Right. And I'll never drop the second shoe. The tantalizing question will be, 'how much does Penelope know?'"

"What do the poor bastards do who are waiting for the second shoe to drop?"

Penelope glanced briefly into the mirror of a gold compact which had taken a week of her income to buy. "They will become my friends." She smiled at Miller. "My real business, Duane, is the friendship business."

Miller ran a freckled hand through his hair. "This is all mighty subtle stuff, Penelope, baby. You're a little beyond my depth, but if you think suppressed gossip is valuable, I'll sell it to you until the world recognizes my true talents. I guess I'm the underground Cholly Knickerbocker."

Duane Miller left at 1:30. Penelope ordered another pot of coffee and studied the entries in a small note book, making notations from time to time with a gold pencil, until Dick Winston arrived. He dropped down beside her. "Hi."

"You're late. Did you have trouble finding me?"

"I brought you here first, remember?"

"I had forgotten."

"You see? That's my trouble. I don't make an impression. I'm like a footprint in the sand."

"Very sad but not original."

"I'm not original either. I'm a duplicate copy."

She gave an impatient shrug. "You don't make sense."

He lit a cigarette and glanced sidewise at her. "You look a little grim. Problems?"

"I've just been thinking about my column. It doesn't really amount to much."

"Ol' Marc says it's a great success and where newspapers are concerned ol' Marc knows what he is talking about."

"Do you like my column?"

"I like it," he nodded positively.

"Why?"

"I don't know. It's about people who seem to have fun, so I enjoy reading about them."

"Do they matter?"

"Probably not. Who does?"

"There are people in Washington who do matter."

"So I've heard, but they are as dry as dust, Penny. Someday they'll grace Statuary Hall or some wax museum. Now they're only slightly more animated."

"Don't you find politics interesting?"

"No, 'tell the truth."

"Why not?"

He smiled wryly. "I'm not used to being profound this early in the day or for that matter any time of day; I leave that to my peers. Ol' Marc, for instance, is profound twenty-four hours a day. He prob'ly thinks profound thoughts in the john."

"Don't be vulgar."

" 'Why doesn't Dick Winston find politics interesting?' has been asked. Answer: because politics is just an organized way of getting yours out of the total national product. I've got mine—had it handed to me at birth by Papa and Mama. So, I don't give a dman. I don't have to crawl over anybody."

"There's more to politics than that."

"If so, its s'caped my notice, but, then, quite a bit has."

"Politics is power. The power to do things you want to see done. The power to do favors for people. The power to make them come to you."

"Don't want them to come to me. Damn boring."

"You described society to me, Dick, as a struggle to advance in the pecking order."

"Right."

"I think that's what politics is, except that it concerns itself with a much bigger field."

"That's a definition. Probably as good as any other. Don't tell me you want to write a political column? There are dozens of those already, all discussing the same topics. *Penelope's Zoo* is much livelier."

"No. I don't want to write a political column. I want to write about the people who are in politics—not about politics."

"Talk to ol' Marc about it."

"I'm going to."

"Let me give you a tip. You know the best time to talk to ol' Marc?"

"No."

"Four o'clock in the morning. He has insomnia. He forces himself to stay in bed until four. Then he gets up. He's told me it is the most frightening time of the day for him. The world is dark, cold, empty, silent. Everyone lies unconscious, enjoying the sleep denied to him. He is alone. The last man on earth. He welcomes a human voice. Even mine. Often he calls me up on the telephone and we talk until dawn. I can't sleep either."

Penelope smiled. "I'll give you both sleeping pills for Christmas."

"'Fore we go pick out Patty's birthday present, I have to pick up Mama and ferry her from a luncheon at the Sulgrave Club to tea with the Dowager Dragon of Washington Society. Her estate covers half of the Rock Creek Park watershed. The public got the other half."

"Your mother doesn't like me."

"Nonsense. She hates you. She hates everybody. That's her *modus operandi.*

"Does she hate you?"

"Of course not. I'm her only son. She merely dislikes me."

"What about Patty?"

"She's decided that Patty doesn't exist. That's the highest rating of all. Someday, God willing, she'll decide that I don't exist either."

"You don't make any sense."

"I make the clearest kind of sense. That is why I have insomnia and insist on drinking as much as is good for me, an amount that so far is unlimited. Will you come and meet the Dragon and Mrs. Winston?"

"What do you suppose they'll have for tea?"

"Ming tea and cucumber sandwiches while a choir of mixed voices sing a litany from the Social Register."

"I think I'd better drive."

"I'm cold sober."

"That's what I mean."

114

❧ 11 ❧

THE alarm clock by Penelope's bed shrilled loudly. She stirred sleepily and reached out with a vagrant hand to turn it off. The pale shimmer of the luminous dial indicated that it was four-ten. It was still dark outside. She lay quietly a moment and then got out of bed and walked down the hallway's creaky floor boards to the bathroom to dress.

At four-thirty she dialed the home number of Marc Haywood. The familiar, incisive, voice answered on the second ring.

"This is Penny, Marc."

"Is something wrong?"

"No. Why do you ask?"

"It is four-thirty, an hour before dawn."

"Oh, good heavens! I woke up very early and I got to thinking about my column and forgot the time. Just because I am up and wide awake I assume everyone is. I'll see you at the office. This can wait. And please forgive me for awakening you."

"No harm done. I'm an early riser myself. What's on your mind?"

"Well, now I feel so silly. I telephoned on impulse."

"Don't make me coax you."

"Have you had breakfast?"

"No."

"Why don't you walk over here and I'll give you something to eat."

There was a short hesitation. "Well, why not?"

"Eggs? Bacon?"

"Just crisp bacon, toast, and black coffee."

"Come along, now."

"I'll be there in fiften minutes."

"The door will be on the latch. The girls are still sleeping."

"So is everyone with a clear conscience."

Penelope poured more coffee into Marc Haywood's cup. "I'm glad you came to breakfast. I usually work in these pre-dawn hours, but sometimes they are a little lonely."

"As a practicing insomniac, I know what you mean."

"Oh, I don't have insomnia. I just don't need much sleep."

"You implied over the telephone that you wished to discuss your column."

"Yes." Penelope's eyes travelled around the small kitchen as she organized her thoughts, then they met Haywood's. "I guess, in a nutshell, I want to enlarge the coverage of the column and include Senior Washington as well as Junior Washington. I also would like to give the column more political content."

"And what becomes of your young friends? The public has become interested in them."

"I'll still cover Junior Washington, but I need more scope. I've about used up the youth in government bit."

Haywood sipped his coffee. "As a matter of fact, we have been thinking along the same lines. You are growing up, so to speak. The column should grow too."

"You put it much better than I could."

"The transition would have to be gradual."

"Oh, yes. I see it that way too. All I want is more people in the Zoo. It will increase reader interest and the column will be easier to put together. I'll have more material."

"We change it from a children's zoo with chickens and

bunny rabbits to a grown up zoo with lions and tigers?"

Penelope laughed. "And a few hyenas."

"You *are* growing up." Haywood lapsed into silence. "I wonder," he said at last, "If you know enough about the predators of Washington to write about them convincingly?"

"I know some things. You would have to help me."

"I think, Penny, you should keep the present style of your column, the light touch, no partisanship, no exposés. Leave the muck to the others."

"I agree. I don't want to be controversial."

Haywood looked at her searchingly until she dropped her eyes and felt color surge into her cheeks. He did not apologize. He finished his coffee and seemed to make up his mind. "Come along with me, Penny. I want to show you something."

She slipped on a green tweed coat and they walked through the growing light of dawn, along the uneven handmade brick sidewalks of Georgetown until they had crossed Wisconsin Avenue and stood before a delicate, small Georgian house on Dumbarton Street. Haywood selected a key from a key ring and unlocked the heavy oak door painted in dull black to match the wrought iron stair rails and bars on the lower windows.

They stepped into the chill, slightly musty odor of an empty house. "How lovely," Penelope said, walking from the entrance foyer into a large livingroom extending the depth of the house. At the far end, the newly risen sun shone through a wall of small handblown window panes arranged in a palladian design around tall French doors. Haywood unlocked the doors and they stepped out onto a shallow balcony overlooking a small garden ten feet below. A row of old magnolia trees masked the nearby houses beyond an ancient brick wall.

"It's exquisite," Penelope murmured.

"It's a gift house," Haywood said, looking at her solemnly. "That is, it is within my gift. How would you like to live here?"

Penelope felt her face going scarlet. Her eyes dropped and

117

her heart began to pound. "I . . . . I . . . . ."

He moved toward her instinctively and embraced her as she stood with her head down. She put her cheek against his chest. He could feel her body trembling. "Darling, I'm so sorry. I'm so tactless. I don't mean it that way at all."

She raised tear filled eyes to his. "I'm such a fool. I've held it in so long. I thought you wanted it that way."

He gently lifted her chin and kissed her. She responded, rising slightly on her toes to reach his lips more firmly. After a moment he gently disengaged himself. "This isn't what I intended," he said, huskily. "I have something quite different in mind."

She smiled up at him. "I love you, Marc, and you love me."

"No. You mustn't think that."

"But we do. We both know it."

"You fascinate me, Penny. I feel very close to you. I want to build your career, but it can't be more than that. It really can't."

"You should divorce Claudia and marry me. I would make you much happier than she does." Her voice was a soft whisper.

"That is out of the question," he said firmly.

She was hurt. "You can't imagine marrying me?"

"I won't divorce Claudia. I don't want that kind of disruption in my life."

"I see. I am a disturbing influence?"

"Very."

She turned away from him. "Why did you offer me this house? You don't love Claudia, not really, not the way you love me. Why have you brought me here? Are you playing cat and mouse?"

He lit a cigarette and stepped out onto the shallow balcony overlooking the garden. "I shouldn't have given in again to the impulse to kiss you. It confuses my motives." He turned around to where she stood in the open livingroom doors. "Am I correct that we meant to discuss your column in my

118

newspaper—not an arrangement?" He tried by his manner to put aside his personal emotions.

She grinned impishly. "We were discussing the one and thinking the other."

He sighed with a little smile. "You aren't helping."

"All right. I'll be good."

Haywood stood a moment gazing down into the autumn colors of the garden, arranging his thoughts. "I am going to speak objectively now, Penny. Your column has done well. Twenty newspapers now take it as a syndicated item. I agree with your idea that it is time to branch out." He drew a deep breath and his voice became more businesslike. "However, you can't write convincingly about something you know little or nothing about. There are too many newspaper people like that, ill-educated, partially informed onlookers, not participants. They fall back on clichés and the traditional imitation of life themes of newspaper hacks to fill their columns. They are bores, but even worse, transparent bores. *Penelope's Zoo* has had some success because you have written in an original way about a life of which you are a part. If you are going to write about Senior Washington in the same fresh, knowledgeable way, you must be a part of Senior Washington. That is what this house is all about."

"I don't understand."

"I am going to lease this house to you at a nominal rent. I'll see that it is properly furnished and maintained. I will see that your acquaintanceship grows in Senior Washington at a proper pace. You will have the whole beat, Congress, the Administration, Washington Society, and Embassy Row. In addition to your talents, which I admire, you will have one advantage that will set you apart from the capital news hens—you'll belong. You will entertain in this house. When you receive invitations you will be invited as a guest, not as a member of the working press. You will repay those invitations with invitations to your home. You will live the part. You will write about *your* life—not the life of others.

119

This will make your column unique. It will make me a lot of money and will pay me back handsomely for the use you make of this house."

Penelope smiled wryly. "You've convinced me that your intentions were honorable, damn it."

"I was clumsy about it, Penny, and I'm sorry. But we have to keep our emotions out of this, darling, or we'll spoil it. I think, working together, we can make you something unique in this town. Don't throw it away on me or on anyone else. I'm susceptible, if you want to settle for less, but don't do it."

Penelope stood silently, her eyes downcast. "I'm not sure I can do it. You want me to become a Washington hostess."

"On a modest scale and within the limits of good taste. Your entertainments will be small and exclusive, not huge catered bashes. Leave those to the gals with big purses and fragile egos."

She raised her eyes. "You'll help me, Marc? You won't let me down?"

"Yes. I'll have my investment to protect, both financial and personal."

She stood, hesitating.

"It's the only way you can make *Penelope's Zoo* what you want it to be."

"All right. I'm scared to death, but I'll do it. I'll try."

"Good." He took both of her hands in a dry, warm grip and squeezed them. "It's a deal then. You will have to live here alone, Penny. You would find sharing the house an embarrassment when you entertain."

"All right," she said submissively.

He smiled at her. "We will have fun."

"Yes, I suppose so."

"Don't feel rejected, Penny, darling. I'm just casting you in a better role. If I didn't think so much of you, I wouldn't bother."

"Thank you. I understand."

"Let me show you the rest of the house."

120

❧ 12 ❧

PENELOPE moved into Dumbarton House, as Marc Haywood called it, in early November. Furnished with the help of Washington's foremost decorator, it was an exquisite and unassuming eighteenth century house, correct in every detail, avoiding any suggestion of self-consciousness or ostentation.

Her first night in the house was a lonely one. Haywood was out of the city and the couple he had hired to maintain her house would not arrive from Warrenton for another week. She fixed herself a scrambled egg and a slice of toast in the gleaming, modern kitchen and wandered through the rooms afterward, a cup of black coffee in her hand. She had an impulse to ask her girlfriends over and even thought about telephoning her mother in Bloomington. She resisted both ideas. She sensed that this move was more than a physical change of location. It was a break with the past. She was about to make a new set of friends and whether he knew it or not her relationship with Marc was entering a new dimension. He was becoming more a part of her life and she of his. Youthful zest and good humor would no longer be enough, neither would informality and frankness. Marc would expect more.

She stood before the long mirror in her bedroom and looked at herself critically. Suddenly it became obvious that she no longer had to watch her wardrobe expenses with a parsimonious eye. It was, in fact, now unwise to do so. She had to rise to her new environment in every way and though she could accept Marc's suggestions on other aspects of her life, she could not risk the humiliation of his critical assessments encompassing her dress. She must anticipate him. She would no longer go to the discount store off the beltway or watch the newspapers for the clearances of odd-lot dresses. No longer would she risk wearing an unfortunate choice that would give her away. She would visit the best shops on Connecticut Avenue and in Chevy Chase and she would buy with the careful understated sense of style she had noticed in both Patty Winston and Claudia Haywood. She would dress with an air of expensive, unadorned, hatless, natural.

She would go to Elizabeth Arden and let them design a hair style and makeup that would fit her new image, a little older perhaps, just a touch of Junior League, but nothing that would obscure her middle western naturalness. She wanted Marc to feel proud of her and at ease. She wanted him to find the idea of marrying her more and more natural. She wanted him to have no doubt that she could be part of his world, but she did not want to set herself off in any way from her past nor from the politicians she would now cultivate, the politicians that sought the support and money of the rich and powerful, but were careful at all times to maintain an attitude that was indigenous in terms of their political base, whether it was urban melting pot, small town, rural, or the vestiges of the frontier.

Her middle western background was neutral and valuable in the political sense. She did not intend to obscure it with an imitation of the patina of the eastern aristocracy. She did not wish to be another Claudia, though she might imitate her dress, she did not aspire to her vague, bloodless, thin lipped look. She only wished to move among Marc's friends unremarked, accepted and belonging as only the secure and self-confident can belong. She wanted to belong because Marc belonged.

As she sat down at a small Sheraton writing desk and as she began to make a shopping list for the next day, she forgot that she was lonely.

Marc Haywood became more than ever her mentor in her human relationships. At occasional lunches or conferences at the newspaper and, more often, at Dumbarton House where he frequently had a pre-dawn breakfast with her or a late afternoon drink he would give her his rather aloof, patrician impression of Washington and its milieu. He leaned one winter Sunday afternoon against the mantel of the fireplace in her livingroom, and explained why he wanted her to confine her entertaining to groups of eight or ten.

"Washington society is different, Penny. In most American cities like Chicago, New York, or San Francisco, society has become a clan-like observance of social convention among a static cast of inbred descendants of the city's first accumulators of wealth and power. Basically their society is closed and really not worth the time of an outsider to breach. In Washington, it is another matter. Washington society is open-ended. There are, at most, a dozen social families in this city that endure from year to year, or even from generation to generation. They are the fixed social points among constant change.

"The rest of social Washington is transient. The Diplomatic Corps is composed of a group of wind-up dolls. They never surprise. They are the prisoners of convention and of time. They appear on the scene for two or three years, mechanically observing the ritual that national prestige or national needs demand and then depart. This is boring, but not particularly unsettling. The Diplomatic List changes, but not the roles. The Ambassador of France is always the Ambassador of France, just as the Military Attaché of Korea is always the Military Attaché of Korea. Protocol rules. One knows what to expect.

"The unsettling factor in Washington society, the element that makes it interesting, that makes it worth your while as a hostess, is the changing pattern of power. Power in most other American cities bears an almost direct relationship to wealth. In Washington, it ebbs and flows, seeks new channels, takes new forms. It changes from election to election, from month to month, even from week to week. It is invariably held by politicians, often without the social graces, who do not value or do not comprehend social traditions. Often they come to Washington from simpler or more primitive environments, determined by an ingrained instinct for political survival not to learn anything or to 'get uppity.' Socially graceless as they may be, they are pursued by Washington society because of their power. If wealth and power create society or the elite, they certainly pass the test of power. So they are a part of society, while their power lasts, and their crudities are laughed off as endearing eccentricities."

He sipped his scotch and soda. "Many newcomers in Washington, on the make, don't understand our society. They mistake quantity for quality. The big party is considered superior to the small dinner. Newspaper coverage is mistaken for influence. There is nothing more pitiful than the 'Washington hostess' standing outside of society, divorced from influence and power, seeking social acceptance by giving huge parties and paying the huge bills. They always can get a crowd, the parties are useful and undemanding, they allow politicians to see one another informally, but the stranger at the party, the real outsider, is the Washington hostess."

He finished his drink and lit a cigarette. "Apart from this, there are the functions where businessmen, lobbyists, diplomats, and politicians are at work. These usually occur in the daytime and aren't society at all."

He was silent for a moment, regarding the smoke curling up from the end of his cigarette. "Why do you imagine that I have been telling you all of this?"

Penelope hugged her knees from her position on a sofa. "It's interesting. It's background—it's important since I wasn't reared in Washington."

"It is interesting, but I have told you this to impress upon you that you must go slowly, now, and feel your way. Penelope's Zoo should remain an exclusive domain. If you are intelligent enough, you can become the insider's insider."

"I want to follow your advice. I just hope I understand it. I didn't realize that human relationships were so complex."

"Nothing is more complex." He thought for a moment. "I suggest that we use an old social device. Do you know what a salon is?"

"Not exactly."

"A salon is an exclusive, informal group that meets occasionally for social purposes. If one is included, one merely appears, usually at a private home, at a given day and hour each week. There is some refreshment, but mostly good talk. It was a popular practice before World War I, particularly in Paris. Unfortunately, like so many civilized practices, it has fallen into disuse."

"Something like an 'at home?' "

"Something like that, only reoccurring regularly for a select group. I suggest we carefully choose a guest list and that you institute a salon in this room each Sunday evening. People are then returning to town from the week end and would welcome a drink and a snack in convivial company before going home."

"It sounds like fun."

Haywood's eyes sparkled. "It will be fun. And I'll predict something, Penny. If we limit it to ten, the right ten, half of Washington will be pounding on your door before the winter is out."

"My goodness. Then what will we do?"

Haywood's expression was mischievous. "We might let the group grow to twenty and call it *Penelope's Zoo*."

"After the column?"

"One is going to feed upon the other. We'll make it difficult to get in either."

"What if the ten won't come to the salon?"

"Leave that to me," Haywood said dryly. "If I can't deliver the right ten bodies, then I've grossly overvalued my influence as editor and publisher."

❧ 13 ❧

MARC HAYWOOD sought Penelope's eyes across the polished mahogany table in the private diningroom at the *Tribune*. "I have here a list of those I propose to invite to your first salon." His expression was touched with amusement. "The group has some things in common. Almost all are under forty; all are brilliant and alive intellectually; all have outsized egos and the driving ambition that goes with it. They represent a variety of Washington types; political and social orthodoxy, urban slickness, professional moral punditry, social rebellion, race prejudices, big business, big labor, militant black power, social uselessness, foreign objectivity, the Italians, the Irish, the Anglo-Saxons, Catholic, Jew, Protestant," he paused—"Rather a good cross section for a group of ten people, I think."

"Do they have power?" Penelope asked.

"Some, but the powerful are often dull. I chose these ten for their amusing qualities."

Penelope sipped her coffee. "Won't they be at each others throats? My livingroom is a rather confined space."

"Not if you prove to be the accomplished hostess I see in you. You must let the conversation become stimulating, but not divisive. I am inviting this menagerie on your behalf in such a way that each will feel subtly flattered to be chosen. The group therapy of mutually massaged egos will create a togetherness that will grow stronger as the weeks pass. They will stop short of conduct that will put them out of the club."

"Who are these fascinating people? Do I know them?"

"At least by reputation." He glanced at the list before him. "*First*, we have Jack Biddle, Junior Senator from California, five years seniority, former Olympic gold medal winner, former Rhodes Scholar, youngest member of the Senate's inner club. He represents the clean-cut American success story—Jack Armstrong type. Brilliant political future unless the voters decide that he's too good to be true. *Second*, there is Jerry Wharton, Assistant Secretary of Defense, partner in a New York law firm, protégé of Samuel D. Barnes, the Governor of New York. He represents the Eastern Establishment, smart, dedicated, perhaps a little patronizing of those with different backgrounds. His Harvard drawl is a bit too broad for his own good. *Third*, Binnie Wharton, née Turnlake, Junior League, well born, but poor, a typical product of a finishing school, socially over-confident and economically insecure. She commutes between Washington and New York where she designs clothes. She represents *Society* in the negative sense."

"I don't think I'll like her," Penelope said quietly.

"No, you won't. No one will. Her role is the gadfly, the straightman for the others. Binnie Wharton is an unconscious genius at goading others into a passionate expression of dissent. Every conversational group needs one. *Fourth*, Parmer Fitzgerald, a professor of political science from the University of Chicago. You may remember him from your White House days as a Presidential Assistant and a speech writer. He represents the academic community, 'sacrificing' a low salary and a dull academic existence to engage in the stimulating and safe game of putting words in the mouth of the President of the United States. He is liberal minded, learned, pragmatic, witty, and the turner of the felicitous phrase. He only becomes bigoted when his Catholic faith is challenged. Of

128

course, he can't stand bigotry in others; he is certain God stands one pace behind him with His hand on his shoulder. *Fifth*, Guido Allessandro, second generation Italian from Providence, Rhode Island, brilliant, articulate, a fourth term Congressman from a district where a non-hyphenated American is an object of mistrust. Guido commanded a Marine company in Korea and came back hating war and despising all things military. He is on the House Armed Services Committee and is a severe critic of military and space expenditures. He's sensitive, an artist at heart. He'd be happier in Italy, but he doesn't know it. He's never been there. *Sixth*, Lionel Jackson, born a Negro, now a black man and so achingly anxious to tell you about it, he can't think of much else. He's the editor of a mass circulation Negro magazine published in Washington called the *Cutting Edge*. His pose is militant dissent bordering on revolution. His mind is rapier keen. He's a specialist at abusive, bruising language. As he would say, 'He likes to get things on the gut level.' However, he has a problem, he's making so much money attacking the system, that he's becoming a part of the system. He's like a child with his bread buttered on both sides. His clean hands are becoming sticky. *Seventh*, Ralph Kerrigan, vice president and Washington representative of GMT, one of our new, sprawling conglomerates growing and prospering through the manipulation of paper rather than through the creation of wealth. Kerrigan passionately believes in this house of cards his management is building and feels that any government interference with its growth is bureaucratic meddling or a Communist plot, or both. He is soft spoken, affable, accommodating. His self-effacing manner masks the fact that he has an almost daily knowledge of how Washington really functions. He knows the power brokers and can give you, from memory, the political temperature within a half a degree of every member of Congress on any morning of the week. If all of his stock options stay healthy, he'll reach the financial Shangri-la he believes is the deserved reward of his type of *free enterprise. Eighth,* Harry Richards, a labor organizer and a professional tough guy when he was in his twenties, he now is a well paid administrator of the labor wing of the status quo. Back when he was battling the Establishment, he was very conscious that he was a member of an ethnic minority. Now with a new name he gives you the feeling that he won't think about it, if you won't. In many ways, he is the most conservative of the group we're assembling. His union is worrying about Negro aggressiveness, Communist infiltration, and non-affiliated union movements. It's ironic that the pursuit of maximum income and profits has tended in recent years to make Big Business flexible and pragmatic in approaching domestic and international problems while the defense of 'labor gains' has made the union movement cautious and conservative. Harry is closer to John D. Rockefeller in spirit than to Henry Ford II. The fun is that he doesn't know it. He has the emotions of a revanchist and the vocabulary of a revolutionary. Combine that with a strangled syntax and you get some interesting comments. *Ninth,* Lynn Hyman, a self-made millionaire in one of the few fields open to women on equal terms—real estate. In twenty years she devastated more quiet Washington residential streets and devoured more rolling farmland than any ten of her counterparts. Eight out of every ten of the ten story cement and glass squares that replaced hundred year old brownstones on H, I, and K Streets were built by Lynn. Two out of every three of the rural housing spores that spread over green hillsides were built by Lynn. Now, in her fifties, a mellowing spinster, she is seeking social approval. She is 'socially conscious' and is spreading more devastation as she plays with people than she did when she played with real estate. Some people leave blight behind them wherever they move. Lynn Hyman is that type, tasteless, unloved and unloving, afflicted with a social and intellectual myopia that only enables her to see and comprehend her current narrow field of interest, she is the hypocrites, hypocrite."

"Why do we have such a creature?"

"She will make you more tolerant of the others and I think it's safer to be friends than enemies with someone who has a sign on her desk 'I serve my fellowman'."

"How ghastly. Does she believe it?"

"Absolutely. *Tenth*, the winning outsider, the uninvolved, objective commentator, Hillary Brummitt, the Ambassador of Canada. Eton, Oxford, born English, a naturalized Canadian, blessed with that detached, wry, English sense of humor, a genius at deflating egos and warring on cant, clichés, and bombast. His personality is so finely balanced that he seems almost immobile, a fixed point of social reference balanced on the point of a pin. He is invaluable at taking an argument, turning it about, and starting it off on a new tack. Like many Oxonians, he dreads a conversation getting serious—he has the instinct of a hostess in that respect. He'll be a big help to you."

"What of their wives and husbands?"

"The Whartons are married to each other, poor dears. Hyman, Richards and Allessandro are unmarried. We'll invite the spouses of the others. They'll be bored and will drop out after a week or two."

Penelope cleared her throat. "I'm not sure that I'm up to it. As you describe them they sound awful. They frighten me to death."

"Of course you are up to it. I'll be there for a few weeks until you have found your métier."

"What if they don't come? Or don't come back?"

"They'll come. One or two may drop out, but eventually you'll settle down with ten to twenty regulars. You have no idea what it will do for your reputation and for the column. People like this are great catalysts."

"I feel nervous."

"You're growing, Penny. It's the sensation of stretching

131

you feel, not nervousness."

She smiled at him. "If you say so, but I would say it's but-terflies in the tummy."

The fire burned low in the fireplace at Dumbarton House. The small Swiss clock on the mantle struck eight unnoticed amid the babble of conversation. Marc Haywood smiled down at Penelope. "I think it's gone well."

"You think so? I've got a headache. What a group of prima donnas you wished on me."

"Go take an aspirin. You'll feel more philosophical."

"I already have."

"I didn't miss you."

"You see? No one knows I'm here or who I am. They're all wound up in themselves."

"They know who you are. And it isn't important that you participate—keep their thirst quenched and they'll think of you as a hell of a hostess. After all, they have indisputable proof of your taste in people."

Penelope put a hand up to her forehead. "Tell me again, why are we doing this?"

"To start the inner sanctum legend about you, darling. These lovely egomaniacs are your backdrop. The backdrop for your column. This is Penelope's Zoo, this is what you write about."

"This?"

"Not literally. But your readers don't know that. No out-sider will. Washington outsiders will struggle to get in. We'll let in a few from time to time if they are sufficiently amusing and good sources of information for the column." He sipped his scotch and soda. "To be exclusive, you must exclude. To be desirable, you must be unobtainable. To be mysterious you must be unknown."

Penelope shook her head. "I don't get it."

"You wanted to graduate in your column to Senior Wash-ington, didn't you?"

132

"Yes."

"You can't pursue Senior Washington. They must come to you. Your competitors' tired prose is due to the fact they pursue Senior Washington. As a result they are on that fringe I once referred to."

"We entice them into the Zoo?"

"Exactly. We'll put them in the Zoo one by one. What does it matter if we start with a few performing bears and a jackel? We'll get the lions and tigers later."

Parmer Fitzgerald got up a bit unsteadily from a sofa and came over to them, drink in hand. He studied Penelope for a moment from half closed eyes which were slightly distorted by the thick lens of his glasses. "Weren't you in my shop at one time?"

"Yes. I was Dave Winslow's secretary."

Fitzgerald snapped his fingers, "Of course. I never forget a face," he leered at Haywood, "Or a figure."

"You are the only person I have ever met, Parmer," Haywood said evenly, "who is arrogant enough to refer to the White House as 'my shop.' "

Fitzgerald waved a hand. "Words of art, words of art. Tell me, Dave Winslow's secretary, what are you doing now?" His insolent gaze turned to Haywood, "Or should I ask?"

Haywood dropped a friendly arm across Fitzgerald's shoulder and turned him from the others in the room. He then struck him with a short, hard jab to the stomach. Fitzgerald turned white and doubled over with a little gasp as far as Haywood would allow him. "No, Parmer. You shouldn't ask."

The color slowly flowed back into Fitzgerald's face. He looked at Haywood from watery eyes. "That was a hell of a thing to do," he croaked.

Haywood tightened his grip on Fitzgerald's shoulders. "If you don't know what Miss Benton is doing now, find out, because if you ever ask that question again, just the way you asked it, I'll let the entire weight of the *Tribune* fall on you."

Fitzgerald nodded. "I stand corrected. I had one too many, I guess."

Penelope's wide eyes were on Haywood. "Forget it, Mr. Fitzgerald."

Lynn Hyman joined them. "You're as thick as thieves over here in the corner. Am I intruding?"

"Not at all," Haywood smiled at her, "We were just discussing college boxing and I was showing Parmer a punch I used when I was intercollegiate boxing champion."

"I know nothing of that," Lynn Hyman's tone was incisive. "What I came over to ask, was when is the *Tribune* going to start supporting my program for urban planning?"

"What is your program?" Haywood asked.

"You are impossible, Marc. Don't you read your own newspaper? You covered it completely in last Sunday's real estate section."

"I never read the real estate section. My stomach isn't strong enough."

Lynn Hyman's expression was sharp. "What does that mean? I never know how to take you." She turned to Lionel Jackson who had joined them, "I'm trying to get this patrician member of the White Establishment to support urban planning, Lionel."

Jackson smiled and fondled the scraggly beard on his chin. "I let you honkies worry about things like that in a place like this. You're just plain gabagonious. No matter what you say, you don't mean nothin.'"

Haywood smiled. "For a Harvard man, Lionel, you have mastered the ghetto Negro dialect very well and no doubt for good commercial reasons, but why inflict it on us?"

"It's the coming thing, man, don't you know that?"

Haywood laughed shortly and said to Lynn Hyman as he moved away, "Sell your urban planning to Lionel. Can't you see that I'm a has been?"

"That man is impossible," Lynn Hyman said looking after him. "He is too detached. Above the battle."

134

Jackson eyed her. "What battle?"

"Why the battle to help the Negro, to clean up the ghettos."

Jackson flashed white even teeth in a humorless smile and spoke to Penelope as he tipped his head in Lynn Hyman's direction. "This babe has a hang up. She wants to help the black man by eliminating him, fold him into the white community like flavoring in a cake batter. If you mix long and hard enough, he'll disappear and you'll never know he's there. She calls that integration. I call it racial suicide." He gave Lynn Hyman a hard, sidelong look, "Then she'll move into the ghetto and tear it down and rebuild it and move back in nice integrated Americans.

"The Nazis put the Jews into the ovens, the honkey integrationist wants to smother the black race in the folds of the white woman's womb. We ain't going to play that game. We got our own black women. We got our own black neighborhoods, we got our own way of doing. We want whitey off our backs—that's all. We don't need no sucking up sweet talk about livin' like whitey. We goin' to get a piece of the action and go our own way, we don't need no white man to tell us we as good as he is. We know that. It's whitey that don't know it."

Lynn Hyman's face was grey. "Really, Lionel. You must be drunk. You sound like the worst kind of extremist and you know better. As a Jew I have a special feeling for minorities." She turned and walked away.

Jackson lit a cigarette and eyed Penelope over the flame. "You dig what I said?"

"I dig. You won't get smothered in my womb."

Jackson suddenly laughed. "That just came to me. I'll use it in an editorial next week." He drew on his cigarette. "Why did you ask me here?"

"Why did you come?"

"Because Haywood extended the invitation. He's the only white man I know who doesn't patronize me to some degree.

Haywood is interested in me to the extent that he is interested in any human being, which isn't much. In his indifference I find true equality. So I'm not self-conscious around Haywood. You have any idea how painful self-consciousness can be?"

"Some."

"No. you have no idea. That's how black people feel around white people, especially those that try to be nice. Jesus, there's nothing in this world that sticks in my gut like having a white man patronize me."

Penelope was silent.

Jackson eyed her. "What do you think of all this?" He asked after a moment.

"You mean what do I think of you?"

"I don't give a damn what you think of me."

"I think you're just a Joe trying to make it. To make it today, you do a big thing of being black."

"Just making it? You don't think I feel anything? That I'm not part of the scene?"

"Sure you're part of the scene. Sure you feel, but you're still trying to make it in the scene you're part of. I am too."

Jackson deliberately dropped his cigarette onto the carpet and ground in out with a shoe sole. "You want me back?" He asked defiantly.

"If you want to come."

"Why should I want to come?"

"No reason, unless you find it interesting."

"Am I interesting?"

"I think you've been pretty boring up to now, Mr. Jackson. But if you stop posturing and relax, I think you will be a person well worth knowing. At least Marc says so. We aren't trying to sell you anything you know."

Jackson looked over the crowded room and was silent for a moment. "I may come back."

"I hope you do."

"But you don't care?"

Not much."

"I guess I'll get a drink."

Haywood drifted back. "You seem to be getting along with our black friend."

"Not really. No one can for a few years."

"Did he annoy you?"

"No. I thought he was rather stupid."

"Jackson isn't stupid. We were at Harvard together. He knows his way around."

"Then he shouldn't act stupid."

"Aren't you enjoying this?"

"Am I supposed to enjoy it?"

"It helps." He glanced at her and found that she was studying him.

"Why did you strike Parmer Fitzgerald? It seemed out of character."

"I shared the urge of millions of Americans. I just had a golden opportunity."

"Thank you, Marc." Her eyes were soft.

He gave an ironic little bow. "My pleasure ma'am. Sometimes it's nice to be a little uncivilized." He looked around the room with a grin. "A real zoo! This *is* fun!"

❦ 14 ❦

PENELOPE ran a questing fingertip over the engraved invitation from Marnie Maane and tapped its edge several times against the top of her desk in indecision. She then dialed Marc Haywood's extension number. "I have an invitation to a reception next month from Marnie Maane. Should I go?"

Marc Haywood laughed. "So Marnie's finally taken notice of you. That's an accolade, of sorts. She's inviting you to her first reception of the New Year."

"It must be the Christmas spirit. Isn't she sort of a cat?"

"A cat, maybe, but no kitten. She's the socially insecure widow of one of those semi-literate oil men who made it big, tearing his body to pieces in the process."

"I've heard of her, of course, but I've never met her. Do I have to go?"

"She's the prototype of the Washington Hostess with a capital H I've described to you before. You should be familiar with the species for your column. Marnie collects celebrities together at a few big receptions during the year and after hiring a public relations firm to see that they are well publicized in the press and on television, lives in the glow of the reflected glory in between."

"I'm no celebrity. Why does she want to collect me?"

"Don't be modest. She doesn't want to collect you. She has identified you as a rival. She wants to look you over. You should look her over. It's a part of your Washington education. Marnie is a walking compendium of don'ts for you."

"She seems popular."

"She picks up the checks," Haywood said simply. "I think I've suggested that anyone that does that has considerable acceptability in Washington."

"Then I should go?"

"This time, but once through the receiving line, avoid her like the plague. She has sharp claws."

"Will you be there?"

"No." Haywood's tone was positive.

Penelope sighed. "O.K. I'll go alone."

"It won't be a total loss. You'll be surprised at the number of people you'll know."

"Uh huh. But you won't be there." Her voice conveyed a pout.

"I'm going to Barbados tomorrow for the holidays. I won't be back until mid-January."

"Oh."

"Have a Merry Christmas, Penny. I'll see you in the New Year."

"Thank you." She hung up the telephone, a hurt expression on her face. She had known that she would be spending Christmas alone, but she had not realized that he would be so far away. She had expected to see him during the holidays. A small gift for him was in her desk drawer. She would now have no graceful way to give it to him. Her eyes misted and she bit her lip, staring unseeingly at the frosted door across her small office. On an impulse she picked up the telephone again and called her mother in Bloomington.

Mrs. Benton arrived the day before Christmas during a brief, shower-like storm of swirling wet snow. When Mrs. Moss opened the door to her ring, she stood on the unsheltered stoop, wet snow clinging to the narrow fur collar of her thin cloth coat and melting in streams down the sides of the red vinyl suitcase she held in one hand. "I'm Penny Benton's mom. Am I at the right place?"

Mrs. Moss's eyes dropped briefly to the sodden shoes and splattered hose before she answered. "Why, Mrs. Benton, come in out of that wet. Miss Penelope was waiting for your telephone call. Mr. Moss was going to come to meet you. Whatever happened?"

"I was on standby on the flight out of Indianapolis so I didn't know when I'd arrive and I wasn't going to pay a king's ransom to those taxi drivers. Why, with their tips they're better off than I am." She took off a small brown felt hat and ran her fingers through her damp iron grey hair. "I'll be just fine when I warm up a bit. The bus dropped me only three blocks away so I didn't mind." She looked around the entrance foyer. "Isn't this just grand? Penny described it in a letter, but I had no idea! My stars!"

"I'll take you right up to your room, ma'am and then you have a hot bath." Mrs. Moss firmly took the suitcase from Mrs. Benton's unwilling fingers.

"Now, don't you baby me," Mrs. Benton said jovially as they mounted the curving staircase. "I'm not used to it. I'll be real spoiled when I go home. Where's Penny?"

"She's at the newspaper, ma'am. She'll be home at five o'clock."

"I can hardly wait to see her. I haven't seen her for ages." She looked around the bedroom with its mahogany four poster bed and chest on chest glowing in the after storm winter sunlight that filtered through heavily draped translucent curtains. "Well, this will do real fine. I feel just like a queen already."

"You relax and take your bath ma'am. I'll let you know when Miss Penelope comes home."

"Thank you, and if you need help with supper, let me know. I like to make myself useful."

"I'll remember, ma'am. Now you just rest yourself."

140

Penelope was sitting by the fire in the living room when Mrs. Benton came downstairs. Other than a small lamp on a pie crust table in the corner, the room was lit only by the firelight and the glow of a Christmas tree in a bow window.

"My stars!" Mrs. Benton said. "It's after six. I must have been tired after all."

Penelope arose from her chair and hugged her. "How are you, Mom?"

Mrs. Benton kissed her on the cheek and then held her out at arms length and kissed her again. "I'm just all choked up, Penny. I really am." She looked around her. "It's all so grand, just like a dream."

"Yes, I'm not quite used to it."

"Can you afford it on your salary? It must cost a lot with help and all."

"The newspaper pays for most of it."

"Oh," Mrs. Benton looked around her. "That's all right then. Those that have money should spend it." She walked over to the Christmas tree. "That's real pretty, Penny. I gave them up since you left home. What's the use? When the students are gone, I'm all alone."

"I'm glad you're here, Mom. We'll have an old-fashioned Christmas."

"Well, I scrimped and saved to get here before this, but something always took the money." She turned to Penelope with a smile. "Not that your checks don't help, Penny, but, even so, there's not much left over for gallivanting about."

"I was glad to send you the money for this trip. It's on me, remember, so enjoy yourself."

"Very generous, I'm sure," Mrs. Benton said self-consciously. "Where shall I sit?"

"Wherever you wish."

"I don't want to take over your favorite chair."

"I don't have a favorite chair."

"Your Dad did."

141

"I know."

Mrs. Benton's face became sad. "God bless him. I wish he was here. He'd be so surprised and proud, just like me."

"I wish he were here, too."

"I always miss him at Christmas, on his birthday, and on the same day each year that he died."

Penelope nodded.

"I keep his memory green, Penny. It's the least that I can do."

"Yes."

Mrs. Benton gazed sadly into the fire for a moment. "What are we having for supper? It smells real good."

"Baked ham."

"I've got a good appetite. I thought they'd feed us on the plane, but they didn't." She turned to Penelope. "I want to go everywhere and see everything while I'm here."

"I'll see that you visit all of the famous places."

"And I want to go with you when you go to these fancy parties I read about in your column."

"You have to be invited to these parties, Mom. I'm afraid that you aren't included."

Mrs. Benton looked hurt. "I'm your mother. Certainly I'm welcome?"

"Welcome, but not invited."

"Well, well," Mrs. Benton said slowly. "That's a disappointment. I was counting on that part of it."

"These affairs are just work for me, Mom. You wouldn't enjoy them."

"Let me be the judge of that," Mrs. Benton's voice faintly suggested a mother's superior knowledge.

"You aren't coming to them. Forget it."

"Are you ashamed to introduce me to your friends? I want to meet your friends."

"You'll meet my friends."

"Well, I should think so. I don't know when I'll be back."

Mr. Moss appeared with a silver tray on which were two

pewter mugs. "Miss Penelope, I've fixed a hot Christmas drink for you and your mother. Mrs. Moss says that dinner will be ready in one-half hour."

"Thank you, Mr. Moss. Have you met my mother?"

"How do you do, Mr. Moss. I met that darling wife of yours earlier. She's a doll."

"Thank you ma'am, and Merry Christmas."

Mrs. Benton sipped her drink. "This is pretty wicked. I have a light head. It may make me tipsy, on an empty stomach and all."

"Merry Christmas, Mom."

"Merry Christmas to you, dear." She studied the Christmas tree with its tiny, candle like lights. "I like her. He's a little snooty. I thought he'd ask about my trip or something."

"He did the proper thing, Mom. Mr. Moss is not here for conversation."

"I stand corrected, I'm sure." She put her mug down on a marble coffee table top. "I hope that doesn't upset my stomach."

Mrs. Benton stood in the rotunda of the Jefferson Memorial. A chill, January wind moved through the great marble columns and whipped at the bottom of her coat. She looked at the words of the third President cut into a marble tablet, a discontented expression on her face. "I never was one for history."

"Would you like to leave?" Penelope asked.

"We might as well." They walked back to the parking lot where Mr. Moss was waiting in the car. "I go home tomorrow, Penny, and you still haven't taken me to one of your parties, not a single one."

"I've had my friends in to meet you."

"Just slips of girls and boys. I want to meet some important people, someone I can talk about back home."

"It isn't that way, Mom. It really isn't."

"I want to see for myself."

143

"I'm sorry. It hasn't been possible."

"You're going out to-night. I saw the invitation. You can take me."

"No. I can not. Besides, this is a duty affair. I'll only stay five minutes."

"It's from that famous Washington hostess," Mrs. Benton said accusingly. "That's what I mean. I want to meet people like that. Her parties are on the T.V."

"You shouldn't read my mail." Penelope said icily.

"It was right out on top of your desk. I couldn't miss it."

"Yes, I know. We have a long history of things you couldn't miss. I had forgotten."

"It isn't prying to be interested in what your only child is doing. Besides, you're changing the subject. This is my last night. Are you going to take me to that reception?"

"No!"

Mrs. Benton compressed her lips. "Very well. It isn't fair, Penny, when it means so much to me, but, very well."

Marnie Maane stood alone, an impressive receiving line of one, just inside the entrance to the cavernous ballroom of the Washington Hilton. Her tall, spare figure was draped in gold lame. Her gaunt neck and claw-like hands were covered with diamonds. Her heavily lined face, dry and deeply tanned from years of dozing on deck chairs and pallets in the sun was ridged into a semi-permanent smile as she greeted her guests. Nearly two hundred of the five hundred guests invited had filed past with a brief greeting when Penelope arrived.

Marnie Maane's sharp eyes appraised her and a catty expression touched her lips. "You're that darling new friend of Marc Haywood's aren't you?"

Penelope felt a swift, uncontrollable surge of anger. "You may have invited me because of Marc, Mrs. Maane. I can assure you that I came only to find out if someone like you could be for real."

144

Marnie Maane's eyes narrowed. "I really don't know why you were invited," she said in a husky undertone. "It must have been a clerical error. You were probably on another list, though I can't think what."

"It's certainly possible," Penelope smiled into the older woman's eyes as she passed on into the room. "I hear that you buy mailing lists for your invitations."

Marnie Maane stood staring after her, a look of malevolence darkening her face.

Penelope swiftly recovered her good spirits. She had given the old dragon as good as she had received—the equivalent of Marc's blow to Parmer Fitzgerald's stomach. Marnie Maane had learned one thing. Penelope Benton was no pushover. She discovered many friends in the crowd, milling about under the curved steel girders that supported the low, concave roof of the room, and managed to be introduced to several prominent members of the Congress who reacted with the politician's absent-minded and slightly weary gallantry to her direct, questing look and ready smile. Instead of five minutes she stayed twenty and left only because she refused to admit to herself that a party of Marnie Maane's could hold interest for her.

She had been gone only ten minutes and the line of arriving guests had shortened to four or five when Marnie Maane turned from the raucous greeting of Congressman Easter and his wife to a rather dowdy middle-aged woman she had not seen before. The woman smiled self-consciously and awkwardly extended her hand. "I'm Penny Benton's mom. Is Penny still here?"

Marnie Maane took the extended hand almost absently as she looked into Mrs. Benton's plain face. A look of incredulity changed to one of pleased surprise and then near elation. "Penny's mom? You are Penelope Benton's mother?"

"Why, yes," Mrs. Benton said, pleased and reassured by the expression on Marnie Maane's face.

"Well, my dear, come right in. What a surprise! What a

pleasant surprise! Penny left a few minutes ago, but I'm glad you came." She took Mrs. Benton by the arm and steered her toward a stiff, gilt trimmed settee along one wall. "My late guests will have to take care of themselves. Let's sit down and relax together. Do you live with Penny, dear?"

"No, I live in Bloomington, Indiana. I run a residence for students."

"A university residence hall?"

"No, my own house."

"You take in roomers, dear?"

"Student roomers."

"How interesting. And you are visiting Penny here?"

"Yes. I go home tomorrow."

Marnie Maane sat smiling at her. "Isn't this nice! Would you like to meet some of my guests?"

"Oh, my yes. I've heard about your famous parties, Mrs. Maane, and I was so anxious to see one."

"I'm so delighted that you came, dear. You have no idea. You've made my day."

Mrs. Benton's face broke into a happy smile. "I think you mean that, Mrs. Maane. I can see you're regular folks. Penny feels, I'm sure, that I can't hold my own out in the world, but I find people are the same all over, if you meet them half way."

"Let's walk among the crowd, dear. I shouldn't keep you to myself. I'm going to introduce you to some well known people and you just speak right up and tell them that you are Penelope's mom. They will be as interested to meet you as I was."

Marnie Maane walked through the crowd introducing Mrs. Benton to selected groups. Mrs. Benton soon overcame her shyness and holding an unaccustomed scotch and soda in one hand and a canape in the other was soon chattering happily to the interested strangers that surrounded her. After a half hour Marnie Maane took her by the arm and led her toward a small stage set against a removable wall that divided the part of the ballroom used by Marnie Maane from an un-used portion that to-night was dark and silent. The stage was surrounded by the mountings of unlit lights and three televi-sion cameras. Four casually dressed cameramen and techni-cians were lounging nearby. "If you are familiar with my parties, Mrs. Benton, you know that they are picked up on television as a part of a program called Capitol View. Usually, they give me a half hour segment during which I in-terview a few of my more interesting guests."

"I've seen that on T.V. My stars! Is this where you do it?"

"This is it. On that little stage. Now, dear," she laid her thin hand on Mrs. Benton's arm, "I'd like you to be my first guest."

Mrs. Benton gave a little gasp. "Me?"

"Yes, dear."

Mrs. Benton sat down suddenly on a nearby folding chair. She felt a little light headed from the whiskey she had drunk. "Me? On national T.V.?"

"Think how proud your neighbors will be."

"But," Mrs. Benton looked up anxiously. "Do you think I can do it?"

"Of course, dear. Be your own sweet, natural self, just as you have been with me and my guests."

"Well, my stars! I never!" Mrs. Benton thought a moment, unconsciously nodding her head. "It will show Penny a thing or two. I can get around on my own. All right! I'll do it!"

"You're a darling," Marnie Maane purred. "An absolute darling."

When the television lights went on, Mrs. Benton blinked into the glare from the cup chair in which she sat and wet her dry lips with her tongue. Her small flowered hat was perched precariously atop her short cropped, slightly disarranged gray hair. Her worn hands nervously fondled the necklace of large imitation amber beads that hung down almost to the waist of her floral print dress.

A young television director who had casually appeared a

few minutes before, fingered his sandy beard and called out, "Sixty seconds, Mrs. Maane."

Marnie Maane smiled an acknowledgement. "Thank you, Jerry."

"Thirty."

"Ten."

The director indicated a live take.

Marnie Maane smiled into the camera. "Good evening, ladies and gentlemen. I'm Marnie Maane and believe it or not I'm giving another party! I just *love* parties, don't you? I have about five hundred of Washington's most important people here to-night and, as usual, we are going to introduce you to a few. Just before the camera came over to me I know you saw this beautiful room at the Washington Hilton just filled with beautiful people. It's glamorous, it's exciting, and it's fun and I'm so glad that you can be a part of it. Now, my first guest to-night is a lovely lady from Bloomington, Indiana. You might say that she is a gate crasher because I didn't expect her, but I have found her a delightfully natural person and I want to share her with you. Mrs. Benton, why did you come to my party?"

Mrs. Benton gave a nervous little cough. "I came looking for my daughter, Penelope Benton, but she had already left."

"Is that the Penelope who writes the column, *Penelope's Zoo?*"

"Yes. That's my daughter," Mrs. Benton said proudly.

"Oh, yes," Marnie Maane spoke with affected vagueness. "I believe she was here."

"She said that she was coming."

"Then I'm sure that she was invited—if she said so. Why didn't you come with her?"

"She said that I wasn't invited and that I wouldn't like it."

"Do you like it?"

"My stars, yes. It's so exciting."

"I think that you told me that you take in roomers out in Bloomington, Indiana?"

148

"I run a residence for students," Mrs. Benton said a little stiffly.

"Of course, a residence for students. That's a better way to put it. Is this your first trip to Washington?"

"My, yes."

"Why haven't you come sooner? None of us who know Penelope know you."

"Well, I wanted to come, but Penny put me off from month to month. I never had the money, you see, and then last month she sent me the ticket money and I came on."

"Do you like Washington?"

"My stars, yes. You should see this house that Penny lives in, a regular palace with servants and a car and everything. It's like a dream. I can't get over it."

"Columnists make a lot of money," Marnie Maane said without inflection.

"Some, I guess, but Penny tells me that the *Tribune* pays for the house, the servants, and the car."

"That's very generous."

"Yes, I thought so."

Marnie Maane hesitated a moment and smoothed a pleat in her skirt. She then looked up and smiled brilliantly at Mrs. Benton. "You're very, very sweet."

"Thank you."

"When do you go home?"

"Tomorrow."

"And will you visit us again?"

"I'd love to if Penny sends me the carfare. Nobody ever got rich catering to students and I'm no exception."

Marie Maane gave a dry chuckle. "When Penelope sends you the car fare. We shall have to see when that is." The director helped Mrs. Benton from the platform during a station break as Marnie Maane turned to greet her next guest.

Penelope sat opposite Marc Haywood at the table in his private dining room at the *Tribune* and toyed nervously with her food. She looked up at him unhappily. "All I did was to return a private insult in private and she crucified me on national television." She burst into tears. "It wasn't fair!"

Haywood got up from his chair and stood beside her, patting her shoulder with a tanned hand. He kissed her gently on the cheek and handed her a linen handkerchief with his initials embroidered on it from the upper pocket of his suit jacket. "The punishment didn't fit the crime, Penny, but the punishment was at hand, a heaven sent opportunity. Marnie couldn't resist it."

"I'll never forgive my mother. Never! How could she be so—so dumb!"

"She's just an inexperienced woman, Penny. She was out of her depth. Marnie took advantage of her. I am sure that your mother had no idea what was happening."

"My God! When I think what she said. I'm so humiliated. Can't we sue for slander or libel or for whatever it is on television?"

"My lawyers have gone over the transcript. There was no slander, if you believe in your mother's innocence, and even if you don't, she's still your mother."

Penelope sighed. "Yes, she is." She dried her eyes. "When did you hear about this?"

"They sent me a transcript in Barbados. The *Tribune* owns the local television station that was the national outlet. That's another reason we can't sue anybody," he added drily.

"What does Claudia think?"

"Imperturbable is the word for Claudia." Haywood walked back to his own chair and sat down with his legs crossed. "I've just finished luncheon. You should eat yours. You can't go to war on an empty stomach."

"Go to war?"

Haywood grinned at her as he lit a cigarette. "You aren't going to quit, are you?"

"I thought that maybe you'd want me to give up the column."

150

"Of course not. A feud with a Marnie Maane is just what you need at this point."

Penelope looked up from her plate dry-eyed. "I won't descend to her level. I hate cat fights."

"That's not necessary. You won't attack her. You'll ignore her and attack with ridicule the whole concept of the 'Washington hostess'. That crack you made about invitations from mailing lists is a pretty good beginning." He began to laugh. "That was priceless."

"How will I ever live down my mother? I'm supposed to know my way around and, let's face it, Marc, my mother came across as an awful hayseed. Some people will say, 'what could the daughter of a woman like that know about Washington?' "

He studied her. "You're too angry with your mother to see the answer to that. It's compassion."

"Compassion?"

"Sure. Marnie used your mother to ridicule you. Most people, even those that laughed at your mother, felt some sympathy for her. If you act angry with her, or ashamed of her, you play right into Marnie's hands. The correct gambit is to show your love for your mother. Emphasize your appreciation of her simple honesty and guilelessness. Direct your anger, subtly of course, against the Washington shrew who exploited your mother's innocence and pride in you."

Penelope spread her hands. "How do I do that?"

"You don't doubt that she loves you, do you?"

"No."

"Then write a column or two about her visit to you in Washington at Christmas time Mention the rooming house. Mention your humble background. Tell about your mother's wonderment at visiting Washington. Include everything the gossips say your mother mentioned at Marnie's party, but tell it from your point of view. The climax of your column will be the visit of this guileless innocent to a phony party, looking for the daughter she loves and who loves her. If you finesse it correctly, you can damn near ruin Marnie and make yourself the daughter of the year."

"Marc, you haven't met my mother."

"And I don't want to meet her. We are dealing with an abstraction. M..O..T..H..E..R in letters ten feet high."

Penelope shook her head and smiled wryly. "I'll try it, though I'm not exactly filled with filial devotion at the moment."

Haywood's eyes twinkled. "I'm betting on you, Penny. You're scratched up a bit, but you are in a good strategic position. You see, Marnie Maane will never have television coverage again on my station or one line of news coverage in the *Tribune*, except as your foil."

Penelope looked at him wide-eyed and caught a diamond hard glint behind the twinkle. "She shouldn't have made the innuendo about Dumbarton House," she said softly.

The expression on Marc Haywood's face became cold. "No, she shouldn't have. It was an expensive impulse. We shall see that she pays in full."

✦ 15 ✦

DICK WINSTON grinned at Marc Haywood as he leaned against the mantel in the Winston living room and forked a portion of scrambled egg in his mouth. "How's ol' Marc this cold, windy morning?"

Haywood sipped a cup of coffee. "Like all the non-hunters, relaxed and at ease. How's Patty after that spill?"

"She has a wrenched shoulder and a lacerated cheekbone. Otherwise, she is fine. She'll be down in a few minutes to do her stuff as hunt breakfast hostess. Mama disapproves of the whole thing and is sulking in her bedroom."

"I thought Mama ruled the roost."

"Not where riding and fox hunting is concerned. But Patty is passionate on the subject and Mama gave way."

"Interesting."

Dick Winston put his plate down on a nearby table. "If Mama had known the hunt ran right through this property she never would have bought it."

"She should have known it. You're a county family."

Dick Winston made an amused grimace. "Even Mama makes mistakes, and usually because she makes herself forget anything contrary to the way she wants things to be."

"I wonder why Patty and Claudia are such passionate horsewomen and love cross country riding and the hunt and yet you and I prefer to stand around, dismounted, conforming only to the extent of wearing riding breeches?

"We have other interests ol' boy. For example, you are busy playing God."

"What do you mean by that?" Haywood asked evenly.

Dick Winston deftly detached a gin fizz from a passing tray and looked at Haywood archly from under partially closed eye lids. "You take a sweet little gal from the corn country and over a period of time turn her into a Washington celebrity. What fun! A real live doll to play with. Maybe you're only playing Dr. Coppelius rather than God. I may have overstated it, but you get the idea."

Haywood's face grew cold. "Dick, I've known you all of my life. It has been my considered opinion since boyhood that occasionally you can be an accomplished jackass. Don't say things that will make me decide that you are a horse's ass as well."

Dick Winston waved his glass and laughed softly. "Got you, didn't I? Even the suave, imperturbable press tycoon can get pricked."

"My interest in Penelope is that of her publisher. What you overlook, from your over-mothered, coupon clipping, rural sanctuary, is that Penelope has become one of the most widely syndicated columnists in the United States and the *Tribune* has made a packet of money off it. As a matter of fact, the dividend increase the *Tribune* pays you as the fortunate beneficiary of a trust probably paid for your liquor this year."

"No matter, no matter," Dick Winston moved a hand. "You've taken the girl over. She has no life outside her damned column and the social schedule you decree for her."

"She's making the best possible use of her time. She's only twenty-five. She can waste her time later when she can afford it."

"She's in love with you, ol' Marc. I think you're taking advantage of that. Makes you something of a cad, doesn't it?"

Haywood stood very still, looking at Dick Winston.

"Don't say that again, Dick. Penelope is taking my advice to the benefit of both of us. I admire her. She's a gutsy little gal. I'll concede she may admire me. Why not? I have taught her more in three years than most women learn in a lifetime."

"What does Claudia think of the tête-à-têtes at Dumbarton House and elsewhere?"

"We seldom discuss them, but I'm sure that she understands them for what they are."

"The understanding wife?"

"The loved wife. You know that, damn you."

Dick Winston shrugged. "I've never doubted that Claudia and you would come out of this intact. The person I am worried about is Penelope."

Haywood slowly lit a cigarette and eyed Dick Winston over the flame of the match. "What are you, a self-appointed guardian? A damn unlikely role, I must say. As for jealousy, there's no basis for it in fact, or, if I'm any judge, on the basis of *your* prospects."

"No, not jealousy, but guardian? Not so damn unlikely. I'm about the only human being she knows that isn't on the make. When *I* look at Penelope I can think of her as a nice young gal with whom I like to have lunch and kid around, nothing more. I'm unambitious, unmotivated, pure of heart as only a contented failure can be pure of heart. I can see that she's rev'd up too fast and you're driving her too hard. You're mesmerizing her."

"Bullshit!"

"No. It's not bullshit. You're such a cold, efficient, son-of-a-bitch, you don't even know what I'm talking about."

"No. I don't and I don't think you do either."

"Well," Dick Winston smiled wryly, "we'll leave it at that. Somehow, that's where all of my conversations end. But I will say this, ol' Marc, people are talking."

Haywood nodded, unsmiling. "I'm the local press lord. I think the gossip will remain discreet and harmless and unrecorded. As such, I'll ignore it."

"You are hard underneath that urbane manner, aren't you?"

"It's a hard world. If you're a doer you have to be as hard as the occasion demands."

Dick Winston looked into his drink. "Guess that's why I enjoy being a non-doer. It's the only truly compassionate religion."

Patty Winston sipped her martini at Sans Souci and gazed out over the crowded restaurant from the table she shared with Penelope on the little balcony at the rear of the room. "You're becoming a celebrity, Penny. I've noticed lately that as we look down into the pit to see who is here, they look up at us."

"You are the President's Press Secretary, not me."

"I've been Press Secretary for over three years. The up-turned faces are recent; it must be you."

"I guess I have been the object of a mild build-up."

"Not so mild from what I can see. The *Tribune's* society editor has orders to keep you front and center. The *Tribune's* weekly news-magazine ran an 'insider's' story last month on your 'exclusive little Sunday night buffets' and breathlessly informed us that your regular guests were happy to be known as *Penelope's Zoo*, after the column of the same name."

Penelope laughed. "That was Marc's idea."

"Of course. I recognized and admire his fine hand."

Penelope looked at Patty quizzically. "Does it bother you, Patty? I have a feeling that you don't approve."

Patty shrugged. "I neither approve or disapprove. I just note that Marc has you on a pretty fast track and he's a driver. How many nights have you had to yourself this last month?"

"I don't know. One or two maybe."

"How about kids your own age? Do you ever see them any more?"

"Not much. They're a bore, really. I like the older, more important people for my Zoo."

"Good God!" Patty said. "You are even beginning to talk like Marc."

"I could do worse," Penelope said with a little smile. "He's wonderful."

Patty eyed her. "You haven't your hopes up there, chick? Marc is a charming, handsome, ice cold operator. He never makes a false step. I wouldn't want you to concentrate on him and let your other chances go by default."

"No one else interests me at the moment."

"Well at least give your generation a chance. Don't bury yourself in a dream world."

"It's as real as this," Penelope said, gesturing to the crowded room.

"This isn't very real; you know that. Sometimes, at night, when I'm alone with the cold cream jar, I wonder if it was all done with mirrors."

"Well, I enjoy my life, Patty. It's exciting." She suddenly grinned artlessly. "Last week I had the French Ambassador, a Supreme Court Justice and Senator Herman Baur to my house for dinner. How about that?"

"Don't tell me they are in your Zoo?"

"Of course not. They are too important. Besides, that is just a publicity gag."

"I suppose it is exciting and thrilling, Penny. I don't mean to minimize it. I think your success is marvelous and you deserve it. You write about Senior Washington as well as you wrote about Junior Washington. And in a subtle way Marc is creating an air of mystery about you. I notice that the better known you get, the less the public sees of you. There have been no recent television appearances, for example."

"Marc says that once you have captured public attention, give the public less information about you than they want. Let their imagination have free rein and they will build a fantasy about you no press agent could concoct."

"Is that what you are doing?"

"I guess so."

"How many newspapers carry your column, by last count?"

"One hundred sixty-five."

"Gazooks! Not bad," Patty said, pursing her lips. "You top me at my best by forty." She lit a cigarette. "Carry on, chick. Who am I to quarrel with success?"

"You look tired, Patty," Penelope said after they had ordered. "Problems?"

"Just family problems. Mrs. Winston isn't at all well. She had a serious stroke last week. I'm driving out to Warrenton this afternoon to see her. I'm a commuter these days."

"I'm terribly sorry," Penelope said with an expression of concern. "I haven't seen Dick lately, and I didn't know his mother was ill. How is he?"

"Confused. He is so used to his mother in a dominating and self-sufficient role that he doesn't seem able to realize that she is helpless. He is rather useless as a result. He expects me to tell him what Mrs. Winston wants of him."

"Will she live?"

Patty sighed. "I can't imagine Mrs. Winston dying. She can't talk at the moment, but she can still gesture in the usual imperial manner."

"You dislike her, don't you, Patty?"

Patty pondered a moment and then slowly shook her head. "No. I don't dislike her. I just regret every moment I have to spend with her. I resent what she's done to Dick. If I didn't love Dick, I'd never subject myself again to one minute of the company of a woman like his mother. If Dick would sever the silver cord, we'd never see that malevolent old woman again. I'm tied to her through Dick. I won't give him up and Dick won't give his mother up. For years the old woman and I have glared at each other across Dick like two dogs over a bone."

"Poor Patty," Penelope said softly.

"You take what you can get and you do the best you can with what you've got. I've got part of the husband I wanted and part of the mother-in-law I didn't want."

"She may resent you, but she's depending upon you now."

"I'm doing it for Dick."

"What will he do if she dies?"

"He may realize for the first time that he's married, has reached the age of puberty, and, according to the Internal Revenue Service, at least, is the head of a household."

It was raining when they stepped out into Seventeenth Street from the restaurant. "My car is parked in my slot on West Executive Avenue. I'll give you a lift on my way to Warrenton," Patty said. "Home or the newspaper?"

"Home. I'm a hostess again tonight."

"Let's see. The Zoo is on Sunday nights with the same crowd and on the other nights you entertain different sets of people?"

"Right."

They walked down Seventeenth Street toward the White House sharing an umbrella. "Doesn't this entertaining bore you?" Patty asked. "Don't you sometimes feel that you are the one in the Zoo?"

"Not really. Most everything is catered and Marc has provided me with Mr. and Mrs. Moss, a couple who serve like a dream. The woman, Lilli, cooks one unusual dish each night to give the dinner a custom made appearance and her husband, Clarence, is one of the best and one of the most attentive bartenders in Washington."

"Does Marc come?" Patty asked with a sidewise glance as she swung her car into Pennsylvania Avenue traffic.

"Not often, now, since, as he puts it, he has me launched." Penelope's voice was pensive.

"Is he coming tonight?"

"No. Tonight is a sort of a repeat, a group interested in foreign affairs, the Under Secretary of State, a couple of Senators, a Congressman, some lawyers and an Ambassador who made his name in a sticky situation somewhere East of Suez.

"No wives?"

"Sure, I invite them but they tend not to come. It's pretty much an evening of man's talk. I just sort of flit about and keep everything running smoothly. There will be three wives tonight, sort of intellectual supernumeraries." She giggled. "Marc says Washington is full of famous men and the women they married when they were very young. I can believe it."

"Pretty shrewd. The wives can't object to their husbands attending what is essentially a male evening with quote one of Washington's most fascinating young women, unquote, if they were invited and chose not to come."

"It works out that way." Penelope was silent until they drew to the curb on Dumbarton Street. "Drive carefully, Patty. It looks like a miserable night."

"Will do. God knows I'm not anxious to see the old dragon. I'll call you when I get back."

The telephone rang as coffee was being served before the fire in the long drawing room. "It's for you, Miss Benton," Mrs. Moss murmured to Penelope. She smiled her regrets to the Senator to whom she had been listening and stepped into the comparative chill of the fireless library. The voice was scarcely audible and at first she could not recognize it.

"Is that you, Dick?" She said at last with a touch of impatience. "Please speak louder, I can't understand you."

The voice, still thick and muffled, rose slightly. "She's dead, Penny. She's dead. They just told me. What shall I do?"

"I'm so sorry to hear it, Dick. I know what your mother means to you. Isn't Patty there? She told me that she was driving out this afternoon."

There was a silence at the other end of the line.

"Dick? Please speak with Patty. I deeply sympathize with you, dear, but this wasn't unexpected and Patty is there. I'll come out in the morning. I have guests."

160

"No, no, you don't understand. Patty is dead, not Mama."

Penelope stood, the telephone receiver in one hand, suddenly sharply aware of the puddle of light thrown from under the red lamp shade onto the mahogany desk where the green telephone base stood, its multiple rows of black buttons mutely staring up at her. She sat down slowly in the ladder-back chair which she had been tightly gripping with her free hand. Her mouth was dry. She felt the beating of her heart in her throat. "What did you say?"

"I said Patty is dead. She had a collision with a truck at the beltway turn off for Warrenton. The police just telephoned me. It seems," the voice broke, "That they had a hard time making the identification. It was that kind of an accident. Happened four hours ago."

"I'm coming at once, Dick. Are you at home?"

"Yes."

"Where is Patty?"

"Don't know. The police fellow called, but after he mentioned Patty's name I forgot all the rest."

"No matter. I'll be there. Does your mother know?"

"That's one of the problems. Don't dare tell her in her condition. She was devoted to Patty."

"I'll be there within an hour."

"God bless you. Never forget it. Never."

The car and driver from the newspaper took her to Warrenton within the hour. It was raining hard as they turned off the narrow macadam road a mile from the turn off for Hollywood and moved up a curving gravel drive toward a large unadorned rectangular mansion of fieldstone set among yew hedges and hemlocks. Dick Winston had apparently been listening for the sound of automobile tires on the rough gravel of the foreyard and stood on the stoop of the open doorway, a raised umbrella in one hand as Penelope emerged from the rear door of the sedan. She embraced him as he held the umbrella over her head. "Poor, poor Dick," she murmured and

161

kissed him on the cheek. He returned the embrace with a convulsive movement of his free hand and though he cleared his throat to speak, he could not.

Silently he took her coat, hung it in a closet near the door and led her down a hallway to a large walnut paneled room where a fire was burning beyond a group of chairs and a heavy mahogany coffee table. He stepped to a sideboard and mixing a scotch and soda handed it to her. He did not take one himself. "Here. You must need this."

"Thank you." She moved over by the fire, but remained standing. "Any more news?"

"They have taken her to the undertakers in Warrenton." He gulped. "She was pretty smashed up. I guess." His voice broke. "We won't see her again, Penny. They advise against it. It will be a sealed casket."

Penelope's throat felt painfully restricted. She tried to sip her drink, but couldn't. "I see. I see." She shook her head. "I can't believe it. I saw her only this afternoon. We had lunch together. Now she's gone. What of her family?"

"They have been notified. I called John Griffin, our family lawyer. He'll take care of all of the details."

"Is there anything I can do?"

He smiled at her. "You're doing it, just being here."

A maid in a grey uniform trimmed in lace appeared at the door. "Your mother is asking for you, Mr. Winston."

He nodded, his eyes seeking Penelope's. "Will you come up with me? She expects Patty. I'm going to have to tell her."

"All right."

They entered the large bedroom at the head of the broad staircase leading to the second floor. Mrs. Winston lay in a hospital type metal bed which had been placed beside the mahogany four poster in which she usually slept. It seemed, in the graceful, well proportioned room with its blue damask draperies masking the tall windows, a note of jarring intru-

162

sion, as if serious illness had perversely found its personification in contemporary steel and chromium hospital equipment that was, in its impersonal utilitarianism, as much a counterpoint to the warm, human surroundings of a Virginia bedroom from the eighteenth century as sickness is to health.

A heavy set, middle aged nurse arose from a chair near the sick bed to greet them with a pleasant smile. "She's resting comfortably, Mr. Winston," she said in a low voice. "She's just a little fuddled. I'll be outside in the hall if you need me. I wouldn't stay over ten minutes."

Dick Winston bent over his mother. "How are you, Mama?"

The strong face with its grey pallor stared up at him, one side twisted by paralysis into a mirthless grimace. A thin line of saliva dripped from one corner of her mouth. He tenderly wiped it away with his pocket handkerchief. She grasped his other hand in a firm grip and beckoned to Penelope. As she approached the bed Mrs. Winston grasped her hand and looked beseechingly from one to the other.

"She thinks you're Patty," Dick Winston said quietly.

Penelope stood staring down into the ravaged face. "What shall I do?" She whispered helplessly.

"Nothing. Nothing at all." He extracted his hand and bent over his mother. "Good night, Mama." He kissed her gently on the forehead. Penelope leaned over and kissed her on a dry, withered cheek. "Good night," she whispered.

Mrs. Winston gave a contented little sigh and her eyes closed in sleep.

The funeral services for Patty were private, attended only by her immediate family and her close friends from the *Tribune* and the White House staff. President Frome came accompanied by his wife and flanked by the inevitable Secret Service detail. He spoke briefly to Dick Winston, Penelope, and Marc Haywood outside the Warrenton church before returning in his caravan of black limousines to Washington.

The rest of the party proceeded to the little country cemetary where Patty was buried among several generations of Winstons. It was a cold, misty day. Penelope turned up the collar of her coat as she turned away from the flower covered burial plot.

"Hello, Penelope." Dave Winslow said softly smiling at her in a tentative way. He stood hatless in a brown tweed top coat, his hand grasping that of a plump, good natured appearing blonde girl beside him.

"Dave, darling," Penelope said, kissing him on the cheek. "I haven't seen you in ever so long."

"I'd like you to meet my wife, Silvie."

"How wonderful! What good news." She smiled at Silvie. "You're a dear. Dave is so lucky. I'm so happy for him."

"Thank you."

Penelope turned to Dave Winslow. "Congratulations, Dave. But I'm hurt that you didn't let me know."

"We just got married two days ago. We went down to New Bern, Silvie's home. We didn't make much of it. It's the second time around for both of us."

"Well, congratulations."

"We didn't expect to spend our honeymoon like this, " Silvie said.

"No. I'm sure you didn't."

"I wanted to come," Dave Winslow said awkwardly. "Of course, Silvie didn't know Patty."

Penelope's eyes had moved across the green cemetery lawn to where Dick Winston was standing with Marc Haywood's arm across his shoulders. "I must go. Thank you, Dave, for introducing me to Silvie."

"Good luck, Penelope," Dave Winslow said quietly. "All the best."

The day following Patty's funeral, Mrs. Winston had another stroke and, after seven hours of unconsciousness and labored breathing, died. She was buried beside the grave of her

164

husband a few feet from where Patty lay, after the same simple ritual at church and graveside.

Dick Winston moved from the Warrenton mansion into a suite at the Sheraton Park Hotel in Washington. It was from there that he telephoned Penelope. "Can I come out for dinner?" He asked.

"Yes. I've cancelled all of my engagements for a month."

"Patty wouldn't have wanted you to do that."

"I am sure that she wouldn't. It's not an empty gesture of mourning. I just don't feel up to facing people yet. Patty was my closest friend."

Dick Winston cleared his throat. "Can I come now?"

"Yes. Come along."

They dined simply on a cheese soufflé and a salad fixed by Mrs. Moss.

"You've stopped drinking," Penelope observed over coffee.

" 'Pears I have. No heroic decision. Just haven't wanted it since I learned about Patty."

"Why is that?"

Dick lit a cigarette and then shrugged his shoulders. "I haven't thought it out. I guess my choice was to quickly drink myself to death or to cut it out. Two deaths in the family seem enough at the moment."

"What are you going to do?"

"I have no idea. I only know one thing for certain. I'm going to sell the Warrenton house."

"It's a lovely old house, but I suppose that it has unpleasant associations for you."

Dick Winston gazed at his feet stretched out in front of him and knocked the heavy soles of his shoes together idly. "Mama left me, no doubt with some misgivings, ten million dollars, mostly in real estate. Under her will, written about fifteen years ago when she had formed her opinion of my ability, it was to be placed in trust until I was forty years old. I guess she didn't notice the aging process in her only son. I was forty-three last August. So all that provision of the will did was to remind me of what she thought of me. The property falls into my incompetent, improvident hands immediately."

"She loved you, above everything."

"Guess so. But mothers can love sons they don't think much of otherwise."

"Would you like more coffee?"

"Please." He sipped his coffee and looked at her. "Penny, what do you think of me?"

She laughed. "Oh, Dick! Let's don't start that!"

"Would you consider marrying me?"

She became immobile, silent, searching his eyes wordlessly.

"I mean it."

She shook her head firmly. "No you don't. You've just lost two women you love. You're looking for a quick replacement."

"No. I mean it. I need you, Penny."

"I'm your friend, Dick. I'll be around. You don't need to marry me."

"Someone else might marry you. Then I'd lose you. I'd be all alone."

She reached over and pressed his hand. "We're all alone, Dick, in one sense or another. You'd be disappointed in me as a wife. I wouldn't mother you. I have my own life. So you have to learn to stand up to things on your own. I can't help."

His serious face was suddenly transformed by a boyish smile. "I notice that you haven't turned me down. I thought you would run for the nearest exit, screaming."

She felt herself coloring. "No, I haven't turned you down, have I?"

"What do you suppose that means?"

"I don't know. I truly don't."

"Will you think about it?"

"Yes. But not for a while. Patty only died last week. It

166

isn't fair to her."

"You mean she's looking down from a nearby cloud with x-ray eyes, feeling we've been disloyal?"

"No. It isn't fair to her reputation among her friends. It would diminish her and she doesn't deserve that."

"I don't give a damn what they think. Not even sure I know to whom you're referring."

"Of course you don't. You are an observer. I'm a participant. I do care."

"About what they think of you, not Patty."

"That was unnecessary. Patty was my best friend."

"You've said that before," he said morosely.

She was silent.

"In spite of what they say, truth doesn't bear repeating. It gets damn boring." He lit another cigarette and looked at her with a wistful expression. "We aren't quarreling, are we? I don't want to quarrel."

She leaned over and kissed him. "Of course, we're not quarreling."

He held her a moment and, seeking her mouth, kissed her upon it. She drew away. "I'm not ready for that, Dick. I've told you why."

"How long must I wait?"

"Some little time. I don't know. I'm not promising anything."

"Six months?"

"Yes."

"Can I see you often in the meantime?"

"Just as often as you did when Patty was alive. I don't want people to talk."

"What shall I do with the rest of my time?"

"Why not try making something of your life?"

"How?"

"You've got ten million dollars worth of real estate, why not develop it?"

"I don't have any idea where it is."

"Find out. Swap, wheel, and deal. It might be fun."

"I haven't the foggiest notion of how to wheel and deal."

"I'm not going to marry you to prop you up, Dick. If you want to marry me, learn to stand alone."

"That was nearly an acceptance," he grinned.

"No. I just warned you how to get turned down."

"It was a provisional acceptance," he insisted.

"No it wasn't."

"It was."

She laughed and fondly touched his cheek. "Sometimes you seem six years old."

" 'Pon my word I'm forty-three."

"Then act like it, darling. All six feet of you."

❧ 16 ❧

DICK WINSTON sat at the round oak table under the huge brass chandelier in the lobby of the Metropolitan Club. He held a copy of *The Wall Street Journal* as a comforting protective coloration among the bankers, brokers, diplomats, and field grade military men who ringed the table reading or talking as they waited for their luncheon companions, but his eyes were on the flames of the fire that had roared up in the room's huge fireplace after an attendant had added two fresh logs. The leaping flames reminded him uncomfortably of the conversation he was to have shortly with Marc Haywood.

He had belonged to The Metropolitan Club for over twenty years, ever since his father had put him up for membership the year he had graduated from Harvard, but he had never felt comfortable there. He remembered wryly the old Washington line that the Metropolitan Club had the money, the Cosmos Club had the brains, and the other Washington mens clubs had neither. He had money and if the old saw were true he should have felt at home with his fellow members. He didn't. He felt ill at ease and he knew that it was because his fellow members were able, intelligent doers; their money, if any, was incidental. A wry little smile touched his lips. As a newly hatched doer, perhaps he would eventually feel more at ease in his own club, but he realized that it was going to take some time. Even the oil paintings in heavy gold frames of eagle-eyed deceased members intimidated him.

Marc Haywood's hand fell lightly upon his shoulder. "Ready, old chap?"

"Hi, there, Marc. Didn't see you come in." Dick Winston laid his newspaper aside, arose and walked with Haywood to the small elevator in the corner of the room.

"Bar or dining room?" Haywood asked, his finger poised over the elevator's floor buttons.

"Dining room. I'm on the wagon."

"A good idea. It's been a respectable length of time now, hasn't it?"

"Glad you approve. Since Mama and Patty died. 'Bout a year."

They were seated in the spacious fourth floor dining room at a table by one of the windows overlooking the blood red brick mass of the Executive Office Building across Seventeenth Street. Haywood entered their luncheon order on the order slip and smiled at Dick. "I hear that the Winston Development Corporation is doing well."

" 'Pon my word I believe it is," Dick said almost bashfully. "I got together with John Griffin, told him what I wanted to do, and he set it all up in proper legal fashion; even found me two bright guys to keep me from overdoing it."

"What are you planning?"

"Been spending most of the year swapping land. In another month, this Virginia gentleman will be disengaged from Virginia and will own several thousand acres north of Frederick, Maryland. My two whiz kids tell me that's where the next surge of noxious urban sprawl will take place."

"And?"

"Well, ol' Marc, I may be sober these days, but I'm shrewd enough to know that I'm no smarter than I ever was. So, I get into a good land position across a growth corridor and then I wait for some smart boys to come along with good ideas. I figure we'll develop the land together. I can't help but make money."

170

"So, at last, you're among the motivated, a land speculator, no less, building the grimy, warped world of tomorrow."

"I'm motivated, but not toward money. I just want to prove to Penelope that I can succeed at something."

"Penelope?" Haywood repeated the name softly. "Why do you have to prove anything to Penelope?"

"We are getting married next month."

Haywood stared at Dick Winston and then flushed deeply. "Damn you, Dick," he spoke after a moment in a husky whisper, "You chose the dining room of this club deliberately to tell me that."

"I thought you would be pleased," Dick Winston said innocently.

"I ought to wring your neck."

"Tut, tut. No scene. We'll both get tossed out of the club."

Haywood forced himself to choke down the fruit cup the waiter had placed before him. He cleared his throat. "I would have thought Penelope would have told me."

"She thought it appropriate for me to ask you for her hand."

"Damn you."

"Well, it's been your whole attitude that you are entitled to give her away. I'm just playing along."

"She's throwing herself away on the likes of you. That is my one and only objection."

"Many thanks, ol' friend."

Haywood quietly folded his linen napkin. "I shall never speak to you again," he said, gazing at the untouched cold cuts the waiter had substituted for the fruit cup. He then rose, turned his back on Dick Winston, and left the dining room.

Haywood sat in his office and looked grimly at Penelope. "You can't be serious."

"We are going to slip off alone for a simple ceremony next

171

month and announce it to friends afterward. We wanted to tell you first."

"You can't marry a weakling like Dick, Penny. He'll ruin your life."

"He's done very well in the year since Patty and his mother died. He doesn't drink and he's active in real estate."

"It's an improvement, but how long will it last?"

Penelope walked to a casement window and looked down Sixteenth Street to the North Portico of the White House, visible in the distance.

"What do you want me to do, Marc?" Her voice was low.

"When you marry, I want you to marry someone worthy of you."

"Like Marc Haywood?"

"I wouldn't be so immodest."

She turned to him, her eyes dark. "Marc Haywood isn't available. We both have known that for a long time."

He looked uncomfortable. "It isn't fair, Penny, to turn my concern against me."

"I repeat," she flared, "just what do you want me to do, Marc? Do you want me to become a spinster, devoting myself only to the column and the newspaper? Am I to spend my life looking at you with adoring eyes, doing everything you suggest, dressing, talking, acting, writing as you direct and never touch you? You want me to go on being made to feel cheap or vulgar, if I even hint that I love you?"

"You don't love me."

"You know that I do."

"Perhaps I sense that you think you do. But it is really misplaced gratitude."

"Gratitude!"

"I'm sorry." He felt an unaccustomed confusion. "I didn't mean that. You have earned your success. It was no gift from me."

"Well, what am I to do? I may be a success, but Dick is the only man who has proposed to me in the last four years

172

and I am twenty-six years old."

"I keep forgetting that you are so young."

"I am old enough, and I am completely sealed off from people of my own age. Anyone in their twenties now thinks of me as a petrified part of the Establishment."

"Surely you aren't interested in twenty year olds?"

"I'm interested in you."

"Are you trying to tell me that since I won't divorce Claudia and marry you, you are going to marry Dick Winston because he is the only man who has proposed to you?"

"Dick Winston is a dear friend. He wants to marry me. We enjoy each other's company. I am deeply fond of him."

"You don't love him."

"I love you. I want to give you children, which is more than Claudia has done. What does she do for you, anyway?"

He turned from her abruptly. "Don't throw yourself at me. It isn't becoming and I don't deserve it."

"Very well," she replied bitterly. "Perhaps Claudia and you are well matched. If you ever get into bed together, you'll freeze to death."

"Are you continuing with the column?" He asked coldly.

"Of course. I don't intend to change my life at all."

A spasm moved almost invisibly across his face. "Are you going to share Dumbarton House with Winston?"

"Do you mind?"

"Yes."

"Then we'll buy a house of our own. Dumbarton House has never been my home. It is the house you provided for your columnist. I shall feel happier elsewhere."

"You needn't say wounding things."

"Of course not. That is a privilege reserved for you. In ten minutes you have slurred my fiancé, again rejected my love for you, and in your inimitable indirect way asked me to leave Dumbarton House. Naturally, after so much consideration from you, I should not say wounding things."

"Your irony is rather ponderous, Penny, definitely not

your forte."

"Are you quite finished? May I go?"

He spoke in a voice flat with defeat. "You may do as you wish."

The wedding took place in Annapolis before a justice of the peace and two casual witnesses at noon on a rainy Saturday. After a brief flurry of coy amenities in the stiff little office, they flew from Baltimore's Friendship Airport to New York and boarded a light green Cunard cruise ship lying alongside a grimy Hudson River dock in the fading winter twilight. They were both tired and tense and napped briefly and self-consciously before going into the dining salon for dinner.

"When do we sail?" Penelope asked after Dick had ordered.

"Eight o'clock. Should be fun cruising the Caribbean. We'll have Christmas off Trinidad."

They were silent, watching the other diners appear, until after the oysters had been served.

"Are you happy?" She asked.

" 'Pon my word, yes. Absolutely floating."

"You look pensive."

"It's the oysters. They have the same leaden stare as my banker."

She giggled more from nervousness than amusement.

"Are you happy, Penny?"

"Of course, dear. I'm floating too."

"They offered to put us at the Captain's table. I thought it was better to be alone."

"I'm glad you refused. I just want to relax on this cruise —be completely anti-social."

"Poor darling. You've been such a butterfly."

She nodded and sipped her wine without replying.

"You like my choice of wine?"

"Lovely."

He turned his own glass, letting the light filter through the red liquid. "My first drink since Patty died."

"Yes."

He glanced over at her and caught the end of a fleeting expression. "I'm sorry, Penny. Damn clumsy of me."

"I don't mind you mentioning Patty. We both loved her."

"Right. Right. But we don't need to talk about it on our wedding night."

She smiled at him. "No, we don't and we won't. What did you order for us?"

"Tournedos Rossini."

"Marvelous."

He filled her half empty wine glass and his empty one. "Wine stewards aren't worth a damn these days. Uncork the bottle and forget you might like to drink some."

Penelope reached across the table and squeezed his hand. "It's going to be a perfect night."

"Sue Cunard if it isn't. That's a promise."

"They guarantee successful marriage nights?"

"Sure, it was in the brochure somewhere."

As they finished dinner they felt the throb of the engines and the movement of the ship. "We must be getting underway," Penelope said, her eyes shining, "Let's go up on deck and say goodbye to New York."

They stood on the lee deck, muffled against the December cold as the ship, free from the tugs that warped her out from the dock, moved majestically down the river and into the channel leading to the sea. Penelope hugged his arm ecstatically. "Isn't this great? It's my first sea voyage. Isn't New York beautiful from the water?"

Dick Winston looked at the massive skyline, a charcoal smudge disappearing behind them in the mist, "Hope we don't get seasick."

"Seasick? Oh, how awful! I never thought of that." She looked at him anxiously. "You don't get seasick, do you darling?"

"Don't know. Sailing boats, yawls, that sort of thing are no problem. Big ship is different, especially below decks. Seems like the whole world has come loose from its moorings, kind of like a fun house with those moving floors."

"Well, we won't get seasick. We just won't!"

"Agreed. Best remedy is a few drinks. Let's go down to the bar and take proper precautions. Cold as hell up here."

"Maybe we can dance if they have music."

He smiled at her gaily. "If they don't, we'll make our own. You haven't lived until you've danced to my humming."

At ten-thirty Penelope whispered into Dick Winston's ear as they danced to the music of a spirited trio. "Shouldn't we go to our cabin soon?"

He spoke in a slurred voice into her ear, "Still shank of the evening. Don't you want to dance at the wedding?"

"We have danced and we've drunk, too."

He held her away from him so that he could see her face. "You going to be a nag, Mrs. Winston?"

"No. But if you drink much more you aren't going to be much good tonight."

His grin was forced. "Aren't you being a li'l indelicate, Mrs. Winston?"

"The truth is sometimes indelicate."

"O.K. we'll go and bed down if that's what the lady wants."

"Who's being indelicate now?"

He signed the check at their table and they walked down a staircase to the deck on which their stateroom was located. The ship was rolling gently in a long swell and there was a muted squeaking from the bulkheads and fittings. "I used to hold my liquor better than this," Dick Winston muttered. "Out of practice."

The stateroom was brightly lit and each of the twin berths had been turned down by the night maid. Penelope walked over to the small writing table between their beds, "Look, a basket of fruit from the Captain. Isn't that nice?"

176

Dick Winston was sitting on the edge of the outboard bunk. "He's a prince. A wonderful guy. It gets you right here." He pushed at his chest with a fist.

"You fool!" Penelope laughed. She hesitated. "Should I use the bath first?"

"Absolutely, rudimentary rule of chivalry." He stretched out on his bunk. "I'll be patiently waiting."

After fifteen minutes she emerged from the tiny bathroom, dressed in a pink negligee, her color high and her heart pounding. Dick Winston was asleep. She shook him. "Dick! Dick, darling! It's your turn." His eyes opened sleepily, a fleeting expression of alarm crossed his face and then he smiled and winked. "Dozed off, didn't I? Hell of a thing to do. I'm wide awake now, though and raring to go."

"I'll wait for you," she said softly. She lay in her berth listening to the sounds of the ship as it moved through the continental ground swells seeking the calmer, warm waters of the Gulf Stream before heading south. Her pulse was still rapid, but her feeling of light headed apprehension had passed. She realized that Dick was not going to be aggressive, that the initiative in their sexual relations might even rest with her. The realization brought a sense of relief. At the same time she experienced a sinking feeling of disappointment.

He emerged from the bathroom and, dressed in new powder blue pajamas, sat on the edge of his berth. She absently noted the shiny glaze of the new cotton and the network of creases marking where it had been folded by the manufacturer. "Why don't you come over here?" She asked.

"Right. Good idea."

"You'd better turn out your light."

"Right you are." He slipped into the berth beside her. She turned and sought his mouth with her lips.

"You're shy," she murmured after a moment.

"Li'l slow to start, maybe. Damn fool to drink so much."

She pressed against him, the warmth of her body radiating through the flimsy, short nylon gown she wore. He put his arms around her as her lips sought his ardently. After a moment she said, "Maybe it's our pajamas. Let's sleep in the raw."

Her nude body pressed against his. His hands moved down over her buttocks and he pressed almost frantically against her. She could feel the perspiration start out on his forehead. His actions became uncoordinated, almost brutal in their desperation and she began to feel abused, thrown about. She pushed him away and pushed the hair away from her own damp face. "Nothing is happening," she whispered. "Am I doing it wrong? This is my first time." Her voice took on a tone of tautness. "Tell me what is the matter, darling. You know these things."

"Maybe it's the wrong night." His voice sounded subdued, far away.

"It's our wedding night. It has to be the right night." She felt tears well into her eyes, prompted by a combination of fear and self pity. "I want to be loved. I want you to take me. I don't want to be the aggressor." She wiped her eyes with the back of one of her hands. "Damn you! Be a man!"

He shivered beside her.

"Be a man!" Her voice was anguished.

He turned and awkwardly seized her shoulders. He pushed his groin against hers in a series of convulsive movements and then lay still. Her hand moved down between his legs and felt the soft, flaccid penis. "You don't have an erection. Don't you feel anything? Am I cold for you?"

He rolled away from her onto his back and drew a tremulous breath. "It's no good, Penny. I've never been able to make it."

A cold, deathlike sensation moved across her body. Her mouth was so dry she could hardly ask the question.

"You mean you can't do it or you won't?"

"I can't. God knows I want to. God knows." His voice broke.

Her voice was flat. "You are impotent."

"Afraid so."

"You never did it with Patty?"

"We tried, after a while we gave up. We gave up on a lot of things."

She began to cry. He reached out to comfort her. "Don't touch me!" She lashed out, "You lying bastard!"

"I haven't lied to you."

"You haven't lied," her voice was low and intense, "You said you loved me and needed me—and we were *married* this afternoon. What did you think I expected of marriage?"

"I love you, Penny. I thought maybe I could make it with you. I'll try like hell. Maybe if you help me, I can do it."

"What are you offering me? A degrading physical exercise twice a week?"

"I didn't think of it that way."

"What were you looking for in this marriage, Dick? A buddy companion? Another mother? Why have you hounded me for a year with your proposal when you knew it would end like this?"

"I didn't want to live alone. I never have."

"What of me? Did you think of me?"

"I hoped I could be a husband to you. I still hope that I can. I'm just nervous, afraid of failing."

She thought a moment. "We could get this marriage annulled. It can't be consummated."

"That would humiliate me."

She was silent.

"Would it be so bad, Penny?" He asked after a moment. "Even if I couldn't make love properly? Do you want children?"

"I don't know. Not at present."

"I adore you. I'll give you anything you want."

"Go back to your bed. We'll talk about it in the morning."

"May I kiss you good night?"

"Hell no. Leave me alone!"

She lay alone, a virgin lying in a narrow bed just as she had

179

lain at night for all of her twenty-six years. Her eyes filled again and again with tears and she bit the knuckle of her forefinger to stifle the sobs. It wasn't fair! It wasn't fair! She had lost Marc forever for this!

After a time, her self pity subsided and she began to think more clearly. Her relationship with Marc was altered forever. She was giving up Dumbarton House. She had to think of her position in Washington. An annulment was out of the question, but not for Dick's sake. She couldn't care less if it humiliated Dick. He deserved it. But an annulment was out of the question because it would ruin her reputation and mystique in Washington. It would make her the favorite object of the off color cocktail party joke. She shivered. She would stay married to Dick Winston all right. He would be eternally grateful and she would see that he expiated his deceit by doing for Penelope whatever she wished.

A chilling thought occurred to her. She would have no children of this marriage. She would be unable to parade her fertility before Marc. She would seem as barren as Claudia. She bit her lip and then relaxed. She would adopt a child and pretend it was her own. She would leave Washington during a supposed period of advanced pregnancy and adopt a new born infant as her own. No one would ever know it was not her child except Dick. Marc would never know. Her eye lids fluttered and she began to drift into sleep. It would all work out all right, Mrs. Richard Winston. All it would take was careful planning.

❧ 17 ❧

Penelope relaxed in a deck chair the first day at sea, gazing out over the blue waters of the Gulf Stream, striped with the lines of white caps whipped by an errant winter's wind. She felt a sudden, welcome surge of happiness that swept away the last of the previous night's bitterness and the little frown that had rested between her eyes was replaced by a half smile playing about the corners of her mouth.

Dick Winston, lying beside her, stealing occasional anxious glances of her face in repose, sensed the change of mood. He wet his lips and turned to her with a nervous smile. "Am I forgiven, d' you suppose?"

She took his extended hand and gave it a quick squeeze. He felt overcome by an overpowering wave of sentimentality. His voice when he spoke was husky. "I do love you, Penny."

"I know."

He waited for her to say more. When she continued to lie in the sun, her eyes now closed, the little smile playing about her mouth, he added, "I'll see that you are happy."

She felt his hand close over her clasped ones and opened her eyes to look at him. He noticed in the strong light how very blue they were, accented now by the blue undertones of the fair skin beneath. A sprinkle of freckles had appeared on her cheekbones. "Will you, Dick?"

"Absolutely and forever."

She closed her eyes again and gave a little sigh. "That's nice." She had resolutely put from her mind the impotent, flaccid proddings of her husband the night before and her first feelings of being used and defrauded. Having rejected an annulment as a publicly admitted mistake she could not afford, she was emphasizing in her mind the advantages of her marriage; a respectable male escort, the social status that automatically went with "Mrs. Richard Perry Winston," the Winston fortune which more than replaced the withdrawn patronage of Marc Haywood.

These were advantages, she realized, that ended her period of apprenticeship, the circumscribed life of the protégé. She could meet Marc Haywood on equal terms at last, more than equal terms, really, because *Penelope's Zoo* and even Penelope were great assets to the *Tribune* and readily salable elsewhere. She gave a little sigh of contentment. The ship was moving southward to tropical islands in warm waters under a hot sun. She was going to enjoy the next two weeks. Last night was a brief, ugly nightmare of humiliation and frustration, but today was not unpleasant and tomorrow had its prospects.

When they returned to Washington they lived in Dick Winston's apartment at the Sheraton Park while they hunted for a house to buy. In February, on a cold, wet day, they found what they were seeking, a graceful home of rose colored brick, secluded among American elms and white oaks in five acres of carefully tended lawn and garden that sloped up gently from a twelve foot brick wall and gate at Foxhall Road.

They both fell in love with the house and Penelope was filled with elation at the prospect of moving into the narrow street of embassy residences and private mansions which so gracefully avoided catagorization as either city or suburb. It was an eminently correct address that freed her of Georgetown and its associations with Marc Haywood, yet stopped short of being a semi-somnolent, anachronistic estate, spilling down the wooded sides of Rock Creek Park. It was in-town enough for the social activity she now planned to pursue single mindedly, yet there was still the aloof suggestion of a country estate not otherwise to be found closer than Potomac or the outer reaches of McLean.

Their first entertainment in their new home was in mid-April when the tulip magnolias and the dogwood were in bloom. The guests moved through the ground floor rooms with their Georgian moldings and Waterford crystal chandeliers and gathered in a salon thirty by forty feet in dimension opening off the wide reception hall extending to the rear of the house, broken only by the graceful, curving staircase ascending to the second floor. Some wandered across the hall into a dining room, sedate and elegant, a gracious room of Sheraton furniture, silver, and evening candlelight, flooded in the daytime through translucent gold draperies with the warm sunshine of a southern exposure, or they found the small parlor, furnished with enough pieces of Heppelwhite to give it a delicate, feminine air, but also furnished with a comfortable love seat by a marble topped coffee table and two contemporary club chairs covered in a neutral, rough linen.

The casual guest did not see the library built off the graveled driveway leading to the garages, paneled in natural, waxed oak with an adjoining room for a secretary. Reached by a separate outside entrance, it served as the office from which Dick Winston could run Winston Development Corporation without more than infrequent visits to the small office on M Street where the rest of his staff was located.

Nor did they visit the second floor where on either side of the broad hallway two separate bedroom suites had been created. Penelope's suite was light grey and pale yellow with a sunny, glass walled room overlooking the formal garden, where Penelope now wrote her columns to minimize her visits to the *Tribune*. There was also a small room for the social secretary, Mary Mehan, who had joined her within the last year and had quickly become indispensable. Dick Winston's suite was furnished in a dark mélange of heavy mahogany furniture he had retained from the Warrenton house. Penelope seldom entered the disordered precincts of his rooms, preferring to talk with him in the white and blue delft room overlooking a small brick paved kitchen garden where they ate breakfast or other infrequent meals together, or in the small parlor.

The French doors of the salon were open to the soft air of early evening. The guests at the reception drifted from the warm, lighted room out onto the terrace and back again. Dick Winston stood on the terrace leaning against the rough brick of the house between two French doors and drew idly on his cigarette. He listened happily to the babble of voices and the intermittent strains of music he could hear from the room behind him. It was a swell party. Penelope really had the knack. Amazing really, a gal from the corn country. He became aware of a plain, spare, pleasant looking woman of middle height with dull brown hair streaked with gray smiling at him. He grinned back, noting that the short bob with the permanent wave, parted on the side, and the red, green, and black patterned dress didn't do much for her.

"You're different," she said.

"You notice that, eh?" ·

"It's the knot in the tie; it's bigger, and the suit lapels, they have a deeper notch and they are slanted differently."

"Bigger and differently from what?"

"All of the other men here." She giggled. "It's kind of like what they say about the Chinese. They all look alike. These men do too, you know: blue and gray suits, ties with small dots or rectangles, round, overfed faces, bald heads, or haircuts where the clippers have climbed too far up the sides, the hearty laugh, the backslap."

"You're a very perceptive gal."

"No. I just arrived in Washington. This is my first party."

"Clear first impressions? That sort of thing?"

"Kind of."

"Where are you from?"

"California."

"You don't look like California."

"You're thinking of the Palm Springs, Pebble Beach bit. I'm from rural California. Upper Sacramento valley."

"Oh. And why did you leave rural California?"

"My husband was appointed Senator by the Governor after Senator Wisheart died."

"That makes you . . . ?"

"Alice Payson."

"Dick Winston."

Alice Payson clapped a worn hand with short clipped nails to her mouth. "You aren't the host, for God's sake?"

Dick Winston leaned forward in a low, confidential whisper. "There is no host. Only the hostess."

Alice Payson continued to stare at him. "What's it like being married to a high powered celebrity type?"

"I think of her as a little gal from the corn country. Otherwise, I'd be scared to death."

"From the corn country?"

"Indiana."

Alice Payson looked past him into the salon where Penelope was chatting with Senator Herman Baur. "That gorgeous gal came from Indiana?"

"We all come from some place."

"I thought women like that emerged from the tip of some wizard's wand."

"A wizard was involved," Dick Winston said dryly.

"You?"

"No."

Alice Payson laughed. "I guess that's all I'll learn from you."

" 'Bout all." Dick Winston looked at her speculatively.

"What's the matter? Do I bug you?"

"I was wondering what Senator Payson is like."

"He's like a Greek god, physically and intellectually superior." Her voice was filled with pride.

Dick Winston gave a mock shudder. "Doesn't being married to a Greek God sort of put you down a bit?"

Alice Payson nodded. "We went to Berkeley together and were married as undergraduates. I couldn't believe it when he proposed. I still can't. He made a fortune on some little electronic gadget and until the Governor appointed him to the Senate, he headed a state commission with super governmental powers to re-organize the state's urban centers. He's known as the urban Hercules—see last month's *Time* cover story."

"Believe there is argument whether Hercules was a god or just a hero."

"Either way, he's traveling too fast for me. I sort of ignored it, you know? The money rolled in. We had a nice ranch type house in Palo Alto. I raised three kids. So far as I could see, Bill's success gave us the kind of middle class life we like and a long row of figures on capital gains.

"The life was real and the figures weren't, you know? Even the urban Hercules bit wasn't real. At least not to me. But this move to Washington is real, scary real. I'm in over my head." She lowered her voice and spoke to Dick Winston's ear. "Parties like this scare the hell out of me."

"Maybe I should get you a drink?"

"Don't bother. I will take a cigarette." She let him light it for her and eyed him over the flame of the match. "Why am I telling this to you?"

Dick Winston gestured toward the crowded room. "Because I'm no more one of them than you are."

"That's a hell of a reason. I talk too much. I've got to watch that."

"Don't worry. This is a gabby town. No one will hear you. We all talk at once. I'd forget the Greek god bit, though, if I were you. Make it just plain ol' Bill. Washington prefers its gods dead and encased in marble. They're safer."

186

"Like I say, I talk too much. Especially when I'm nervous." She squeezed his hand. "Thanks. I've made one friend anyway. I think I'll go look for that drink."

Senator Herman Baur smiled down at Penelope. "A nice little party, Penny, as always."

"Thank you, Senator. I'd never get to see you if I didn't give a party. You stay up there on Capitol Hill, surrounded by staff and secretaries like Jove on Olympus."

"That's where my life is. I have no use for Washington parties. But I like yours. I relax and enjoy myself."

She reached out and playfully patted his cheek. "You are a dear. How you have managed to remain a bachelor all these years is beyond me."

Herman Baur laughed heartily, showing a gold tooth in the front of his lower jaw. "You're a flirt, Penny. But at my age it's damn nice to be flirted with." He grew serious. "Could we go into another room where we can chat for a moment?"

"Of course. Come this way." She left the crowded salon and crossed the reception hall to the closed door of the parlor, turning to a sallow faced waiter furnished by a catering firm as she passed, "Bring the Senator and me a bourbon and branch water. We'll be in this room."

"Yes ma'am."

She sat down on the love seat and patted the down cushion beside her. "Sit here, dear."

"I was hoping you wouldn't put me in a chair," he said gallantly.

The waiter entered and put their drinks on the coffee table before them.

"I didn't know bourbon was your drink, Penny. I figured a gal like you that knows all these diplomats and rich folk drank pink champagne."

"Don't you believe it. We are both from southern Indiana. That's bourbon country."

"It is at that." He sipped his drink and looked at her

187

through narrowed eyes. "I remember the first time I met you, Penny. It was at that party April Rumbaugh gave for Charlie Frome at that golf club."

Penelope was pleased. "I was so green. Heavens! I never would have thought you would remember. It's nearly six years ago."

"You're that kind of girl, Penny. I think it's the combination of the sweet smile and the direct, open gaze. Very few women look at a man like that."

"You're sweet."

"And, you've grown up since then. Grown up in a nice way. I've kept my eye on you. How old are you?"

"Twenty-seven."

"Jumpin' Jesus! Twenty-seven!" He smiled at her benignly. "Imagine me knowing anyone twenty-seven." He drained his glass. "Well, it bears out what I've always said, you're born with common sense and good judgment. Age hasn't anything to do with it."

Penelope laughed. "How awful, Senator. I thought you were going to flirt with me and you tell me that I have common sense."

He waved her comment aside with an impatient gesture of his hand as if his thoughts had already gone on to another subject. "You mentioned my black angus herd in your column last year. It was a charming story, did me a lot of good back home, but you couldn't have written that story without knowing also the part that could have done me a lot of harm. That part you left out."

"I'm not out to write a column to do harm. There are plenty of columns that are near libelous exposes. Mine is about the happy, positive side of Washington."

"I appreciated the part you left out, Penny. It could have been explained, but a smear of the tar brush always leaves a few stains. A politician who has to explain too often is going to get licked, even if he is a good explainer."

Penelope's voice was soft. "Senator, I wouldn't harm you

188

in any way for the world. You're too important to the country. And I don't expect you to be perfect."

"Well," the voice was gruff. "I do thank you. And there are others who have noticed the same thing in your columns. Those of us who know where the skeletons are in this town recognize the part of the story you're writing and we know the part you aren't writing. That means you have discretion. You can be trusted. That's why I come to your parties, when you're kind enough to invite me. I know I can relax. I won't get a knife in my back from you or from your guests."

"I'm just awfully pleased," Penelope said, giving his hand a pat.

"Well, let me get to the point. I like you. I admire you. I trust your judgment. That's why I want you to do me a favor. It's not personal, but I will be grateful if you will do it."

"Of course I'll do it."

He turned and took her hands in his. "We have a new Senator in the Senate, William Payson of California. Governor Lakeland appointed him to Wisheart's unexpired term. This man already has a national reputation as a scientist, as a businessman, and as an expert on urban affairs."

"Yes. I know of his reputation. He was supposed to join us tonight, but he had to make a quick trip to California. His wife came instead." Penelope's nose gave an unconscious wrinkle.

"Exactly. This man, when he was appointed to the Senate, was a bigger man in California than Lakeland," he smiled wryly. "That may have had something to do with his appointment. He is presidential timber two years from now when President Frome's second term expires. He only has one problem—that wife of his. Unless she shapes up, dies, or becomes invisible, she'll ruin his presidential chances."

"You usually don't pick a candidate this early, do you?"

"I'm not picking Payson. He is one of several possibilities. I won't pick my man until my support is crucial." He glanced

189

sidewise at her, a mischievous twinkle in his eyes. "That's the secret of being a kingmaker, Penny. It is also the secret of a happy relationship with the man in the White House." His face became serious again. "But we haven't so many good candidates that we can afford to mishandle one— particularly if that one is a fresh new face with an appeal to the urban areas."

Penelope sipped her drink. "I don't offer murder services. I can't make people invisible. That leaves shaping her up."

"Exactly."

"Dear, you don't know how one woman resists being 'shaped up' by another. You don't know what you're asking."

"Yes I do. I don't suppose there's anything you can do with an odd ball woman in her late forties, but we have to try. She's just arrived. She needs friends. Those who help her now will become her pals. I'm not asking you to show her how to dress. A certain dowdy inelegance may even be appealing to the voters. Look how Eleanor Roosevelt caught on; but she does have to learn the do's and don'ts of this town, of politics. I don't know where in hell Payson has been keeping her for the last twenty years, but she has emerged right out of the suburban egg."

Penelope laughed. "What did she do to you?"

"I had Payson and several other Senators and their wives to my apartment for dinner, a gesture at getting acquainted because I'm impressed with the man. This wife of his brought a ouija board and thought we'd ask the occult for guidance after dinner."

"What was Senator Payson's reaction?"

"He thought she was quite amusing."

"Perhaps it was a joke."

"It was no joke. You have to hear the conversation of this woman to believe it."

Penelope laid a smooth, cool hand over his gnarled ones.

"I'll cultivate her and see what happens. I can't promise anything."

"I know that, but it's worth a try. He's a good man, apart from his taste in women."

"Does he have a mistress?"

Senator Baur looked mildly shocked. "A mistress. Why would he have a mistress? He loves her. It's very clear in his manner. She's the problem, not him."

"I'll see what I can do." Her hand continued to rest on his. "Now, I want you to do something for me."

He looked at her quizzically without speaking.

"I want you to come to my Sunday evenings at home."

His eyes twinkled. "You want the old lion of the Senate at *Penelope's Zoo?*"

"Yes."

"Why?"

"Because you are the most important man on Capitol Hill. I would be most honored to have you feel that my house is yours."

"I hear you have some pretty toney people at those buffets. I won't fit in. I'm a Senate cloakroom man. I'm no good at light conversation."

"That's why I want you to come. I'm bored with bright conversation. I want some solid men about." Her hand tightened over his. "Say you will come."

"Next Sunday?"

"Yes."

"When?"

"Any time after five. Stay as long as you are enjoying yourself."

"All right. I'll try it once. I have enjoyed your other parties and dinners."

She leaned over and kissed him on a rough cheek. "You're a dear."

He cleared his throat and got up. "I can't remember when

191

I've been kissed by a girl your age. I'll be acting like a rejuvenated old goat next. Pity you've got a virile young husband, Penny dear. I might just throw my hat in the ring."

She arose, and taking his arm, walked toward the door opening on the reception hall. "I'll see you Sunday, dear, and I will do what I can about our problem."

Dick Winston stood in the dressing room off Penelope's bedroom surveying the rows of dresses, shoes, coats, furs, and accessories hanging neatly behind glass doors. "Takes a lot to clothe a high flying Washington gal, doesn't it?"

"I like to dress well," Penelope said evenly. "Any objections?"

"No. Just a comment." He lit a cigarette. "Nice party."

"Thank you." Penelope, sitting at her dressing table, made an entry with a pencil in a red leather note book.

"Interesting gal there tonight—sort of appealing."

"I'm glad."

"Wife of a new Senator from California. Very perceptive gal. Maybe too frank for this town."

Penelope glanced up, interested at last in his conversation, the pencil eraser held against one cheek. "Mrs. Payson?"

"Yes. Alice Payson."

"Alice?"

"We became ol' pals talking on the terrace. You scare the hell out of her."

"Me? Whatever for?"

"You're the glittering Washington hostess and columnist and she's scared of Washington."

"That's ridiculous."

"Maybe. I kind of know how she feels."

"You know how she feels? If anyone was born to Washington society, it's you."

"I don't mean that. I mean feeling not up to it, particularly around people who seem so damn self-confident."

Penelope's eyes grew cold. "Are you trying to tell me

192

something?"

"No. No," he said hurriedly, "I don't mean us. I mean I just know how she feels about you."

"Yes?"

"I don't feel that way about you—she does. I feel that way about ol' Marc for instance."

Penelope loosed her hair and began to comb it. "You sometimes make no sense at all, darling." She gave her hair several vigorous strokes. "Perhaps we should have her for lunch. Just we three. I understand her husband is in California."

"Why should we do that?"

"I don't want her to be afraid of me, heavens knows. That's an awful position to be in."

Dick Winston smiled. "Why include me?"

"I gather you are her pal. It will give her confidence."

He moved behind her and fondled her hair. "Am I your pal, too?"

She smiled into the mirror at him. "Of course, idiot."

❦ 18 ❦

PENELOPE turned impatiently to Dick Winston on the settee at The Jockey Club. "Where is she, anyway?"

"She'll be along in a minute. Maybe she got lost."

"That I can believe."

"If you don't like her, why are we having her to lunch?"

"I want her to like me. God knows I don't want her to be afraid of me. She's a Senator's wife."

" 'Pears to me you are paying more attention to that remark of mine than you do to most."

"It bothered me," Penelope admitted. Her eyes met his, "With your embellishments."

"I explained that."

Penelope glanced at her wristwatch. Its hands pointed to one-twenty. "Did you tell her one o'clock?"

"I did."

"Well, damn it. I have to get down to the newspaper by two-thirty. Marc wants to go over a new syndication contract with me."

"How is ol' Marc?"

" 'Coldly correct' I believe best describes it."

"He won't speak to me. Even ignored me in the Metropolitan Club elevator the other day and that's so small you're eyeball to eyeball."

"He is acting like a child. After all, he didn't own me body

194

and soul."

"He's in love with you, Penny. Like I am."

She was still a moment and then carefully reached for the drink before her. "Don't be ridiculous. I was a sort of real life Barbey doll for Marc. When I married you I shattered that illusion to bits. Now, I'm just a business associate of whom he mildly disapproves."

"No. He's in love with you, but he feels an obligation to Claudia."

"He loves Claudia, period. He loves Marc Haywood. He loves order. He loves the even, uneventful continuity of his life. He loves his possessions, his name, his clubs, his reputation, his power as a publisher. There isn't room for anything else."

"S'pose not. But that doesn't mean that he doesn't love you. Ol' Marc can only take one emotional involvement at a time. He'll never look beyond Claudia—so relax. I was just trying to explain why he is acting so damned childishly."

"Isn't it rather unusual for a husband to try to persuade his wife that another man loves her?"

"I'm rather an unusual husband, and I'm not throwing you at him. If you made any advances he'd be thrown into utter confusion and bolt for Warrenton and Claudia."

Penelope frowned into her drink. "You do talk such nonsense sometimes."

"Here comes Mrs. Payson. Brighten up or you'll continue to scare hell out of her."

Penelope looked up with a brilliant smile at the distraught, windblown woman following the headwaiter to their table.

"My God," Alice Payson said. "Go ahead, shoot me. Shoot me right now. I'm a half hour late."

"Are you really?" Penelope said pleasantly. "Dick and I were chatting and didn't notice."

"You're sweet. Do I sit here?" She dropped down between them where Dick, who had risen, indicated. "I took this taxi, driven by a sweet boy from Jamaica. He's going to school in

Washington and drives a taxi part time. We had a wonderful conversation and it was ten past one before we both realized that we hadn't the foggiest idea where this restaurant was. He vaguely thought it was a private club in Georgetown. We finally went into a filling station and got a map and the address out of the telephone book. Well, I'm so sorry, but I thought any taxi driver would know where to go, but leave it to me to choose an out of town medical student."

"You need a drink," Penelope said easily. "We have loads of time, haven't we, Dick?"

"Absolutely."

"What are you drinking?" Alice Payson asked Dick Winston.

"Penelope is having bourbon on the rocks. I'm a reformed drunkard. This is tomato juice dressed up to look like a Bloody Mary so I won't lose cast."

Alice Payson giggled. "I never know when to believe you."

"Mama always said that you can trust a man who drinks tomato juice. I pass on free of charge that profound comment from a long and observant life."

Alice Payson giggled again and eyed Penelope. "Isn't he a scream? Living with him must be a ball. If he hadn't been around I couldn't have gotten through that awful party the other night." She stopped and put a hand over her mouth. "My God! What am I saying? That was *your* party!"

Penelope laughed in genuine amusement. "I thought it was pretty awful too. And Dick does help." She smiled at him affectionately.

"Well, you're acting like an absolute doll. Some days I can't stand myself. I'm afraid this is going to be one of them."

"I like that pin," Penny said, nodding to a small, irregular dull gold rock fastened to Alice Payson's tweed jacket.

"You like? My hubby gave it to me last year. It's a gold nugget from the Mother Lode. It was sort of a private joke. He always says, 'Ali, you're as good as gold' so he gave me the nugget made into a pin."

"How sweet," Penelope said, flashing a warning glance at Dick Winston.

Dick Winston grinned. "It's a good thing he doesn't say, 'ali, you're a brick.' You'd go around with a permanent list to port."

Penelope kicked him under the table. Alice Payson smiled uncertainly. "Is that a funny?"

"Meant to be ol' girl. Maybe I over shot."

"Well, it's lovely and unique," Penelope said briskly. "Now let's order something scrumptious."

Over coffee she glanced at her wristwatch. "Two-fifteen. Dick has to run, but why don't you and I stay a while for some hen talk?"

"As an abandoned wife I have nothing but time on my hands—but aren't you just terribly busy?"

"Not this afternoon." She blew Dick a kiss. "I'm sorry you have to run, darling."

"So am I. I always miss the most interesting part," he said, rising to his feet, "But I'm just a slave to my unquenchable thirst for power and money. Usually I have crackers and milk at my desk for lunch, Mrs. Payson. The last tycoon. That sort of thing."

As he left them, Alice Payson turned to Penelope. "I just love that man, but he says the most off-beat things. Do you understand him?"

"Yes. I understand him."

Alice Payson sipped her coffee. "You're not like I imagined. You're just folks. I'm really enjoying this."

"I'm glad. Dick says I'm a gal from the corn country. It's true though Bloomington is a little south of the real corn belt, I'm proud of it."

"People back home said that Washington is a jungle; that people go in for double talk, the double shuffle, and double dealing. Frankly, I came down here scared to death. I'm no good at anything but frank, straight talk. If people don't mean what they say—I just don't know what to do. I really don't."

"I'm like that too."

"You are? Well, doesn't Washington throw you?"

"No, but I entered this town as a green college kid looking for a job. I had time to look around and to take on a protective coloration before anyone noticed me. You're a Senator's wife so you have no time to reconnoiter. You're front and center right away."

"I wish I could take on some kind of protective coloration. I am so desperately anxious not to let Bill down and I'm trying, but I seem to say and do the wrong things in Washington. Remarks that would wow them in the supermarket check out line in Palo Alto fall flat here."

"You're trying too hard. Relax."

"But what do I say to all of these people? Senators, Supreme Court Justices, Cabinet Members, people I have seen in the society pages suddenly looming up before me in living color, Ambassadors, even. I don't mind telling you, Mrs. Winston, it scares the hell out of me."

Penelope put a hand over hers. "Penny, Alice. Penny."

"You're sweet, Penny, just like the gals in my coffee klatch when I get to know you. The other night in that gorgeous home of yours I had an opposite impression."

"That's the point." Penelope signaled the waiter for more coffee. "I have two suggestions that I think will help you. First, remember that everyone in Washington is a little insecure. Everyone but the cliff dwellers are here on somebody else's sufferance. The politicians have the problem of re-election and the financing of expensive campaigns. The diplomats have fickle governments to appease and usually a chronic money problem. The lobbyists live from success to success, always fearing the lurking failures that might plunge them from the heights. The glamour girls on the fringes that might bug a genuine person like you are the most insecure of all. A change in style or mood can send them to the reject pile.

There is nothing more perishable than Washington's 'amusing people.' When they stop amusing, they've had it."

"What does 'cliff dwellers' mean?"

"The local great families, like my husband's family. There aren't many of them. Most great American families spring from a successful predator, now happily obscured in the mists of time, to borrow a corny phrase. There never has been much to prey on in Washington, so most of the cliff dwellers are imported. They have their own form of insecurity. They fear that they really don't matter in this capital city, that they are tolerated because they foot the bills, politically, socially, and charitably."

Alice Payson sipped her coffee. "Well, I must admit it makes me feel better to realize that I'm not the only one chewing my fingernails. But, I still don't know what to say to these people. I prattle on and the first thing I know they are staring at me bright-eyed with a little smile on their face. I feel like bolting for the ladies room."

"That's my second suggestion. Don't say anything. Listen. The commodity in the shortest supply in this town is good listeners. This is a town of talkers. They talk to project their egos. They hunger for an audience that will listen and respond. They frequently must have an audience that will reaffirm their high estimate of themselves, because it is only an estimate, fragile, tentatively arrived at, chronically subject to chilling winds that blow in from home."

"That sounds simple."

"It isn't. Listening is the hardest thing in the world to do and in human relations, at least, perhaps the greatest art."

"It's easier than talking."

"It's less dangerous. Nothing is easier than talking, especially if you are repeating yourself, which is ninety-nine percent of Washington talk."

Alice Payson leaned back and lit a cigarette and then a slow smile stole across her face. "What guardian angel sent you my way?"

Penelope laughed, thinking of Herman Baur. "Dick told me that as a hostess I frightened you. That really bothered me. I have my insecurity hang-ups too, you know. I don't want to become a Washington type and forget that I'm really a simple, uncomplicated girl from Indiana that's had a few breaks."

"That was a silly remark of mine. I should have been listening."

"Your husband has made quite an impression. You're his wife. People will seek you out. Just smile, listen, and say a few non-committal, gracious things. Don't try to be witty, original, or cute."

"I feel like we're old friends, Penny."

"I hope we'll be good friends. I think we shall." She smiled. "I've known you less than two hours and I'm already telling you my trade secrets."

"I don't deserve it."

"Oh, yes you do. The Paysons are going to be important in this town. I have admired your husband by reputation for a long time, and you measure up to him in every way."

Alice Payson flushed with pleasure. "Isn't he wonderful?"

"Yes. He's wonderful."

"I still feel like a school girl about him. Isn't that silly?"

"You're lucky."

"Don't you feel that way about your husband?"

Penelope glanced at her wristwatch. "I have another hour. Have you decided where you will live yet?"

"I think in an apartment. Where, I don't know."

"Let me drive you around a few neighborhoods, dear. Then you will have a better idea of where you want to look with the Senator."

Alice Payson arose with Penelope. "The Senator. I still can't get used to that."

"You'll be surprised how soon you'll get used to it. It's the 'Bill' you'll forget."

200

Alice Payson turned serious eyes toward her. "Oh, he'd hate that. He truly would."

Marc Haywood glanced at the gold digital clock on his desk as Penelope entered his office. It read four-thirty. "You are usually prompt," he said dryly.

"I'm very sorry, Marc. I had Alice Payson for lunch. She asked me to show her some of the nearby neighborhoods."

"You could have telephoned."

"I know. I was thoughtless."

His calm face bore no expression. "That was it, was it?"

"I said it was. I'm sorry."

"No matter." He lit an oval cigarette. "Alice Payson. Is that William Payson's wife?"

"Yes."

"I wouldn't think you'd have much in common."

"We both love our husbands."

He cleared his throat. "I see. Well, Senator Payson is a good man. Perhaps a great man."

"Shall we discuss the new syndication contract? I have to get home and change for a dinner at the Peruvian Embassy."

"In a moment. I want your advice first."

"*My* advice?"

"As my currently severest critic."

"I'm devoted to you, Marc." Her brisk voice made the words meaningless.

"Tomorrow's the deadline for filing in the Virginia primary for Senator. I'm thinking of running."

Penelope sat down gracefullly on a straight chair and crossing her legs smiled at him. "I'm surprised."

"Why?"

"I think of you as an aristocrat, even an autocrat on some days. I would not have thought you would submit yourself to the democratic process. It's a little more intimate than your current way of life."

He put the fingers of his two hands together, the tapered cigarette glowing between the index and forefingers of his right hand. She noticed that he wore star sapphire cuff links and a heavy gold signet ring on the ring finger of his left hand.

"Inherited wealth like mine is aristocratic and the publishing business is autocratic. However, in politics I'll make an admirable democrat."

"Why?"

"It's the style in both parties. It's the formula for success for someone like me. If I ran as a conservative, I'd immediately be accused of representing wealth and Big Business, which, of course, I do represent. But if I emerge as a fighting liberal, my wealth, my upper class accent, my manner, places me above suspicion. Since I appear to favor giving it all away, my disinterest is immediately established and I emerge as an accredited champion of the common people. You and I can both name a score of wealthy politicians that prove the point."

"Are you going to give it all away?"

"Of course not. No more than they have. They all continue to live on their cloistered estates, send their children to select private schools, and only support charities and foundations with the most beneficial kind of tax impact. They rumple their hair and let it grow long, fail to press their suits and mistie wrinkled and spotted cravats under soft button down collars. They avoid hats and neither shine nor half-sole their shoes and the people love it. They tell the people they deserve more and more and the people willingly tax themselves to pay for it. It never occurs to them that we rich should do the paying. The richer one is, the more radical he has to be to get elected. I figure that I should be in the middle range of the left of center group, based upon my net worth."

"Which party do you belong to? I've never known."

"President Frome has asked me to run in Virginia, so there is your answer. The *Tribune* is independent and I've been apolitical personally. If I take the plunge tomorrow, I'll emerge as a tousle headed liberal."

Penelope cocked her head to one side. "That could take some doing."

Marc Haywood arose wordlessly, took off his coat and vest, and roughing up his hair pushed it over to one side with his fingers. He cast the vest aside and slipped the coat back on. He pulled his tie loose and slipped it to one side. "This is how I'll look when I file tomorrow," he grinned. "Better?"

"Better. Better yet, wear some of your country tweeds and a shirt with barrel cuffs fastened with humble mother of pearl buttons. And don't forget to remove that ring."

"Should I do it, Penny? Or will they laugh at me?" He came around the desk and held her at arms length, both hands cupped around her shoulders, looking earnestly into her eyes.

"What does Claudia think?" Penelope asked, her tongue moving along her upper lip as she looked up at him.

"She hates the idea. I have her ultimatum that she won't cooperate."

"That figures. You haven't said why you want to do it."

"I'm bored. As a publisher I've been more of an observer than a participant. I feel cut off from real life. I live entirely within a business my father left me and within a social world he arranged for me. I want to break out, do something on my own, develop a new personality. I might even contribute something toward solving the problems I editorialize about."

"Don't tell me you're developing a social conscience?"

"I'm restless. Maybe that's my conscience stirring."

"Why do you ask me what to do?"

"You know why."

Penelope was silent. She moved away from him, sat down, and spent several minutes looking at her hands folded in her lap, thinking. "I'd do it," she said at last.

Haywood exhaled gently. "That's what I wanted to hear." He smiled at her boyishly. "Now we have a joint project again. I have something to do that's exciting."

Penelope raised her eyes to his. "I have some news for you. I'm going to have a baby."

Haywood paled and then flushed deeply, dropping his eyes. "Very well, very well," he said after a moment, sitting down at his desk.

"Aren't you going to congratulate me?"

"No. I'm not."

"Aren't you being a dog in the manger?"

"Possibly. I don't feel like a false gesture and I'm not going to make one."

Penelope arose and reached for her purse. "I am two months pregnant. I'm going to leave Washington before it shows. I'll be gone six months."

"What about the column?"

"I'll have advanced copy and we can arrange for guest columnists."

"I guess I have no choice."

"I'm afraid not, dear. This is biological."

"Does Dick know?"

"I'll tell him tonight."

Haywood looked disconsolate. "I hoped I'd have your help in my campaign."

"I'm afraid not. I'll be rooting for you, of course." She touched her hair with one hand. "Do you want to discuss the syndication contract?"

"No. Let's do it tomorrow."

"I have to go to the doctor tomorrow."

"All right, damn it. Name your own day."

"Friday, at two."

"Very well."

She walked around his desk and lightly kissed him on the cheek. "Good luck, Senator."

He glowered after her as she left the room, then he moved around the desk and stood staring out of the window with its view down Sixteenth Street, his hands in fists jammed into his pockets. "God damn it," he muttered, "And God damn her."

Penelope smiled sweetly at Dick Winston over breakfast coffee the next morning. "I have news for you, Dick. I'm going to have a baby." She watched Dick Winston's face as it was swept by a rapid series of expressions and then burst out laughing.

"I don't think that's so damn funny," he said, deeply hurt.

"I'm sorry, Dick. It's such a conventional remark, at least for other couples, that I couldn't resist it."

"Damn poor taste, ol' girl. I really mean it."

"So do I."

"What in hell does that mean?"

"I'm going to arrange to adopt a baby boy."

"Oh." Dick said uncertainly. He looked slightly confused. "O.K., I guess, if that's what you want."

"I want."

He got up from the table and coming around to her side, hugged her. "I'm sorry, Penny, darling. Of course you do. You just sprang it on me in a way that took me off balance. When did you decide this?"

"Yesterday."

"Well, swell." He hesitated. "How do we go about it?"

"I know a place up in Pennsylvania where you adopt a suitable child a few days after birth. No one knows it's not your natural child."

"You don't have to do that for me, Penny." He said quietly.

"I'm thinking of the child. It's better that it never knows it was adopted."

"I see."

"I thought a boy. We can get the same ethnic background, even coloring."

"O.K."

205

"Richard Perry Winston, Jr."

He grinned. "Gee, that's swell. I like boys."

"I will go up and make the arrangements next week. I'm planning to leave town and live in seclusion for the last six months of the 'pregnancy.' No one but you and me will know that he's not our son."

"That's a lot of trouble for the little fellow, Penny. You're very thoughtful."

She smiled at him. "We're going to make this a real marriage, Dick."

He nodded, returning her smile. "You betcha."

Marc Haywood, dressed casually in the flannel bags and well worn tweed jacket he often wore at Hollywood walked up the flight of stairs on Seventh Street that led to the editorial offices of the *Cutting Edge*. Lionel Jackson was waiting for him in a small office set off from the rest of the room by a six foot high partition of frosted glass framed in scarred walnut stained wood. He extended his powerful black hand in a firm grip. "Glad to see you, Marc." He noticed the informal clothes. "You taking the day off or is that what you think you ought to wear on Seventh Street?"

"I'm out canvassing for votes."

"Oh, yeah. I heard. You're running for Senator in Virginia against the machine. I hear Frome talked you into it." Jackson grinned widely. "That man doesn't like you, Marc, baby. You got no chance at all."

"I think I have. Northern Virginia is more liberal than it used to be; the independent vote is larger. If I can get most of the black vote I might squeak by the primary. If I can win the primary, I can win the general election."

Jackson offered Haywood a cigar and carefully lit one after Haywood refused and shook a cigarette out of a crumpled pack. He gazed at his visitor through a cloud of smoke as he got the cigar drawing to his satisfaction. "Why would a black man want to vote for you, Marc?"

"I've always run a liberal, progressive newspaper. I've supported civil rights. I'll be that kind of a Senator."

"You haven't answered my question."

"Isn't that enough?"

"Not any more. Not to me, even if I was invited to the *Zoo*."

"What is enough?"

"Maybe nothing is, man."

"Come on Lionel, lay it on the line. If I can't buy it I'll tell you so."

"You buy it, man, like you buy the farmer's vote, the labor vote, the veterans vote, the Italian, Polish or Irish vote. You find out what we want; not what we deserve, not what we need, not what you can afford, but what we want. Then you deliver, man, you deliver."

"Why do you keep saying, 'man' to me? You didn't talk like that when we were undergraduates at Harvard."

"Harvard? Oh, you remember me at Harvard? I figured you just thought I was background in those days. You and Hasty Pudding and the *Crimson* and the like."

"I remember you."

"Many thanks. Well, I'll tell you why I say, 'man.' It's a polite way of reminding you that I don't forget we are different. You whites sort of sidle up to us blacks these days, sort of on your good behavior, and sort of simper and pretend you don't notice anything. You know, the black skin, the pink palms, the thick lips, the kinky hair. When I say 'man' I'm telling you I'm not buying it. There are other ways of saying it you would like less."

Haywood calmly drew on his cigarette. "O.K., Lionel. Can we get down to cases? How do I get the black vote in Virginia?"

"Let's take a walk." They went down the stairs into the street. "I thought you might like to see the neighborhood." They walked slowly northward past burnt out stores, stores still open where unpainted wood planks with "Soul" or "Soul Brother" crudely painted in white paint had replaced glass

207

windows, stores with heavy iron bars or iron latticework across display windows. The street was full of people, most of them aimlessly standing about. Newspaper and paper wrappings blew about in the late afternoon breeze. After a few blocks there were no white people, only blacks. "Feel uncomfortable?" Jackson asked.

"A little."

"Why not? You're a whitey. They hate your guts."

"I don't believe you."

Jackson grinned. "Then why is the flesh crawling on the back of your neck? Why do you wish you had eyes in the back of your head?"

"You have the hopped up imagination of a political pamphleteer, Lionel. You can't believe that people seldom think of politics, white or black. You think they hang on your every word."

"I tell them to cool it. Your flesh ain't crawling because of me, Marc. It's because of what you sense out there. You ain't safe on Seventh Street and you know it. You ain't safe on Connecticut Avenue, in Georgetown, or in Warrenton either, but you think you are."

"I was talking about the black vote in Virginia, not in the District of Columbia."

"It's all the same. A whitey gets the vote if he delivers."

"Delivers what?"

Jackson waved his hand at the shoddy street. "You're now a politician, Marc. You know you have to do something about this."

"I'm going to do something about it."

"Now, man. Don't talk about the children or the next generation. Now, man. The Negro voter wants it now."

"I'll only be one Senator."

"One more. It all adds up."

"Will you support me in the *Cutting Edge?*"

"Take a few full page ads. I'll see how you do."

"That could be misinterpreted."

Jackson grinned. "Could it now, man?" He exaggeratedly shrugged his shoulders. "I wouldn't know. Show me a little soul, man, and we'll get along."

"How do I do that?"

"It will come, Marc baby. First you learn the words and the tune just comes to you."

"I'll take a full page ad."

"You're getting the words man. You're beautiful. You really are."

Haywood looked uncomfortable. "I'm really sincere, Lionel. I really am. I hate racial prejudice."

Jackson stared at him unsmilingly and gave a jerky nod of acknowledgment. "Good for you. Good for me. We're going to end racial prejudice and when we end the prejudice, we still have opinions and what do we do about that?"

"You're more pessimistic than I am, Lionel."

"I got reason to be, man. I got reason to be."

❧ 19 ❧

THE string trio briskly made music in the green and crystal room at the Sulgrave Club valiantly, if unsuccessfully, trying to dominate the high pitched cacophony of the two hundred women gathered there. Penelope and Alice Payson stood near the doorway, an abbreviated receiving line of two, and exchanged tired smiles. "Is that the lot?" Alice Payson asked.

"I believe everyone is here," Penelope looked over the crowded room.

"It was so nice of you to give this reception for me, Penny. With your sponsorship they know I'm not a West Coast freak."

"The freaks are in there," Penelope answered. "I think we can leave this doorway soon and mix with our guests. Most of these women, though, are lovely ladies. When you know them better they will like you and you will like them."

"Right now they are just a blur. I didn't catch a single name. I stare at people when I get introduced and get transfixed by a mole or a pierced ear or some other minor detail and don't even hear the name or see the face. Of course," she gave a short, hoarse laugh, "I'd know the mole anywhere."

"You're human," Penelope nodded. "Let's move on in and I'll try to single out a few types. If you understand the types, you'll understand Washington women, at least as far as they are understandable." She lowered her voice slightly. "First, we'll take the Washington swinger. The tallish gal with the thick chestnut hair down to her shoulders is Mary Louise Pica. She looks bored to death because there are no men about. Her makeup and manner is a little obvious to the women here, but it really raises the hair on the male chests. Enough anyway, to keep Mary Louise occupied."

Alice stared. "Is she . . . ? Does she . . . ?"

"No. She isn't. She probably does on a selected basis. At least she wants the men to believe that. She's married to a speculative contractor who has built more marginal office space than any ten other men in Washington. She's flashy, and he's proud of her, but I doubt that he plays the cuckold. He probably knows that her bite is smaller than her bark."

"What's she trying to prove?"

"Nothing. Nature heavily endowed her and she's none too bright mentally. She's restless. One of these days a sexy young Ambassador will come along from one of the oil countries and she will allow herself to be swept off her feet after an appropriate settlement. It may make a few newspaper stories and a few stray shots may be exchanged, but no one will really be hurt and the whole thing will soon be fogotten."

"It all seems so superficial, as if they are living entirely on the surface."

"This type is. Remember that, dear." They moved through the crowd. "Mary Louise," Penelope said, "You look more gorgeous than ever. How do you do it?"

Mary Louise's restless, gray eyes touched Penelope's and then moved out over the crowd, unconsciously seeking the men that weren't there. On a man she could fix an intense, flattering regard and gaze into his eyes for minutes on end, seemingly oblivious to all others around her, but with women a quick meeting of eyes was the most she attempted and if her eyes were not darting about the room, they were downcast. "Elizabeth Arden's," she said. "They redo me every so often." She giggled. "You should see the bills. Marvin hates it."

"I'm so glad you could come and meet Mrs. Payson."

"Yes. Well, you asked. I didn't know it would be all women."

"This is a woman's club."

"Oh." Mary Louise took a canapé from a passing tray and popped it in her mouth. "I love these little things, but I have to watch it. I'm damned if I'll wear a girdle."

"Or a bra," Alice Payson said.

Mary Louise's eyes rested on Alice's for the first time. "That goes without saying."

Alice Payson laughed. "It sure does, sweetie, and do I envy you."

Mary Louise looked away again and moistened her full lips with her tongue. "Well, thanks, Penny. I've got to run. I'm due at an Embassy next. Marvin's got a deal." Her eyes flicked over them as she gave a quick smile and moved away.

"Marvin's not the only one," Alice Payson said sotto voce.

"Now, Alice," Penelope said, laughing in spite of herself. "I suppose I can scratch that one."

"No. You said just the right thing. She'll remember you fondly as the woman who admired her breasts."

"That remark was a happy accident. I'll probably really mess the next one up."

"Well, you see that there is no reason to be afraid of a Washington glamour girl."

"No. Actually, I feel rather sorry for her. I have the feeling that her relationship with Marvin, or with any other man is a pretty brutal thing."

"I see Mrs. Ponford, the wife of Justice Ponford. Let's chat with her."

Mary Ponford smiled at them as they approached. "It's a lovely party, Penny dear, and so nice to have this chance to meet you, Mrs. Payson. The Justice so admires your husband and he will be glad to learn from me that he has a lovely wife."

Alice Payson smiled back at the tall plain woman with

muddy grey hair that escaped in long wisps from beneath old fashioned tortoise shell combs. "Thank you. You make me feel so welcome."

Mary Ponford closed a boney, heavily ringed hand over Penelope's. "I do enjoy your column so, Penny. As the Justice was saying the other night, it leaves you feeling happy. It isn't full of all of this terrible Gothic foreboding and negativism. It is about a Washington we can all recognize." She turned to Alice Payson. "I think these columnists and newsmen that describe Washington day after day to the rest of the country as a corrupt Rome do us a grave injustice. People are beginning to lose confidence in our country." Her grip tightened on Penelope's hand. "This girl doesn't do that. Her column is amusing and wholesome."

"And accurate," Alice added.

"And accurate. The Justice and I have read it daily for nearly five years. We have no quarrel with it."

"Thank you, Mrs. Ponford," Penelope said gravely. "That really inspires me. How is Justice Ponford?"

"Better. Better. He had a bad fall last winter. He's eighty-six, you know. It worried him so. Not the fall, he's a good soldier about physical things. He worried about not keeping up his end of things at the Court. For a time he was even thinking of retiring, but he's in a better mood now."

"Give him my love."

"I shall. I shall and we shall have you and our new friend here to a luncheon very soon after the Court recesses. The Justice avoids evenings out." She released Penelope's hand with a squeeze and smiled at Alice.

"At eighty-six he *thought* of retiring?" Alice whispered to Penelope as they moved off, "When do Supreme Court Justices retire?"

"There's no age limit. It's the same with Congress."

"Is he that good?"

"Frankly, no. He just repeats everything he had learned by thirty. Fortunately, I'm told, that is what judicial precedent is all about."

Alice Payson shrugged. "Well, she's a dear."

"So is the Justice. He may be straight out of Gilbert and Sullivan, but that is better than Marat-Sade."

The first arrivals began to seek them out to say their good byes and they moved back toward the doorway. When the last guest had departed, Alice Payson grimaced, "I feel as if my feet were planted in cement. Is there some place we can sit down?"

Penelope led her into the small barroom and smiled at her from the end of a small chintz covered sofa as the bartender served them martinis. "Do you have a better sense of what the women of Washington are like?"

"I'm beginning to sort them out. The funny thing is, taken one by one, I can identify the same types we have in Palo Alto. Mary Louise reminds me of the wife of one of our used car tycoons and Mrs. Ponford could be the wife of one of the more elderly professors at Stanford."

"That's the way it is. It's one world. When I began to write my column it helped to equate Washington types with people I knew in Bloomington."

"In the mass, women are frightening. At my first reception after Bill and I arrived, it was a Congressional wives bash, I felt like I was a British sentry being stormed at Khartoum by the legions of the Mahdi. When I have someone like you to hold my hand I calm down and see them as individuals." She sipped her drink. "Is it unladylike to borrow the men's gag and say we all put our pants on one leg at a time?"

Penelope winked. "Except Mary Louise."

Alice laughed. "Well, sure. I know what you mean."

"Have the Senator and you been invited to an Embassy dinner yet?"

Alice looked alarmed. "An Embassy? Are foreigners going after us, too?"

"Your husband is a Senator. That automatically puts you on the list. When they discover that he is going to be an influential Senator, the dinner invitations will flow in."

"Gosh! Sit down dinners?"

"Yes. Very formal."

Alice looked stricken. "My God! What will I do? I hate the very idea. I like buffets or barbecues where you can make a few *gaffes* and no one notices. In Palo Alto we don't even have a dining room."

"It isn't too hard. It's all ritual. Once you have learned the rules it's like dancing a slow minuet with food."

"It sounds boring as hell, a very expensive way to get a belly ache."

"You will have to attend a few during the year."

"Bill's specialty is urban affairs. Can't we just stick to Americans?"

"You're going to have to raise your sights, Alice. Senator Payson is going to be bigger than that."

Alice looked at her anxiously. "I know, Penny, and I just don't think I'm up to it."

"Don't be a goose. Dick and I have an invitation to the French Embassy in three weeks. Ambassador Piccard is an old friend of mine. I'll ask him to include the Senator and you."

"You mean ask for an invitation?"

"You have to start sometime and I'll be there with Dick. I'll coach you on a few rules ahead of time. You'll do fine."

Alice sighed. "I thought after today we could relax for a while."

The Norman facade of the French Embassy on Kalorama Road glowed in the light reflected from its score of mullioned windows. The gathering of limousines standing in a glistening black file with their chauffeurs chatting together in groups nearby indicated that a party for the rich or powerful was in progress inside.

Alice Payson turned to Penelope in the ladies' powder room where they had left their wraps. "How do I look?" She asked nervously. Penelope looked at the plain face with its erratically applied makeup, the casually brushed mouse colored hair, and the long black unadorned gown that hung from the spare frame.

"You look lovely."

"You say he's a bachelor?" She asked nervously.

"Yes, and very courtly with the ladies."

"I'll bet. He's probably one of these smooth Frenchmen. I won't know what to say."

"The French are smooth because they put you at your ease. You can't object to that."

"No, if that's the way it works. Well, let's go join the boys."

Ambassador Piccard greeted them warmly, standing just inside a spacious, impeccably furnished salon. Crystal and gold chandeliers supplemented by soft table lights bathed the priceless French furniture, art objects, and paintings in a subdued glow. "Penny, dear," he said, kissing her lightly on the cheek as he held both of her hands, "How lovely you look, the American girl incarnate. You always bring me a little joy. Dick, I am so pleased to see you."

"This is Senator and Mrs. Payson, Mr. Ambassador," Penelope said. "Bill, Alice, the dearest man in Washington, Monsieur Piccard, the Ambassador of France." She smiled at the elegant, slight man before her in a dinner jacket closely tailored to his figure. A red handkerchief protruded from the jacket upper pocket in the familiar fluted pattern he affected. "Dear Yves," she said squeezing his hands.

"Hello," Alice Payson said artlessly with a tight little smile.

Ambassador Piccard bent over her hand. "Madam, you honor me." He smiled into the blue eyes of Senator Payson, noting the scholar's face and the faintly appraising squint. "Senator Payson, I have heard of you as the man from the West who doesn't ask questions; the man with the answers."

William Payson gave a dry laugh. "You have been reading too much of my political literature, Mr. Ambassador."

"But, of course. And I believe what I read."

Payson's shrug was deprecating. "The advertising men got a little carried away. I only know the answers if they ask me the right questions."

The Ambassador half turned from them. "Come in and meet my other guests. Tonight we are an intimate little group of twenty."

A few minutes later Marnie Maane laid a claw like hand on Penelope's forearm. "Penny, dear," she said in a hoarse whisper. "Isn't that the new Senator from California I have heard so much about?"

Penelope turned and spoke in a faintly patronizing tone. "Hello, Marnie. Yes. That is Senator Payson."

The shrewd eyes, surrounded by puffs of dry wrinkled skin, gazed speculatively across the room. "Is that his wife beside him?"

"Yes."

"It never fails, does it? Someday we're going to get a charming *couple* in this town."

"Don't underestimate her, Marnie. There's something there. I have a feeling that in a few months she's going to more than hold her own."

Marnie Maane gave a rough edged chuckle. "I hear that you've been sponsoring her, Penny, and I've wondered why. Is he that important?"

"Don't be a cat, Marnie. He's important enough for you, and so is she."

Marnie Maane looked hurt. "I didn't mean it that way. I just wanted your opinion. I might invite them to my next party."

Penelope's eyes twinkled and she spoke tartly. "In my opinion they are eligible."

Marnie Maane's small mouth drew back in a tight little smile. "Well, I'm not as exclusive as you, dear. That I will admit. I *try* to be democratic."

Penelope's face grew cold. "Don't be tiresome, Marnie. And don't assume that we have the same interests."

Marnie Maane's face flushed. "I don't assume anything, but I can remember when you were a little more accommodating, or, if you don't mind, dear, anxious to please."

"I have a good memory, too, Marnie," Penelope said evenly. She turned away and walked over to Alice Payson. "Who was the old dragon you were speaking with?" Alice Payson asked.

"Marnie Maane."

"What does she do?"

"She collects people." Penelope looked across the room at Marnie Maane with a little smirk. "Fewer and fewer each year."

"I don't get it."

"She's a 'Washington hostess.' She collects celebrities together at a few big receptions each season. However, she's had her day. She's been on the skids for the last three years."

"That sounds sad."

"It is sad. If she weren't so easy to dislike, I might feel sorry for her these days."

"She's staring at me."

"That means that she'll soon come across the room and give you an invitation."

"What do I do?"

"Turn it down. Bill doesn't need it and neither do you."

Ambassador Piccard came over to them. "I offer you my arm, Penny dear. I'm taking you into dinner."

"What about me?" Alice Payson asked. "Do I rough it?"

"A gentleman with your name in a small envelope which he was given at the door will seek you out, Madam. He will be your escort and will sit on your left."

"Oh. That was a *gaff*, wasn't it?"

"Not at all, Mrs. Payson. Quite understandable. I merely explain our custom."

William Payson, at Penelope's right at the table, leaned toward her. "I appreciate your kindness to Ali, Penny. She thinks the world of you."

"I think she's wonderful, Bill. I enjoy her company."

"She needed a friend. All of this is something different for both of us. I can take it in stride. I have other things to preoccupy me. But a woman concentrates on these things. You know, 'What should I wear?' that sort of thing. She needs another woman to talk it out with. As Ali says, 'A woman without claws.' You're that kind of woman and that kind of friend. I want you to know that we both appreciate it."

"I'm delighted to help, Bill. After all, I'm only a newspaper columnist. Alice and you are the important ones."

William Payson gave a thin smile and waved the comment away with a gesture. He looked down the long table with its flowers and two tall silver candelabra, the white damask covered with china and crystal, the two files of diners on either side, the blue, silver, green, and pink of the ladies gowns set off by the regular spacing of pink cheeked, silver haired men in white and black. "Pretty, isn't it?"

"Yes. It's a lovely setting."

"Very civilized, the apex of social intercourse."

"Ambassador Piccard would be pleased to hear you say so."

"I find myself wondering what the relationship of this is to what's going on in the city outside."

Penelope sipped her wine. "Does it have to have a relationship?"

"Perhaps not, though I happen to think what is going on outside is more important."

"That's because cities are your specialty."

"No. Cities are my specialty because I think they are important."

"Ambassador Piccard has been in Washington twelve years. I don't think he would bother with the expense and trouble of parties like these if he didn't think that they served some purpose."

"What do you think the purpose of this party is?"

Ambassador Piccard had turned from the woman on his left and heard the question. "The purpose of this party, Senator, is to honor my good friend, Penelope Winston, and her husband. They have both been very kind to me."

Senator Payson flushed slightly at being overheard asking a tactless question. "They also have been kind to Mrs. Payson and me, Mr. Ambassador. We're delighted to join you at a party in their honor."

The Ambassador's eyes twinkled. "I didn't hear all of your conversation, but I imagine you were attempting to answer a larger question, that is, what is the value of diplomatic entertaining?"

"Something like that."

"We are both practical men, Senator. Men of affairs. We can't afford to waste our time. So while we are happy to honor Penelope, there may be other similar occasions we should avoid?"

"Well, I haven't come here from California to entertain or to be entertained."

"Of course not. Nor have I come from France for that purpose." He smiled. "But even the most important, the most complex of affairs are conducted, after all, by human beings. Problems don't exist in a vacuum. Solutions to problems aren't found by applying abstract formulae. We come to grips with problems when we confront men. We solve the problems when men decide upon a workable solution or compromise. Entertainment in this Embassy or elsewhere in Washington brings us together. We get to know one another. We can judge one another. This is an essential for negotiating together."

Senator Payson glanced down the table. "Are we all potential negotiators at this table? That seems hard to believe."

"Of course not. That would be uncivilized. We must have

220

amusing people at our table. We must repay social debts. We have friends of whom we ask nothing. But you must not think that this is not 'real' on that account. It is very real. After a few months in Washington you will realize this. This is a very complicated city and we communicate on many levels. The national and international capital is just as real as the urban environment in which it rests, and, forgive me, Senator, more important."

Senator Payson smiled. "My interests are probably parochial, Mr. Ambassador. I'm the first to admit that. I admire a man who can express himself so eloquently, and in another man's language. Certainly, as a Washington newcomer I should withhold judgment. In any event, we're delighted to be here and I hope that you realize my comments to Penny were table conversation. This lovely dinner is an end unto itself."

"Of course, Senator, I understand. Someday soon I want to call on you at your office and you must lecture me on urban affairs." He laughed. "Turn about is fair play."

The ladies moved into the salon for coffee while the gentlemen remained around the table for port and cigars. A dark, intense woman with closely bobbed hair and a dimple in her chin approached Penelope.

"Well, hi. I haven't had a chance to say 'hello.'"

"Hi, Judy. How many of these have you covered for your column this week?"

"This is my third dinner party. Then I've attended two luncheons, four receptions and a tea. Of course, it's only Thursday."

"I don't see how you do it."

"Speed, footwork, and fractured prose. I'd give a lot to have your kind of column. You don't write about what you've seen and heard, at least not directly. I've noticed that you're one of them. They forget you're a newspaper woman. I'm an outsider. Conversation becomes stilted when I join the group. They know that my flapping ears and X-ray eyes are transmitting tomorrow's story to my brain so they are on their good behavior. Take these gals. I could sum them up in three words, buxom, bland, and boring."

"You do your column so very well, Judy. I couldn't begin to do it. I'm not observant enough and I'm not enough of a quick study."

"You're sweet to say so, Penny."

"Have you met Mrs. Payson yet?"

Judy giggled. "Have I? And is she quotable! What is she, the West Coast Mencken?"

"Take it easy on her, will you? She needs a little time to adjust to being a Senator's wife."

"Well, O.K.," Judy agreed reluctantly. "She's furnished the only color I've got for tomorrow's column."

"I can imagine. She's nothing if not quotable."

"Rumor has it that she's your social protégé. Can I use that?"

Penelope hesitated. "Well, O.K., go ahead, but drop the protégé bit. It sounds patronizing on my part. Just say we've become good friends."

"Will do."

Alice Payson joined them. "You know, I'll never learn. I forgot about the damn finger bowl and took some fruit from a tray with those fancy tongs. Where did I drop it? In the finger bowl! I hadn't removed it and that doily what's-it from my plate. I tried to pass if off by pretending I was a raccoon washing her food." She laughed heartily. "Fortunately that cute baldheaded banker next to me was boiled. He didn't even notice."

Penelope grinned at Judy. "As I say, she's quotable!"

Alice looked at them. "What gives? Have I missed something?"

"Judy is a newspaper woman."

"Here? Well, I'll be damned. Is the place bugged as well?"

"I won't quote you, Mrs. Payson," Judy said easily. "I'm a society page vulture. I'll just describe what you're wearing."

"I'd rather be quoted," Alice said glancing down at her frock doubtfully, "And it would be easier on you."

"Is it an original?"

"It sure is, honey. The only long dress I've ever owned."

Judy joined Penelope and Alice in laughter. "This gal should be a standup comedian, Penny, so help me God."

"It may be funny, girls," Alice said, reaching for a cigarette, "But it's the awful truth."

Ambassador Piccard approached and took Penelope by the arm. "You ladies are laughing? Then we gentlemen will worry no more about the state of the world. May we join you?"

"That was a fun evening," Dick Winston said at breakfast the next morning.

Penelope sipped the black coffee and nibbled on the toast which had constituted her breakfast since she had noticed that her weight had increased from 115 to 120 pounds. "Piccard is a dear. What did you think of Payson?"

"She did O.K."

"I meant the Senator. For better or for worse Alice is becoming a known quantity."

"Don't b'lieve I noticed anything special. I suppose every comic like Alice needs a straight man."

Penelope looked at him with interest. "Sometimes, darling, you say the most penetrating things. Now that you've said it, I find I've been thinking the same thing."

Dick Winston smiled at her and winked. " 'Pon my word, I've become a political commentator."

"Did you know that he is a possibility for the party's nomination the year after next?"

"I'm not surprised. Presidents, by and large, are a pretty dreary lot. After all, who would choose Atlas for light conversation?" He chuckled. "But I could go for Alice as first lady. Wow!"

"He's some sort of genius in urban affairs."

"Great. Garbage collection, sewage and water lines, public housing, poverty, crime, pollution—he'll make a real fun president."

Penelope shrugged. "Herman Baur thinks that he fits the mood of the country and no one reads the mood of the country better than Herman Baur."

"Is Baur for him?"

"Not yet."

"Well, I've noticed that we've been developing a sort of negative rhetoric about the country, the antithesis of the old fourth of July patriotic speech. Payson may be just what we're looking for, a sort of political shroud. Does he ever smile?"

"Sometimes. Usually he pops his eyes."

"Good God!" He sat smiling at her.

She smiled back and extended her hand. "The nice thing about you, Dick, is that you're always gay."

"When in season, I'm irresistible. I wonder if you have an hour or two this morning? I'd like to show you something."

"This morning?"

"Please."

"Well, all right. Is it far?"

"No."

They drove to the narrow, three story brick building with the restored colonial front and green window shutters that housed the offices of Winston Development Corporation on M Street in Georgetown. He pulled his Mercedes convertible into the parking space and they entered through a rear door into a hallway that bisected the building. "My office here is upstairs. What I want to show you is in the drafting room." A tall, thin, dark complexioned man with a mole on his left cheek looked up as they entered. He was dressed in brown tweeds and had pulled loose the knot of a green knit tie below the open collar of a buttoned down shirt. He moved by two draftsmen busily at work in their shirt sleeves to greet them. "Morning, boss."

"This is Jerry Stern, Penny, one of the sharpest brains in real estate development. Jerry, Mrs. Winston. I want to show her what we're up to."

"Delighted, Mrs. Winston. I wondered if I would ever meet you. I always read your column."

"Thank you."

"Well, let's see; I guess we can lay the plans out on this table. Then we can show the colored slides in the projection room." He swung a heavy roll of blueprints up on an empty drafting table and smoothed them out. "Would you like to explain them, Mr. Winston?"

Dick turned to Penelope with a broad grin. "That pile of blueprints represents a new town we are building on our own land north of Frederick. It's called Heitzing. Eventually, it will cover several thousand acres and will have a population of fifty thousand people."

"I thought you were just land owners for capital appreciation?"

"I thought so, too, but when you study this business, Penny, you learn that the real money is in the development and sales end. If we are farsighted enough to obtain a good land position, why should we give a windfall to a developer? Besides, this is where the action is, the real fun, the sense of accomplishment, right Jerry?"

"Right, sir."

"Doesn't it take a lot of money?"

"It sure does, but we aren't having any trouble with the financing. We put up the land, two Maryland and one D.C. bank are providing interim construction loans, and insurance companies, savings and loans, and bank mortgage departments will finance the ultimate purchases of homes. Winston Development Corporation will own the shopping center with long term leases out to the stores that will occupy it."

Penelope looked over his shoulder as he turned the blueprints, explaining the details in a staccato voice that revealed his pride and excitement.

225

"Where are the people coming from—north of Frederick?" She asked.

Dick Winston struck his forehead with an open palm in exasperation. "Of course! I forgot to tell you the most important part. I bought up all of this land over a year ago as a long term appreciation deal on Jerry's advice. But several weeks ago the Office of Education announced that they are relocating the Office near Frederick. We got our first hint, when we began to get nibbles about buying our land from political types. Jerry and Steve Bates, my financial man, he's up front, I'll introduce you later, both said, 'Go slow, something's cooking here,' and they were so right! When we learned what was going on, we didn't take long to decide that we would develop it ourselves and Heitzing was born!" He gave her a little hug. "Isn't that great? Isn't that just great?"

"Yes, I heard about that move. It's part of the government office dispersal program, isn't it?"

"Exactly, and a bonanza for us! It's just like having millions fall into your lap."

"It sounds wonderful. I'm very impressed."

"We'll start growing like Topsy soon. I've been over coordinating our plans with those of the Office of Education. They will need housing in about one year—we'll have to scramble to meet that deadline. Now, let me introduce you to Steve and the office staff and then we'll show you slides and movies of the site." He laughed happily. "Then you will know as much about the Heitzing project as we do."

"Well, what do you think, Penny?" He asked in the car on the drive back to Foxhall Road.

"I'm staggered. It's a huge undertaking, isn't it?"

"Fifty million dollars in the first phase alone."

"Are Jerry Stern and Steve Bates that smart?"

"Sharp as tacks. You met them."

"Yes, they seemed bright," she bit her lip. "What's in it for them, while you're making millions?"

"I've given each of them a five percent equity in the company."

"That's very generous. No wonder they are so enthusiastic."

"I've done something else, too, on tax counsel's advice, before Winston Development Corporation's net worth soars through the ceiling."

"Oh?"

"I've put forty percent of the shares in trust for you."

She turned to him, "Oh, Dick, what a kind, thoughtful thing to do!" She leaned across on the seat and kissed him on the cheek. "I do love you."

"In spite of everything?"

She moved next to him on the seat and hugged his arm. "That something isn't everything. We can't complain about something that neither of us can help."

"Are you proud of me?"

"Yes, I am."

He sighed and put his arm around her. "I guess this is the happiest day of my life."

As they turned into the driveway of Foxhall House she asked, "Who is the trustee?"

"John Griffin. He'll vote your shares and he is our general counsel. He'll keep our feet on the ground."

She looked at him earnestly before they got out of the car. "Dick, you'll get the very best advice?"

A faint expression of petulance crossed his face. "I have and I will, but let's remember, this is my show."

"I'll remember that it's your show, darling. I'm about to start on my own show anyway." Dick Winston looked at her quizzically. "The baby, Dick. Next week I go off on my six months disappearing act."

"I'd forgotten. Is it all arranged then?"

"Yes, several unwanted babies will be born in about six months and a boy will be given to us."

"Won't they give us more details?"

"No. We have to rely on the agency to properly match families. The identity of all parties is protected. I want it that way too."

"I'll miss you, Penny. Where are you going?"

"I'm going to stay at a little Inn on the Delaware River under the name of Mrs. Rockwell. Edith Rockwell."

"Can't I visit you? After all, I'm in on the secret. I'm the father, sort of."

"No. Some snoop will try to find out where I've gone. You'll lead them to me if you visit me. Absolutely nothing must go wrong. Nothing. In six months I intend to come home with a new baby. We'll announce it as our natural born child. I want no one in a position to challenge that."

Dick Winston sighed. "It seems like a lot of trouble for the child."

"Six months isn't long. I'll enjoy the rest."

Penelope stood in the window of the rustic bedroom of her small suite in the old brick inn and watched the rapid flow of the Delaware River down its ancient course to Philadelphia and the sea. The water was brown from the winter rains and carried with it dead limbs and debris from its numerous tributaries upstream. She had been living at the inn nearly four months under her assumed name with only a few short trips into equally remote and rural surroundings to ease the tedium of her existence. A hundred times she had regretted the impulsive announcement to Marc Haywood which had resulted in this enforced exile. With the coming of winter, it had become less like an exile and more like an imprisonment and she found herself marking off days on the calendar in the manner of a prisoner waiting for a parole.

She had made casual acquaintances at the inn, but had shunned even the incipient intimacy that could lead to curiosity or to questions. She would consent to make a fourth at bridge in the little lounge after dinner and would join in the light conversation between the rubbers, but she ate alone at a small table by the dining room windows and politely re-buffed all attempts to draw her into a larger group.

As the curiosity of the staff mounted with the length of her stay, she had felt compelled to infer to the innkeeper that her husband was on a perilous overseas military assignment and that she was keeping vigil until his return. This invested her with an aurora of stoic patience and impending tragedy which made the innkeeper her protector and encouraged the staff and other guests to give her the privacy she sought. Yet, her position was most awkward and unnatural. To stifle her natural gregariousness and to seek lonely solitude was one of the most difficult things she had ever undertaken. The frustration of dissembling kept her under permanent strain.

As she stood at the bedroom window she reflected somberly that she had to endure this twilight existence for two more months. It seemed as if an eternity had already passed since her arrival. She turned on the radio by her bedside and then, as soon as the music sounded, turned it off again. She picked up the local newspaper and glanced at an inside page to see if the movie offered at the only motion picture theatre in the nearby village had changed. It had not. She threw the newspaper aside impatiently as a firm rap sounded on the door of her small livingroom. She walked through it from the bedroom and opened the door. Smiling at her from the hallway was her mother.

"Hello, dear. Surprise!" Mrs. Benton threw back her head and laughed like a school girl.

Penelope's face drained of its color. She felt as if she had received a hard blow to the stomach. She seized her mother's right arm and quickly drew her inside the suite. Her breath came in shallow gasps. "What in hell are you doing here?"

Mrs. Benton's smile had faded into an embarrassed caricature of itself. "Why, I'm here to help."

"Help?"

"With the baby when it comes."

Penelope ran her tongue over her dry lips. "How do you

know about the baby?"

"Mrs. Moss told me."

"Sit down," Penelope said, indicating a maple framed chair with green and yellow cushions tied to the seat and back. She dropped down herself on the edge of a matching settee. "I want to get this straight."

Chilled by Penelope's attitude, Mrs. Benton's voice took on a defensive edge. "I sold off part of the house lot in Bloomington. They rezoned it so I could. Nellie Wilson next door agreed to look after the boys and the house so I could get a little vacation. I had some money ahead for a change, so I just got on a bus and came to Washington to see you. It was three years, Penny. I hadn't met your husband or seen your new house. I'd say it was about time for a visit."

Penelope looked at her mother wordlessly. After a moment she said in a brittle voice, "Your last visit to Washington wasn't exactly a success."

Mrs. Benton's face clouded. "I thought we'd forgotten about that. You wrote those nice columns about me and all."

"I've had to live down your performance, Mom. It's as simple as that. It hasn't been easy."

"Well, I'm sorry. A body has to make some mistakes. Besides, in your column you seemed to like it."

"When did you arrive in Washington?"

"Yesterday. Mrs. Moss told me about the baby so I rode the bus up here to-day."

"Mrs. Moss promised me that she'd tell no one where I was, not even Dick."

"She told me that, but we thought you'd want your own mother to know. As Mrs. Moss said, a girl needs her ma at a time like this."

"Did you meet Dick?"

"No. He was off some place."

"Have you told anyone who I am?"

"My stars, no! I know it's a secret, though I can't think

230

why. I must say you're carrying the baby just fine. When is it due?"

"In two months."

"It will be a small baby. I can see that. You were like that. I hardly knew I had you." She smiled. "Until you were birthed. Then you let us all know you were here."

"Mom, you can't stay here. Within a few hours everyone will know who I am. I know you."

"Penny, I can keep a secret."

"My name is Edith. Edith Rockwell."

"I know that, Penny."

"You are leaving. Or I am. Tonight."

"All I want to do is to keep you company for a few days and then I'll come back for the birth of the baby."

"No!"

Mrs. Benton stared at Penelope. "You don't want me?"

"That's exactly the point!" Penelope's voice was low and intense.

Mrs. Benton's eyes snapped. "I'm not going to be kept away from my own grandchild!"

"You aren't going to have a thing to do with it until I bring the baby to see you in Bloomington."

Mrs. Benton's lips compressed. "I don't understand you, acting this way to your own mother!"

Penelope sat erect on the settee, her hands clasped tightly, her eyes an electric blue in a face pale with strain. "Mother —"

"I always know when you call me 'Mother' that you are going to say something unpleasant," Mrs. Benton sniffed.

"Mother," Penelope repeated, "We must have an understanding."

Mrs. Benton nodded. "Go ahead and say it, whatever it is. Hurt my feelings after I've come to you half across the country."

"You have to realize that your place is in Bloomington, not

231

Washington. I write to you. I send you money. I visit you. We are in touch. You don't have to come east."

"You came to Bloomington twice in three years, Penny. Duty visits. That was clear enough."

"Call them what you will. I made them." Penelope glanced down at her clenched hands and then up again. "I intend to make myself clear. You are not to visit me again in Washington. I am building a life there, creating a certain image. You don't understand the world I now live in."

Mrs. Benton's voice thickened. "I suppose, then, that it would suit you better if I was dead. I raised you. I sacrificed for you, and this is the thanks I get. You don't want me. You get a good education and meet fancy folks and then you don't want me."

"Oh, for God's sake!" Penelope said as her mother began to cry. She did not go to her, but arose to her feet and clasped her arms in a gesture that indicated her inner tension. "Your place is in Bloomington. You belong there. My place is now in Washington. I'm leading a different life that you can't possibly understand. When you come to Washington, it takes me a year to repair the damage you do in a week."

"I may not fit, but I get lonely. I want to know what's going on. That's human enough."

Penelope bit her pale lips. "Mother, I'm going to give you an ultimatum. I'm not going to argue. Either you stay in Bloomington or we won't see each other again."

The words hung in the silence of the room. Mrs. Benton's eyes rose to Penelope's and held them. "That's clear enough, I must say," she said at last. She dried her eyes and sat looking at the floor for a moment. "Folks aren't ashamed of me in Bloomington. I'm quite a person there, you know."

"I'll bring the baby to visit when it's three months old." Penelope's voice was faintly coaxing.

"You promise?"

"I promise."

232

"I don't want to cause you trouble, baby. I just get lonely."

"I'll write and visit you more often. But you must understand that you can't come to me. I must come to you."

Mrs. Benton nodded, avoiding Penelope's eyes.

"Do you have enough money?"

"Yes."

"I can give you some."

"No, not now."

Mrs. Benton got to her feet. "I'll go now." Her eyes met Penelope's. "Somehow, you're better at a distance. I had to learn that."

"I'm sorry."

"Thank you, I'm sure."

Penelope crossed the room and placed a dry kiss awkwardly on her mother's cheek. "Good-bye, Mom. I'll bring the baby to Bloomington."

Mrs. Benton turned away to the door. "I don't understand you," she said in a flat voice. "I swear to God I don't."

Mr. and Mrs. Moss stood at the door of Foxhall House looking with anticipation down the driveway to Foxhall Road. "She ought to be here any minute," Mrs. Moss said. "She called from the airport twenty minutes ago."

"I don't see why she didn't have the child right here, like other folks would," Mr. Moss said. "Running off for six months. It sure seems silly to me."

"It's not silly at all. She's a society woman and very well known. She wanted to have the child in peace. Besides, maybe she didn't want folks to see her swollen figure."

"That's pretty old fashioned talk."

"Maybe it is, but Mrs. Penelope Winston is a pretty prideful woman, or hadn't you noticed?"

"I notice just as much as you. I also notice Mr. Winston hasn't much to say. He wasn't even there when this baby was birthed and no one has even told him she's coming home."

"You notice too much." Mrs. Moss straightened her dress. "Here they come now! My! Isn't this exciting! It's a boy, you know. She told me on the telephone."

"I know. I was listening on the telephone extension."

The dark blue limousine rolled over the beige gravel of the driveway and came to a halt before them. Penelope emerged smiling and after a glance of greeting in their direction reached back into the car, taking a bundle of blue blankets in her arms. "Here he is," she announced proudly. "Richard Perry Winston, Jr."

Mr. and Mrs. Moss peered into the bundle and saw the pink face of a sleeping baby. "My!" Mrs. Moss said, "Isn't he handsome! Why I can see a lot of Mr. Winston in him, and you, too, ma'am," she added hastily.

"He favors you, ma'am," Mr. Moss said positively.

"Thank you both," Penelope answered smiling. "I suppose he favors both his mother and his father." A neat, efficient looking woman in her middle thirties got out of the car and joined them. "This is Miss Lucy Kerry. She is joining us as a governess for Dick, Jr. She will have the room next to the nursery. Lucy, this is Mr. and Mrs. Moss who take such good care of me."

"I'm delighted," Miss Kerry said with a slight Irish accent. "I'm sure we'll get on."

Penelope handed the baby to Miss Kerry. "Mrs. Moss will show you up, Lucy. I must freshen up and make a few telephone calls. Where is Mr. Winston?"

"He's playing golf at Chevy Chase. He didn't know you were coming when he left."

"That's all right. We'll surprise him when he returns. The baby may be awake then." She giggled. "He has the bluest eyes. Wait until you see them!"

❦ 20 ❧

HERMAN BAUR smiled at Penelope as she entered his high ceilinged office in the Old Senate Office Building through a series of connecting outer offices filled with the cluttered desks of members of his staff. For a brief moment she had been reminded as she passed of the months she had spent at a small table in a corner of Dave Winslow's office during Congressman Frome's campaign for the presidency. The earnest, intense secretaries had glanced up at her with shy, but inquisitive smiles as she passed, noting the casual elegance of her pale blue suit and the subtly contrasting effect of the long gloves in a soft leather the color of rich cream. They had been brushed by the light scent of the perfume made especially for her in Paris and the atmosphere of a wider, richer world which swept with her through the crowded offices. The brief memories of the past brought an unexpected sense of depression and Penelope instinctively shrugged them away. Had she once really found this environment exciting? Even romantic?

"Penny, dear," Senator Baur said, rising from the tuffed, high backed Victorian chair of dull black leather in' which he sat to walk around a huge, heavily carved desk toward her. "How nice to see you. We all have missed you while you have been gone." He gave her a courtly kiss on the cheek and holding both of her hands in his stood away from her at arms

235

length and beamed. "Why is it you always look so alive? So full of happy anticipation? Is it because you are a new mother?"

Penelope laughed up into the heavily lined face, now transformed into ridges, folds, and hollows by an unaccustomed broad smile. "I'm just hungry, Senator, and I'm eagerly waiting for lunch."

"And that you shall have." Herman Baur glanced at an old pendulum clock in a plain rectangular walnut case standing on the blue veined marble of the mantel of a fireplace. "It's high noon. Let's go over now."

They walked down the cavernous hallway outside his office, brightened by the reds, blues, greens, and yellows of secretaries' extended umbrellas, to the elevator marked "Senators Only." "The umbrellas look gay," Penelope said. "I always remember them filling the hallways on a stormy day."

"Strange custom," Herman Baur said, pushing the elevator button with the same incisive poke of his index finger he used in Senate debates. "Is it still raining outside?"

"No. It's clearing and windy."

They descended in the elevator and followed a sign which read, "Subway."

"I love to ride on this little subway," Penelope said taking his arm with a hug. They climbed into the waiting open car with its four hard bench seats and soon were moving rapidly along through the well lighted tunnel leading to the Capitol.

"It saves time and is a great boon to old goats like me," Herman Baur glanced sidewise at her with a little smile. "I've never understood why the House hasn't built a proper one."

"The one to the Rayburn building is terribly short."

"Your bottom no more than hits the seat until it's time to get off. They still have to go shanks mare most of the way and some of those fossils over there are twenty years older than I am."

"Senator," Penelope said in mock reproof, "If you keep pretending you are an old man, I'll stop dating you. After all,

236

I have to keep Dick jealous."

Herman Baur gave a gruff chuckle. "All right, Penny, I'll watch my p's and q's."

They stopped and greeted several Senators and members of the Senate staff in the hallways leading from the subway to the Senate restaurant. A smiling white jacketed black waiter took them to the table for two against the far wall which Herman Baur had reserved. As she removed her gloves, Penelope looked out over the spacious room with the steamboat Gothic crystal chandeliers hanging from the high ceiling, the heavy green draperies masking a row of majestic windows framed in limestone, and the tables surrounded by sturdy walnut armchairs with soft green velvet seats. "I'm always so flattered to be invited here. It's very impressive."

Herman Baur grinned. "That's the idea, for the folks from home. I'm surprised we can still impress you, Penny. You know too much about us."

"I'm very impressed," she repeated with a smile.

"What would you like to order?"

"I wouldn't miss the navy bean soup for the world. And, I'll have a chef's salad."

"Good. I'll have the soup and the braised beef. I need a little more than fancy grass to get through the afternoon."

They were frequently interrupted as they ate by Senators dropping by to say a few words of greeting. "It pays to eat lunch with the Lion of the Senate," Penelope smiled impishly. "You meet more people and shine in reflected glory."

"It's not quite like this every day," Herman Baur growled. "I think you are the attraction."

He carefully lit a cigar as their coffee was poured. "Well I'm too old and you're too smart for sweet talk. Let's get down to cases. I really appreciate your efforts with Mrs. Payson this last year. She's doing much better. I don't expect her to change, but she's at least looking now before she puts her foot down."

"I'm trying, dear. Part of her trouble was that she was just plain scared. Some people try to put up a front when they are scared. Unfortunately, Alice's front is what she thinks is blunt, frank, smart talk."

"I don't know what it is, but smart, it ain't." He drew on his cigar. "According to the newspapers you've become close pals."

"I've taken her through the Washington scene with a word to the wise at critical points. She and her husband seem to appreciate it. I think that you are underestimating her. She's really quite a unique and genuine person."

"I didn't say she wasn't unique or genuine. I said that she was a kook."

"Well, don't worry, dear. She isn't going to rock the boat. She's mastering the art of silence and a few pat phrases like, 'How well you put that' and 'I'll have to think that one over,' in short, the art of being non-committal."

"If she masters that, I'll be much obliged."

Penelope's eyes sought his. "You were just awful sweet to come to some of my Sunday evenings at home."

"I enjoyed it," Herman Baur said gruffly. "If I hadn't, I wouldn't have come back."

"Now that I've returned to Washington again, I'm going to reorganize my Sunday evenings a bit. I want more men like you to come, men with power."

His eyes twinkled. "Power, eh? Why?"

"Every Sunday night for over two years I entertained. Originally, the idea was that of my boss on the newspaper, Marc Haywood. He thought it would add prestige to my column. His idea was to invite amusing people with high visibility."

"Penelope's Zoo," Herman Baur said without a smile. "Haywood's a good promoter."

"That's what it came to be called," Penelope dropped her eyes modestly. "But before I left to have my child it had gotten into a rut. It was a bit of a bore."

"Well, as I say, I've enjoyed it the few times I was there,

different breed of cat than I ordinarily talk with."

"I think those who came enjoyed it. I'm talking about the hostess. At first, the whole idea scared me to death and I'd stand around on the sidelines worrying about all of the details, food, liquor, ash trays. If there was one moment of silence my heart would sink. I'd think people were silent because they were bored or incompatible. Marc participated at first and I left it all up to him. At the end of the evenings I had the jitters and a splitting headache."

"Why didn't you drop it?"

"It was the boss's idea." Penelope waited while the waiter refilled their cups. "After a time, Marc faded out and I had to participate more. I began to get involved in the discussions. It was exhilarating. Ideas flew all over the place, civil rights, the quality and quantity of education, the nature of crime, the concept of justice, the problems of urban civilization, foreign policy—you name it, we had it. I began to have the illusion that I was in the center of things."

Herman Baur eyed her through the smoke of his cigar. "When did you begin to realize that it was an illusion?"

"When nothing happened."

There was a sage nod from across the table. "Exactly."

"We talked and talked, but it began to remind me of my seminars at college. We were pure soldiers for right and justice and we would not compromise one ideal or one objective in that fight. We argued passionately and maintained our purity to the end. Our deeply moved professor gave us an A and we all went home for spring recess. I expected more in Washington."

"I see. You were disillusioned. Then what?"

"While I was away I began to wonder if it weren't a waste of time to spend every Sunday evening talking about what should be, or of what might have been, or of what was, however brilliant the talk. I began to want to hear talk about what will be."

A long white ash dropped from the cigar. "That kind of

talk isn't as interesting, Penny. That kind of talk is earth-bound. It doesn't soar way up into that wild blue yonder." Senator Baur gestured with his cigar. "That kind of talk is laconic and when it isn't laconic, it's banal. Sometimes it isn't the talk that counts, it's the long silences over bourbon and branch water. Sometimes it isn't the words, it's the pursed lips, the drooping eyelid, the amused snort or the hearty laugh. You have to know how to read these signs."

Penelope's eyes sparkled. "That's what I mean. That's what I want at my Sunday evenings."

"In your Zoo?"

Penelope gave an impatient shrug. "That's newspaper talk. You know I'm just a woman with a few good friends."

Herman Baur chuckled. "That could describe Du Barry."

Penelope looked hurt. "Now you're poking fun at me."

"No. I'm not poking fun. Don't underestimate yourself, Penny. I don't. I've been around too long. You are an instinctive seeker of power—no less because you are unaware of it."

Penelope's eyes dropped. "Somehow that doesn't sound quite nice," she said in a low voice.

"I'm an instinctive seeker of power, too, so let's don't worry about it."

Penelope raised her eyes to his quizzically.

"You can't function in Washington unless you understand power, Penny. That's what this town is all about. It is the simple art of making people do what you want them to do. You've been busy on that with me for some little time and I've been making you pay. I've been making you do what I want you to do." His eyes twinkled under his craggy brows. "Now, what are we talking about? What is it you want me to do?"

Penelope wet her upper lip with the tip of her tongue and looked earnestly across the table. "I want Senator Baur to persuade Senator Green, Representative Davies, and Representative Waverly to come to my Sunday evenings when I resume them next week."

Herman Baur's face was as passive as if he were playing a poker hand. "That's the Chairman of the Senate Finance Committee, the Chairman of the House Ways and Means Committee and the Chairman of the House Rules Committee. What about the Senate's Majority Leader, the Speaker of the House, and the Majority Whip? What about the minority party?"

"I don't want to be obvious. No one will come."

Herman Baur began a deep, heaving chuckle. His cigar ash fell on his vest front and his face became purple as the eruption progressed. He continued, oblivious to Penelope's anxious and embarrassed regard, until tears rolled down his weathered cheeks. Several diners in the room looked at him in amazement as his amusement slowly subsided and he sipped a glass of water and vigorously blew his nose. "That's the best laugh I've had in years. You've added ten years to my life."

"Are you all right?"

Herman Baur nodded. He wiped his eyes. "I say only a fellow Hoosier could think of that. We are born to politics, Penny." He peered at her. "You've left out one name, Senator George Wysong, and we shouldn't ignore the minority members . . . you can't use power unless you can push against something."

A radiant smile spread across Penelope's face. "You mean you'll do it?"

Herman Baur nodded. "It's a nice place for a Sunday evening. I'll recommend it, especially the smoked turkey."

"Oh, my gosh! I could kiss you, Senator! You are the dearest man."

Herman Baur fussed with his cigar. "I'll make you pay. Never fear," he said gruffly. "It's no favor. I think a nice cozy place to talk things over might be useful, especially with a good looking, discreet gal to furnish the bourbon."

"I'm so *proud*. I really am."

Herman Baur touched a match to his cigar to relight it and eyed her over the flame. "Is Haywood coming?"

"He's always felt that he could come when he wished."

"He's a promoter. He's promoted himself into the Senate as a 'fighting liberal,' whatever that means. He seems rather forward for a freshman Senator. He's been up here less than sixty days and he's already challenged the leadership twice. He's even introduced a bill, for God's sake."

"I can't tell him that he's unwelcome. He's still my boss."

Baur drew on his cigar meditatively with hooded eyes. "Perhaps he will yield to reason in a private environment away from the Senate. He's got to learn that he can't preach from the Senate floor the way he has preached from his editorial columns."

"You won't stay away on his account?" Penelope asked anxiously.

Baur's eyes caught hers. "I never abandon the field, Penny. That's my first precept."

Eight men sat silently in a semi-circle of easy chairs around the fire at Foxhall House. The only sounds were the crackling of the oak logs behind the massive limestone mantel and the scratching sweep of a magnolia tree's limb as the gusts of raw March wind flung it back and forth against a nearby window. Herman Baur puffed slowly on his cigar. "I'm agin' it, Senator," he said after an interval.

"Why?" Marc Haywood challenged. "You have agreed that it is economically sound and the right kind of program to solve the problem. Why take an obstructionist position?"

Baur's face remained impassive, "Don't confront me with labels, Marc. That isn't going to help. I'm agin' it because there aren't enough votes to pass it—in either house. There weren't in the last Congress and there won't be in this Congress."

"Aren't you putting the cart before the horse, to use one of your favorite clichés? Don't we decide upon the program, frame the legislation, and then rustle up the votes?"

"Not where I went to school," Herman Baur said easily. "We count the votes first."

Haywood looked at Baur with an expression that fell only slightly short of patronizing disgust. "You call that leadership?"

Baur drew on his cigar imperturbably. "I don't call it anything. It's the way the system works. This is a great, restless, growing continental empire with scores of major interests in conflict and hundreds, even thousands, of minor interests in conflict. We're a democracy, for the lack of a better name. That means that you can't make anybody for very long do anything against what he conceives to be his self interests. You can confuse him for a time, you can appeal to the emotion of self-denial for a time with patriotic or religious appeals, but you always come back to the bedrock for the long pull, his self interest; you govern by putting enough of those self interests together to make a voting bloc and you put enough voting blocs together to make a majority. With the majority you pass legislation. I've been counting heads on this bill of yours and you haven't got the votes, so I'm agin' it."

"But, Herman, God damn it, I don't have the votes because you won't support it!"

Baur's grin was saturnine. "Thank you, Marc, for the compliment, but I don't carry votes around in my trouser pockets. I have some influence in the Senate because I can count votes. After twenty-four years in the Senate I have some feeling for what will go and for what won't. If I started acting like I control more than one of the two Senate votes from Indiana my Senate colleagues would cut me down in a hurry."

"Now you're being cute," Haywood said in disgust.

Congressman Davies, the Chairman of the House Rules Committee, accepted a bourbon over ice from Penelope. "Thank you, sweetheart." He turned to Haywood. "Herman's right. You haven't got the votes in the House either. It won't get out of Committee and onto the floor."

"You have it bottled up," Haywood said accusingly.

Congressman Davies slowly shook his head and rubbed a forefinger under his prominent nose in a characteristic gesture. "It isn't bottled up. It hasn't got enough political horsepower to move."

"Let it get to the floor in both houses. Let the people speak," Haywood challenged. "If the leadership stops obstructing it, it will pass and President Frome has said that he'll sign it when it reaches his desk."

Davies gave a dry chuckle. " 'When it reaches his desk,' is the qualifier. The President isn't taking much of a chance and he knows it. He pleases those who are for the bill and since he knows it won't pass the Congress he knows he'll never have to offend those who are against it."

"I don't believe the President is that much of a cynic!"

"He's a damned fine politician," Davies said calmly.

"But he supported something very similar in his State of the Union Message last January."

Davies made a little gesture of dismissal. "The State of the Union message is a mosaic of platitudes, serious proposals, and pious hopes. Your project was a pious hope."

Haywood turned to Penelope who was sitting on a sofa, her legs drawn up under her listening to the conversation with shining eyes. "What do you think of this talk, Penny? Isn't it disillusioning? If the public heard it, they would retch and then revolt."

"I think it's fascinating," Penelope said in a low voice.

Herman Baur's voice was hard. "Maybe we've been too polite with you, Senator. You're beginning to demagogue it a bit. Why in hell do you think you're the repository of the people's conscience? Where do you get your pipeline to God, your revelation of the ultimate truth? You hammered it up a bit in Virginia and won your seat. Fair enough. We are all hams, but the applause has gone to your head. You have confused your constituency with the news media. You're too well known nationally for your own good. You're still a freshman Senator, remember that. You still have to get re-elected, and let an old political in-fighter tell you something, it's the people of your state that will re-elect you, not the newspaper or television commentators or the editors of ladies fashion magazines, or even your Negro pal and his *Cutting Edge*. The people of your state will re-elect you if you have been tuned in to what they want."

"They need this reform legislation. The nation needs it."

"They may need it, but they don't want it. You'd better check at home."

"Don't try to interpret the people of Virginia to me. I live there. They've just elected me to the Senate."

"I don't need to. Check at home. We want you back for a second term. We don't want you to be a one term wonder."

Haywood glared into the fire. "Oh, to hell with it. You'll never understand." He took a sip of his drink and munched nervously on a handful of peanuts he had scooped up from a dish on a table before him. "The people need leadership. They don't always know what they want. Forward looking leadership anticipates the future and prepares for it."

Herman Baur leaned quickly forward and punched Haywood's knee with a boney forefinger, "Oh, so we've come to that, have we? The people need to be given what they need whether they've asked for it or not? What are we 'leaders' supposed to do? Sit around in Washington and decide what we think is desirable and ram it down their throats? Do we try to condition them with such an avalanche of government propaganda that they react in a favorable Pavlovian way to what we've decided they should have? And if they don't react properly, should we put a few criminal penalties in the law to assure that they accept it? Just a little duress to take over where the persuasion broke down?"

"You overstate the case." Haywood's voice was exasperated.

"Really? I don't think so. You have just dismissed us as a group of old political fossils, unresponsive to the public will, and, strangely enough, the public will happens to be what you want it to be. Now I'm leveling with you, Marc, in these pleasant off-the-precincts surroundings Penny provides. As a politician you're still wet behind the ears. You're committing the arrogantly dangerous mistake of confusing your ideas with those of your constituents. What's worse, you don't think that there should be any difference and that if there is, your views should prevail. With that attitude, you don't belong in the Congress. You ought to go back to your newspaper, or serve on a Presidential Commission, or go up to the Brookings Institution. Those are the places where ideas should gestate; those are the places to dream of the perfect society. I don't minimize that kind of dreaming—someday the American people may buy part of it, but it is in the Congress of the United States that they decide what they will buy and it is the high function of the 535 Senators and Representatives to decide what they will buy. That's the essence of democracy.

"If a legislator can pass a law that people will accept, that's self-enforcing, then he's done his job. To accomplish that he has to develop that special rapport with his constituency, that sensitive judgment that enables him to represent them. He has to judge the validity of all the pressures put upon him from all sources, high and low, respectable and unrespectable, interested and disinterested and come out with a position that also takes into account his own beliefs and intellectual intregrity. It's one of the hardest responsibilities in the world to discharge and there have been damn few countries, past or present, where we got the chance. It's too important a function to prostitute by propaganda and it's too precious to endanger by the totalitarian doctrine that the 'leader' knows best.

"So when someone comes up with a good idea, Senator, and I do think you have a good idea, and I say 'we haven't got the votes,' I'm not being faint hearted or uninterested. I'm saying that the people aren't ready for it. It won't be the kind of accepted, self-enforcing law we have to have in a democracy. I'm saying, Senator, be patient, make your case with the people and when the Haywood bill is finally passed and some President signs it into law, it will be a legislative monument. It will be accepted and it will last."

Haywood munched silently for a time on the peanuts. He cleared his throat. "Well, you have some points there, Herman. I'll think them over. I'm not going to abandon this fight, but I understand the position of the leadership a little better now." He got up. "Time to go." He looked down at Herman Baur. "I've never heard you talk more eloquently, Senator. You have a reputation of being taciturn."

"I speak out when there's a reason for it," Herman Baur growled. "Maybe I think you're worth it."

An easy, companionable silence fell over the group after Haywood had left. "He's a good man," Congressman Waverly said.

"Yes, he is," Herman Baur agreed. "Like all new Senators without previous experience in the House or a State legislature, he tends to minimize the legislative process, but maybe he'll learn. If I didn't think there was a chance of that I wouldn't waste time on him. Of course, as a freshman, he shouldn't have been brash enough to introduce a major bill. He expects too much of it. For years, he's sat in that newspaper empire of his and favored us with Olympian judgments on our works. Now he has descended among us and must deal with the nitty-gritty, answer roll call votes on the issues. We'll find out what kind of a man he is when he's gone through the fire."

Senator Green cleared his throat. "Right now, he's acting like a phony. It elected him, but I'm not impressed. What committee is he on, Herman?"

"Foreign Affairs."

"Well that can't do any harm. It's a good place for the broad brush boys."

Penelope hugged her knees and giggled.

"Was it that funny?" Green asked.

"It's just that I know how exacting he was on the *Tribune*," Penelope answered. "It's amusing to hear him described that way."

❧ 21 ❧

IT had been a hot, humid June day, but a breeze had sprung up in the late afternoon and, with decreasing humidity, it became quite pleasant. Penelope sat on the flagstone terrace overlooking the garden waiting for the first members of the Zoo to arrive. Mrs. Moss stepped onto the terrace and called her to the telephone. It was Senator Herman Baur.

"Don't tell me we won't see you today, Herman," she said as soon as she heard his voice.

"No. I'm coming and I have a pleasant surprise for you. The President is coming with me." Penelope's involuntary intake of breath was audible over the telephone. "I just wanted to be certain that he would be in congenial company."

Her voice was a note higher with excitement. "How wonderful! I'm thrilled and honored. It will be the first time he has been in my house. It will be all right. We will only have part of the Zoo. Let me see, Congresswoman Mays, Justice Bronton, Congressman Waverly, Senator Green, Senator Payson, Congressman Davies, oh," she interrupted herself with a little laugh, "I'm flustered, Herman. This is a surprise." She put a hand to her hair absently. "No one else is coming."

"That's all right then. The Secret Service detail will arrive in about twenty minutes. They'll crawl all over the place, I'm afraid. It's according to the drill. They'll telephone the White

House and we'll come along at once. We should be there within the hour."

"I'll be waiting." Penelope placed the telephone back in its cradle and looked about her with shining eyes. Was there anything to do? She could think of nothing. Mrs. Moss had prepared for the Zoo for years and there were no details unattended. She went into the parlor and brought an inscribed picture of the President into the salon. She stood with it a moment and then placed it on a table in the corner where it could not be seen on entering the room but could not be overlooked after remaining in the room a few minutes or in passing through it to the terrace.

She glanced down at the simple blue frock she was wearing and decided to change to a yellow shirtwaist dress with white piping. President Frome had once complimented her on a yellow dress she had worn when she was on the White House staff and she remembered that Mrs. Frome often wore yellow. She hurried into the kitchen, informed Mr. and Mrs. Moss to expect the arrival of the Secret Service men, and hurried up the backstairs to her dressingroom. After she had slipped on the dress, she examined herself critically in the mirror. The color brought out the red tints in her hair. She removed her lipstick and applied a slightly paler color. She dusted her face lightly with a powder designed for her pale translucent skin and then touched her face lightly with a piece of cleaning tissue. The freckles across the bridge of her nose and a sprinkle on one cheek again became visible. The President had once joshed her about her freckles. She put a simple topaz ring on her right hand. With her wedding band and a short, single strand of pearls, it was all of the jewelry she would wear. Her eye makeup was unnoticeable. Elizabeth Arden had recommended only a thin line of mascara to emphasize the blueness of her eyes. With her long lashes and the natural blueness of the skin under the eyes, this was enough. After one last glance she hurried back downstairs.

When the members of the Zoo began to arrive she sup-

250

pressed her excitement and greeted them with her usual casualness. She did not mention the President.

William Payson rocked back and forth on his heels, looking out across the sweep of green lawn from the terrace. "There seem to be several plainclothesmen about, Penny. I noticed two by the gate down at Foxhall Road and there is one on the other side of that boxwood hedge. I hope you haven't been robbed?"

"No. Nothing like that." Penelope smiled at him, her eyes bright and sparkling.

"I see," William Payson said non-committally and did not pursue the subject, but the others had heard the question and the evasive answer and began to sense the air of expectation in Penelope's manner. Conversation started, faltered, and died.

"Where is Herman?" Congressman Davies asked. "He's proud of always being a first arrival any place. Is he coming?"

"Yes. He'll be here shortly." Penelope turned about on the cushion of the wrought iron lawn chair on which she had been sitting as Mrs. Moss whispered in her ear, "He's here, Mrs. Winston. They're passing the gate now."

"Thank you." Penelope arose and left the others on the terrace with an enigmatic smile. She was standing just inside the open front door when the black presidential limousine drew up with a crunch of gravel. The President emerged, glanced up toward the eaves of the house in a characteristic manner and then dropped his eyes to Penelope's as she emerged from the doorway, both hands extended in greeting, "Mr. President," she said. "How delighted I am that you have come with Senator Baur."

Charles Frome's face crinkled into a smile and he bestowed a kiss on the cheek turned slightly toward him. "Penny, you're as bright as ever."

"You remember!" Penelope said, giving him a little hug. She moved past him to Herman Baur and kissed him on the cheek. "You old dear," she said, "What an inspired idea to bring the President!"

"Well, we were talking shop at the White House. The President's family is at Camp David and he was going to eat alone in that mausoleum so I suggested that he join us here."

"And, I was curious, Penny," Charles Frome said smiling. "I wanted to learn what the magic of Penelope's Zoo is. Herman Baur is a cantankerous, anti-social old bachelor and you've charmed him away from the Sheraton-Park nearly every Sunday evening for months. How do you do it?"

"Come in and see, Mr. President."

They walked down the hall to the salon. Charles Frome stopped as they entered, surveying the graceful, sunlit room, filled with summer flowers, and the small group on the terrace beyond, respectfully standing, waiting for him to greet them. "A lovely room," he said. He started for the terrace and then noticed his picture on the table in the corner.

"I was a little trimmer and considerably more innocent then," he said, picking it up. "That was taken for my first campaign." He turned to her. "Those were the exciting days, Penny, and you were there."

"The best days of my life."

Charles Frome laughed. "You're too young and too pretty to say that, or to believe it, but thanks. Let's see, what did I write on this picture?" He peered at it closely, unwilling to put on his reading glasses. " 'To Penelope Benton, a staunch fellow warrior.' " He grimaced. "Now you'd think I could do better than that."

"It's my most valued possession, Mr. President."

"I'll send you another. An older face, but a more original sentiment."

Charles Frome walked out onto the terrace and greeted the others. He then dropped into a chaise.

"This is relaxing time, Mr. President," Herman Baur said. "We don't sit around in this heat like boiled owls. Loosen your tie and take off your coat."

Charles Frome smiled at Penelope. "You don't mind?"

"Heavens no! Herman is right. Mrs. Mays and I have on light summer dresses. Why should you men be uncomfortable?"

Charles Frome removed his tie and coat and accepted a tall scotch and soda from a tray. He gave an involuntary little sigh as he looked out over the lawn. He said nothing, but gradually some of the lines of strain in his face softened. No one interrupted the silence. "I see what you meant, Herman," he said at last. "No one but friends can sit together in a compatible silence. It's wonderful."

"It's the thing you need most, Mr. President."

"I know." He gazed out again over the lawn. "Is that a volley ball net down there at the end of the yard?"

"Yes," Penelope answered.

"Do you have a ball?"

"Sure."

"Good. We're in business. Let's get up a game."

"I'll be scorekeeper," Herman Baur said hurriedly. "I'm not going to drop dead in the middle of Penny's lawn—not even for the President of the United States."

An hour later, Dick Winston, returning from his Sunday round of golf at the Chevy Chase Club, stepped out on the terrace and looked smilingly down at the shouting group playing volley ball. He turned to Mr. Moss as he crossed the terrace carrying a tray full of empty glasses. "What happened to the egghead discussion group and why all the Humphrey Bogart types outside? If my name hadn't been on my golf balls I don't think they would have let me in."

"The President's here, Mr. Winston."

"The President of what?"

"The President of the United States."

Dick Winston stared down into the garden. "Imagine that, and Mama couldn't stand him."

The President dropped in at Foxhall House three more times during the course of the hot summer on Sunday when he had been forced by events to remain in Washington over the weekend. His visits were unannounced and unreported in the press. They were informal interludes of shirt sleeve relaxation. On a humid, overcast August afternoon he turned to Penelope with a smile. "I'm becoming a repeater. Does this make me a member of the Zoo?"

"Oh, Mr. President! I wouldn't be so presumptuous as to include you in anything of the sort. You're always welcome. I'm just so pleased that you find my house relaxing and pleasant enough to revisit."

"You take me on my own terms. You don't ask anything of me and you don't fuss over me. That's a rare quality to find in a hostess. Especially if you're President of the United States."

"It must be a terrible burden," she murmured.

"Not unbearable. I sought it. I'll miss it when it's gone." He lit a cigarette and looked out across the garden to a small grove of crepe myrtles hung heavily in bloom. "The hard part, Penny, is that you can't put the burden down, even for a moment. It's there day and night. That's why an hour or so in your garden among people with whom I can relax means so much to me." He lightly touched her cheek and chin with his cupped hand. "I thank you for it."

She met his eyes. "It's my privilege, sir."

"There are certain people we treasure when we are at the apex of politics, Penny. I've discussed this with a few of the men who have shared the problem, our living former Presidents and one or two heads of other states where I have a personal relationship of sorts. The people we treasure are those that can act natural around us, make no demands, and make us laugh. There are days, we all agreed, when one feels overwhelmed by humanity, the drives and ambitions of billions of the living, the memories and traditions left us by billions of the dead, the consideration that must be given to bil-

254

lions of the unborn. People, past, present, and future are with me all of the time. Not as individuals, but as a huge mass with gabbling spokesmen for every conceivable interest or point of view."

"I didn't realize it was that bad, Mr. President."

"Oh, it's not so bad. I've learned to live with it. It's surprising how quickly one can accept the role of a superman and, on some days, at least delude oneself that one is playing it rather well."

"Sixty percent of the people agree that you do it rather well, according to the latest poll."

"Fifty-nine point three percent to be exact," Charles Frome grinned. "I read them all, you know." He pushed out his cigarette in a ceramic ash tray on a glass topped table. "Do you know why I came that first Sunday last June?"

"Because Herman Baur asked you to?"

"No. And not because of your famous hospitality. I came because I always thought of you as having fun, getting a kick out of life, smiling, a sort of impish smile sometimes. I decided I needed a little bit of that. I'm glad you haven't changed. It's more important than all of this." He waved his hand to encompass the house and grounds.

Penelope felt herself coloring, but she continued to look into the President's steady, brown eyes. "I'd rather hear you say that than to receive the medal of honor."

"Someday we may think of something appropriate." He studied her for a moment. "I don't believe you have ever received a formal invitation to the White House?"

"No. I've only seen it from the working level."

"We'll correct that. In September, when the social season begins, we'll include you and your husband in some amusing function."

"That would be lovely."

"Not as much fun as your Sundays, but if you don't do it too often it has its points."

"Dick and I will be thrilled."

"He's a builder, isn't he?"

"Yes. He's building a new town out beyond Frederick. It's named Heitzing after his maternal grandfather."

"Yes, I've heard of it. Is he making money at it?"

"Not yet. That comes later."

"Good." The President looked about. "I've never met him, you know."

"He's playing golf. He never attends my Zoo. We have our separate interests. Washington life is a bore to him. With me it is a passion and my career."

"Very few passions can be shared."

"I've learned that."

"I'll look forward to meeting him at the White House," the President said. He looked over to the group sitting at some distance on the terrace. "I wonder if I could get up a volley ball game from among that over-indulged group?"

The Winston's limousine swung off Executive Drive, stopped briefly at the open massive iron gates where the pass included with their invitation was inspected, and moved slowly up the narrow, curving driveway to the south door of the White House. Penelope emerged from the limousine dressed in an ankle length empire style white satin gown, a mink cape across her shoulders. Dick Winston followed in white tie but hatless. An attendant helped Penelope to the door leading directly into the large oval of the diplomatic reception room with its scenic wallpaper depicting in shades of gold and green views of an earlier America. A young White House aide smiled at her and nodded at Dick Winston. "Good evening, Mr. and Mrs. Winston," he said, identifying her from newspaper pictures and television appearances, "Please pass into the passageway. The guests are gathering in the East Room. A young lady will escort you there." His smile broadened. "I don't imagine that we have to guide *you* about the White House, Mrs. Winston."

"What I knew started from the West Wing and the Press

256

Room. I'd get lost in a hurry down here," Penelope answered.

Most of the hundred guests for the state dinner for the President of the Ivory Coast had arrived and were gathered in an irregular and informal semi circle just inside the door when Penelope and Dick entered the huge East Room. There was an air both of expectancy and unease among the guests. The conversational murmur was low, even subdued. "It's going to be a real fun evening," Dick murmured in her ear. "This is the kind of room where you could stage a basketball game in periwigs."

Penelope laughed in spite of herself. "Dick, now stop it!" They moved into the crowd. Ambassador Piccard joined them, kissing Penelope's hand.

"I'm so glad to see a familiar face," he said. "I have been included because the Ivory Coast was lately French territory, but who are these other people?"

"We'll learn that from the guest list in tomorrow's newspaper," Penelope said. "Other than the West African section of the State Department, they are probably from out of town."

Piccard sighed. "I am relieved. If you don't recognize them either, they can't be important. For one horrible moment I thought that the Ambassador of France after twelve years in this capital, was friendless."

A pianist had appeared at the great mahogany piano at one end of the room which was supported by three huge gilt eagles with folded wings, and began to play a series of light musical comedy airs.

"Well, hi!" It was Alice Payson.

"Madam," Piccard said with subdued enthusiasm. He bent over her hand.

Alice Payson giggled. "I can never get used to that." She looked down the great salon, its waxed parquet floors gleaming from the light of the great chandeliers. "Get a look at the eagles on the piano," she said. "There are gold eagles everywhere. I didn't know we were so imperial."

Piccard smiled. "Americans were less self-conscious when they were less powerful."

"Where's Senator Bill?" Dick Winston asked.

"Coming. He had to get the last word in on a crummy little bill on meat inspection on the Hill tonight. He'll just beat the ruffles and flourishes. I've warned him. Someday he'll get tossed out on his ear. I never could stand people who come in late to dinner."

Penelope looked over her shoulder. "I see Senator Haywood over there by the fireplace admiring the portrait of Martha Washington. Virginians stick together."

"Not always," Dick Winston reminded her.

Penelope gave a temporary farewell with a quick smile and walked over to Haywood. "Hello, Marc."

He turned to her. "I was wondering how I'd get you away from that insufferable husband of yours."

"He asked to be remembered to you, too."

"I hear he's building a noxious little swarm of sub-standard houses out in the red clay belt."

"You look like the Senate agrees with you."

He smiled for the first time. "Your usual good taste. Why should we discuss Dick Winston when we can discuss me?"

"We see less and less of you at the newspaper."

"Don't tell me you miss me?"

"Frankly, yes." Her eyes met his. "I always miss you, Marc."

He was momentarily serious. "That's very kind and much appreciated." A wry grin touched his face. "However, the *Tribune* has a good editor, an avaricious managing committee, and the nation's top columnist. It can do with less of its publisher. Besides, I find, somewhat to my surprise, that being a Senator is a full time job. You have no idea how many hands I have to hold. I can't figure out if I'm a messenger boy or an oracle."

"How is Claudia? I don't see her here."

"Claudia is disenchanted."

"Oh?"

"She disapproves of me."

"Be serious."

"I am serious. After I filed for the Senate, I discovered that she didn't merely disapprove, she actually hated politics. She can't stand the corduroy, peanut butter, and beer side of people. So, to use a favorite phrase of my administrative assistant, she copped out."

Penelope stared at him.

"She's divorcing me."

Penelope felt the icy chill of shock. Her face muscles became stiff and she could not speak. After a long pause she said, "She's a fool, and she has lousy timing."

He squeezed Penelope's hand and looked deeply into her eyes. "I've thought that too. I also thought that she was a better sport. She refused to attend political rallies. She wouldn't receive political visitors. She wouldn't be photographed. She also detests my liberal views."

"Doesn't she know it's a game?"

"No. And I'm not sure that it is. After years as a scoffing critic I'm beginning to feel something."

"Good heavens! You are changing," her voice was now under partial control, affectionately mocking.

"You have to commit yourself to something, Penny. I'm in politics now. I can't just be an observer or a reporter."

"I'm sorry you don't attend the Zoo anymore, Marc. I see very little of you."

"I can't endure Herman Baur's efforts to educate me in the ways of the Senate. I intend to go my own way."

"You could drop by some other time."

"I might run into Dick."

"That's childish, you know."

"Perhaps. That's the way I feel."

"I guess I'll have to come to you."

He looked at her solemnly and then made a little depreciating gesture. "How is your young son?"

259

Penelope's eyes dropped to the floor. "He's doing beautifully. He's learning to crawl about now. Miss Kerry has to keep a sharp eye on him."

"I hope he resembles his mother."

"Enough. I think."

The Marine band in the mansion's great cross hall struck up ruffles and flourishes as President and Mrs. Frome with the President and First Lady of the Ivory Coast began to descend the main stairway from the yellow Oval Room on the floor above.

"Thank God!" Haywood said, relieved. "I wondered how long we had to wait. We still have to go through the receiving line."

"Goodbye, dear, take care," Penelope's eyes met his for a long moment, then she turned and rejoined her group.

The familiar figure of President Frome with a strikingly tall black woman in a gold gown on his arm appeared in the doorway of the East Room to a pattering of applause. Behind him, smiling broadly, a wide red ribbon slashing across his chest, was the President of the Ivory Coast with Mrs. Frome on his arm. The quartet moved to the south end of the room and formed a receiving line.

"How's ol' Marc?" Dick asked.

"Claudia's divorcing him." Penelope's voice was flat.

"I'm sorry to hear that. Why?"

"Politics."

Dick Winston smiled faintly and looked across the room at Haywood. "They say politics make strange bedfellows. There's nothing strange about Claudia."

During the rest of the evening in the receiving line and at dinner in the state diningroom around the great horseshoe table sparkling with the gold and green presidential china, the delicate crystal, and the gold urns that held great bouquets of chrysanthemums, asters, and daisies, she stole glances at Marc Haywood. Later, during the entertainment in the East Room, she convinced herself that he looked unhappy. She wondered

260

if he were as unhappy as she was. He would soon be free of Claudia, free to marry her, and she was married to Dick Winston. She could divorce Dick. He would have to give his assent to conceal his impotence, but would Marc marry her under such circumstances? Probably not. It would appear to be a scandal and Marc Haywood abhorred scandals. He would fear what it might do to his political career. A chilling, mortifying thought came to her. After two years of marriage she was still a virgin, how could she ever admit this to Marc? On their nuptial bed he would realize that her marriage to Dick had been a failure, her pregnancy and birth a fraud and deception. She couldn't face that humiliation, not with Marc. She looked across at him unhappily. He seemed more remote than ever, less obtainable yet she loved him and he would soon be free. A mood of desolation swept over her.

⚜ 22 ⚜

THE first chill of autumn was in the air. Penelope had worked on her column at a table on the terrace until the warm October sun had left it and she had begun to feel cold. The fire in the parlor before which she was now sitting, completing her proofreading, was welcome. She had felt an unaccustomed tenseness all day which she recognized as the way fatigue manifested itself in her. She could truthfully say that she was never physically tired, and rarely sleepy, but she did feel the rise of nervous tension when she was driving herself too hard. She decided that she had to get away for a week of rest. When she felt tense she had to carefully control her human relationships. If she were not watchful, she knew that then her wit became a little too sharp, her reactions too quick, the nervous tapping of her fingers obvious and disconcerting. She laid her column aside and sipped the tea Mrs. Moss had placed before her on a small pie crust table.

The door from the hallway opened. Dick Winston thrust his head in. "Am I interrupting? May I come in?"

In her present mood his diffident courtesy, interpreted as obsequiousness, annoyed her. "Of course. You're the master of the house. Why not?"

He shut the door behind him. "Mrs. Moss told me that you were working on the column. I didn't want to drive away an inspiration."

"You didn't. I'm doing a foul job."

"Nice fire," he said, moving toward it. "They say the temperature will take a real dip tonight." He stood with his back to her, looking into the flames.

She watched him for a moment. "Is there something on your mind?"

"Yes."

"Well, what is it? You're acting like a schoolboy."

He turned toward her. In the brightness of the fire's glow which accentuated the lines of his face, now serious and drawn, he suddenly looked old. "I'm in trouble with the Heitzing project," he said.

"It's not like you to worry about business. Is that all?"

"It's enough. I mean serious trouble."

She put down her cup and spoke sharply. "What do you mean? Now, Dick, don't exaggerate or dramatize. Just tell me what you mean."

He lit a cigarette and tossed the match into the fire with an underhand motion.

"Dick, what's gone wrong?"

"The Office of Education isn't going to relocate north of Frederick, after all."

There was an interval when the only sound was the crackling of the fire. "How bad is that?" She asked in a flat voice.

"Every cent I've got is in the pot. In addition, I've a fifty million dollar line of credit from a group of banks for construction. So far, I've drawn down around twenty-three million."

"You must have something for all of that money."

"Sure I do. I've got a hundred acre tract under development and twenty-three million dollars worth of half finished homes, mud roads, partially installed utilities, a dry lake, and a skeleton shopping center. I'm committed to every contractor and supplier in Maryland. I'm in hock to three banks for the construction loans. They're short term advances to cover me until I start selling units and the buyers arrange for long

263

term financing. When the banks hear the news, the money is going to dry up, there will be no further advances. With no cash flow from sales I won't be able to service the loans. It will become apparent that I'm over extended and the wolves will move in. The banks will sell off the assets at a few cents on the dollar. I'll have to file a bankruptcy petition." He spread his hands. " 'Pears that's about it."

"Did you put everything in it?" Penelope whispered.

"Yes. It looked like a sure thing. I thought I'd double my money in three years. It worked out that way on paper."

"No hedging?"

He shook his head with a rueful little smile. "I read somewhere that A.P. Giannini once said, 'Make up your mind and then back your judgment to the hilt.' I thought that was one tycoon talking from the grave to another. 'Pears I overlooked something."

"For one thing, you're not A.P. Giannini."

" 'Pears not."

"I have understood from you and from others that the plans to move the office to Frederick were firm."

"They are firm. But the move has been postponed, economy reasons. The General Accounting Office and the Bureau of the Budget see eye to eye. They were very considerate. They called me over to General Services Administration this afternoon and broke the news, since as they put it in the century's understatement, 'I have a special interest in their plans.' There will be a press release on it in seventy-two hours. Then the roof falls in on Winston Development Corporation."

"It will leak before that," Penelope said soberly. "Where information is concerned, this town is a great big sieve." She scowled into the fire. "You've been pretty stupid, Dick. Even school kids know the old saw about not putting all of your eggs in one basket."

" 'Pears so." The voice was almost inaudible.

She turned to him and addressed his profile. "Why didn't

264

you get some outside advice? Why didn't you tell me that you were risking everything?"

Dick Winston sighed. "I wanted to do it on my own. I wanted to show you what I could do. And ol' Marc and others," his voice trailed off.

Penelope got up and turned on a lamp in the corner. She walked over to the window and stood looking out at the firey, leafy manes of the maples and beeches, now turning into silhouettes in the rapidly fading light. She spoke aloud, but not to Dick Winston "You gave me this house. I have a few hundred thousand dollars invested. My income is growing from the column. We can keep up appearances. We'll cut down, but we'll keep up appearances."

He did not speak and a silence settled over the room.

"But that isn't the answer," Penelope continued, turning around into the room. "That would be a defeat. We'd be losers. It would be humiliating. We'd look like fools. Damn it, Dick, there's a fortune at stake here. We have to fight for it!"

" 'Pears so," he answered listlessly.

"Well, for Christ's sake, Dick," she burst out in white anger. "Are you just going to sit there on your, on your *ass?*"

He got up wordlessly and walked to the sideboard. He poured a third of a tumbler full of scotch and drank it down. He poured three fingers more into the glass and walked back to the fire, standing with his back to the flames. He grinned at her crookedly. "You're really beginning to get stirred up, aren't you? Money is at stake."

"Of course money is at stake, you silly fool! Ten million dollars of old money is at stake and millions of new money in profits as well. Even your Mama would fight bare knuckled for money like that. It's Winston money. To her that made it sacred."

"I'm the last of the Winstons," he said pensively, sipping the whiskey. "Mama had an heir. She looked at things differently."

265

"You have an heir," she reminded him.

"Not really. He's not mine. Ol' Kerry hardly lets me see him."

"That stuff isn't going to help," Penelope said, indicating the glass, "And you know that you can't handle it."

" 'Pears I can't handle much of anything."

She turned on him, her hands on her hips. "Well, damn it, what are you going to do?"

He looked at her. "You're Scotch-Irish, aren't you? Never thought of it before."

"I don't know what in hell I am," Penelope said angrily. "I just want to know what you are going to do. I don't want to discuss family or ethnic origins. Stick to the issue."

"We've looked it over from all angles. 'Pears there's nothing to do but walk the plank."

Penelope turned from him back to the window, biting her lips. After a moment, she spoke in a calm voice over her shoulder. "What if they decide to go ahead now with the move of the Office of Education?"

"Lisa'd be saved from the ice, sho' 'nuff."

"Could we hold on?"

"Yes. We cut it thin, but if they move it will all work out."

"Then that's the answer." She turned from the window. "I'll see what I can do. The publicity types say I'm 'the most powerful woman in Washington' and I've never even asked to get a parking ticket fixed. It will be interesting to see if I really do have some friends in this town. Damn it, they've got to reinstate their plans. They can't do this to us!"

Dick Winston drained his glass. "Hope it works out."

"Well, don't you care? It's your business and your money. You seem to want to take a licking, to fail."

"I have failed, Penny. I've mucked it all up. For once, I had a chance to try something on my own and I couldn't make it. If you work it out for me, it's the same old story, poor, silly, impotent Dick Winston being nursed and moth-

266

ered by a woman." He sat down on a hassock and covered his face with his hands. "I don't think I can go back to that. I really don't."

"Forget that nonsense. Right now we have to think of the money."

"I don't give a damn about the money."

"That's because you've never been without it. You can't imagine life without money."

He looked up at her. "And you can't imagine life without self respect. I've spent all of my years that way. I thought, after Mama died, I could do something, prove myself, get some self respect and now I've ruined it all." Tears began to run down his cheeks. "Money? What in the hell do I care about money? Pull your strings here in Washington, bribe somebody. Sleep with somebody. Save the show. What in hell do I care? You win. I lose, no matter how it comes out."

"You're getting mauldin," Penelope said in an even, cold voice. "You can't hold liquor and you never could. I want you to take me down to your office and show me all of the details. We're going to fight. This involves me as much as you. I won't be a loser!"

At seven-thirty Penelope telephoned Herman Baur at his Sheraton-Park apartment from the M Street office. "I must come and see you at once, Herman. Will you be home tonight?"

"Yes. I've just got in. I'm a little tired, Penelope I've been on the floor all day. Could we do it tomorrow? At breakfast, perhaps?"

"It's most urgent and personal, Herman."

"Then come right along, dear."

Penelope walked down the long tunnel-like entrance leading from the automobile entrance to the lobby of the Sheraton-Park apartment wing and took the elevator to the fifth floor. Herman Baur, in his shirt sleeves and in worn leather slippers opened the door himself. "I told Mrs. Mac to go home early. Come in, Penny."

The living room had the worn, disarranged, look of a bachelor home where comfort and convenience are prized above appearances. Leather chairs with cushions made wrinkled and concave by use were placed beside well lighted tables overflowing with books and papers. Herman Baur removed a tied stack of Senate bills from a chair. "Sit here, Penny. How about a drink?"

"I'd love a good strong bourbon and water," Penelope said with a little sigh as she sat down. "I'm all a-jangle."

He handed her the drink and dropped into a nearby chair.

"I can see that you aren't in the mood for small talk, dear. What's on your mind?"

Penelope started to speak and then bit her lower lip and looked down at her trim alligator pumps. "I'm so confused," she said after a moment in a small voice. "I only learned about it this afternoon."

Herman Baur reached over and covered her hands with his. "Pretty bad, is it? It can't be so bad that we can't fix it up."

Penelope began to cry.

"Here, now. Here, now," Herman Baur said helplessly. "We can't have this, you know."

The tears flowed unchecked for a moment as she muffled her sobs in a handkerchief hastily snatched from the square alligator handbag on her lap. "I feel such a fool," she said at last. "I've never done this before."

"Doesn't matter. Doesn't matter," he said gruffly, "But I can't help you if you don't tell me what the problem is, can I?"

She smiled at him, bright eyed through her tears, like a small child beguiled away from some minor grief by a kind adult.

"No, you can't. And I'm being awfully feminine. Please forgive me."

"Nonsense," the voice was gruff. He reached into a humidor and took a cigar. "We can wait," he said, lighting it. "Talk when you feel like it."

Penelope blew her nose and wiped her eyes. After a moment she sipped her drink. "You have heard Dick speak about Heitzing?" She said, her eyes meeting his.

"That's the big development out beyond Frederick?"

"Yes."

Herman Baur nodded. "Quite a spread about it in the newspapers last month."

"Dick is terribly extended on it. Every cent we have has been put into its development. I'm afraid that he has been foolish. It will all come out right if everything goes according to plan. He hasn't allowed for contingencies, for the unexpected."

Herman Baur continued to gaze at her as he puffed on his cigar, but made no comment.

"It all depends upon a big demand for housing in upper Montgomery and Howard counties created by the relocation of the Office of Education near Frederick. As you know, this is part of the federal government dispersal program."

Herman Baur nodded.

"General Services Administration advised Dick this afternoon that the move is being postponed for economic reasons. The Bureau of the Budget and the General Accounting Office concur. I can already feel that this decision is cast in bureaucratic cement."

Herman Baur cleared his throat. "We're after Charlie Frome up on the Hill. He wants another tax increase. We won't give it to him without a cutback in spending. If we don't tidy things up a bit we're in trouble for the presidential elections next year."

Tears flooded into Penelope's eyes. "Well, it's so *unfair*, Herman. Dick has been trying to build a model community for government employees. He doesn't deserve to be ruined."

"No one deserves to be ruined. Was he depending entirely upon the Office of Education's move?"

"Yes. Later, subsidiary employers might be attracted, but initially the demand for homes would come from government employees."

Herman Baur puffed on his cigar in silence.

"It's not fair, Herman."

"Maybe not. That doesn't help us much. Dick's a big boy. He took a chance." The gray eyes looked at Penelope quizzically. "He wasn't going to share the profits with the government, was he?"

"No. Of course not."

"Well, then, let's don't talk about fairness. It's just as fair for him to be broke if Education doesn't move as for him to be a few million richer if they do."

Penelope arose from her chair and dropped down on a hassock before Herman Baur. She looked into his eyes. "Herman, this involves *me*. It will limit my usefulness in Washington. I won't be able to afford all of the things I do now."

His eyes held hers and then slid away to watch the smoke curl up from his cigar. "I would have to go to the President personally on this one. There's no other way to head it off. A direct Presidential order will create talk. There may be criticism."

"I realize that. That's why I came to you. The decision has to be reversed within twenty-four hours. He's the only one who can do that."

"And what do I tell him?"

"Tell him that if he doesn't reverse the order Penelope Winston will be ruined."

"Just the naked truth?"

"I think too much of both you and the President to engage in hypocrisy. There are times one must ask ones friends for a personal indulgence. I'm asking for one now. I think there are also times when one has to realize that some abstract *bono publicas* consideration isn't the only weight on the scale. Personal friendship and loyalty are also important in politics."

Herman Baur grinned saturninely. "You aren't quoting me

270

back to myself, by any chance?"

"By every chance. I believe what you tell me. I'm an apt pupil."

Herman Baur threw back his head and laughed. "By jingo, you are a girl!" He rolled the cigar between his fingers and continued to chuckle as he gazed at her. "Were the tears real?"

"Why, yes!" Penelope said, taken aback.

"They didn't do any good, you know."

"Sometimes you say the most wounding things, dear."

"You finally got around to the only argument that fits the problem, Penny. This big, impersonal juggernaut of government is about to step on a friend of mine. We can't have that."

Penelope flung herself in his lap and kissed him. "Oh you angel. I love you dearly!"

"Now, now. You don't have to do that and the President may turn me down."

Penelope looked into his eyes with alarm. "You don't really believe that?"

"Not really. This will be a matter of personal privilege. He won't say no. Besides he admires your spunk, just as I do."

"Will it cause trouble, Herman?"

"None we can't handle. There was a good reason for the move in the first place. We'll tell the bureaucrats that those reasons are overriding. We don't have to explain anything to the press. If they ask, we deny that a postponed move was even considered."

"You don't know what this means to me."

"Oh, yes I do. I'll remind you of it from time to time."

"You're so sweet."

"I suppose I am, once in a while. I treasure friends, Penny. And the only thing more valuable in politics than a friend, is a friend in debt to you. Remember that."

❧ 23 ❧

THE downstairs rooms of Foxhall House were empty when Penelope returned, lit only by the chandeliers and an occasional table lamp. She found Dick asleep across his bed. There was a strong smell of whiskey and she could not arouse him. She angrily lifted his head by the hair, shoved a pillow under it, spread a blanket over him, and left the room, slamming the door behind her.

She did not greet him when he appeared at breakfast the next morning, ignoring his furtive glances across the table as she ate her grapefruit. He poured himself a cup of coffee from the pot on the sideboard and sat down. Mrs. Moss brought him his usual scrambled eggs and bacon. "Good morning, sir."

" 'Morning, Mrs. M."

"Lovely October morning as I was tellin' the missus."

" 'Pears so."

He cleared his throat after Mrs. Moss left the room. "Guess I tied one on last night."

The eyes that met his were ice blue. "I would say so."

"Awfully sorry. It doesn't take as much as it used to. I misjudged."

"I missed you," she spoke with heavy irony. "It would have been nice to have you around."

"Sorry. However, it isn't every day a millionaire becomes

272

a pauper. 'Peared to me I should at least acknowledge it."

"You aren't a pauper."

"Sorry. Forgot I was married to a breadwinning wife. Damn farsighted of me."

"For God's sake, stop saying you're sorry. I talked to Herman Baur last night. There's no truth in the rumor about the Office of Education. They're moving to Frederick on schedule." The blue eyes met his. "You didn't need to give me such a fright."

"It's no rumor. G.S.A. told me so."

"It was a rumor."

"I'll call G.S.A. back and ask."

Penelope sipped her coffee and gazed at her appointment book. "I'd wait until tomorrow, if I were you."

"What does that mean?"

"Just what I said."

" 'Pears I'm well connected."

"Does that hurt?"

"Matter of fact, it does."

Penelope glared at him. "Yesterday you were acting like a bastard, dear. Don't act like an ungrateful bastard today."

"Don't worry. I'm good at being grateful. I've spent most of a long, dull lifetime being grateful."

She arose from the table impatiently. "I have my work to do. I suggest you do yours." She left him morosely hunched over his untasted breakfast.

The voice over the telephone was diffident. "Mrs. Winston?"

"Yes."

"This is Jerry Stern at Winston Development."

"Yes, Jerry?"

"I'm sorry to bother you, Mrs. Winston, but we haven't seen Mr. Winston down here for a week, ever since we got that scare about the office. Is he sick?"

"He hasn't felt well, Jerry. Is there anything I can do?"

"We have some decisions that have to be made pretty quickly."

"I'll speak to him."

She found Dick Winston in the lower end of the garden on a small two hole putting surface stroking a golf ball. The ball curved along an invisible rise of ground and fell into the hole with a 'plop.' He looked up with a grin. "I 'most never miss. Wish I knew the greens at the Chevy Chase Club as well. My handicap would improve."

"Your office called. They asked if you were ill."

"What did you say?"

"I said you were."

"Good girl. Lie for Papa."

"It was no lie."

He leaned on his golf club. "I never felt better in my life."

"What are you trying to prove, Dick? I've heard of small, spoiled brats refusing to play, but I have never heard of a grown man ignoring his business at a critical moment."

He stroked the ball. "Funny, isn't it? I just don't give a damn."

"There's no problem about the move of the Office. Everything is going on as before. Why are you acting this way?"

"Poor, old, silly Dick Winston would have lost it all, but his wife used her political influence and saved him. I told you he was useless in anything practical."

"People aren't saying that."

"Give them time. They will."

"There are only three persons that know about this, beside you. None of them will talk."

"You know. You must despise me."

"Of course I don't despise you. Good God, you made a human miscalculation. Everything is all right now. Go back, build Heitzing. Make millions. What if I did help? I'm your wife. Why wouldn't I help?"

"I had to do it on my own."

"I couldn't help?"

274

"Especially you. You don't understand that, do you?"

"No. I don't. You must be crazy. Are you going to throw it all up, just because I helped?"

"I just don't care about it any more. It doesn't prove anything."

She stared at him. "Don't I mean anything to you?"

"Everything. That's the trouble."

"Then straighten yourself up and run Winston Development Corporation. Make me proud of you."

"Can't do it."

"You mean that you only allowed yourself one mistake?"

"One mistake so big that only a powerful woman could right it. For me, one mistake like that is enough. I've got a thing about powerful women."

"Dick, I don't know this side of you. You're all mixed up. This doesn't make sense."

"Clearest kind of sense to me."

"Well, what are you going to do with your life?" She flared. "Drink yourself to death?"

"No. I discovered the other night I was cured of that stuff. You don't need to worry. You won't have a drunkard husband."

"Well, what will you *do?*"

He swung the golf club back and forth in one hand. "I'll think of something."

"You act as if you dislike me."

"No. I pity you."

"Pity me?"

"You're married to me. You're damn right I pity you," he said bitterly.

Tears flooded into her eyes. She started to speak, then bit her lips and ran headlong back across the lawn to the house.

Penelope sat in the small conference room of Winston Development Corporation with Jerry Stern, Steve Bates, and John Griffin. The three men looked embarrassed and uncomfortable as she spoke. "I may as well be frank, gentlemen. My husband is in a strange mood. I have tried to convince him that he should see a psychiatrist, but he refuses. He also refuses even to discuss this business or to have anything to do with it. We are going to have to run it without him. Mr. Griffin drafted a power of attorney in my favor to vote the fifty percent of voting shares my husband owns. Mr. Winston has signed it, so one hundred percent of the voting shares are represented around this table."

John Griffin cleared his throat. "The purpose of this directors meeting is to accept Mr. Winston's resignation as a director and as president and to elect Mrs. Winston in his place. I think we can dispose of this matter and other details informally and I'll draft formal minutes and resolutions later."

"I'm agreeable to any arrangement Mr. and Mrs. Winston favor, of course," Steve Bates said.

"I am also," Jerry Stern agreed.

Penelope nodded. "I count on both of you as well as Mr. Griffin for advice. I know next to nothing about business and I am involved in this only because of my husband's aberration. I hope that he will decide to resume his responsibilities soon. In the meantime I'll do the best I can."

"I've known Dick for a long time, Mrs. Winston," John Griffin said. "He has always been erratic. His sense of values seems different than that of others. He refuses to be involved, at least for very long. He dislikes responsibility. I suspect that he got tired of Winston Development Corporation as he has gotten tired of so many things and has walked away from it. I wouldn't call it more than eccentricity, but no matter what we call it, it places you in a very difficult position. When his mother died, Dick removed all of his fortune from the prudent investments where it was lodged and, against my advice, I must add, decided to buy real estate for appreciation— this has gradually been transformed into a very speculative venture, the Heitzing Project. Since he has abandoned it, we four must look after it." He cleared his throat. "What is his

276

new interest, by the way?"

"Flying. He's taking flying lessons out near Gaithersburg." Penelope shrugged with a little smile and raised her eyes to the ceiling.

"I'm very sorry about all of this from a personal point of view, Mrs. Winston," Steve Bates said rubbing a palm across his thinning sandy hair," But from a business point of view you have nothing to worry about. We're going to make a lot of money."

"I think it will be exciting," Penelope smiled. "As long as I have to do it, I'm going to be a good pupil." She looked around at the men and said solemnly, her smile fading. "I only require one thing. I want winners around me. Only winners."

It was warm for late April and Alice Payson was lunching with Penelope on the terrace of Foxhall House. "It's amazing, Penny, how beautiful the dogwoods and azaleas are in spring along the Potomac. A month ago everything was so dreary."

"It is beautiful. Spring in the middle west is a pale imitation."

"In California we have so much irrigated and fertilized foliage that spring is hardly noticeable. I think of it as the season when the rain stops. Here it's like a rebirth. I wish human affairs were like that."

"People are happier in the spring, more romantic. They at least stop and look around."

"We stir when we ought to be transformed."

Penny finished her salad. "How is Bill these days? I notice that the Payson Urban Redevelopment Act has made him a sort of hero. Yesterday's *Tribune* editorial referred to him as a latter day combination of Herbert Hoover, Bernard Baruch, and Albert Schweitzer." She laughed. "Marc would never have allowed them to get so emotional."

Alice grimaced. "No one loves or admires Bill more than I do, but stuff like that makes me uneasy. I have the feeling that it's some sort of a buildup, but I'm damned if I know for what."

Penelope looked at her quietly. "Don't you know? It's for the presidency."

Alice looked horrified. "You've got to be kidding! We just got here!"

"It's been two years."

"But, my God. I've just learned to cope with being a Senator's wife!"

"Bill is the man with the answers to the problem that worries the country most. Some men have made the White House on less than that."

"But Bill hasn't said anything. We always share."

"He doesn't realize it. That's part of his appeal. Before Madison Avenue began to nominate candidates, the office used to seek the man. People like to watch a public figure qualify for the presidency without thinking of the office. It's reassuring. Bill's like that so he seems real, not contrived."

"What about Governor Breen of Ohio and John Wittecomb, that big international banker? I thought that they were the front runners?"

"They are."

"Well, Bill doesn't want it. They can have it."

"Are you sure?"

Alice Payson gazed at Penelope. "Sweetie, you sure know how to scare the hell out of me."

Dick Winston finished his breakfast coffee and opened a magazine on flying.

"Dick?" Penelope asked.

"Yes?"

"We're having a directors meeting of Winston Development Corporation this morning. Wouldn't you like to come?"

" 'Pears not."

"There will be some good news, our first dividend."

"Glad to hear it. I'll be flying. My flying club wing is going up to Buffalo today."

"We're considering opening up a new tract."

"M-m-m."

"It will be called El Segundo."

"Very original."

"We are succeeding, Dick. Don't you care?"

"Not a damn. Glad to hear it, of course, for your sake."

She got up and stood by him, a hand on his shoulder. "If you were happy, Dick, that would be one thing, but you aren't. You're miserable. I can tell. Why are you doing this? Heitzing was your idea. You should be building it."

He was silent, looking at the open magazine, but not reading it.

"Well?"

He shrugged. "Let's leave it as it is."

She stood looking down on him. "Very well, I won't mention it again. You seem to enjoy being a failure. You seek after it like some men pursue success."

" 'Pears so," he said indifferently.

"Dick, I'll ask you again. Won't you see a doctor?"

He raised his eyes to her. "About my mind or my reproductive organs?"

"You can be viciously spiteful, can't you?"

"I just wondered where the itch was before I scratched."

She turned away from him in a white hot flash of anger. "I can leave you alone and I will. Apart from you, my life is stimulating, exciting. I'm not going to let you spoil it."

"Wouldn't dream of it. Tell you what we'll do. You live your life and I'll live mine. I won't moralize you, if you don't moralize me. You leave me alone. I'll leave you alone."

"Why did you marry me, Dick?"

"I had something in mind. Don't remember it now."

She began to cry, more in frustration than in anger.

He folded up his magazine and stood up. "This doesn't do us any good. Can't we leave each other alone?" He turned and left her.

Marc Haywood looked into Penelope's office at the *Tribune*. "Am I interrupting?"

She smiled at him. "Darling, of course not."

"Darling?"

"Now that you're divorced, you have to expect that from women."

"Married women?"

"This married woman."

He looked at her wordlessly and then entered her office and sat down on a cane ladderback chair. It creaked under his weight. "You don't expect people to stay long, do you?"

"It's a pretty chair."

He lit a cigarette, shaking it out of a popular priced pack.

"I miss the cigarette case," she said mischievously.

"So do I." He watched the smoke rise from his cigarette for a moment. "How's Dick?"

"Busy developing Heitzing."

"I hear differently."

She did not answer.

"I just want to remind you that I've known Dick since we were boys together."

"Thank you, Marc. I'll remember."

"Claudia got Hollywood in the divorce settlement," he announced. "That's the only part of Virginia in which she has an interest."

"It must have been a wrench. You loved it too and had done so much with it."

"I have welcomed a few wrenches. I was in a rut, a comfortable, aristocratic rut, but a rut. I'm better out of it in my new reincarnation."

"Where are you living?"

"At the Watergate. I sold the Georgetown mansion. I also

have a pied-á-terre in Alexandria for political domicile purposes. Dumbarton House is all I now own in Georgetown, but I don't feel like living in it."

Her eyes softened. "And what have you been doing?"

"Fighting for the right, the true, and the beautiful."

"How nice to know what it is."

"The Americans for Democratic Action guide me. My rating from them last year on legislation was one hundred percent. I must say it makes me look like a political zombie. I'll have to find an issue to buck them on this session just so they won't begin to take me for granted."

"Specifically, what have you been doing?"

"I'm coming out for Payson for President at a press conference this afternoon."

Penelope leaned her chin on one hand and looked at him. "Really? Isn't it early? April?"

"Late April. Nearly May."

"Why are you for Payson?"

"He's honest, intelligent, and I think he's going to win." He smiled wryly. "The reasons appeal to me in reverse order."

"Win? Why? He's a rather colorless, humorless man and he hasn't even entered the primaries."

"Haven't you noticed? He suits the mood of the country. Payson looks and acts like a consulting psychiatrist. With the whole country on the couch, so to speak, that's reassuring. He talks like a compendium of urban and sociological clichés, and that's reassuring, too. He's dead earnest. So is the country. As for the primaries, we both know they are only marginally effective. Payson is following the sound strategy. He's letting the country and the politicians come to him."

"But he lectures the country like a school teacher."

"Don't forget we elected Woodrow Wilson."

Penelope laughed. "So he's a man of his time?"

"Exactly. Charlie Frome is the last of the personable, pretty boys for a time. Youth and indulgence is at a discount.

The pendulum has swung. The country wants to feel the rod, verbally, at least."

"Well, I'm for him too, but don't ask me why. I haven't figured it out."

"Don't be coy with me, Penny. It's very simple and altogether creditable. His wife is your best woman friend. I might say," his eyes twinkled, "Your only woman friend."

"If I'm a friend of Alice, I'll keep her out of the White House. The idea scares her to death."

"She'll get used to it. They all do."

"Is Herman Baur for Payson?"

"I think so. I'm almost embarrassed to be on the same side with Herman. We can't even agree on what time it is, but he's too shrewd not to realize that Payson is the man this year. He'll wait, of course, and see how he stands up as a candidate, but I'm pretty sure he'll be behind Payson before the convention and end up masterminding the final drive."

Penelope hugged herself. "Isn't it great to be going into a presidential year? It's going to be such fun!"

"For the winners."

"Of course," Penelope said, surprised. "That's what I mean."

William Payson sat in his suite at the Century Plaza in Los Angeles and listened with a half attentive, half embarrassed air to Herman Baur. "God damn it, Bill," Baur said earnestly, "We've almost got it sewed up downtown, but you'll have to accept Governor Breen as your running mate."

"I don't think Breen is fit to be President."

"I don't either, but he'll make a great Vice President."

"There have been no great Vice Presidents."

"That's what I mean."

"I may die in office."

"Look, Bill. You won't die in office if we don't nominate and elect you. It's a chicken and egg proposition."

"There's no other way?"

282

"No. We've canvassed the convention hall from the johns to the T.V. platforms; without Breen's votes General Witte-comb is going to head you off. You won't make it on the first ballot, you'll lose some of your first ballot commitments on the second. Wittecomb will get it on the fourth, or it might go five."

"Can Wittecomb win in November?"

"I don't give a damn about November, Bill. This is July. Can I make the deal with Breen?"

William Payson gave a little gesture of resignation. "Go ahead. I'll start taking vitamin pills."

The keynoter at the convention was Marc Haywood, cho-sen to placate the party's young turks in the Senate and House and because, in a convention dominated by Payson supporters, it was recognized that he was the first prominent politician to unequivocally declare for Payson for President and prejudge the amazing preconvention tide of popularity that swept Payson toward the nomination almost without a campaign and with only friendly neutrality from Charles Frome. Haywood appeared before the television cameras with shaggy hair and an unpressed suit projecting a fiery image that his friends in private life scarcely recognized. Claudia Haywood, watching him on television at Hollywood rail bitterly against privilege and the status quo, exclaimed in disbelief and went to bed with a migraine headache.

Senator Payson was nominated on the first ballot and after the usual pandemonium and cascade of balloons the hoarse delegates nominated his choice for vice president, Governor Stanton Breen of Ohio, by acclamation. In his acceptance speech Payson promised a task for everyone in the recon-struction of America. "I proclaim a renewal," he said almost sternly, "A renewal of faith, a renewal of challenge, a re-newal of work, a renewal of responsibility. We are going to move America forward, honoring the doer and castigating the shirker. We are going to rebuild America and in achiev-ing its aspirations we shall live its ideals. I proclaim the Responsible Society with a task for everyone. If you are satisfied with your country and yourself, if you are satisfied with less than full performance, don't vote for me. But if you want to excel, if you want to do better, if you want to see your country do better, then follow me, because I intend to lead the way." When he had finished the great hall was hushed and then the thousands of people arose spontaneously in a standing ovation and began to sing 'America the Beautiful.'

Herman Baur leaned over to Congressman Davies sitting next to him on the platform. "He's caught the country's Gothic mood. Like an old time evangelist he'll tell them to come forward on election day and be saved. They'll come by the millions, glorying in a kind of self-flagellation."

"Damndest thing I ever saw," Congressmen Davies muttered. "I've been practicing the cheerful smile all of my life, even when I have a bellyache, and now it's out of date."

"It will come back, Cary. After Payson we'll run another happy warrior. The country will be ready for it."

"What is your projection, Herman?" William Payson asked in the private cabin aboard the chartered airplane taking them to Payson's final campaign before the election in his opponent's home state of Illinois.

"With ten days to go it looks like a comfortable margin," Herman Baur said cautiously, "Maybe a landslide, but don't let up until we get the horse in the barn."

"I thought George Stuart would conduct a better campaign. He's a two term Governor, astute, and much more photogenic than I am."

"The country wants a change of pace, Bill," Herman Baur said easily. "The more George imitates Jack Kennedy, the more you imitate Calvin Coolidge."

"But I'm more like Kennedy than Coolidge," Payson protested. "I want to get this country moving. I want to go out and meet the future!"

"You may feel like Kennedy, but you come across like

Coolidge. Don't worry. That's what the country wants. Look at the polls."

"I thought they were listening to what I said, not the way I said it," Payson replied with a slight edge of irritation in his voice.

"When did they ever do that? They want someone to disapprove of them and put them on the road to righteousness. This is the beginning of a wave of national puritanism following twenty years of hedonism. You're going to ride that wave right into the White House."

"You make me sound like a stuffed shirt."

"You are a stuffed shirt. Thank God your time has come."

Penelope generously contributed time and money to the Payson campaign. It was a happy, busy three months during which she was able to spend more time with Marc Haywood than she had since their days of easy intimacy before her marriage. She felt that they were growing closer together again, sharing their common interest in politics. As she explained on a television interview show, she did not feel that she had abandoned her non-partisan posture as a Washington columnist. "I'm not partisan. Everyone in Washington knows that, but everyone also knows that Alice Payson is my dearest friend and that I adore her husband. Naturally, I want to see him in the White House, and politics has nothing to do with it."

William and Alice Payson decided after voting in Palo Alto to await the election returns in a suite at the Fairmont Hotel in San Francisco while over a thousand campaign workers milled about in the hotel's huge ballroom, their enthusiasm held in low key until they could erupt in a victory rally later in the evening and cheer themselves hoarse when their victorious candidate appeared. The Breens returned to Columbus and the Governor's mansion for their vigil. Marc Haywood and Penelope voted in their home precincts and then flew together to San Francisco to join the Paysons and a few others in the suite.

Penelope sat on a sofa with Alice Payson. "I wish to God that I could relax," Alice said, pouring herself another cup of coffee from a pot on the table before her. "Win or lose, I'm going to have to go on national T.V. with Bill. I'm so taut I'll probably grimace like Martha Raye and let out a blood curdling yell."

"He's going to win, Alice. So think pleasant thoughts. Think what it will be like to be First Lady."

Alice groaned. "That's what's bugging me. Can you imagine me in the White House? Can anybody?"

"Yes."

"Well, I'd better go to the can. All this coffee. You never know when you're on camera these days and I don't want the whole country to see me as First Lady elect, or whatever in hell you call it, for the first time and then realize that I'm not only nervous, but that I've got to go."

Penelope laughed. "They will realize that you're human."

"I'm nothing else, if not human."

Herman Baur walked over to Penelope after Alice left for a bedroom. "How's our girl doing?"

"She'll be all right. She's saying all of the wrong things now, off camera."

"You've performed a great national service with that gal, Penny. You've taught her how to keep her mouth shut in public. On television she compliments Payson, sort of a Myrna Loy twinkle about her. Of course Alice is pretty plain and Myrna Loy was that rare thing, a beautiful woman with a sense of humor."

"Why Herman, I never knew."

"I had my passions, Penny," he grinned. "I can still get fired up for short periods."

Marc Haywood joined them. "The first returns are coming in from New England; pretty spotty. Where's Bill?"

"He's taking a nap in the next room," Baur said.

"That's self-control for you."

286

"Self-control he's got."

"What's he going to say when he's won?"

" 'Thank you. Now let's get to work.' "

A pretty young girl who was answering the telephone and taking and receiving messages came up to Penelope. "Mrs. Winston? It's long distance for you. The telephone on the table in the foyer."

Marc Haywood was sitting alone on a sofa before one of the television sets, sipping a scotch and soda a white jacketed waiter had handed him. Penelope dropped down beside him.

He glanced at her and noticing her pallor asked, "What's the matter, darling?"

"Dick is dead," she said. "He crashed his airplane." She swallowed with difficulty. "Near Leesburg."

"An accident?" He asked without thinking.

Her eyes sought his. "I don't know. I've never known about Dick."

He took her hands in his. "We'll fly home together, darling. I'll take care of everything."

She fought back the tears. "I'm so sorry about him, Marc. You'll never know." She bit her lip and cast down her eyes.

"Yes," he said quietly. "I think I do. Let's go home."

❧ 24 ❧

MARC HAYWOOD looked in on Penelope at her office at the *Tribune*. "How are you?" He asked with a quiet smile.

"Just fine." She returned his smile. "I don't know whether to invite you to sit down or not. Are you here as friend or enemy? As a United States Senator or as the publisher?"

"As the publisher. The Board of Director's meeting is tomorrow and I'm boning up on a few matters, but I'll sit down anyway."

She watched him light a cigarette. "It's strange, Marc. Dick slipped away so easily. I know you'll understand when I say it's as if he never were here, and it has only been a month since the accident. I think his fellow flying club members have missed him most."

Haywood nodded. "He had pretty well disengaged himself otherwise. We called him, 'a pioneer developer of Washington's outer northwest corridor' in the real estate section. He would have laughed at that as typical obituary language. He was realistic enough to realize that after John Griffin memorializes him for a few months as 'the decedent' in probate and tax proceedings he'll be reduced to that red granite grave stone inscribed 'Richard Perry Winston' between those of Patty and his mother in the Winston family plot. As I recall, that means that horrible Victorian family monument in the middle of the plot has received its last satellite and the only further thing that can be done for the Winstons is plot maintenance under the perpetual care contract." He gazed soberly at the tip of his cigarette. "Still, that's better than I will do. He at least left a son."

Penelope met his eyes. "Yes, I have Dick, Junior. That's a great comfort."

"I'm sure it is. I have always regretted that Claudia and I didn't have children."

Penelope dropped her eyes. "Some women are prolific, and others aren't. I have always wanted a large family, myself, but I'm one of the lucky ones. Poor Claudia wasn't. You can't help that."

"No, of course not. A thing like that just happens."

Penelope's tongue ran along her upper lip. "Marc, it's too soon after Dick's death to ask anyone else, but everyone will understand in your case. I'm the chairman this year of the annual charity ball in New York for newspaper people. Will you take me to New York and escort me to the ball?"

"When?"

"Three weeks from yesterday."

"Where?"

"At the Waldorf."

He pushed out his cigarette in an ash tray on her desk. "I'm honored, Madam Chairman. I'll be delighted."

She came around the desk and kissed him.

"I hoped you would do that."

"How could I resist?"

"I'll make the arrangements through the newspaper. Separate suites at the Regency. O.K.?"

"Lovely."

"Let's stay over a couple of days afterward and have some fun," he said impulsively. "A few night spots, a couple of plays. It will be a nice change from Washington and it's time you kicked off your shoes and enjoyed yourself."

"Oh, Marc! I would adore that!"

They flew up to New York in a twin engined jet owned by the *Tribune* in time to drop in briefly at several pre-ball cocktail parties and receptions. Penelope gave a short welcoming speech at the ball and after enduring the crush and heat of the crowded ballroom for the minimum time required they escaped at midnight to a small bar on upper Madison Avenue where a piano player stroked his keys in a light and languid manner, creating an undulating curtain of soft music that floated through the room, muffling, but not quite extinguishing the low murmur of voices and the clink of ice cubes against the crystal glasses. Penelope leaned against Marc and sighed. "Darling, what a relief! How wonderful to be alone together."

"At least we have that ball behind us. We can enjoy the next two days."

She lightly brushed his cheek with her lips. "It will be so wonderful. I was just thinking I never get away from Washington."

"Then it's about time we did the Big Town together."

They danced between drinks on the small, crowded rectangle in the middle of the room to the flowing, sensual rhythms and when they returned to their small, secluded table between dances they conversed with each other as lovers converse, not by the murmured, obscure, disconnected phrases frequently interrupted by low, errant laughter, but by soft, caressing glances and the warm, lingering touch of fingertips, cheeks, and lips, finding the frequent opportunity to reaffirm the wonderful reality of their nearness to one another.

They emerged into a pre-dawn coolness about four A.M. and walked down Park Avenue to their hotel. He stood before the door to her suite.

"Would you like to come in?"

"For a moment."

Inside the closed door, in the dimly lighted foyer with the simulated mottled mirrors and the useless reproduction of a

Louis XV bench, he took her in his arms. His kiss was casual, polite, considerate, but as her lips clung submissively to his it became questing, ardent. As he held her tightly to him her passion began to rise to meet his own. "Must we stay here in the foyer?" He murmured, moving his lips caressingly across her cheek.

She wordlessly drew him into the small sittingroom. He pulled her to him on a sofa placed in front of windows muffled against the noises of the avenue by heavy draperies. His lips again sought hers and his body slowly pressed her backward against the soft pillows. Her arms encircled his neck and drew him to her as her back arched slightly to thrust her body against his, then she remembered that she could not have him without humiliating herself. She broke away, giving him an affectionate little hug as she did so.

"What does that mean?"

"It's very late, darling." She turned on a table lamp.

"I thought we knew each other better than that," he said irritably.

"We're both free now, darling. We have all of the time in the world."

"Time be damned. I want you now."

"No. Not now."

He lit a cigarette and then glanced up at her. "You aren't still leading me on, for God's sake? Not after all these years?"

She looked hurt. "I was never aware that I 'led you on' as you say."

"I have a different impression."

"You aren't being very gallant."

He arose. "Gallant, hell. I don't understand you. What kind of relationship do you want with me?"

Her eyes were downcast. "You know how I feel about you."

"I'm not sure that I do. Tell me."

"Marc, let's don't quarrel. It's late. We're both tired."

"All right. I'll go to my own rooms and take a cold

291

shower."

She walked with him to the door. "I had a lovely evening. Thank you."

"My pleasure."

"Won't you kiss me goodnight?"

"No." He opened the door and pulled it closed behind him with a click.

Penelope stood still in the foyer clenching and unclenching her fists in frustration. "Damn it to hell," she whispered to her faint image in the mottled mirrors. "What do I do about him? How do I handle him?"

The next day as they went about the city together her eyes sought his, seeking with soft caressing looks to draw from him a response. He remained attentive, courteous, but remote. "You are angry with me, aren't you?" She asked over dinner at L'Aiglon.

"No."

"Marc, you are. I can tell."

"Penny, I'm too damned old to play games. Last night I gather I presumed on our relationship. You held me off. I'm not going to let you play the coquette with me. You are going to have to decide what our relationship is to be."

She was silent, looking at her untasted food, her tongue moving across her upper lip.

"For years, I've understood that you were in love with me. Claudia and then Dick stood in our way. Now they are gone. We can do what we wish. It's childish to act like a shy virgin with me. I don't deserve it."

"Marc, it's more complicated than that."

"Don't tell me you want an old fashioned courtship?"

"Are you proposing?"

"No, I'm not."

"You want an affair?"

"I want some intimacy with you. I want us to give ourselves to one another. I want to end this feeling that we are always verbally sparring at arms length. I don't intend to take any chances. I won't endure another bloodless, passionless, correct marriage such as I had with Claudia. I wouldn't think you would want another husband like Dick. I want passion, commitment, ardor. I'm not going to settle for an embrace or a peck on the cheek."

"You want me to go to bed with you?"

"No, damn it, not just like that." He pushed his plate away from him. "I just want a warm, unreserved, human relationship. You're holding back, Penny. Why, I don't know. It makes me wonder what your feelings for me really are."

"Marc, don't. Please. Don't drive me to the wall like this."

"Very well," he said quietly. He glanced at his wristwatch. "We'd better go. We'll miss the curtain."

Alice Payson smiled at Penelope across the polished mahogany surface of the telescoped dining table in the dining room of the presidential apartments at the White House. "We sort of rattle around in here, just two gals, eating alone."

"It's a beautiful room," Penelope said looking about her. "I love the pictorial wallpaper against the white wainscoting."

"It's the smallest and most intimate diningroom in this historical museum. I doubt that we could comfortably seat more than twenty in here."

"I think it's beautiful."

"Beautiful, yes, but, my God, it's lonely, Penny. You have no idea."

"I think I do. I live alone, except for the baby and the servants."

Alice impulsively put out a hand and squeezed Penelope's where it lay on top of the table. "Of course, dear. I'm so stupid. What I meant was that you would think, living here with the President, with people crawling all over the place, that I couldn't be lonely. Well, you know the old bromide, alone in a crowd? It's like that. Bill is the President of the

United States. I am the First Lady. We are the centers of circles of attendants and activities that are completely impersonal. Mine are really incidental, trivial, I might say, but he had the weight of humanity on him. I can sometimes get away, like now, and think like Alice Payson. He never can. He's not really with me any more, even when we are alone. It's frightening, what they have done to him. He is a stranger. So I'm alone. And I never wanted it, Penny. You know that."

"He's making a great President."

"Yes, I know. I'm very proud of him. I'm glad that he is fulfilled in this way. I'm also glad that seven more years is the most it can go on." She lit a cigarette and smiled at Penelope. "I'm so fortunate to have a friend like you, Penny. One to whom I can speak frankly, a good companion."

"I treasure your friendship, too, Alice."

"Do you get bored being asked to come and stay with me everytime Bill is whisked away somewhere in that damned helicopter?"

"I love to come. I enjoy you, Alice, and I'm still enough the gal from the corn country, as Dick used to say, to be thrilled to spend nights in the White House. The little empire guest room you put me in is a dear."

"You miss Dick, don't you?"

"Of course."

"Are you going to remarry?"

"Who?"

"You meet hundreds of attractive men."

"If you eliminate the married, the aged, the preoccupied and the foreign diplomats who would expect me to leave Washington, there aren't too many."

"There are younger men."

"I suppose so. But I'm thirty and identified with the Establishment. That scares them off."

"What about Senator Haywood? I notice he is frequently

your escort since Dick died."

Penelope smiled. "Marc 'discovered' me as a young White House secretary and made me a Washington columnist on his newspaper. I've been rather at a disadvantage with him ever since. He has a way of blowing hot and cold. Besides," she said, dropping her eyes to her extended left hand and inspecting her rings, "I find I rather like being a rich widow."

"How about more children?"

"I've never been very interested in sex."

"That isn't what I asked."

"I think you did. One biological step leads to the other. Surely the mating instinct preceeds the maternal instinct.?"

"The two came pretty close together in my case. I'm not sure which was first. I saw, fell in love, and wanted his kids." She snuffed out her cigarette in an ash tray before her. "Didn't you feel that way about Dick?"

"No. Dick was a special case. We never considered a large family." She smiled wryly. "I'm not certain he would have welcomed the competition."

Alice Payson glanced at her wristwatch. "I asked them to show us a movie tonight, in color, and without a message. Should we go?"

"I love movies. I never see one, except here."

"There's no popcorn, but the price is right."

They had a scotch and soda and some finger sandwiches before the fire in the family sitting room after the motion picture.

"You really ought to encourage the President to relax, Alice."

"He will go up to Camp David for twenty-four hours. That's it."

"He never comes to my house as President Frome did, and he used to come as a Senator."

"He feels that as the President, he shouldn't be identified with your Zoo or with any other clique."

295

"President Frome wasn't a part of the Zoo. I wouldn't expect Bill to be. The Zoo legend is part joke and part publicity. Marc started the idea on my behalf years ago. I do nothing to perpetuate it, though everyone likes to believe that there is an insider's Washington and it's natural to wish to be identified with those on the inside. I realize that the joke shouldn't include the President. Ask him to come and relax. He knows that it's off the record."

"I'll see what I can do with him, Penny. Old friends are best, he and I both know that. It's sweet of you to ask."

Penelope sipped her drink and lapsed into silence.

"What are you thinking?" Alice Payson asked after a long interval.

"I'm sorry, dear," Penelope said. "I didn't mean to be rude. I've been thinking for some time of building a country home for weekends. Perhaps that might appeal to the President. Some place on the Eastern Shore, perhaps."

"Penny, don't be ridiculous."

"No, I'm serious. Bill needs a place among friends where he can unwind, a place where you two can be together for a few hours as you used to be, a place as unlike the White House and Camp David as possible. I'll build an eighteenth century manor house on the Chesapeake with a small boxwood garden down near the water for meditation. You two can go there alone if you wish. I won't even be present."

Alice Payson regarded Penelope for a long moment. "You heard Bill mention the meditation garden he loved when he studied in Europe, didn't you?"

"Yes. It sounded so like Bill."

"Penny, you're sweet and extravagant. We'll find some way of encouraging Bill to relax without you spending a fortune on an estate he can use."

Penelope's eyes were dreamy. "Money is cheap. It's friends that are dear, besides, I've always wanted something I could call my very own, something that's all me." She gazed into the distance. "I think I'll call it 'Pennysworth'."

John Griffin and an accountant sat with Penelope in the parlor of Foxhall House. Griffin leafed through some papers. "That's about it, Penny. Most of the first tract at Heitzing has been completed and sold. The Winston Shopping Mall is leased for minimum five year terms. The estate is now settled, and as Dick's sole heir you are now a very rich woman. He left his son in your care with a bequest of one thousand dollars." He shook his head. "Rather unusual, I must say, I tried to persuade him to set up a trust for the little fellow, but he said you were the mother and you would provide and, of course, you will."

"How rich?" Penelope asked, interrupting the lawyer's monologue.

"I would rather tell you what you own, Penny. Its value depends upon a number of variables and assumptions."

Penelope turned to the accountant. "He always talks like that. You must have a total to those figures of yours. What is it?"

"Twenty-five million, Mrs. Winston, in round figures."

She smiled at him. "Thank you. That's a nice, round figure."

"Too much of it is in the Heitzing and El Segundo Developments, Penny," John Griffin interjected. "In your own interests you should diversify."

"I agree. Now aren't you surprised, John?"

"A little, yes. And gratified. I'm going to make an appointment with Warren Hodson. He's the best investment counselor in Washington. We'll go see him this week. It will mean selling Winston Development stock."

"I only want enough to keep control."

"Good. We're talking the same language."

"I also want a million in cash."

"Whatever for? You shouldn't be that liquid."

"I intend to build an estate in Maryland. I want a place in the country."

"Where?"

"The Eastern Shore."

John Griffin snapped his briefcase shut. "You might want to give that a little thought," he said dryly.

"I've thought about it off and on for years," Penelope said, stretching with her arms out in front of her, "And now I'm going to do it."

Penelope turned her station wagon off the highway and drove up the rutted dirt road through a small forest of pines toward the peninsula of meadow on which the silhouette of a large house with huge twin chimneys was rising by the Chesapeake Bay. She parked near a cluster of automobiles belonging to the workmen and the contractor and pulling on knee high boots walked over to a tall, well built grey haired man dressed in a grey suede driving coat with a sheepskin collar.

"I can see some changes since last week, Mr. Chauncy."

"Hello, Mrs. Winston. We're making progress. That handmade brick was hard to get in sufficient quantity, but we are all right now."

"Is there enough for the garden walls?"

"I'm that sure there is. I'm seeing Bevill, the landscape architect, tomorrow. We'll check his requirements again."

Penelope looked up at the rose colored facade rising before her and smiled happily. "It looks just grand."

"It's going to be a show place. We haven't built one like it for over fifty years."

"Am I going to be able to move in by next summer?"

"That was a promise, Mrs. Winston, and I'll keep it. Of course, the garden will take a little more time, possibly autumn. We can't rush the seasons."

"That's fine. As long as I'm in the house. I'll enjoy watching the garden."

She spent nearly an hour in the cold March air walking about the rough meadow, following the wooden stakes driven by Mr. Bevill to mark the shape of the landscaped grounds to be created, turning on her heel from time to time to see the house from yet another angle.

She was completely happy. Pennysworth was altogether her own. No one had guided her or instructed her. She had found the site after weeks of searching; she had determined what the architect, the contractor, and the landscape gardner were to create upon it. Even in the rough, unfinished early stages of construction she had developed a fierce attachment to it. It was hers. It was the material expression of all she had accomplished in nearly ten years in Washington. It made those accomplishments seem more secure. If readers tired of her column, if her friends turned away from her, and if the restless, essentially faceless crowds that accepted her public and publicized parties failed one day to materialize, she would still have Pennysworth.

She had found security here in a way that was inconceivable during her ingratiating Washington beginnings, under Marc's patronage, or when married to Dick Winston. She drew a deep, tremulous breath of contentment and shoving her hands deep into her coat pockets walked back to her car. She felt secure and independent, Marc's equal at last.

She sat in her car a moment before starting the motor. What was she going to do about Marc? In recent months she had seen him only infrequently. He seemed to be waiting for some sign from her. What if he proposed? Her heart sank. What if he didn't? He might even marry someone else. She found herself grappling with her familiar dilemma. What was she to do about Marc? What if she lost him?

❧ 25 ❧

SHE stopped at her *Tribune* office on her return to Washington and worked for an hour or two on her column. She began to feel tired and hungry and left the *Tribune* building for a little bar and restaurant on L Street frequented by members of the newspaper staff. After a drink and something to eat maybe she could rewrite the column the way it should be. Somehow it seemed cloy and banal. Maybe it was the material. A feminine Senator at best was a dull subject. Once you marveled over the fact that she had been elected at all, there was little more to say. Because of the double standard in politics she had to be a lady to get re-elected and ladies made poor copy. Just for the sake of good material she would like to see a few actresses in politics with the flair an actress can bring to unladylike conduct. If there were a few male rogues in the Senate, why not a few female rogues as well? Why did women in Congress have to be grandmothers, widows, or blameless spinsters?

It was nine-thirty and the restaurant dining room was nearly empty.

"Can you serve me something, Charlie?' She asked a heavy-set man in a shiny black headwaiter's suit. "Cold cuts or a salad is O.K. if the kitchen is closed."

Charlie's face broke into a broad smile. "Miss Penelope," he said in his low, hoarse voice, "Why do you ask Charlie a question like that? Of course we'll serve you. A steak with French fries and onion rings, how's that?" He took her arm in a proprietary way. "We'll put you at this corner table in the bar, O.K.? Then I get no guff from the dining room waiters about after hours work. "I'll serve you myself." He placed her at a table and soon returned with a table cloth, a place setting, and a small wrought iron lamp with a candle inside a pink frosted globe. "At night I don't see you much. Working late?"

"I goofed off and drove into the country today. Now I have to make it up."

Charlie rocked his head back and forth with a little smile. "So? Even you do it." He patted her shoulder as he turned to go. "With you, I approve. It's O.K. You work hard. You deserve a day off. Tell the boss Charlie says it's O.K."

Penelope sipped her martini with a little smile. Charlie treated her the same as he had when she first came to work on the newspaper. To him she was a working girl. Period. The rest didn't count. So what? It was nice. Charlie was genuine.

A tall, powerfully built man at the bar smiled at her and gave a little salute with one hand. Without the glasses she wore only when driving or at the theatre she could not make out his features. Assuming he was someone from the *Tribune*, she gave a little nod and a tentative, half smile in greeting. He immediately walked over to her table with his drink and sat down on the bench beside her. He was a total stranger. "Hi." His strong, white teeth flashed in a deeply tanned face.

Penelope felt an unaccustomed thrill of excitement mixed with alarm. My God, what was this? "You've made a big mistake, handsome," she said coldly. "March right back to the bar."

"Then why the come-on?"

"I couldn't see you well at a distance. I thought I might know you. In any event, it was no invitation."

"You want me to go?"

301

"Yes."

He gazed at her a moment, a little smile playing about his lips, then he leaned back comfortably. "You don't want me to go. I can tell. I turn you on."

Her eyes dropped to the martini glass she was rapidly turning with her fingers. "Don't be ridiculous."

Charlie appeared with her steak and looked at the man beside her suspiciously. "Is the gentleman ordering?" He asked her pointedly.

Penelope hesitated and the man spoke casually and easily, "I've had dinner. I'll just keep her company."

"You see?" He said confidently as Charlie moved away. "You want me to stay."

Penelope felt her face burning. She had an overpowering sense of physical disorientation. She tried to cut her steak, but her hands trembled so that she lay down the knife and fork and placed her hands in her lap. "Who are you?" She asked in a low voice.

"Jon Hamilton." The match with which he lit his cigarette flared in the semi darkness.

"What are you?"

"A professional golfer."

"Where?"

"I'm on the town. I'm sitting a few out just now. Who are you?"

Her eyes met his. "I work on a newspaper."

"What a waste. What's the name, chick?"

"Penny Winston."

"That sounds real."

"It is real. Why wouldn't it be?"

"My name isn't real. It replaces a real jaw breaker."

She looked at her tightly clasped hands in her lap, feeling his physical presence, his eyes upon her.

"You don't want that steak," he said. "Let's go somewhere and dance."

She didn't answer.

He threw a twenty dollar bill on the table. "Come on," he said, taking her arm authoritatively. They left the barroom together followed by the doubtful eyes of Charlie. They went to a small smoky nightclub on Wisconsin Avenue with a rhythmic trio and a minuscule dance floor. He held her tightly as they danced in a firm embrace that crushed her breasts against him.

"You shouldn't hold me like that," she said breathlessly.

"Why not?"

"It's not nice," she said as he pulled her closer. "It really isn't."

"You like it," he said after a moment. "You know you do."

"I do," she said into his ear in a husky whisper, "but it isn't nice. Not here."

Wordlessly he led her from the dance floor, pausing to hand the headwaiter a bill and to indicate their abandoned table. "Where are we going?" She asked as he hailed a taxicab in the street.

"My pad on New Hampshire Avenue. You'll like it."

She felt a strange helplessness, a detached submissiveness. She had never seen this dominating male before and he did not know who she was. This was not happening to her. She didn't need to take any responsibility for it. It didn't count. The sudden, inexplicable surge of passion she felt when he touched her was overpowering, it had never happened before, it was delicious, she wanted him on any terms he offered and since he didn't know who she was, she could have him. She could have the experience Dick Winston had denied her. She could end her virginity and validate her pretensions to Marc about her sexuality. Her thoughts whirled dizzily around in her head, a bewildering combination of desire and an almost intellectual calculation.

The apartment was small, cheaply furnished, an unimaginative replica of tens of thousands of minimal living spaces being grouped in cement and stainless steel towers among the rubble of older buildings in the city's inner core. It had been reached through a brightly lighted lobby with stone faced walls and stiff red furniture by means of a self service elevator with high glass plastic panels colored a chemically simulated peach.

It was so revoltingly different from everything Penelope was used to that she felt further freed from any lingering inhibitions. She was suspended in time and in space with no remaining obligation to her real life. She could pursue her passions where they led in this unreal environment with this attractive man with the unreal name.

The bedroom was small and cramped. The window frames were of dull aluminum. A shallow closet was concealed by a drawn ribbed plastic curtain of simulated cream colored leather. The bed was hard and cold. It was a brutal room, appropriate for a hard, loveless, brutal passion. She sat on the edge of the bed watching him disrobe, shivering as she saw the powerful, tanned body with the black hair on the forearms and heavily matted hair on the chest. He removed his shorts revealing the whiteness of his flat abdomen and buttocks.

He reached out for her and began to roughly tear away her clothes. He threw them into an unceremonious heap in the corner with his own and, laying her on the bed without removing the thin green cotton bedspread, fell across her body. His lips sought hers and as his mouth pushed forward cruelly, his hands cupped over her buttocks and pulled her against him. She briefly felt the boney projection of his thigh bones and then drifted into a state of semi consciousness as the pain of the penetration grew. He was relentless, unfeeling. She clung to him tightly, meeting his thrusts, seeking the pain, until at the moment of orgasm she felt disembodied and released from torment, swept away by euphoria.

When she opened her eyes she realized that they were both covered with perspiration and that she lay beside him on soiled, disheveled bedding, finding strangely pleasant in the lassitude of passion spent the animal odors she would have ordinarily found revolting.

He lay beside her, his face half lit by the glow of the city outside the darkened room. "Honest to God," he said, "I didn't know that you were a virgin."

"It's time I stopped being one, don't you think?"

He looked at her in the darkness, unable to see her face in the shadows cast from the window. "It's O.K. then?"

She reached over and seized him, drawing him to her. "It's O.K.," she said, biting his ear.

The second time was easier than the first and less frantic. They slept for a time and in the grey of the dawn had each other a third time. He rolled away from her at last. She lay with her eyes closed, listening to the shower running. He came back into the bedroom wearing a terry cloth robe and sat on the edge of the bed smoking a cigarette. She lay in the rumpled bed, lazily stroking his forearm with her fingertips. "The shower is all yours," he said.

She gave him a pinch and got up. When she emerged from the shower, he had removed the bed linen. She walked over to him and kissed him. He fondled her hair, "I feel a little cheap," he said.

"Don't feel that way, Jon. I've never been so happy."

"I know, but I pick you up, buy you a few drinks, and bring you here. I've treated you like a tramp, Penny, and I don't feel that way about you. You're really something special. I should have taken my time, courted you a bit. I didn't have to act as if I were raping you."

"That isn't the way it was. It was love at first sight and we just sort of exploded. I think it's wonderful. If you had tried to court me, I would have been aggressively unladylike."

"But you were a virgin. This was the first time for you."

"Someone had to deflower me. I must have been waiting for you and when you touched me I couldn't wait any longer."

"Let's drive out to the ocean," he said impulsively.

"All right."

"Let's go now."

She telephoned Mrs. Moss from the garage while he had his white Jaguar brought around and told her that she would be gone a few days.

"I'm so glad you called, Mrs. Winston. It wasn't until ten minutes ago that I realized you hadn't been home last night. I was a little worried."

"I stayed with a friend. Don't worry, dear. I'll telephone you when I'll be home. I'm going to take a little rest."

"Good for you, ma'am. It's fair enough, the way you work."

Jon Hamilton drove fast and hard eastward through the barren, sodden fields of Maryland and Delaware until they reached the Atlantic at Bethany Beach. They parked the car and walked together along the deserted boardwalk in a soft, damp breeze off a lead colored ocean with long smooth swells that broke on the grey beach with just a thin edge of surf. It was unseasonably mild for March. There was the suggestion of rain in the air. Penelope grasped his firm hand, feeling the golfer's calluses, and gently swung her arm back and forth as they walked. She was completely, mindlessly happy, living entirely on a sensual level, aware as never before of the physical world about her, the lap of the gentle surf, the cry of the sea gulls, the hollow impact of their heels on the boardwalk. She felt a great sense of relief. She had no fear of a sexual humiliation now. She had been drifting into a mental spinsterhood. Now, with a stranger, she had become whole at last. She squeezed his hand and looked gratefully up into his eyes, but as she did it and thrilled to his response, she was thinking of Marc. Her happiness grew. Poor, foolish, bloodless Claudia! What a fool she was to give Marc up. In Penelope he would find the total wife, passionate, helpful, devoted to his political career. They would have several children.

Hamilton smiled down at her. "Happy?"

"Oh, yes. Completely."

"No regrets?"

"None."

"Good."

They entered the coffee shop of a motel, open throughout the winter with a reduced staff and had a sandwich and coffee at a formica topped table from which they could see the boardwalk through windows dulled by an accumulation of salt from the sea air. Jon Hamilton glanced at his wristwatch. "It's one o'clock. We can head back to Washington or we can spend the night." His eyes sought hers.

"I don't want to go back to Washington."

"Then let's drive down the coast to Ocean City."

They drove down the narrow Victorian streets of Ocean City, slashed across with modern fronts and bands of neon lighting until they found a small department store where they could buy what they needed. When they emerged into the street Penelope said, "I'll wait in the car while you buy the luggage. You'd better visit the drug store. It's the right time of the month, but we'd better not take another chance as we did last night."

They found a large modern motel north of Ocean City and registered as Mr. and Mrs. Jon Hamilton. Their room on the fourth floor had two double beds, a blue tiled bathroom with a paper band fastened around the toilet seat and two drinking glasses sealed in plastic envelopes, and a utility kitchen from which the motor of a small electric ice box purred audibly. Hamilton walked across the room and drew brown draperies with a polynesian design in red, green, and yellow across the window wall opening onto a small weather stained cement balcony. "There's nothing out there we'll miss," he said.

The next morning he watched Penelope as she emerged from the shower and began to dress before an electric heater. She smiled at him. "This tweed suit of mine is looking pretty sad. That's what happens when you run off with a man on the spur of the moment."

"Penny."

"Yes. dear."

"Let's get married."

She stood quietly, looking at him and then walked over to the bed and kissed him gently on the mouth. "Thank you, dearest, but that's not possible."

He looked both surprised and discomfited. He had expected an ecstatic assent. "Why not? We really have a thing together."

"I don't want to get married."

He sat up on the edge of the bed and groped for a cigarette from the night table. "I don't understand you," he said, lighting it. "Are you one of these emancipated women?"

Penelope laughed. "Yes. I guess you would say that I'm emancipated. You emancipated me."

He smoked for a moment as she brushed her hair before a mirror in a dressing table that was a part of a combination stained mahogany assembly running along the wall until it reached the folding louvered doors across the utility kitchen. "You are different than you were that first night. I was in charge then. You seem in charge now."

She looked at him with melting eyes. "You are in charge, dear. I've done everything you wanted."

"Maybe. I'm not sure."

"I'm thirty, Jon. I may have been backward in terms of sexual experience, but otherwise I'm the product of my years. How old are you?"

"Twenty-four."

"You're just a baby."

He looked nettled. "I don't believe you're thirty. You're putting me on."

She applied her lipstick. "I wish I were. I'm being honest. No woman adds to her age, you know."

"Well, what was this?"

"An affair."

"I don't think of you that way, Penny. I know I've gotten off to a pretty quick start, but you aren't just a woman to

308

bed down with. I want to marry you."

She came over and sat down beside him. "And then what would we do?"

"I'd take you on the tour, we'd hit the Crosby at Pebble Beach, the Desert Classic at Palm Springs, and right on through to the Masters, the Open, and the P.G.A." He grinned at her boyishly. "We'd have a ball, honey. We really would. You can't imagine. I think you'll bring me luck. I may get up into the big money, purses, then endorsements, a good pro job at one of the better country clubs."

She hugged him and then got up. "You tempt me, Jon. You really do. But I can't."

"Why not? Throw over your job. It can't be that important."

She stood, smiling down upon him. "You're really much, much nicer than I had any reason to expect."

He glowered up at her. "I recognize that as a brush off."

"Let's go down to breakfast."

They walked on the beach. When they returned he bought a newspaper and two magazines at the newsstand. She looked at him with amusement in the elevator as they ascended to their room. "You're settling in. Maybe it's time to go."

"I've just been turned down," he said. "That sort of turns me off. I'm funny that way."

She squeezed his arm, but said nothing more.

In the room she turned to him. "I'm going to wash my hair."

"Why not?" He said sullenly, opening a magazine.

He was sitting quietly, the magazine open on his lap, when she emerged from the bathroom drying her hair on a towel.

"So you're that Penny Winston," he said in a flat voice.

She looked at him from under the towel. "What do you mean?"

"You're Penelope."

She glanced over his shoulder at a double page spread of one of her parties at Foxhall House. "There is a resemblance,

309

isn't there?"

"No wonder you wouldn't marry me."

She met his eyes. "We both took an awful chance, Jon. You got stuck with a celebrity."

He looked at her bleakly. "I'll forget marriage. That would be a joke. Do we stay friends?"

"How can we?"

He looked down at the magazine. "What were you doing in that bar," he said savagely. "Slumming?"

"I'm a newspaperwoman. I've gone to that bar for years."

"A newspaperwoman," he said scornfully. "You're a Washington rich bitch."

"I'm a newspaperwoman first—and last. The rest just happened."

"Yes *Mrs.* Winston," he grinned at her sardonically.

She stood very still, poised. He continued to look at her but said nothing more. "Are you going to throw that up at me?" She asked.

"No."

"I'll deny it, if you do."

"Mr. Winston must have been a real loser."

She eyed him calculatingly. "I'll give you fifty thousand dollars to forget this whole episode. That's more than you'll make on the tour in a good year."

He turned white and then flushed a brick red. "What kind of a woman are you?" He asked thickly after a moment.

"A realist. Everyone has to have some motivation for what they do—or don't do."

"I could take your money and come back again." He looked at her bitterly.

She shook her head. "You have to tell your story now. I'm here and they'll have to believe you. Once I'm back in Washington, no one will believe you. I'm in the public eye. There are always a few scurrilous stories about public figures. I deny them all. The story will reflect on you, not me."

"I could get a few witnesses."

She smiled. "Don't be naive, dear. I've played this game much longer than you."

"Charlie?"

"Charlie is a friend of mine. So are a few other people whose names you would recognize."

He looked at her thin lipped. "I don't want your money."

"I want you to have it."

He got up from the chair. "Let's go back to Washington."

She looked frightened. "What are you going to do?"

"I'm going to play golf."

Her eyes sought his anxiously.

"And keep my mouth shut."

She walked across the room and impulsively hugged his rigid body. "I was so lucky in you, Jon. Forgive me."

He pushed her away from him in distaste. "We both should have been so lucky."

He refused to talk to her on the return trip to Washington but as they swung onto the beltway he asked, "Where do I drop you?"

"Sixteenth and L. You'll dispose of the luggage?"

"Yes."

"I'm really ashamed of myself, Jon. Please forgive me. I'm used to writing about some pretty predatory types. I figured I had met one in real life."

He did not answer for a moment, then he said gruffly, "That's O.K. I sure acted like a heel on the make. It's not surprising that you thought I was one." He concentrated on traffic. "I would like to see you again." It was a request, almost shyly spoken.

She hesitated.

"On your terms. I know I struck pretty hard. I'd had a few drinks, but I meant it, Penny."

"I meant it, too, Jon, as far as it goes. I'm not a wanton, just a little sex starved, I find."

"Can't it go a little further? Do we have to call it quits?"

She squeezed his arm. "All right. Call me in a week."

311

"A week?"

"I intend to get control of myself, Mr. Hamilton. I want a friendship, at most an affair. I don't want a scandal and so far you affect me scandalously."

"Me too," he grinned.

"Then simmer down. One week."

"O.K." He turned to her. "I'll bet you have an unlisted number."

"I do. I'll give it to you." She wrote the number on a plain white card from her purse and stuck it in his coat pocket. "Satisfied?"

"No. But at least I'm not getting a brush-off."

"No. You're not getting a brush-off."

❧ 26 ❧

THE receptionist in Senator Haywood's outer office in the new Senate Office Building looked up as Penelope entered from the public passageway and then smiled with the shy expression of recognition of a celebrity that people who had never met her in person often assumed.

"I'm Mrs. Winston. Is the Senator in?"

"He's over on the Senate floor, Mrs. Winston. We can try to reach him."

"I'd like to speak to him on the telephone, if possible."

"I'll see what I can do."

Penelope ignored the inhospitable straight chairs placed against the walls of the cramped waiting room and examined, in wooden racks, several of the unimaginative leaflets and guides to Washington which were a part of the handouts for visitors of every member of Congress. The receptionist handed her a telephone with a smile. "He's on the line."

"Marc? Can I capture you for lunch?"

The voice on the telephone was faintly surprised. "Today? I'm expecting a vote, Penny. You would have to wait for that."

"No matter. I'll wait."

"Then come over to the Senate Reception Room and send in your name with a page. I'll join you as soon as I can."

She walked across the shaded grounds to the Capitol, admiring the majestic, timeless, beauty of the great white marble building containing the nation's two great deliberative halls and scores of rooms and corridors already heavily encrusted with art work and statuary indicating the accumulation of time and tradition. She knew the members of Congress so well, she was so familiar with the details of the building, that she was watchful for any tendency on her part to take it for granted. She didn't want to lose the sense of awe, of wonderment, the sense of great purposes served, she had felt when she first came to Washington and saw the glow of the Capitol's great dome against the backdrop of a June night sky.

Instinctively she knew that it was this sense of wonderment combined with knowledge and wit that made her column a continuing success. So, from time to time, she preferred to avoid the prosaic subway or the labyrinthian tunnels connecting the Capitol with the office buildings that housed congressional members and staff and approach the building across its grounds, as it sat on its natural pedestal overlooking Washington, dominating even the great oaks, elms, and maple trees that shaded the curving pathways leading to it.

She climbed the great center staircase to the Rotunda under the Capitol dome and at its top turned to look eastward toward the classical Greek simplicity of the Supreme Court Building and the sprawling Victorian ornateness of the Library of Congress. This was the view newly inaugurated presidents looked upon as they felt for the first time the full weight of responsibility and power. This was the view that retiring presidents looked upon as they felt the power and responsibility lift from them, leaving them greatly relieved but also greatly diminished. Penelope drew a tremulous breath. How wonderful it was! She wouldn't want to live anywhere else. She was a part of the most exciting city in the world.

She entered the coolness of the great Rotunda, echoing hollowly to the voices of the groups of tourists walking slowly around its circumference, admiring the huge oil paintings on its walls, and walked down the ornate, almost Byzantine corridors leading to the Senate wing. She entered the Senate Reception Room and sat on one of the hard black leather upholstered benches while a serious faced young page took her name into the Senate Chamber to Senator Haywood. In a few minutes he joined her, his characteristic, tentative smile playing about his lips. He kissed her. "Hi, darling. I don't believe we've ever met here before. Isn't it fantastic?" His eyes moved around the room with its mosaic floor, its frescoes, murals, and sculpture, its heavy Victorian chandeliers. "I always feel that I'm on a Hollywood set in this room and we are about to film one of Garibaldi's greatest moments in Rome in 1866."

"I like it," Penelope said. "It seems historical."

"It's the work of an over emotional Italian American patriot. The only thing in the room that honors the Anglo-Saxon Puritan ethic are these benches. They're hard enough to satisfy Cotton Mather."

"Have you voted yet?"

"No. Senator Berry is droning on. He's one of these Senators who is so loquacious he even filibusters bills he's *for*. I give him another half hour, then we'll vote."

"I'll wait."

"I could buy you a quick lunch in the Senate restaurant, subject to interruption by the roll call bell."

"No. I want to buy you lunch—in a less official place."

He sat down beside her and lit a cigarette. "That sounds inviting. I'll keep you company until we are called for the vote."

They sat together on the soft leather cushion of the restaurant booth surrounded by old brick, weathered timbers and artifacts that sought to create the atmosphere of an old colonial inn in the basement of a modern building. He smiled into her eyes and took her hand. "After two martinis and osso buco, I'm not going to feel much like shouldering the duties

315

of the Work Horse of the Senate."

"Good heavens! Is that what they call you?"

"No. That's what I call myself."

She laughed and leaned toward him. "You do enjoy it, don't you, Marc?"

"Yes, I do. It's very real, you know. Sooner or later you have to stop talking and vote. I like real things."

"So do I," she said softly. They looked deeply into one another's eyes and their lips met. "Was that real?" She murmured.

"Very real."

"Would you like to try again?"

"Here?"

"That's why I chose a booth and an inattentive waiter."

His lips met hers again. "You do connive."

"Of course, otherwise you would brood in the Senate, waiting for roll call votes until we were too old for romance."

"Are you still seeing the poor man's Arnold Palmer?"

"Jon? That isn't fair. He does fairly well."

"So I've heard."

She smiled at him. "You're jealous, Marc Haywood. How simply marvelous."

"He isn't your type. It's a comedown for you. I don't like to see it."

"Who is my type?"

"I am."

She leaned close to him, her voice low and seductive. "I've always said you were, but you've always refused to believe it—or do anything about it."

"I tried in New York."

"Oh, that," she dismissed the memory with a little gesture. "Try again."

"All right. Let's get married."

She sat very still, her eyes searching his, then her face flooded with happiness. She took his face in both of her hands and kissed him. "Darling, I never, never thought you were going to say it. Let's. As soon as possible."

"An elopement?"

"Not quite, but soon. Within a month. Just our close friends."

He sat back with a grin and looked at her. "I can't believe it."

"Neither can I." She toyed with her fork for a moment. "Darling, I have something I want to show you out in Maryland. Can you take the afternoon off?"

"Not that Heitzing development of yours? If so, I visited it last week as a member of a Government Operations Subcommittee. We gave you restrained cheers."

"No. This is on the Eastern Shore and more personal."

"I must be back at seven." He smiled sardonically. "I'm attending a black tie dinner for those who feel very deeply about poverty. Though not the principal speaker, I'm scheduled for a few inspiring remarks."

"I'll get you back."

"O.K. Let me advise the office and we can go."

She looked at him with a vulnerable expression as they stood before the completed facade of Pennysworth. "What do you think?"

"Why do you need it?" He asked shortly.

She looked at him in surprise. "I don't need it. I want it."

"Why?"

She bit her lip, taken aback. "I only wanted an opinion, Marc. Not an analysis."

He stared at the house, his hands shoved into his coat. "You need both. What are you trying to prove?"

Tears of anger and disappointment flooded into her eyes. "I admire the fine old country houses in the East. I'm trying to build one. I'm not trying to prove anything."

He continued to glower at the house. "I don't think it's becoming of you to imitate the great historic houses of Maryland or of Virginia. You come from the yoeman tradition of the Middle West. This is the last third of the twentieth century. We have contemporary problems. We can't take refuge behind eight foot hedges of English boxwood, particularly hauled in and transplanted from somewhere else."

"Well, I asked," she said, trying to control the tremor in her voice. "And you have told me."

"I'm simply saying that you have more relevancy being what you are. You don't have to pretend to be something else."

"I think you're jealous."

"Jealous? What a fantastic idea!"

"No. What really upsets you is that I'm building an estate as lovely as Hollywood or Westgate and as a little nobody from Indiana I shouldn't do such a thing."

"Don't be absurd, Penny. I question your judgment, not your right to do it."

"Most of you Virginia and Maryland country estate types are phonies anyway. The rich German burgers of the nineties built replicas of medieval castles on the Rhine and dreamed Wagnerian dreams. Your families brought New York or Pennsylvania money to Virginia or to the Maryland Eastern Shore and built replicas of colonial plantations for use as horse farms and pretended that you were landed gentry. You deprecated it all to me, Marc, but you still liked it. You still like it, but you pretend you don't because you don't want to spoil your political stance. There isn't a decent estate in Virginia that isn't maintained by contemporary money. Even museums like Mount Vernon or Gunston Hall require contemporary support. You've accepted the new money that built the estates of the 1920's, but it's posturing for me to build a similar estate half a century later."

"I was not critical, Penny, because I thought you were imitating Hollywood. Frankly, the thought didn't occur to me. I was critical because what you are doing is an anachronism. I'm willing to concede that Hollywood may be too. I feel

318

well rid of it."

"It's not an anachronism. The rich have always built great houses. I'm rich. I'm building a house that pleases me. I intend to entertain my friends here—live, relevant contemporary friends."

"Penelope's Zoo?" He asked quietly.

"That was your term, remember? Not mine. I know you coined it tongue-in-cheek."

Haywood lit a cigarette. "If you want to play Du Barry or Pompadour go ahead. Build your palace."

She turned away from him in a fury. "Oh you're such a perfect—perfect, son-of-a-bitch!"

He did not answer. In a moment she turned around and saw him smiling at her, a twinkle in his eye. Impulsively she threw herself into his arms. "Oh, Marc. I love you so!"

He held her tight and kissed her ardently. "And I love you."

She looked up at him. "You do?" Her blue eyes were wide and appealing. "But how can you, really? I'm such a bitch."

"Only when provoked. I was pretty provoking."

She held his arm, looking at her raw, new home. "You're right. I'm a showoff. I'll abandon it. We'll call it Penelope's Folly and sell it off."

"No. Don't do that. It will be a lovely house."

"Will you come and live in it?"

He gazed at the house seriously for a moment then he said slowly, "No. I'll never even visit it."

She looked at him uncertainly. "What does that mean?"

He lit a cigarette and stood looking down for a moment at the dry grass on which they stood. "It means," he said carefully, "That where politics is concerned you and I are going to lead separate lives. This has been a problem in the back of my mind for some time. This house symbolizes it."

"But I'm not in politics!"

"Don't be absurd. You are in politics up to your neck. You've changed your Zoo in the last few years until it's known on the Hill as Herman Baur's unofficial caucus. We all know that you sponsor the meetings of the congressional hierarchy. You are an intimate of the presidential family. You write the most devastatingly political column this town has ever seen without mentioning politics. You have become a Washington political institution. Unfortunately, you don't practice my kind of politics."

"I'm what you taught me to be."

"You've gone a few light years beyond that. Don't misunderstand, darling. I don't disapprove. I admire you for it. As Marc Haywood, publisher of the *Tribune*, I'd marry you and look on with pride and amused tolerance. As Marc Haywood, freshman Senator, you frighten me to death."

"Oh, Marc. How melodramatic! That doesn't sound like you."

"I'm making a reputation in the Senate. It's a small reputation, but it's my own. It's solidly based on my own voting record and performance. I don't want to marry into Penelope's Zoo. I don't want to be a part of Herman Baur's clique."

"Well, of course, you don't have to come to the Zoo just because you're married to me. Dick never did."

"I won't come to the Zoo and I won't be a part of whatever you have in mind for this estate, though I can guess."

Penelope's face looked pinched with disappointment. "Very well, you needn't."

He took her in his arms. "Darling, don't you understand? You're a famous wife. You're better known in politics than I am. If I were a smart dedicated politician I wouldn't marry you. I'd stay as far away as possible. But I love you and I want to marry you. This thing has grown between us for years and I am not going to resist it any longer. For some people that means I'll join your Zoo, Herman Baur's Zoo. I'll have to take a chance on that. I can't help misunderstandings. But, in fact, I won't have a thing to do with it. I'm making my own way politically. I want to feel free to oppose Herman Baur and the President, too, if I feel I must."

"All right," Penelope said grudgingly. "I think you are exaggerating the situation, but if that's the way you feel— that's the way you feel."

"Then it's understood that my political life is my own. It is separate from our marriage. You won't interfere with it in any way and you won't expect me at your Zoo or out here at this, this, palatial spread?"

"It's understood. But you've hurt my feelings. You really have. I feel rejected, sort of put down, as if part of me were unclean."

"Not at all, darling. Where politics is concerned I'm an independent. I intend to stay that way."

"Herman Baur is a fine man."

"Of course he is. But you can't be a political friend of Herman Baur unless you agree with him all of the time or trade off something you believe in. I don't agree with him all of the time and there are beliefs I won't trade on."

Penelope smiled suddenly. "O.K. It doesn't matter. I won't interfere. Politics don't interest me any way."

Haywood laughed. "I believe you really mean that."

Penelope was wide eyed. "Of course I do. I wouldn't say it, if I didn't."

They were married on a Saturday afternoon at St. Johns before a small group of twenty close friends and after a wedding luncheon at the Sulgrave Club flew to Antigua for their honeymoon. A classmate of Haywood's at Harvard gave them his house and servants for the ten days they wished to remain. They were on the island incognito and spent their time on the terrace overlooking the sea and a small natural beach or swimming lazily in a kidney shaped pool framed in pink marble. They ate simple salads and barbecued chicken with their fingers, peeled fresh fruit and drank tropical drinks of rum and juices. They laughed and talked at random of nothing in particular and as they relaxed in the warmth and glow of the low latitudes they grew closer together in the in-

321

timate silences that reflected their love and understanding of each other.

Alone, sleeping nude together in the soft humidity of the Caribbean, their skin gently stroked by the almost imperceptible movement of the night air, they found a oneness in the union of their bodies neither would have believed possible. Penelope could only compare the groping ineptitude of Dick Winston and the brutal, explosive passion of Jon Hamilton to the sustained and considerate ardor she was now experiencing. Marc Haywood, childless after nearly twenty years of marriage to Claudia, could only compare her fastidious and infrequent submission, her pallid and restrained affection, to the questing, seeking love of Penelope who endeavoured in a dozen unconscious and subtle ways to please him. For the first time in her life she felt in his arms wholly content, wholly secure, able to relax. She felt that she had completed the journey at last and was safely home.

The day before they were to fly back into the gray, noxious shroud of air that covered New York she embraced him as they stood toward the shallow end of the pool, the cold azure salt water reaching to their breasts, lapping against them in a strong on-shore breeze. "Marc, darling. I want to give up my column. I don't want any part of my old life. I want this to be a beginning of a new life. I just want to be the wife of Senator Marc Haywood. I want to devote myself to you, to your career. I don't want us to be separate in any way. I want us to be together in everything, just as we are here in Antigua."

He kissed her, but did not reply.

"What are you thinking?" She asked.

"I was thinking how much I love you and that I'd like to remain right here for the rest of our lives. Things can't be like this back in Washington."

"Then let's stay here."

"You know that we can't."

"Why not? We'll buy this house or another like it and live

happily ever after."

"We have our obligations. We can't just walk away, because if we did we could never walk back again. I don't think either of us could live the rest of our lives in lotus land."

She looked downcast. "You're pushing me away a little, aren't you?"

"Just a little, darling. I want to run my own political life."

"I could help. I desperately want to help."

"You can't help. We must see each other as we are. I have a political identity separate from Penelope's Zoo. You are Penelope. Neither of us can help that."

"I didn't realize that I was such a baleful influence."

"You aren't, darling, but you and your Zoo have such a vivid public personality, you would destroy my independent political identity if you entered my political life. I helped create your public image and as your publisher and husband I'm proud of it. But as a politician I want no part of it."

"But, darling. You are excluding me from the most important part of your life!"

He kissed her. "An important part, yes. Not the most important part. You are the most important part and I want you as you are, independent, magnetic, glamourous, intelligent, Penelope of Washington. Don't forget I've watched all of that emerge from a pert, vivacious college girl. It's very important to me. I'm not at all certain the political career of the Junior Senator from Virginia is worth one-tenth the career of our Penelope, but for whatever it's worth, I want to develop it."

"Do you regret marrying me?"

"Don't be a dunce."

"I'll never let you go, you know."

"Nor I you."

"Let's take an afternoon nap together."

"We didn't get up until eleven."

"I know."

"You're shameless."

"I always will be. I warn you."

"Penny."

"Yes."

"Thank you for entering my life and refusing to leave it, even when I was acting my worst."

"I have always loved you, Marc."

"I don't deserve your love. I never have. But I'm so grateful to have it."

She kissed him a long, lingering kiss as he helped her out of the pool.

❧ 27 ❧

THE autumn leaves had turned at Pennysworth. The great stand of beech which had been bisected by the broad lawn reaching from the terrace of the house to the pier and boathouse on the Chesapeake Bay now framed the view to the water in files of gold, rippling in the restless breeze that swung about, from northwest to southeast, surged and subsided, suggesting under the pale blue sky and the still warm sun that harsher weather might soon come. Penelope had come up to the house from the tennis court where she had just finished a fast paced singles game with young, angular Congressman Gresham, a protege of Speaker Blount. Having lost 6-4, 4-6, and 6-1, she had abandoned the field to others and joined Alice Payson who was sitting alone, looking pensively out on the Bay. Penelope sat down on the limestone cap of the low flagstone wall running along the edge of the terrace and swung her racquet idly back and forth.

"Good game?" Alice Payson asked.

"Oh, yes. Harry is a real heads-up player. Much too good for me. He carried me along for two sets and then really polished me off in the last one."

"Brute," Alice said, lighting a cigarette from the one in her hand.

"You seem on edge, Alice. Is anything wrong?"

"Nothing I can talk about."

"Where is the President?"

"Down in the boxwood garden with a book and three bored Secret Service men."

"He's looking better, now that Congress has adjourned."

"You think so?"

"Yes, I do."

"I'm glad to hear you say it, dear. I'm not sure myself." Her mouth gave a little twist. "They always kill the man in the White House, one way or another. They have had nearly three years to work on Bill. I think it's showing."

"Don't worry so, Alice. I know Bill is under a terrible strain. Presidents must be. There is no way to avoid it, but he has the best and most attentive medical attention in the world. They won't let him overdo."

Tears flooded Alice Payson's eyes and she looked down.

Penelope laid her racquet down and came over to her. "Alice, something is wrong. Let me help."

Alice Payson blew her nose and shook her head. After a moment she cleared her throat and looked at Penelope. "I just have to share this with someone. It's tearing me apart inside."

"Then share it with me, dear. I'm your friend. That is what friends are for."

Alice nodded without speaking.

"Let's walk down the lawn together. No one can overhear us," Penelope suggested. They walked slowly, arm in arm, across the sloping lawn. They had progressed over half way toward the pier when Alice Payson spoke in a strangled voice.

"Bill is sick. Very sick, Penny."

Penelope turned to her wordlessly.

"He has arrested cancer of the liver. If it gets out of hand, it's terminal. He will go very quickly."

"Oh, Alice," Penelope said, tears filling her eyes. "How terrible. How perfectly dreadful." Her hand, grasping Alice's through her arm, tightened.

326

Having uttered the words, Alice seemed more in control of herself. "Bill doesn't know. Doctor Fyfe has only told me. He doesn't know what to do. You see," she said brokenly, "Bill is the President of the United States."

"Oh, Alice," Penelope repeated.

Alice cleared her throat. "If Bill were a private citizen, we wouldn't tell him. Why force him to live his remaining time under the burden of knowing that he has this ugly, quiescent thing inside him? But he is the President. Do we owe it to the country to tell him, to let him resign or refuse to run again? The doctor can't answer that question and neither can I. And, of course, apart from that, I think of Bill. I know now that I'm going to lose him, sooner or later, and that there will be years and years and years without him." Her voice broke. "I don't think I can stand that, Penny, or the look that will come into those fine, intelligent eyes and stay there when he knows."

"Don't tell him." Penelope's voice was husky with emotion, but her mind was racing.

Alice Payson sought her eyes. "You're sure, Penny? That not telling him is right? Because it's what I want to hear. You aren't telling me what I want to hear to be kind, are you, Penny? We have to do the right thing. We really must. This is the presidency."

"No," Penelope spoke slowly. "I'm not just thinking of you and Bill. He has been elected by the people. No one knows how long he has to live. He may live out this term. He may live out a second term. He may outlive both you and me. Who knows when it will flare up? Perhaps it never will. The diagnosis may be wrong. We can't put this additional burden of knowledge on him. We can't play God. I think you should say nothing and let the future take care of itself."

"And even run for a second term next year? That's unthinkable!"

"Why? If Bill feels like running and the people want him? We can't destroy a great man one day before God does.

327

That's why the doctor is remaining silent. Doctors fight illness and death every day. They know better than to try and play God."

Alice blew her nose and then kissed Penelope on the cheek. "You've been my good friend from the day we arrived from California, Penny. I don't know what I'd do without you. You are right. I feel so much better. We'll live this thing from day to day, Bill and me. I'll be stoic and keep it to myself. I'll have faith that it will all come right, that a great and good man won't be struck down before his time." She smiled. "And I count on you, dear, to keep me going if I weaken."

"I'm devoted to you both, Alice. You know that."

"I know it and Bill knows it. That's why this is the only private estate he'll visit. He knows that you want him because he's Bill Payson and in spite of the fact he is the President. He knows a President is a poor guest, descending upon a place accompanied by a locust swarm of Secret Service men and aides, leaving it afterward a publicity wasteland, an object of withering public attention. You endure his entourage, the weight of the human millstones about his neck, and you blunt the publicity. He can come and go unmentioned in the press, even in your column."

"I'd never mention it in the column, Alice, and it helps to be married to a press tycoon. They are the only ones who can call off the working press."

Alice powdered her nose and examined her eyes anxiously in her compact mirror for tell tale signs of red. "Are you happy with Marc, Penny? After eighteen months of marriage?"

"Ecstatically, Alice. He is my one, great, enduring love."

"That's so wonderful to hear, Penny. I never heard you talk of Dick that way."

"No. Dick was sweet and I loved him, but Marc, well, I adore him. He's everything to me."

"Yet, I seldom see you together. There are even rumors

328

that you don't get on."

"Our private life is our own. It is all the more wonderful because it is intimate, limited, and intense. Our public lives are apart. Marc insists on his political independence, even from me."

Alice smiled and squeezed her hand. "I'm so pleased to see you happy, dear. Especially since I can never be completely happy again." She looked out over the water where a score of white sails caught the rose glow of the late afternoon sunlight. "Let's join the President," she said. "He should come in now, it's getting chilly."

Herman Baur sat before the fire with Penelope at Foxhall House. "It's nice to have this chance to talk with you, Penny, before the other members of the Zoo arrive."

"I wanted to talk with you alone, Herman. I have something important on my mind."

Herman Baur sipped his bourbon and branch water. "I assumed that you did," he said dryly. "That's why I was so prompt."

Penelope glanced out of the window and watched the heavy snowfall for a moment. "I guess I might as well come directly to the point."

"It saves time."

"I have overheard you say that you might drop Vice President Breen from the ticket this year."

"You overheard right. Breen drinks too much, and talks too much. He'll be a drag on the ticket. The President thinks so, too. If anything happened to President Payson, we'd have another Harding in the White House."

"I think you should put Senator Haywood of Virginia on the ticket."

Herman Baur stared at her unblinkingly for over a minute. Penelope calmly and serenely met his gaze. "Well, young lady, you are full of surprises," he said at last. "I didn't guess the subject of this pow wow." He sipped his drink and his shrewd eyes sought hers again. "What put that idea into your head?"

"You need to balance the ticket geographically. Virginia will balance California. You need a young appearing, vital man to offset the President's rather pedantic manner. You need a liberal to appeal to the Negro and the independent vote. Payson hasn't moved left as fast as that vote and Senator Haywood has. You need a good speaker to carry the bulk of the campaign in the hustings. You need a southerner to get the South to swallow a liberal ticket. You need a good press and Marc can practically guarantee that."

Herman Baur nodded. "As a matter of fact, Haywood's a name on my list, but not for those reasons. I admit he has those qualifications, however."

"Why is he on your list?"

"I want to get him out of the Senate and into the political graveyard of the Vice Presidency," Baur said brutally as he put down his drink and slowly lit a cigar. "Of course, Payson might die and we'd have Haywood in the White House, but that's a chance we have to take. In politics we ignore death. Our profession specializes in the living and the needs, wants, and weaknesses of the living. There's no way to deal with death except to accept it. That puts it outside the deals of politics."

"Then we want the same thing," Penelope said.

Herman Baur rolled his cigar between his lips. "I'm surprised that Haywood wants this. It means joining the *Club*. I thought he rather preferred being the party's Senate gadfly."

"Marc knows nothing about this."

Baur held her eyes in a searching gaze for a minute. "I see." His face was impassive. "Why are you tinkering with this? Why do you want it for him?"

"I think it's about time he rejoined the Zoo. I'm getting a little tired of my husband being the critic of my political friends in public. Also, I'm a little more impressed with the

Vice Presidency than you are."

"How do we persuade him to leave the Senate?"

"We don't. At the convention he's suddenly chosen and nominated. He won't refuse the President."

"What if he issues a Sherman statement and refuses to run?"

"He won't. I can at least promise that."

The cigar smoke curled slowly upward toward the ceiling. "Very interesting idea, Penny," Herman Baur said at last. "There are quite a few obstacles, but it's an interesting idea."

Penelope looked at him unsmilingly. "I'm dead serious about this, Herman. I really want it for him. I'll work right with you on it."

"I can see that you want it intensely, though as yet I can't see why, but it may come to me. There are several months before the convention."

"I told you why."

"So you did. So you did, but wouldn't I be foolish to believe all a woman tells me or believe she tells me all?"

Walter Tucker sat in Herman Baur's livingroom at the Sheraton Park, his big hands resting easily on his knees. He looked from Penelope to Herman Baur with dark eyes partially obscured by heavy brows. "I like Senator Haywood right where he is. Why should I support him for Vice President?"

Baur looked at the long ash on the end of his cigar. "You are a Negro politician, Walter. Wouldn't you like the Senate's newest glamour boy, its fighting Southern liberal on the ticket? He's been a friend of your race."

Walter Tucker smiled broadly, throwing his heavy face into furrows and ridges. "Herman, until recent years you've never given a damn for the Negro. You don't give a damn now. You deal in power and votes. So do I. I don't know what you mean by 'Southern liberal.' So don't try to sell me something using phony political clichés. Haywood's a nice

331

fellow, he's got the black vote in Virginia until we can do better, but he doesn't know how to make a deal. He just talks about things. If you are here to make a deal for him, let's get down to cases."

"I want you to visit President Payson and tell him the American Negro wants Haywood on the ticket. Present it as your own spontaneous idea. Leave me out of it. I'm willing to give you something in return."

"I'm listening."

"What do you want? I never make an offer."

"I want a five billion dollar federal program for my state. I'll give you the details later."

"Education? Slum clearance?"

Tucker laughed, showing his strong, even white teeth. "Man, we're going to get that stuff anyway from Payson as part of the urban package. We both know that, so don't give me a snow job. I'm talking about something extra, public works, pork barrel, you know, Herman, space, defense, roads, rivers, and harbors. After the election, I'll give you a list."

"Five billion is too high."

"What figure you thinking about?"

"One."

"I'll take three billion, one cabinet appointment, and two federal judgeships."

"I don't know that I can deliver that. I can only advise the President."

Tucker grinned at Penelope. "Ain't he cute?" He turned back to Baur, the grin still playing about his lips, but his eyes were hard. "You want Haywood out of the Senate, Herman. He's beginning to draw the young Turks of the party around him. You want to kick him upstairs. So fish or cut bait."

"We need you, but we don't need you that bad. The President may choose Haywood anyway. Mrs. Haywood is a close friend of the Presidential family, as you know. The President sometimes listens to what I have to say. Other factions are supporting Haywood."

Tucker shrugged. "You may not need me to say 'yes', but what if I say 'no'? What if I come out for another term for Breen? Attack the 'dump Breen' movement?"

"That would hurt, maybe not enough. It might cause a convention floor fight, nothing more."

Tucker looked up at the ceiling and intoned, "White racist, bigot, aristocrat, millionaire."

"Are you suggesting that as a description of someone?" Penelope asked hotly.

Tucker's expression was bland. "No, not at all. That's just a little litany I go through now and then. It keeps me up tight when I might let down."

Baur drew on his cigar and made a decision. "I agree to your terms. It's late April. You'd better see the President right away and deliver the endorsement. But not a word to the press or anyone else or the deal is off."

Tucker slapped his knees with his open palms and got up from his chair with a little grunt. "You are a great, farseeing statesman, Herman. I've always said so. I may even say it in public some day."

Baur grinned. "Check it out with me first. I'm not sure it would do me any good where I come from."

"That's right. You act so civilized I sometimes forget you live close to lynching country."

"No. We have never had a lynching in my state though we sometimes crossed the border to watch them in our southern neighbor."

Tucker nodded. "I apologize. I didn't realize that you were only onlookers."

"When are you going to start lynching whites up in your northern urban black belt?"

"Man, you don't know, do you? We're lynching them now, but we call it guerrilla warfare and we use lead instead of hemp."

Baur returned to his chair when Tucker had left and lit a

fresh cigar.

"What an awful man!" Penelope said. "Do we need him?"

"Yes," Herman Baur said. "We need him. And Walter's all right. He's a politician. He's projecting his constituent's view and language, but he's inside the system. I can understand Walter. We can get along."

"But he hates you."

"No he doesn't. That's his bargaining stance."

"Isn't he a crook?"

"Not at all. His political bargains aren't for himself. I'll bet Walter is worth less then $100,000."

"I don't like him."

"You should. He's the rarest kind of bird we've got, an independent Negro political leader. Both black and white militants are outside politics. They are the totalitarians, using duress and propaganda techniques to seize power. They can't accommodate. They can't compromise. They advocate Armageddon. Walter is inside politics like me. His power is democratic. What he gains for his people will last because it's based on negotiation and accommodation—tough, hard negotiation and reluctant accommodation, but negotiation and accommodation nevertheless. Walter and I are both in that business. We understand each other."

"Where are we now?" Penelope asked.

"I think with Tucker we're over the top. I've been wheeling and dealing. Within the last month Payson has been told in private conversations that labor, farmers, the party's congressional leadership, and several fat cat contributors from the business sector want Haywood. I think he's about convinced."

"What if there's a leak before the convention?"

"There won't be. The President realizes that he shouldn't reveal his hand prematurely. There may be rumors. With several people involved, enough information to fuel rumors may get out, but we'll keep several other names in the ring. That will confuse everyone, including Haywood. I'm pre-

334

tending to Payson that I'm not yet convinced Haywood is the right man. When I fall in line, it will put Haywood over."

Penelope walked to a window and looked off toward the Potomac and the thin white needle of the Washington monument glowing in the twilight. "I do want this for him."

"He won't thank you. He wants to stay in the Senate even though in my opinion he doesn't respect it and refuses to work within its traditions."

She turned and nodded. "I know that he won't thank me. He mustn't find out. He would be furious."

"If he does, deny everything. That's what I always do. Accusations and denials aren't like truth and lies. They're the tools of politics, used in the necessary probing and fencing to find a position you can stand on."

28

THE convention was held in Miami Beach in July, a dull and colorless political caravansary held of necessity to re-nominate as presidential candidate a popular, but essentially dull man. The delegates, dressed in soft shapeless summer fabrics worked into imitations of winter business suits for the men and gaudy print dresses for the women, festooned with buttons, medallions, and ribbons moved restlessly from the chill stale drafts of air conditioned hotels into the heavy, humid air of crowded streets and parking lots acrid with the exhausts of numberless motor cars, and back again, fighting the colds, muscular aches, and sinus infections the contrasts induced with copious quantities of alcohol interspersed with hurriedly eaten sandwiches or cold canapés. They held the outward forms of power of the convention, but in fact they were passing the time in a carnival atmosphere waiting for the moment when they would nominate an incumbent president by acclamation and nominate his choice for vice president as a matter of course.

Penelope and Marc Haywood sat at breakfast at a small table placed in the livingroom window of their suite. Beyond a narrow balcony they could see the edge of a huge swimming pool five floors below, a narrow strip of beach and the blue of the ocean beyond. Penelope sipped her second cup of coffee and watched the gentle breakers move in irregular

336

lines to the beach.

"When do you see the President?" She asked. Marc Haywood glanced up briefly from the newspaper he was reading. "At ten o'clock. You know," he said, changing the subject, "The layout and type of the *Tribune* is much better than this Miami newspaper. I understand its circulation and advertising volume have been dropping. If I weren't involved in politics, I think I would buy it. It's just mismanaged. It should do much better."

"Don't be too hard on it. After all, it carries my column."

"That's the only thing in it worth reading."

"Marc, aren't you just a little excited to be asked to see the President, this morning, of all mornings?"

"No. Why?"

"Well, the Vice President will be nominated today. The President may ask you to join the ticket."

Haywood grinned. "No danger of that."

"Why not? Your name is among those mentioned in the news reports."

"Surely, you know enough by this time to discount news reports."

"What if he asks?"

"I'll refuse."

"Marc!"

"Look, darling, it isn't going to happen. I haven't lifted a finger and I'm not an organization man. Baur's man will get it and that's that. Payson and I are close, but he won't buck Baur on a matter like this."

"Who is Baur's man?"

"If you don't know, I don't know. You're the Zoo keeper, not me. All I know is that I'm not Baur's man and Baur's man will get it."

"Well, why does he want to see you?"

"Probably he'll ask me to give a seconding speech. If he asks, I'll do it; that's a harmless enough exercise."

He left the suite at ten minutes of ten to go to the Presidential Suite on the tenth floor. Penelope sat on a blue linen sofa and waited for his return. She held a book, but her heart was pounding and she was too excited to read it. What would Marc do? What would he say? Would he guess that she had a part in it?

He was pale and silent when he returned. He sat down in a chair opposite her wordlessly.

"Darling," she heard herself say, "What is it? You look almost ill."

He lit a cigarette and sat staring at her. "It seems," he said after a moment in a flat voice, "That I am Herman Baur's man."

"You mean that the President asked you to run as Vice President?"

"Yes."

"Oh, Marc! How wonderful! I'm so proud." She ran across the room to embrace him.

He endured the kiss and pushed her away. "Just a moment, Penny. Don't be premature. I want to sort this out."

"Sort what out?"

"I'm not Herman Baur's man, you know. Why did he choose me?"

"The President did, darling. Not Herman."

"We both know better. Herman proposes, the President agrees where politics are concerned. Payson can't worry about politics, he is busy thinking thoughts for the ages."

"Marc!"

"And as a politician Baur repels me. He is one of these narrow gauge types that confuses legislative experience with wisdom. To him a deal is real, a principle is an abstraction. That means to be a realist, you can't have principles."

"Herman's a better man than that. You aren't fair to him."

"Baur is a slave of tradition, of time hallowed method. What's so damn exalted about the past? What have we accomplished, generation by generation, other than 'making it?'

338

I believe to make it now we have to solve our problems in our own context. Baur is absorbed with nailing one plank to another. I want to use modern construction methods. That's why I'm a thorn in his side in the Senate. I'm gaining converts to my point of view and I worry him."

He pushed out his cigarette and lit another. "I think I've got it," he said suddenly. "The wily old bastard wants me put out of the Senate. He thinks he's sending me to the political graveyard." He laughed. "I'm glad I didn't accept it. I outsmarted him."

"You didn't accept it! The Vice Presidency?"

"I refused. Payson told me to think it over until eleven A.M. I've thought it over. It's now 10:50. I'll telephone him and tell him to get another boy." He reached for the telephone.

"Marc! You can't throw it away! You can't! I worked too hard for it."

He slowly put the telephone down again, the color draining out of his face, "What did you say?" He asked quietly.

"I've worked behind the scenes for months, Marc, to get you this nomination. It just didn't happen. Herman Baur had to be convinced. Others had to be convinced. The President had to be convinced. You can't refuse now."

His eyes blazed. "You had the effrontery to do that? I told you to stay out of my political life. Who in hell do you think you are?"

"I'm the woman who loves you, who wants you to be Vice President."

He got up and began to pace the room. "All of this intrigue going on behind my back? Don't you see the position it puts me in? Who will believe I wasn't a party to it? My own wife was involved. What's the price, Penny? If Baur's involved, there's a price."

"There's no price that concerns you."

"That concerns me?"

"Yes," she said angrily. "That concerns you. You're cultured, intelligent and high minded, Marc, but what you don't know or refuse to acknowledge about practical politics would fill several books."

"So now we're discussing *practical* politics." He glanced at his watch. "It's nearly eleven. I'm getting out of this."

"Marc! If you refuse that nomination I'll leave you."

"The two have nothing in common in my mind, Penny," he said, carefully controlling his voice. "I thought we kept our private lives separate from all of this."

She bit her lip, "We do. I'm sorry."

"Then I am saying no."

"No, Marc, I mean it."

He looked at her solemnly and reached for the telephone.

"I'll destroy you in politics, Marc. I'll turn on you with all I've got. You couldn't survive it."

"The truth won't hurt me, Penny."

"Who said anything about the truth?"

His voice came in a whisper. "You are utterly ruthless, aren't you? You'll do anything to force me against my will."

"You must be the Vice President. For that I'll fight until I drop."

The telephone in his hand rang. He spoke a monosyllable and listened for a few moments. His eyes sought Penelope's. "That's that, then, Mr. President. No, I understand. I wouldn't put you in that position. I'll be honored. I'll do my best." He put the telephone back into the cradle. "That was the President, Penny. Through some mix-up my selection as Vice Presidential nominee was released to the news media at ten-thirty. He pointed out that if I refused to run now I would be publicly repudiating him. Of course, I wouldn't do that. I agreed to run."

"Oh, Marc!" Tears began to run down her cheeks.

"It's too bad he didn't telephone a minute sooner. You wouldn't have had to reveal to me how little our marriage means to you when it conflicts with your ambitions."

"My ambitions for *you*, Marc."

340

"No. We haven't been discussing me." He smiled at her wryly. "We're a long way from Antigua, aren't we?"

She began to sob. "Marc, please, please."

"I have been asked to join the President. Pull yourself together. You'll want to be loyally at my side on the platform when I am nominated and television notices red eyes."

"They could be tears of happiness."

"Yes, if they mistake you for a wife with normal emotions."

Alice Payson stood beside her in the wings of the great hall as they waited to step onto the dais with their husbands and accept the cheers of the convention. "I'm so pleased Marc is on the ticket with Bill." She said in an aside. "Bill has always liked and admired him, Penny. But knowing what we both know about Bill and the presidency, aren't you afraid for Marc?"

"Nothing is going to happen to Bill, Alice. All he needs to keep his health is a strong Vice President he can lean on. Marc will work his heart out for him. He's that kind of man. Besides, Bill and the party wanted him. It would have been selfish for me to insist that he refuse."

"You're more generous than me, Penny. I hate them all for swallowing Bill up in politics. We were happy when he was just an engineer in California. We didn't need all of this."

Penelope squeezed her hand. "You don't mean that, Alice."

"I sure as hell do and if that second rate band out there gives one more oom-pah, I'll seize a microphone and tell them all off. You'd think Professor Zilch and his performing dogs were on next—not the President of the United States."

She stood with Haywood beside Bill and Alice Payson as the roar of the convention delegates engulfed them and the sound of a gigantic amplified organ, replacing the band, echoed and reechoed throughout the huge flag draped hall. No one noticed that the glittering smiles of Senator and Mrs. Marc Haywood were empty and that they did not look at or touch one another.

They left Miami Beach that night on a *Tribune* company plane. Penelope returned to Washington, but Haywood flew on to the hunting cabin he had in northern Ontario in forest land owned by the newsprint producing subsidiary of the *Tribune*. "Can't I go with you?" She had asked on the flight to Washington. "Alice has accompanied Bill to California for a rest. Won't it look strange if you leave me behind?"

"I want to think," he said shortly. "Outsiders have laid violent hands on my political career. I want to re-orient myself."

"Marc, I love you. I won't interfere. I won't even speak. I just want to be with you. Especially now after this misunderstanding."

"Especially now I don't want you with me. I want to think. I don't want to be manipulated."

She turned from him in the swivel armchair and stared out of the small cabin window into the black night. After a few minutes she said quietly. "Will you let me participate in the campaign?"

"Of course. We should be seen together. You are my wife."

His cold, factual tone brought a lump to her throat and she did not speak for a moment, blinking back the tears that came. "I'll think about that while you're gone," she said at last. "I'll try to think of some good campaign ideas."

"Good campaign ideas will be welcome," he said evenly. "See Jerry Frame, my administrative assistant."

"Marc," she said beseechingly, laying a hand over his. "Let's don't leave it like this. Not when I won't see you for ten days."

He withdrew his hand. "Leave me alone, Penny," he said sharply. "I have had quite enough for one day."

She sat silently, utterly miserable, until a thought occurred to her. Like it or not, he was the party's nominee for Vice President. The immediate problem now was the election. She would worry about her relations with Marc later. By the time they landed at Dulles airport she had thought of an idea or two and had recovered her good spirits. She leaned over him as she prepared to leave the plane and kissed him on the cheek. "Enjoy yourself, dear. I'll miss you."

"Thank you, I hope to come back tanned, rested and a little wiser."

"Just come back."

Mr. Moss grinned at her beside the limousine which had been allowed to come out to the private airplane parking apron. "It was great news, Miss Penelope. Me and the missus watched it on the color T.V. We just about busted our buttons and that's a fact."

Penelope laughed for the first time that day and embraced him. "Wasn't it great, Clarence? Wasn't it really great? The home team did all right."

"Yes, ma'am. It sure did. Mrs. Moss and me we chilled a bottle of champagne and thought maybe you'd join us. We'd like to show you how we feel."

"I'd love to, Clarence. I'm sorry Mr. Haywood had to fly on to Ontario, but you don't know how kind you are being." She sat an hour later in the large kitchen of Foxhall House and ate a huge plate of Mrs. Moss' scrambled eggs as she joined them in drinking the champagne. "It's good to be home," she said. "If things look this bright from my kitchen table, we're going to do O.K."

"Sure we're going to do O.K." Mr. Moss said. "We always do."

Marc Haywood returned from Canada to his apartment at the Watergate. Penelope saw him for the first time in his office at the *Tribune*. "Aren't you coming home?" She said. "Or is this sulk of indefinite duration?"

"It's not a sulk," he replied evenly. "I intend to run an independent campaign. I don't intend to subject myself to outside influences."

"I see. You appreciate the fact, of course, that you are in

343

the second spot on the ticket?"

"That was my understanding. I'll coordinate my campaign with the President's, but I'm not going to destroy my own political image in the process. You kingmakers should have realized that you were taking the risk I might have a few ideas of my own."

"Oh, Marc. Don't be ridiculous."

He lit a cigarette. "What's on your mind?"

"I want to discuss your campaign."

"All right. I've given you the ground rules."

"I really do agree, darling, that you should project a distinct image in the campaign. Until now you have not been well known nationally. Bill Payson's image is that of the pragmatic, understated technician, the problem solver. You should bring charisma to the ticket, relate it to youth, idealism, joy, happiness, the new day, that sort of thing."

He eyed her critically. "I agree with that, but I don't think it will make Herman Baur happy."

She shrugged impatiently. "I'm thinking of you, not Herman Baur. Please get it out of your head that I wanted to destroy your political career."

"I don't think you want to destroy it. But you aren't going to run it either."

"I have no desire to run it. I merely want to help elect my husband to the Vice Presidency. Judge my suggestions on their merits."

"Fair enough. What do you suggest?"

"That you completely abandon the campaign format. It's a tired cliché at best."

"And?"

"Give the impression that you are wandering through the country talking with people so that you can be a better Vice President. Your appeal for their votes would be secondary."

"How do I wander through the country on camera?"

"You might make your first pitch to young voters. Organize a campfire at the beach, no speech, just good conversa-

344

tion around the fire and then answer questions. No side. You're the one who wants to learn from them."

Haywood gazed into the distance for a moment. "I like that, Penny. I'll have Jerry set it up for the Labor Day weekend as the kick-off for my campaign. We'll use the *Tribune* television station gang. They'll handle it right for the boss. We'll film it the night before release to be certain we can edit out any awkward spots. We'll have to round up the right group of kids, interested, smart, but not too hostile. No kooks. No pay. We'll offer a free barbecue and a chance to be seen on television."

He thought a minute, a little frown on his face. "And, we'll do it on our own. I don't want the National Committee within ten miles of this one. All I want from them is the television time."

"I agree." She grinned at him. "It's like old times, except we're building you up, not me."

He did not return her grin. "We're playing with something a little more important. We don't want to be too slick. Let's be human."

"I'd like that." Her gaze was challenging.

His smile was remote. "I feel human, but platonic. Don't try the sex bit on me, Penny. I'm going to play this cool and detached—all the way."

"But I'm your wife."

"I'll overlook that for the time being."

It was a few minutes before sunset on the stretch of Atlantic beach south of Rehoboth. The area had been cordoned off for some hours by reddish brown drift fencing provided by the Delaware Highway Department. A crowd of several hundred people were scattered along the fence, attracted by the television sound trucks, the cameras, and the heavy cables that ran to the periphery of a group of people gathered around a roaring fire. From time to time floodlighting flared on with sudden brilliance as reflectors were positioned and shifted, then winked off again. The fifty participants interviewed and invited the two preceding days by a hard working Haywood task force from college age groups in the area were gathered in a semi-circle facing the ocean around the large fire of six foot split logs burning in a saucer like depression surrounded by a circle of field stones.

Haywood dressed in white swimming trunks and a loose fitting red terry cloth beach jacket stood in the middle of a tent errected a few hundred feet from the fire, but inside the drift fencing, and held a cigarette in one hand while he patiently allowed a makeup man to dust his face with powder. "Now, don't overdo it, damn it," he said irritably. "This has got to look natural."

"Just enough to avoid the reflection of light on your skin, Senator," the makeup man said soothingly. "That won't look natural either, you know."

"How much time do we have, Jerry?" Haywood asked, turning to his aide.

"About three or four minutes."

"Now, let me run through this again. I go over and join the group. We talk and get to know each other a little. Then we sing a song or two, *Home on the Range* and *Beautiful Ohio*, right?"

"Right."

"These kids know these songs?"

"They've been rehearsed and we have ten professional mixed voices among the group to be certain everybody sings out."

"Good. Then as we do the songs a second time we are on camera. Right?"

"Right. We want to film this thing between sunset and dark when the fire will be visible, but when we need a minimum of artificial light for the faces around the fire."

"Once the camera rolls, we go right on. No breaks. If we goof, we edit it out. Right?"

"Right. This has got to be natural. Some goofs will make it

seem more natural."

Haywood threw down his cigarette on the sand floor of the tent and pushed sand over it with a bare foot. "O.K. Let's go."

Penelope sat alone in her bedroom at Foxhall House, watching the end of an old movie as she waited for the Haywood Campfire program filmed the evening before to appear on her television screen. Haywood had telephoned her earlier in the day. He thought it had gone well, but he seemed uncertain of its effect on television viewers. "Maybe it was too static, Penny, too old fashioned. Maybe I should have filmed it at a college hangout with amplified music, psychedelic lights, the whole bit."

"You would have been lost in stage business."

"I guess so."

"I'll watch it tonight."

"I wish you would. I have to fly to Cleveland for a campaign conference with the party's middle western governors. Let me know the worst."

"Have a good trip."

"Thank you."

"I love you."

There was a moment's hesitation. "I'll see you tomorrow."

Penelope had hung up, conscious of her cheeks burning. Imagine, throwing oneself at one's own husband and being rejected. But she would never give up until she had re-established the personal relationship she had destroyed at Miami.

The station symbol was replaced by a scene of a group singing around a campfire. Beyond the faces lit by the firelight a long, slow ocean surf surged against the beach. For about forty-five seconds the voices singing *Home on the Range* filled the room, then a pleasant male voice cut in over the singing which receded into the background. "Ladies and gentlemen of America. Like many of you, Senator Marc Haywood is spending this Labor Day holiday at the beach with a group of young people. We thought you would like to join him." The voice was replaced again by the singing. The camera slowly panned around the circle showing the faces of the young singers including Marc Haywood sitting with his arms locked into those of a girl on one side and a boy on the other. His eyes were on the campfire as he sang and he rocked gently back and forth to the music. *Beautiful Ohio* followed *Home on the Range* and when the song was finished the camera zoomed in on Haywood's face for a close-up.

"Fellows and girls," he said in an easy conversational tone of voice, "I have been thinking as we sang how fortunate I am to be able to spend my Labor Day holiday in this manner. Until a few days ago I had planned to use this time to discuss one of our major national problems. As the Vice Presidential candidate of my party, I have been giving a lot of thought to those problems. But, it occurred to me, why can't I just share the holiday with some of our young people? It took a little arranging, as you know. It isn't a private party. But the chance to share this typically American, uniquely American, holiday in this way with millions of people across America is, I am sure you will agree, worth a little inconvenience. In fact, I think I'm sitting on a power cable right now, but I hope I don't look like it." As the laughter of the group subsided he continued.

"One of the great things about a beach party is that we don't make speeches. The fire, the atmosphere, the posture on the sand don't permit it. But when Americans gather together around a fire they do like to talk and I hope that is what we'll do tonight. I modestly hope you'll ask me a few questions and I hope that they will reflect what is of concern to you because it is your concerns that must be the business of this country in the years to come." He stopped and took a sip from a soft drink can.

"Senator," an intent young man with a crew cut and a deep tan asked, "I don't mean to be impolite. It is just that this question really interests me. Why are you running for Vice President? What makes you so special?"

Haywood looked into the boy's eyes and grinned. "I don't think I'm so special. There's only one reason I'm running for Vice President. I want the office badly enough to try for it. I've wanted it badly enough to serve my country in the Senate to prepare for it. I've wanted it badly enough to study and to master the problems that face our country today. I've wanted it badly because I think I can use the office the way it ought to be used, to advance the interests of the people of this country. When you live in a country like this with its unlimited opportunity you have an incentive to prepare yourself. You have an incentive to qualify yourself. As of tonight, I think I'm the best qualified person in the United States for the Vice Presidency because those incentives galvanized me. I hope you'll vote for President Payson and for me. I also hope you'll think that this great office, this great opportunity for public service, is worth trying for, worth preparing for and that I'll have a chance to vote for you. Not because you're so special, either, but because you cared enough to try to qualify for a position of great trust."

A thin faced boy with horn rimmed glasses and long hair hugged his bare, boney knee and leaned forward. "Do you really think you are relevant?"

Haywood spontaneously threw back his head and laughed. "Relevant to what?" He asked easily.

"To the contemporary world."

"What is the contemporary world?"

"If you don't know you shouldn't be running for Vice President." The boy's eyes glinted mischievously, "Or maybe that's just what you should be running for."

Haywood joined in the laughter. "Oh, none of us overestimates the Vice Presidency. A Vice President is sort of a political valet, isn't he? He tidies up where the President asks him to; but we aren't here to discuss the constitutional limitations of the office. Presumably, we are asking questions and giving answers. You, if I may say so, are asking a non-question. It deserves a non-answer. But I'll try to do a little better by you than you've done by me. The word, I believe, means pertinent, bearing upon the matter at hand. I think all of us are pertinent, or relevant, if you choose. A human society should be concerned with human beings and that is all it should be concerned with. Everything else is an abstraction. Because I'm concerned with human beings, I think I'm relevant."

"That's why we want to restructure this society," a red haired, freckled faced girl spoke from the edge of the firelight. "It's not relevant."

Haywood smiled. "You don't frighten me with the term restructure. I happen to think we do need some changes in our society pretty fast. You will disappoint me if you don't know what you mean by the term."

"It means destroying the system that allows some human beings to exploit other human beings."

"Why are you so convinced the system is at fault—not the human beings?"

"Well, something's got to give. What we've got is unacceptable."

Haywood sipped a coke. "You know," he said thoughtfully, "You are trying to say something important, but you aren't saying it. Your mind is the prisoner of clichés. Maybe you have a flaming idea, I don't know," he grinned disarmingly, "But you're using a pallid cliché to express it and it's damped out. I hope, as an editor turned politician, a wordsmith, if you will, you'll let me try to articulate for you.

"You are dissatisfied with our society. Good for you. I'm dissatisfied with it, too. So is the President. So are most progressives in politics. But before you can do anything constructive you have to think things out a bit, decide what is 'bugging you.' A lot of discontented people shouting clichés at each other aren't going to get anywhere on or off the campus."

"We've tried working within the Establishment. Where

350

has that got us?" The thin faced boy's voice was heavy with disdain.

"You're throwing words around again," Haywood said sharply. "Used like shrapnel, words can have the same effect, a sort of indiscriminate wounding of the sensibilities. I doubt that you can give me an intelligible definition of 'the Establishment' and I suspect that you have only worked within it in the sense that to date you have accepted what's been given to you."

"Answer my question," the boy challenged. "Stop the double talk."

Haywood's eyes gazed off camera for a moment. The camera left the thin faced boy and came to rest upon a small, dark haired girl.

"What do you think concerned college kids should do, Senator Haywood?" she asked quietly.

Haywood grinned boyishly. "You are actually asking my opinion? I guess there isn't a generation gap, after all." He waited for the laughter to subside. His face then grew serious. "I think you ought to give your shining ideals and warm emotions the kind of support they deserve, the support of cool intelligent analysis and research. The college years are the years when you can single mindedly devote yourself to the selfless, objective pursuit of knowledge. Don't muff it. Don't let your emotions run away with you. The rationalization of emotions has always been man's hardest task. The world will give you a few brownie points for your concern, we like the warmhearted, but if you want to be admired and honored, if you really want to realize your ideals, then you must match those warmhearted stirrings with knowledge and apply that knowledge to the problems your emotions tell you must be solved. Otherwise, you are like a child throwing a tantrum in his nursery and breaking all of his toys because he is bothered with prickly heat. If you itch, learn how to scratch."

The following questions came rapidly. Haywood answered

351

them frankly and humorously. With five minutes of the half hour left he held up his hand. "Let's take a breather. We'll come back to the questions later. I'll stay here with you until midnight, if you wish. But right now, I'd like to sing again. Somehow a song puts things in perspective. How about *Down by the Old Mill Stream?*"

The singing filled the room. With twenty seconds of the half hour left, the announcer's voice cut in again over the singing, "Ladies and gentlemen, thank you for joining us on this Labor Day. The friends and supporters of Marc Haywood for Vice President appreciate it." The singing surged in again until both sound and picture slowly faded out.

Penelope sat with a little smile on her face after she had turned off the set. It was great. It was the formula for making Marc Haywood into a national figure. It was the perfect counterpoint to the dignified, pedantic President Payson. Penelope tried to imagine Bill Payson sitting around a campfire singing and couldn't.

An hour later by pre-arrangement she telephoned him in Cleveland. "What did you think?" he asked.

"It's going to put you in the White House."

"The White House?"

Penelope was momentarily confused at her slip of tongue. "I mean that the public will recognize that you are Presidential timber."

"It was that good?"

"Yes, darling. It struck just the right note."

"It was a tricky balancing act. I wanted the kids with me, but it's their parents that vote. I was trying to be a swinging square and that's not easy."

Penelope laughed. "You came across as a responsible political leader who understands and sympathizes with kids who are less responsible."

"All but one of the kids questioning me were plants. Could you detect that?"

"No, really? Which one wasn't the plant?"

352

"The kid who asked if I was born in a log cabin."

"Are you coming home tonight?"

"Tomorrow." He was silent a moment. "I guess this means that we'll do it again."

"Yes, but with different groups. Cowhands in Arizona, farmers at a ploughing contest, factory workers at a lunch break. It doesn't always have to be an occasion either. We could film you afoot. 'Across America with Haywood' we could call it. You could walk through slums to be rehabilitated, forests to be saved, along rivers to be cleansed of pollution and at every stop we project Marc Haywood, young, contemporary, concerned, anxious to meet the people and to learn."

Haywood laughed. "You know, I may even vote for myself."

"We've never doubted that President Payson could get reelected, Marc, and carry you in as his Vice President. But think how much more influence and authority you will have as Vice President if the polls show you strengthened the ticket."

"Yes, I think that is important."

"Think what it would mean if you were more popular than the President."

"Whoa, now. Let's don't get carried away. You'll make me into a usurper."

"You're mine, darling," Penelope said in a low voice. "Alice can worry about her own man."

"I'm overwhelmed, but out of all this I gather that you feel this should be my campaign format?" He had deliberately made his voice impersonal.

"Absolutely." Penelope said the single word with a lilt, trying to hide her disappointment at his reaction.

"Then we'll get cracking."

"Goodnight, darling."

"I'll see you tomorrow at the office."

✣ 29 ✣

HERMAN BAUR sat in the cluttered livingroom of his apartment with Senator George Wysong. A rollaway table from room service pushed to one side held the remains of their dinner. They sat quietly with the easy intimacy of old friends and political allies watching the television set, sipping tall glasses of bourbon and branch water.

"Do you see the trend yet, Herman?" Wysong asked.

"It's only seven-thirty. In half the country the polls aren't closed yet. It's too early to spot a trend."

"The television boys say it's a landslide for the ticket."

Baur snorted contemptuously. "They can't reduce politics to computer tape. Never will. As usual, they miss the point. There never was any doubt of Bill Payson's re-election. He's an incumbent President. The interesting political question is how strong is the lift Haywood is giving the ticket?"

"They say, Herman, that, as usual, you engineered a good choice." The words came dryly.

Baur inspected the end of his cigar with a wry little smile. "I may have been had, and by a woman at that."

"Penelope?"

Baur nodded. "I thought we were using her, George, to maneuver Haywood out of the Senate. He acted like a reluctant candidate, but since his nomination he's been campaigning as if he's inspired. It's been damn effective and Penny has

354

been helping him. I can recognize the touch."

"You can't fault her for that. She's his wife."

"She's a damn ambitious and canny woman. That's a dangerous combination." He puffed on his cigar contemplatively.

"Haywood's put on a good campaign and helped the ticket. I say good for him."

"He's campaigned too well, George. He's used her money and his money and all of their combined knowledge of publicity techniques and politics, which is considerable, to make himself an *erzatz* national figure in two months. He's been helped by Payson's colorless personality. Haywood's the new darling of national politics. He has charisma, empathy, he's with it. Call it what you will, he's almost overshadowed the President in this campaign. It's been those damned campfires, the factory lunch circles, the college skull sessions. Damn it, he didn't even seem to be campaigning; he acted as if he already ran Washington and merely wanted some consultation and advice."

"He says 'inspiration', too, Herman."

"Yes, damn it. Inspiration too. If there's one thing I mistrust it's inspiration. It's one of those terms that hide rather than reveal, like 'conscience' or 'morality' or 'religious beliefs'. When they throw terms like those at you they mean they are running away from a rational discussion. They're demagogic."

"He'll fade away after the election, Herman." George Wysong said comfortably. "Vice Presidents always do. The Constitution requires it."

Herman Baur mixed them each a fresh drink. "I'm not so sure. Penny is a close family friend of the Paysons. I don't think she has fading away in mind for Haywood."

"You're exaggerating the problem. She's only a woman, after all."

Baur peered at Wysong over his glass. "I'm a bachelor, George, and you've been married twice, but I'd never make a remark like that."

355

Wysong laughed. "You'd think Penny was going to be Vice President."

"No, Haywood will be his own man, but Penny will give him that extra dimension."

"Get Haywood back in the Zoo."

"Yes. I'm going to have to do that."

Penelope sat under the ornate Victorian chandelier in Herman Baur's high ceilinged Senate office and smiled at him. "To answer your question, dear, I'm tired and happy."

"You should be. Your husband was the real winner in the campaign."

Penelope's eyes widened. "What do you mean?"

"He's become a national political figure, a highly visible Vice President elect."

"He did do well in the campaign, Herman. I'm proud of that. I like my people to do well."

Baur's eyes met hers. "I still have my reservations about his politics, you know."

"Yes, I know."

"That's why I wanted him out of the Senate."

"I know."

"Perhaps I made a mistake."

"Perhaps you did."

"I think Haywood and I should work together. He's too popular for me to ignore and he can't function as Vice President without political allies on the Hill. That office has no political role."

"President Payson will give him a political role."

Baur shrugged impatiently. "I know, the President's deputy in space programs or civil rights programs, the alter ego. There's no power or influence there, Penny. Marc needs to work closely with the Senate leadership. He needs to recognize the party hierarchy. Otherwise, popular as he is today, no one will remember his name in two years. That's the fate of Vice Presidents."

Penelope looked enigmatic. "It might work that way."

"It will work that way. Depend on it. I can imagine Haywood as the party's Presidential nominee four years from now if he plays his cards right. If he doesn't, he'll just fade away."

"What do you suggest?"

"He might attend the Zoo for a beginning; get to know us better."

"Marc has already asked me to give up the Zoo."

"And what did you say?"

"I told him I wasn't ready to, yet."

"I think that was wise. The Zoo can be a big help to him."

"He feels that meeting as it does in my, our, house, it suggests cronyism. He wants to be a Vice President for all of the people."

Herman Baur's laugh was one of real amusement. "That's a good one. He'll soon learn he's Payson's Vice President and no one else's and Bill will ignore him as he did Breen, out of absent mindedness, if nothing more." He carefully lit a fresh cigar.

"Penny, don't you see? Haywood is still a political novice. He thinks he can be effective by communicating with the people through the news media or directly. He is suspicious of the nuts and bolts of politics. He is suspicious of me. He thinks I'm a backroom operator and therefore less pure than he is because he operates entirely in public view, or so he pretends. Well, I am a backroom operator and proud of it because that is where the agreements are reached between political factions that enable us to run this country, and our business is to run this country. We aren't running a newspaper, trying to fill the front page with eye catching headlines and sub-heads, we're trying to run a country. Unless Haywood learns that he won't be Presidential timber. He can't live in an intellectual mansion on the hill and issue proclama-

357

tions of dogma to the peasants down in the valley."

"I agree with you, Herman. Marc has to learn to stop edi-torializing and performing. The campaign is over."

"Good," Baur's voice was gruff. "Get him to the Zoo. All he needs to do is come down the stairs of his own house. The rest of us make more effort."

"Marc doesn't live with me, Herman. He stays in his apartment at the Watergate."

Baur looked mildly surprised. "Why?"

"I committed the unpardonable crime. I interfered with his political career. He feels that I connived with you to get him the Vice Presidential nomination."

"So you did."

"So I did and he won't forgive me."

"He took your money and ideas in the campaign, I no-ticed."

"Yes, he did, but you must remember we have worked to-gether years longer than we've been married. It was the mar-riage I shattered, not the old relationship. He welcomed my help in the campaign once he was committed to it, but he won't forgive me for committing him to it. I'm the last one who can influence his politics."

"Well, we can't have a wild March hare one heart beat from the Presidency."

Penelope smiled. "No, we can't. March hares don't make good Presidents."

Baur looked sour. "We're talking in circles. I gather that it's up to me to talk with him?"

"Yes, Herman, it is. I've got to concentrate on saving my marriage, if I can."

"If your marriage is in danger, the man is a fool. You're his greatest political asset."

"No. He has a very strong sense of personal privacy and integrity."

Baur sighed. "He should have been a monk. Why in hell

358

did he get into politics?"

"Out of a sense of duty."

Baur looked as if he had tasted something bitter. "Jesus. This is worse than I thought. I've got a hypocritical, inflexible, novice on my hands with political charisma. He even confuses his political ambition with a sense of duty." He glanced at Penelope. "I don't mean to annoy you, honey. I'm speaking of him as a politician only."

Penelope arose to go, pulling on her gloves. "I'm not annoyed, Herman. You're probably right. All I am saying is that from now on you deal with the politician. I'll deal with the man."

Herman Baur struggled up out of his chair and kissed her gravely on the cheek. "I wish us both luck, Penny. He doesn't deserve either one of us."

Penelope sat beside Marc Haywood on the wooden seats erected under the temporary white colonial portico on the east steps of the Capitol and listened to the second inaugural address of President Payson. The familiar, flat western twang of the President slowly became an unintelligible background monologue as her thoughts turned inward. She looked out over the crowd toward the box like tower of the television correspondents opposite, who peered back through their large plate glass windows at the rows of distinguished guests on either side of the ceremonial wine red carpet leading from the interior of the Capitol. Beyond the television tower the bare January trees partly obscured the white Corinthian columns of the Supreme Court building across the Capitol grounds. She was now the lady of the Vice President of the United States. Her eyes rested on Marc Haywood's solemn profile and then moved to Alice Payson. Alice Payson was watching her husband speak with a somber pride, never taking her eyes from his face. Penelope shivered in the January cold and dropped her eyes to her gloved hands. Marc Haywood's eyes rested on her. "It will soon be over," he whispered. "It's a miserable time of year for an outside ceremony."

Penelope sat in one of the upholstered seats of the reserved gallery of the Senate Chamber and watched the low key, seemingly aimless proceedings on the floor below. Not more than eight or nine Senators were on the floor. They sat or stood near their mahogany school boy desks peering at papers, whispering to one another, and, in one case, reading a newspaper, seemingly oblivious to the impassioned speech Senator George Wysong was giving from the approximate location of his desk in the front row three seats away from those of the majority and minority leaders. Senator Wysong was a master of histrionics and he paced a few steps up and down the aisle, making his points for the gallery and the Congressional Record while he eyed the clock above the dais of the President of the Senate, Vice President Marc Haywood. It would soon be time to vote. The whips of both parties were mustering their forces from the Senate lobby, the cloakrooms, the hearing rooms and offices of Capitol Hill. He was conscious of the increasing movement of Senators on and off the floor behind him and of the muted squeak of the ornate swinging doors at the head of the aisles as Senators left or entered the chamber from the cloakroom where the last minute bargaining before the vote was taking place. He would restate his last two points again. That should about do it.

Haywood sat in his presiding officer's chair, a look of polite attentiveness on his face, hiding his essential boredom. From time to time he turned his head to one side or the other and listened to his aides, clustered around him at a lower level, nodding his head briefly. On the floor, Senator Wysong leaned his lionine head to one side to hear the comment of his party whip, finished his sentence and said, "I therefore commend this bill to my colleagues, Mr. President. It serves the interests of all of our people well." He sat down with evident relief at his desk.

There was a short conference at the presiding officer's dais and Haywood said, "The question is on the passage of the bill."

Senator Byron Corson, the majority leader, slowly rose to his feet at his desk. "Mr. President, I ask for the yeas and nays."

"The yeas and nays have been ordered. Those voting in favor of the bill will vote yea, those opposed will vote nay." Haywood nodded to the legislative clerk to call the roll.

The Senate chamber had rapidly filled within the last few minutes and most of the seats other than those of Senators who were ill or out of the city were filled. The roll call droned on and finally ended. An aide handed Haywood a talley sheet. Haywood cleared his throat. "Forty-five Senators having voted in the affirmative and forty-three in the negative, the question is carried."

A little collective sigh moved across the Senate floor and the Junior Senator from Illinois moved the next order of business.

Haywood relinquished his gavel to the Junior Senator from Texas and left the chamber. Penelope sat quietly for a moment after he had departed. How handsome he looked. How much in command of himself he was. She was so proud of him. The Vice President of the United States! And looking every inch like a President. Her eyes moved around the emptying galleries rising like steep theatre balconies to the outer extremities of the huge chamber where gold brocade on the walls in a liberty bell design and more than a score of white marble busts of famous men suggested the Senate's preoccupation with its Roman origins; she sat quietly for a moment then reached for her handbag and left the gallery. She found her way through the halls, heavily encrusted with ornamentation, down a great marble staircase, and through the frescoed Senate reception room to the Vice President's office. His receptionist looked up with a smile. "Go right on in, Mrs. Haywood. I'm sure that it's all right."

He was standing with his back to her, gazing out of one of the windows behind his large carved desk. The desk was empty except for a single green telephone. "Good afternoon, Mr. Vice President," she said.

He glanced into the huge gold framed mirror above the mantel of a grey marble fireplace, saw her reflection, and turned around with a little smile. "Good afternoon, Mrs. Haywood, I didn't realize you were among us."

"I wanted to watch you preside over the Senate. It was great fun. You looked scrumptious."

Haywood gave a short hard laugh. "That's about it. My function was about as empty and ceremonial as a uniformed coachman on the Queen of England's state coach. I was praying for a tie vote so I could actually contribute something. That's the only reason I bothered with this charade. A tie vote was predicted. Unfortunately, Senator Berry switched. He yawned. "I'm sorry, Penny, but there is something somnambulant about this office. It's overdecorated and underused. I'm going back downtown where the action is."

"I thought you might take me to lunch."

"No, I'm sorry. I have a delegation to meet at the Executive Office Building."

"What delegation?"

"I've forgotten. It doesn't matter too much. It's good exposure. Jerry fixes these things up."

"I guess I'll have to see Jerry."

"We'll get together very soon."

"How nice." She pulled on her gloves. "Well, you did look gorgeous." She turned to go.

"Penny?"

"Yes?"

"What about the Zoo and the column. Are you giving them up?"

"I haven't decided yet."

"I've mentioned this before."

362

"I know."

"It doesn't look well, my wife writing a column for my newspaper, even if all my holdings are now in trust."

"The *Tribune* could sell the column and stop carrying it."

"I'm not sure that would answer the critics."

"I have to have some role, Marc."

"You are the wife of the Vice President."

She met his eyes. "That role hasn't been very demanding."

He slowly lit a cigarette. "Also, your continued association with Herman Baur concerns me."

"Herman is an old friend. He at least takes me to lunch. I never discuss you or your politics with him. I've told him that I have no political influence with you at all."

"Nevertheless, I am uncomfortable."

"I'm sorry, darling. I don't like to see you uncomfortable."

He made a little gesture with his cigarette. "Think it over, please."

"I have and I shall. But I must have a role to play."

"You said that before."

"I know I have. It's important to me."

"Incidentally, I've given up the Watergate apartment. I'm moving to Dumbarton House."

Her eyes darkened. "That's a dear little house." She said softly. "I loved the time I spent there."

"Well, you have moved on to grander quarters. I'm afraid you would now find Dumbarton House rather confining."

"I must run along," she said, forcing a smile. "Have fun with your delegation and be sure to have Jerry tell you who they are before you start talking." She left him with a backward wave of her white gloved hand.

Herman Baur sat dourly in the leather chair before Marc Haywood's desk in the Executive Office Building. "I appreciate your seeing me here, Mr. Vice President," he said with heavy irony. "We seldom see you on Capitol Hill."

"The Vice Presidency is an empty office, Herman. It's

even emptier on the Hill."

"Nevertheless, you are the President of the Senate. You owe some gestures of respect and interest to it."

"You maneuvered me out of the Senate, Herman, and I'll never forgive you for it. So don't lecture me on my duties."

"Politics is politics. You were a burr under my saddle."

"You even stooped to using my wife."

Herman Baur slowly lit a cigar. "Where I come from," he said slowly, "We don't discuss ladies."

Haywood's lips compressed. "What do you want, Herman? You haven't come downtown just because you miss me as the Senate's presiding officer."

"No, I don't miss you, Mr. Vice President. I prefer a Senate man in that chair and you have never been a Senate man."

"That's a matter of definition and opinion."

"I've said you were a burr under my saddle when you were in the Senate. You are now a burr under the President's saddle."

Haywood's eyebrows arched. "Really? I see the President nearly every day. He hasn't complained."

"No. He won't. He's not that sort of man. And, I suspect he is not well. Nevertheless, in a Constitutional sense, you are causing the President trouble."

"Oh, my! Now we have the Constitution involved." Haywood smiled tolerantly. "It has interested me, Herman, how you always have your point of view buttressed by 'the sense of the Senate', 'legislative tradition', 'the unwritten rules of civility' and now, at last, the Constitution itself. What's the problem? Don't you have any confidence in your opinions? Can't they stand alone?"

"These publicity techniques of yours, I'll admit that they were effective in the campaign. They made you a national figure. But it's unseemly for you to continue to use them as Vice President."

"I'm afraid you will have to be more specific, Herman."

"I refer to these so-called 'seminars' you are holding in La-

364

fayette Square."

"Ah."

"It is unseemly for the Vice President of the United States to sit on a park bench across the street from the White House and engage in televised rabble-rouser talk with a group of political irregulars dressed for a masquerade."

"Most people think it is charming. We have quite a good rating for a political show."

Baur gestured impatiently with his cigar. "You are taking advantage of the fact that you own the local outlet of a national television network. You are upstaging the President and his press conferences."

"The President can borrow the idea, if he wants to. Personally, I like the format. It's participatory democracy." He grinned at Baur. "I'm good on television, Herman. You can't criticize me if I use it. What bothers you is that I'm getting directly in touch with the people."

"We have elections and a representative system of government for that, Haywood." Baur's voice hardened.

"You maneuvered me out of the Senate, Herman. You tried to bury me in the Vice Presidency. I'm refusing to be buried. I'm finding a format for staying alive politically." He paused and pushed out his cigarette carefully before raising his eyes to Baur's. "And if you don't like it, you can go straight to hell."

Baur got stiffly up from his chair. "I shall pray every night, Mr. Vice President, for the health of the President of the United States."

Haywood's lips were in a straight line. "I am going to succeed him, Senator Baur, by nomination and election and I give you notice right now I won't need or welcome the help of the Lion of the Senate, kingmaker or not."

Baur jerked his head up angrily and left the room without a backward glance.

❧ 30 ❧

IT was nine o'clock in the morning. Washington already simmered under an overcast sky in the humidity of mid-July. Within the Potomac River Basin there was no movement of air. A grey mist with bluish overtones had accumulated during the days of stillness, reducing visibility until the spires, domes, and monuments that were so white against blue skies on clear days seemed dull shadows floating and shimmering in waves of heat.

Alice Payson looked up, a vulnerable, pleading expression in her eyes as Doctor Fyfe entered the family sitting room on the second floor of the White House. She wet her lips. "How is he doctor?" The voice was dry and brittle with strain.

Doctor Fyfe shook his head. "I'm going to move him to Walter Reed, Alice."

Alice Payson cleared her throat to ask the haunting question, but it died on her lips as Doctor Fyfe gently reached out and took both of her hands in his. "We expected it, sweetheart," he said gruffly. "Now it's here. We'll make him as comfortable as possible."

"May I see him now? It will be different at the hospital." Her voice thickened. "Somehow he will seem out of my reach there. They will take him away from me."

"Yes. Remember, he's under sedation. He may not know you."

366

She entered the familiar, high ceilinged bedroom, now transformed by the atmosphere of sickness and death, and moved to the side of the President's bed. He lay quietly with his eyes closed, his angular face ashen gray, breathing shallowly. She took the boney hand with the long, tapered fingers and the familiar mole above the index finger and held it in a gentle embrace. "It's me, Bill, darling," she said softly. "I'm here." His hand stirred in hers, but he did not open his eyes or speak.

She turned with a bewildered, stricken expression to Doctor Fyfe who stood behind her. "It's the sedation, dear," he said softly.

"It's not possible," Alice said in a hoarse whisper. "This can't be happening to him."

Doctor Fyfe put his arm around her and drew her away. "You should get some rest now. You've been up all night."

"Can I go with him?"

"Later. We'll prepare a suite for you near him. Let us get him settled first."

"How long will . . ." her voice trailed off.

"A few days. It moves fast once it gets out of control." He looked at her closely. "Are you all right? I can give you something to help you through this."

She shook her head. "I'm all right."

"You should have someone with you. Shouldn't your children come?"

"I'll call them when I can. I can't do it now." Her voice broke.

"You should have someone."

"Yes. I'll call Penny." Her voice strengthened. "And Senator Baur. We must think of the country, too. I'll speak to my secretary."

Penelope was sitting on the terrace of Foxhall House drinking a glass of ice tea and watching Dick Junior play on the lawn under the supervision of Miss Kerry when the call came. Mrs. Moss appeared through the French doors of the salon trailing the cord of the extension phone behind her.

"One moment, Mrs. Haywood," the soft, cultured voice of the White House social secretary said, "Mrs. Payson would like to speak with you."

"Penny?" Alice Payson's voice was tight and strained.

"Yes, dear."

"Can you come at once?"

Penelope's heart began to beat faster as she interpreted the tone of voice. "Of course."

"Plan to stay with me."

"Yes."

"Can you do it? It isn't an imposition?"

"Alice, I'll be with you within an hour."

There was a short silence and then Alice Payson controlled her voice and could speak. "I'll call the South Gate entrance. God bless you, sweetheart."

She was waiting for Penelope in the family sitting room. Her face was pale and she had been crying, but she was now composed. She arose and kissed Penelope on the cheek. When they were alone she locked her arm in Penelope's and walked with her to the windows overlooking the great lawn which stretched away from the mansion, the distant mist-muted view of the Washington Monument and the Jefferson Memorial beyond framed in the dark green midsummer foliage of ancient trees.

"Bill has always loved this view."

Penelope squeezed her arm. "It's a lovely view."

"Oh, Penny!" Alice turned and buried her face in Penelope's shoulder. "He's ill again. He is so ill!" Penelope embraced her wordlessly. "It's terminal." Alice Payson uttered the hated words in a hoarse gasp.

Penelope began to cry. Alice stood back and then embraced her again, now the comforter rather than the comforted. "There, there, baby. I know how you feel."

"Alice, I'm so sorry for Bill and for you. I really am so

sorry." Her voice broke.

"I know, baby."

"I should be comforting you and you are comforting me."

"I know, but it helps to have someone with me who cares as a friend. You don't think of Bill as the President. You and I are the only ones around here who don't. And it isn't the President that's ill, Penny, some stuffy abstraction for the history books, it's Bill, my Bill. The boy I married. You are the only one who senses that." They stood quietly a moment in their embrace.

"What about the children?"

"I will telephone them soon. I wanted to get a grip on myself first. Also, I've sent for Senator Baur. I need his advice on what we tell the country. He can deal with the staff and the cabinet."

Penelope nodded pensively. "Marc is in India, in the midst of one of those oriental celebrations he's come to love."

"He was notified last evening when the President's condition worsened. He's flying back now."

The door to the room opened and Herman Baur entered, his face drawn into lines and furrows. He took both of Alice's hands in his and after looking her searchingly in the eyes kissed her on the cheek. "I had no idea, Alice. Simply no idea. Bill looked tired recently, but I didn't guess it was this serious."

"Other than Doctor Fyfe, only Penny and I knew it was arrested cancer. Even Bill didn't know."

Baur turned and kissed Penelope. "I see. I see." He looked at Penelope curiously for a moment and then made a courtly little gesture to Alice. "I'm at your service, my dear. What can I do?"

"Handle this so the country isn't alarmed. I know a President is . . ." she forced the words ". . . is dying and there are public problems to consider. I'm a private person and for me this is a very private death. That's all I want to think about. So I want you to see that all of the public things are done correctly as Bill would wish and leave me with my husband."

Herman Baur nodded. "You shouldn't be burdened with such things. I'll see that what needs to be done is done. Where is the Vice President? Is he still in India on that state visit?"

"He's been notified. He's flying home."

"Good. He must be here." Baur stood a moment, his head down, his face heavy with thought, then his eyes met Penelope's. "I'd like to have a chat with you, Penny."

"You can have it here," Alice Payson said wearily. "I've been up all night. I'm going to my bedroom and lie down."

When they were alone, Baur dropped into a chair and motioned to Penelope to sit down. He looked at her for several seconds and then dropped his eyes as he slowly lit a cigar. "You've been fishing in deep waters, young lady."

"I don't know what you mean." Penelope tucked her feet under her on a sofa and carefully smoothed her skirt.

"I mean that Marc Haywood is Vice President of the United States and the President is a sick and dying man."

Penelope's tongue flicked over her lips and she smiled, but she said nothing.

"Mrs. Payson said you knew of the President's condition. How long have you known?"

"Nearly two years."

Baur drew on his cigar, regarding her steadily through the smoke. Penelope calmly met his gaze. "You're a bit of a conniver, aren't you?" He said it without inflection as a simple statement of fact.

"It was arrested cancer. Alice, the doctor, and I prayed it would stay arrested. We saw no reason to play God."

"But you did what you could to make your husband Vice President, didn't you?"

Penelope looked at him defiantly. "Well, why not?"

Baur grinned wryly. "Why not, indeed? You haven't been

370

entirely frank with me, have you?" His anger briefly sur-
faced. "Not by one God damned hell of a long shot."

"Who's entirely frank in politics, Herman?" Her voice
was soft, without an edge.

He eyed the end of the cigar. When he spoke he had controlled his temper. "I have no doubt you will make a stun-
ning First Lady, but I doubt that your husband should be the
President of the United States."

"Why not?"

Baur made a little gesture. "I could keep you here for an
hour answering that question, but you wouldn't really be listening. I'll sum it up this way; Marc Haywood has a con-
tempt for the democratic process. He is a publicizer, an image
maker, a manipulator of emotions."

"You mean he's a good politician."

"No, damn it, I *don't* mean he's a good politician. A politician uses the Constitutional system and builds his
constituency on the issues. Haywood demagogues it."

"It seems to me it's a matter of degree, Herman. Marc
plays the same game you do, dear. I think you're just afraid
that he plays it better."

Baur flushed deeply. "You see no difference between us?"

"Not really. One is the old politics and the other is the
new politics, but you are both politicians."

"You think that matters of state should be handled in the
streets? Do we put the parliamentary issues to the mob? Do
we whip up their passions with all of the modern techniques
of the media and then put the question to a voice vote?"

Penelope laughed softly. "Herman," she said reprovingly,
"You are exaggerating."

"I hope to God I am. Have you watched this husband of
yours lately?"

"Well, Herman, what do you want me to do? He's going
to be President. I can't change that and I don't want to."

Baur sat staring at her morosely. "Do you honor your
debts?" He asked at last.

371

"Of course I do."

"I mean real debts, not money debts: debts of gratitude."

"I'm afraid that I don't know what you mean."

"I mean I saved Winston Development Corporation for you."

"Oh, that."

"Yes, that. I won't cry over the spilt milk of Haywood's nomination. We both had our motives there and you outsmarted me. But for Winston Development Corporation you owe me a political debt, Penny. I want to collect on it."

Penelope eyed him warily, her lips compressed. "How?"

"I want you to use all of your influence, all of your wiles, to persuade President Haywood to work within the Constitutional system, to work with the Congress. It's one thing to demagogue it as a candidate, it's another thing to demagogue it as Vice President, it's unthinkable to demagogue it as President of the United States. If he continues with his public mob scenes, his 'participatory democracy', if he ignores and then browbeats Congress with his version of public opinion, he'll destroy the country. I want you to persuade him to work with me." He bit on his cigar. "We hate each other's guts, but we must work together."

"Herman, I've told you that where politics is concerned, I'm the last one to influence Marc. I've ruined my marriage to get him in the White House. I'm now going to concentrate on the marriage, not politics."

"Exactly, concentrate on the marriage, then bring him around."

Penelope smiled at Baur and then laughed out loud. "You are surprising, dear."

"I'm a realist. Between us, one way or the other, we've put the wrong man in the White House. We have to make it work."

"I think he's the right man in the White House, Herman, and I happen to love him, but I agree we have to make it work. He'll be a strong President, but I know he has to work

372

with the Lion of the Senate."

"Is it a deal?"

She smiled. "I don't like to call it that." Her smile became mischievous. "Just say that when I'm in bed with him, I'll speak kindly of you."

Baur made a sour face. "That kind of talk shocks me, Penny."

"Does it really, dear? I doubt it. I doubt it very much."

Marc Haywood arrived during the afternoon at Andrews Air Force Base and was brought directly to the White House by helicopter. He joined Penelope and Alice in the family sitting room. He embraced Alice and kissed her gently. "I'm so very sorry about this, Alice. I'm stunned."

"It's terminal," Alice said dully.

Haywood slowly shook his head. "I can't believe it. I just can't believe it."

Alice patted his arm. "You have other things to think about, Marc. Penny will stay with me. My only regret for you is that you are going to have to assume Bill's burden. I know what that is going to mean to both of you."

Haywood released Alice and stepped over to Penelope, kissing her on the cheek. "Hello, dear."

Penelope embraced him wordlessly, her eyes full of tears.

"She's a strong heart, Marc," Alice Payson said. "She's shared this terrible burden with me for months. I had to tell someone. Even Bill didn't know."

Haywood stood still. "Then this isn't the first attack?"

"No. The doctor diagnosed it two years ago, but it was arrested. He left it up to me to tell Bill, but I couldn't. I had to tell someone so I told Penny. She's been wonderful. I can never repay her."

Haywood's eyes sought Penelope's. She met his gaze unflinchingly. He kissed her cheek again with dry lips. "Well, well. What you have been through." His thoughts turned inward for a moment, then he roused himself. "I am going to

373

my office. I must be briefed as fully as possible as quickly as possible so that I can make the decisions as Bill would wish me to do until he recovers. Then I'm going to Walter Reed. I'll have to hold a press conference this evening. The rumors are already beginning."

"He isn't going to recover, Marc," Alice Payson's voice was strained to the point of cracking. "Don't say these things for my benefit. They don't make it easier."

"I'm not saying them for your benefit, Alice," Haywood's voice was gentle. "I was describing my Constitutional position and posture. I must assume that his disability is temporary."

"I'm sorry. Forgive me. I keep forgetting that a President is dying, too."

Haywood winced in spite of himself. His grave eyes sought Penelope's again. They held them a moment and then he left wordlessly, picking up in the hallway outside the door the entourage that would now follow him everywhere.

Alice Payson turned to Penelope. "I feel so sorry for him. This damned town. I hate it. Everyone in it is on the make."

Penelope looked hurt. "Everyone? Do you think I am on the make?"

Alice forced a smile and reaching out, patted her hand. "I never judge my friends, Penny. That's my first rule of friendship."

Shortly after an early dinner Alice Payson excused herself and went to bed. "Forgive me, Penny, if I'm not good company. I feel sort of drained." She kissed her on the cheek. "It means so much to me just to know that you're in the house. You won't find it too deadly?"

"As long as I can help, Alice, I'll be here."

"I can probably go to Walter Reed tomorrow. Will you stay with me there? At least until my children come?"

"Of course, Alice."

Alice Payson touched her hair with a vague, disjointed gesture. "Of course, you have so many important things . . ."

"Nothing is more important at the moment than Bill and you."

Alice squeezed her hand. "Bless you, dear. Goodnight."

Penelope was thankful at last to be alone with her own thoughts. It had been a tiring, tumultous day. She felt the strain in a faint headache she had developed, but she was not sleepy. She retired to her bedroom on the third floor and after taking a hot shower slipped into a filmy summer nightgown and negligee. She turned out the lights and parting the curtains at the window looked out across the darkened ellipse toward the flood lighted needle of the Washington Monument, glowing rose in the humid summer air. The lights of National Airport were visible near the horizon. From time to time she could see the winking lights of ascending and descending jet aircraft.

She sighed and hugged herself happily as she leaned against the windowframe. In a few days time this tragedy of Alice and Bill Payson would be over and Marc Haywood would be the President of the United States. He would be a great President, a man of vision, drive, and compassion. Perhaps compassion was overstating it—Marc was too clinical, too detached, but he had built his political career on the prospects of social change and he would continue to advocate that change, perhaps a session of Congress or two before his political adversaries. His acute sense of timing and sense of things to come would be mistaken for compassion, but what was wrong with that? Whether he was compassionate or adroit, the results would be the same. And she would be a brilliant First Lady.

She smiled into the darkness and then the smile turned wistful. She had risked her marriage to get Marc into the White House. Would Marc think her ruthless and unfeeling? Whom, after all, had she harmed? Certainly not Bill or Alice. Her cheeks grew hot as she thought of Alice. Alice knew—but she didn't even need to forgive her—Alice refused to judge her. Would Marc find the Presidency only ashes because of the way he had won it? She thought not. Marc was as she was; he wanted to win. Winning was the answer to everything. The slate was wiped clean when you won. You only had to explain things when you lost.

She grew happy again. She was married to the greatest winner of them all. Soon she would be the First Lady. And more than that, she was a winner in her own right, Penelope of Washington. Her brow drew down slightly. Was she at thirty-four the youngest First Lady in history? Or was that Jackie Kennedy or Dolly Madison? Her brow cleared again. She would look that up in the morning.